Praise for #1 *New York Times* bestselling author Ellen Hopkins

COLLATERAL

"Hopkins examines the difficulties often overlooked in military marriages, such as limited communication, infidelity, worry over injury, loneliness, and the physical and mental issues of returning veterans. . . . The story will appeal to many readers."

—*urnal*

"Hopkins brings much passion to her wor

—*ews*

"Hopkins's point is well made: collateral da   en extends to soldiers' families."

—*st*

"Supremely realistic. . . . It was so great to   t recognized the struggle that those left behind by military members face. . . . I loved that for once there was a character in Ashley that I could identify with."

—*Booktacular*

"Holy wow. . . . I was blown away. . . . A hard-hitting, emotional story."

—*TriangleMommies*

TRIANGLES

"A raw and riveting tale of love and forgiveness that will captivate readers."

—*Publishers Weekly*

"Absorbing . . . told in beautiful blank verse."

—*EW.com* (A "Must-List" pick)

"A real gem. . . . Heartbreaking, yet eye-opening."
                                        —*RT Book Reviews*

"The sheer emotion almost tipped me over the edge a few times. I barely paused to look up."
                                        —*A Curious Reader*

"My favorite aspect of this novel is that Ellen Hopkins writes about relatable adult issues that many women and families go through."
                                        —*Moonlight Gleam's Bookshelf*

"The thing about Ellen Hopkins is she writes about the stuff that everyone knows happens, but nobody is willing to admit to. She gives emotion and reason to why people make the choices we do, and what they feel like in the middle of a messy hurtful situation."
                                        —*The Life and Lies of an Inanimate Flying Object*

Also by Ellen Hopkins

Triangles

Young Adult Novels
Crank

Burned

Impulse

Glass

Identical

Tricks

Fallout

Perfect

Tilt

COLLATERAL

A NOVEL

Ellen Hopkins

ATRIA PAPERBACK

New York   London   Toronto   Sydney   New Delhi

ATRIA PAPERBACK

A Division of Simon & Schuster, Inc.
1230 Avenue of the Americas
New York, NY 10020

First Atria Paperback hardcover edition July 2013

ATRIA PAPERBACK and colophon are trademarks of Simon & Schuster, Inc.

For information about special discounts for bulk purchases,
please contact Simon & Schuster Special Sales at 1-866-506-1949
or business@simonandschuster.com.

The Simon & Schuster Speakers Bureau can bring authors
to your live event. For more information or to book an event
contact the Simon & Schuster Speakers Bureau at 1-866-248-3049
or visit our website at www.simonspeakers.com.

Designed by Jill Putorti

Manufactured in the United States of America

10 9 8 7 6 5 4 3 2 1

The Library of Congress has cataloged the hardcover edition as follows:
Hopkins, Ellen.
    Collateral : a novel / Ellen Hopkins.—1st Atria Books hardcover ed.
        p.   cm.
    1. Single women—Fiction.   2. Marines—Fiction.   3. United States.
Marine Corps—Military life—Fiction.   4. Man-woman relationships—
Fiction.   5. Novels in verse.   I. Title.
    PS3608.O647C86   2012
    813'.6—dc23   2012029864

ISBN 978-1-4516-2637-7
ISBN 978-1-4516-2638-4 (pbk)
ISBN 978-1-4516-2639-1 (ebook)

This book is dedicated to America's warriors and their loved ones, whose patriotism and sacrifice cannot be overstated. Be strong. Be safe. Let love conquer the loneliness.

ACKNOWLEDGMENTS

Many thanks to everyone who shared their stories of deployment with me: Abi, Amanda, Amber, Ashley, Ash, Corrina, Elyse, Jen, Jenna, and Rick, plus several who shared them in passing. To all of you, and any I may have forgotten, please know how important your stories were to creating this book.

With a huge shout-out to Kylie Alstrup and Mary Claire Boucher, whose stories served as special inspiration for characters you'll meet in these pages. Thank you, ladies. And thanks to Connor and Dana, too.

Finally, to Deb Gonzales. Thanks, m'dear. You were so right.

AUTHOR'S NOTE

With *Collateral*, my goals are to put a spotlight on our returning warriors and to hopefully increase interest in providing the resources they need. As more and more return home, the help they require will become harder to find, because of the struggling economy and also because of the growing anti-war sentiment in this country, which may very well be valid. But our service people didn't take us to war, and they lay their lives on the line for our freedoms every single day.

I have a special interest in traumatic brain injuries, and the cumulative effect of smaller, often undiagnosed traumas that can result in devastating consequences. A lot of this research is relatively new, and it's hugely important that both military families and civilians understand the possible outcomes.

This is not a book meant to dismiss or lessen the sacrifice of our soldiers. It is highly researched. Cole's Marine battalion does, in fact, exist, and was deployed to Iraq and Afghanistan over this exact timeframe. I followed them through news stories, battalion newsletters, and Facebook accounts. I also read accounts of coalition forces, watched hours of videos, movies, YouTube postings, and more. Plus, I scoured Iraqi and Afghani news sources, seeking information largely never seen in the U.S.

Collateral illustrates war from the warrior's POV, as well as its effects on both soldiers and loved ones and, yes, even those who live in the countries we've occupied. It is not a "romance novel" (though love is a driving factor), nor does it make light of the impact of war. I have the utmost respect for those who choose to serve our country, either overseas or on home shores. And, while I currently have no close family members in the service, I do have many friends there, and many readers there, and their stories speak to me.

Within my fiction, I write the truth always, and I have to believe military families want to read the truth about themselves, and to have this truth realized by those who live dissimilarly. Civilian or military, will you like every fact you read in these pages? Probably not, but I can't whitewash war, any more than I can prettify addiction or prostitution or abuse. Surely military families don't want their realities scrubbed of pain or danger or love or what that love might evolve into, when war is the driving factor.

Ashley is one of thousands of military girlfriends trying to build a future from the scraps of her present. The peripheral stories here are just as important, and the heart of them all came to me from real soldiers' spouses. Some military relationships survive, and even thrive. Others simply can't. That is fact. I truly believe military families want books that represent their daily lives, not some scrubbed version. Knowledge is power, I often say. And so is understanding.

—Ellen Hopkins, July 2012

UGLY IN BLACK

As Earth returns to chaos, her women brace to mourn,
excavate their buried faith, tap reservoirs of grace, to mourn.

Soldiers steady M-16s, search stillborn eyes for welcome
or signs of commonality. Ferreting no trace, they mourn.

Few are safe, where passions swell like gangrened limbs
you cannot amputate. Sever one, another takes its place,
and you mourn.

Freefall into martyrdom, a bronze-skinned youth slips into the
crowd, pulls the pin. He and destiny embrace, together mourn.

Grenades are colorblind. A woman falls, spilling ebony hair
beside the blond in camouflage. Death's doorman gives chase. All
mourn.

Even hell capitulates to sudden downpour. Cloudburst sweeps across
the hardpan, cracks its bloodstained carapace. Hear God mourn.

Up through scattered motes, a daughter reaches for an album. She
climbs into a rocking chair to search for Daddy's face, and mourn.

Downstairs, a widow splinters on the bed, drops her head into his
silhouette, etched in linen on the pillowcase, to mourn.

Alone, the world is ugly in black. When final night descends
to blanket memory, drops its shroud of tattered lace, who will
mourn?

POETS WRITE ELOQUENTLY

About war, creating vivid images
of severed limbs, crusting body fluids
and restless final sleep, using nothing
more than a few well-crafted words.

Easy enough to jab philosophically
from the comfort of a warm winter
hearth or an air-conditioned summer.
But what can a sequestered writer know

of frontline realities—blistering
marches under relentless sand-choked
skies, where you'd better drink
your weight in water every day or die

from dehydration? Flipside—teeth-
cracking nights, too frigid for action,
bored out of your mind as you try
to stay warm in front of a makeshift fire.

How can any distant observer know
of traversing rock-rutted trails,
hyperaware that your camouflage comes
with a built-in bull's-eye; or of sleeping

with one ear listening for incoming
peril; or of the way fear clogs your
pores every time you climb inside
a Humvee and head out for a drive?

You can see these things in movies.
But you can't understand the way
they gnaw your heart and corrode
your mind, unless you've been a soldier

outside the wire in a country where
no one native is really your friend,
and anyone might be your enemy.
You don't know till you're ducking

bullets. The only person you dare rely
on is the buddy who looks a lot like
you—too young for this, leaking bravado,
and wearing the same uniform.

Even people who love soldiers—
people like me—can only know these
things tangentially, and not so much
because of what our beloveds tell us

as what they'll never be able to.

LOVING ANY SOLDIER

Is extremely hard. Loving a Marine
who's an aggressive frontline marksman

is almost impossible, especially when
he's deployed. That's not now. Currently,

Cole is on base in Kaneohe, awaiting
orders. The good thing about that is

I get to talk to him pretty much every
day. The bad thing is, we both know

he'll go back to the Middle East as soon
as some Pentagon strategist decides

the time is right, again. Cole's battalion
has already deployed twice to Iraq

and once to Afghanistan. Draw-down
be damned, Helmand Province and beyond

looks likely for his fourth go-round.
You'd think it would get easier. But ask

me, three scratch-free homecomings
make another less likely in the future.

OF COURSE, IF YOU ASK

Me about falling in love
        with a guy in the military,
                I'd tell you to about-face
                        and double-time toward

a decent, sensible civilian.
        Someone with a fat bank
                account and solid future,
                        built on dreams entirely

his own. I'd advise you
        to detour widely around
                any man who prefers fatigues
                        to a well-worn pair of jeans;

whose romantic getaways
        are defined by three-day
                leaves; who, at age twenty-
                        six has drunk more liquor

than most people manage
        in a lifetime. He and his
                fellow grunts would claim
                        it's just for fun. A way to let

their hair down, if they had
        much hair to speak of. But
                those they leave behind,
                        devoted shadows, understand

that each booze-soaked
        night is a short-lived
                retrieve from uncertain
                        tomorrows, unspeakable

yesterdays. Service. Sacrifice.
        The problem with that being,
                everyone attached to those
                        soldiers must sacrifice, too.

So, as some Afghani warlord
        might say, put that in your
                pipe and smoke it. Okay, that
                        was actually my grandpa's saying.

But it works, and what I mean
        is, think long and hard before
                offering your heart to someone
                        who can only accept it part-time.

TOO LATE FOR ME

I didn't go looking for some dude
with crewed yellow hair and piercing
golden eyes. It just happened.
So here I am, in the second year
of my MSW program at San Diego
State, while he brushes up his sniper

skills twenty-six hundred miles away.
Some people consider Hawaii paradise,
an odd place for a Marine base. Except,
if you consider war in the Pacific Theater.
Except, why not? I'm elbow-deep in
Chaucer when his call, expected, comes.

> *Hey, babe.* His voice is a slow burn,
> melting all hint of chill inside me.
> *Word came down today. Two weeks.*
> *How fast can you get here? I need*
> *serious Ash time. And, I've got a surprise*
> *for you. Something . . . really special.*

"Sounds intriguing. No hints?"
He refuses and I consider what
it will take to reach him. "I'll look
into flights and let you know. Probably
next weekend." It will be a pricey ticket.
But I have no choice. Cole Gleason is my heart.

WE TALK FOR AN HOUR

About nothing, really, at all.
       Finally, we exchange love-
       soaked good-byes and I do my best

to go back to Chaucer. I've got
       a paper due on Friday. But it's hard
       to concentrate. The couple next door

is having one of their regular
       shouting matches, and the thin walls
       of this apartment do little to dampen

the noise. Every time they go off
       on each other, it plunges me straight
       back into my childhood. My parents

argued regularly, in clear earshot
       of the neighbors or their friends
       or even at family gatherings. And

they always made up the same
       way, so everyone could hear, taking
       special care to let my little brother,

Troy, and me understand that
       no matter how much they had grown
       to dislike each other, that paper

they signed in front of the priest
        was a forever contract and meant
        more than personal happiness.

Their own brand of sacrifice.
        I grew up equating public displays
        of affection with private problems

and, when I found out about Dad's
        affairs, with covert actions. Hmm.
        Maybe that's why I'm so attracted

to someone who specializes in
        ferreting out the truth. Ha, and
        maybe my parents don't like him

for the same reason. Mom claims
        it's because anyone who signs up
        to kill innocent people right along

with the bad guys must be either
        brainwashed or brain-dead.
        Of course, she has a personal

relationship with the military
        through her father, a Viet Nam vet
        who came home irreparably damaged.

I NEVER MET HIM

Nor my grandmother. Both died when
Mom was eleven. She was raised

by her dad's mother, "crazy Grandma
Gen," as she calls her. I don't know if

Genevieve was really crazy, or if that's just
how she seemed to Mom. But I do think

losing both parents in the same accident
plowed deep into Mom's psyche. To a stranger,

she'd seem standoffish. To her friends,
a challenge to know. To Troy and me,

she is a river of devotion beneath a thick
veneer of ice. To Dad . . . I'm not sure.

Sometimes, when she giggles at one
of his ridiculous jokes, or when he looks

at her in a certain way, I see a ghost
of what they once meant to each other.

What I do know is when I truly need support,
she always comes through, at least once

we make it past her counseling sessions.
But, hey. She's my mother. It's her job

to assail me with advice. As her daughter,
it's my prerogative to take it or leave it.

When it comes to Cole, I mostly ignore
what she has to say, and completely shun

> Dad's sage wisdom—*I don't understand*
> *why you want to commit to someone*

> *whose entire life is following orders.*
> Dad doesn't care much for rules, except

for the ones he makes. He's brilliant,
but hated school, and could never

have worked for someone else. He never
had to. In college, he became obsessed

with technology, way down to nano
level. His crazy scientist inventions

have kept us living well, especially out
in the country, a very long commute

to the Silicon Valley. Dad is impatient
with conventions, or silly things like

my longstanding desire to teach.
Stupid is actually what he called it.

Too little pay, and even less respect.
My liberal arts BA, according to Dad,

was, *A serious squander of time and
money.* I figured it gave me options.

Dad says it just proves I'm wishy-washy,
and maybe he's right. I chose an MSW

over an MFA. Social work seemed like
the right direction at the time. But writing

and teaching call to me, too. Which explains
why I'm taking poetry as an elective.

"Creative expression as therapy" was
the explanation I gave to my advisor.

I have, in fact, encouraged the veterans
I've worked with at the VA Hospital

to write as a means of sorting through
the scrambled thoughts inside their heads.

A few showed me their ramblings. I could
fix their grammar. But not their memories.

STILL, TO A POINT

The writing seemed cathartic.
        I might use that as my thesis,
                if I get that far next year. I went

for a three-year program, hoping
        to give myself a little breathing
                room. I talked Dad into paying

for it, so I guess it's fair he's a bit
        pissy, especially because he also
                agreed to let me quit my part-time job.

I loved working at the preschool, but
        it didn't pay very well, and it crowded
                my days. And a couple of incidents

made me question why some people
        have children. A certain mother made
                me a little crazy. Jacked up my stress

factor, not to mention blood pressure.
        Parents like her are why the world
                needs social workers. Poor, little Soleil

deserves better. Every kid does. Dad
        says I can't change the world. Maybe
                not. But I'm damn sure going to try.

IN THE MEANTIME

I suck it up, put distraction away,
and try to jump into writing my paper.
I kind of love most poetry, though
I do prefer writing it to dissecting

some of it, especially Chaucer. He is not,
as the English (Old, new, or anywhere
in between) might say, my cup of Earl
Grey. Still, I manage almost three pages

on his contributions to the *Oxford English
Dictionary* when my cell signals
a new text message. Happy for
the interruption, I go ahead and

        investigate, discover it's from Darian.
        HEY, GIRL. A BUNCH OF US ARE GOING
        OUT ON SATURDAY NIGHT. WANT TO
        COME WITH? Some best friend.

Zero communication for weeks at a time,
then she invites me out with a "bunch"
of her new pals. Military wives, none
of whom I know. The ones she hangs

out with. Works out with. Goes out
with, more often, obviously, than
she does with me anymore. I suppose
I should be grateful she thought about

me at all. Part of me is. And part
of me wishes I had a valid excuse
to say no. But I really don't, and how
would saying no make me a better

friend than she's been to me lately?
Anyway, I could use a few hours away
from here. Out of this apartment,
and into the land of drunk living.

I text back: SOUNDS FUN, BUT I HAVE
TO BE CAREFUL OF MY CASH. LOOKS LIKE
I'M FLYING TO HAWAII NEXT WEEK.
She, of course, knows why. Which reminds

me: HOW'S SPENCE? Her husband,
and Cole's good buddy, has been
in country for several months. Behind
the wire, at some uber-protected

Afghanistan airfield—wherever they
keep the helicopters that need a little
tweaking. Spencer is a self-proclaimed
master copter mechanic. Darian's answer

> is slow to come. In fact, I'm just
> about ready to believe she has put
> away her phone when: OKAY, I GUESS.
> WE HAVEN'T TALKED IN A FEW DAYS.

STRANGE

Spencer should have fairly easy access
to a computer, if not a phone. E-mails
and even Facebook are rarely prohibited

when a soldier is safely behind the wire.
Communication, the brass believe,
is the key to harmonious long-distance

relationships. You're not supposed
to give away any really important
information, of course. Nothing

the enemy could use to his advantage.
But discussing family or work or school
(on this end) and what to put into care

packages (on the other) are encouraged.
Connection to home and loved ones
helps keep a warrior grounded in

a reality that doesn't revolve around
war. Except when the current battle
happens to involve someone at home.

> When I ask Darian what's up with Spence
> and her, she responds: *WE HAD A FIGHT*
> *LAST TIME WE TALKED. SAME OLD BULLSHIT.*

MEANING IMAGINED CHEATING

Wish I could jump straight to her defense.
But there's a lot I don't know about her

at this point. And a lot more that I suspect
myself. Once, I could have come right out

and asked her if she was sleeping around.
Darian and I have been best friends since

the fourth grade. We used to tell each other
everything—confessed big secrets and little

lies. San Diego State was a shared dream,
mostly because, growing up in Lodi, the idea

of moving south and living near the ocean
seemed akin to heaven. We were stem-to-stern

California girls. Funny we fell in love with
heartland guys. Spencer is a corn-fed Kansan.

And Cole's a Wyoming boy. Both were raised
gun-toting, critter-hunting, Fox News–loving patriots.

They met in basic training at Camp Pendleton,
became instant friends. We connected with them soon after.

JANUARY 2007

Darian and I were roomies then,
sharing an off-campus apartment.
She grumbled a lot about school.
About feeling shackled. About men—
the ones she'd been dumped by,

the ones she couldn't seem to find.
One Friday she seemed ready to lose
it, so I suggested a night of drunken
revelry. "Who knows?" I prodded.
"Maybe you'll find Mr. Wonderful."

We chose an Oceanside hotspot, too busy
for the bartender to give our fake IDs more
than a quick glance. We ordered margaritas,
found two seats at a table not too close to
the speakers pounding base-infused music.

> I didn't notice Cole and Spencer walk
> in. But Darian did. She nudged me.
> Hard. *Check it out. Hot Marines.*

Military issue was not my type,
at least I didn't think so then. I did
have to admit, however, that whatever
hoops they'd been jumping through
had left them buff and bronzed.

Which one do you want? she asked,
as if hooking up with them was in
the bag. *I kind of like the dark one.*
Spencer swaggered. That's the only
word I can think of to describe the way

he moved. "Cock-sure," my grandpa
would have called it. Definitely more
Darian's overhyped style than mine.
Cole, I wasn't sure about. He carried
himself straight up and down, stiff

as a log. He looked deadly serious,
until he smiled, revealing a hint
of something soft—almost childlike—
beneath his tough infantryman veneer.
Some things are meant to be, it seems.

I mean, we weren't the only women
in the club. There were way too many
vampires—girls hoping to hook up
with a military sugar daddy. Someone
whose paycheck would see them

through when he was sent away.
I didn't know about them then,
but it didn't take long. That night,
they prepared to swoop in on Cole
and Spence. Except, there was Darian.

I'VE NEVER BEEN MUCH OF A FLIRT

Darian, though, is flirt enough for
        two. Not to mention, bold enough

        to move in before the vampires
                could reconnoiter. *I'll be right back.*

She walked straight up to the bar,
        insinuated herself between Spencer

and Cole, ordered drinks, even
        though the ones we had were barely

half gone. Then she turned and
        looked Spencer square in the eye.

        *My friend and I want to thank you
                for your service. Next round's on us.*

It wasn't a question, and one minute
        later, I found myself thigh to thigh

next to this quiet guy with intense
        topaz eyes. It wasn't love at first sight

or touch or whatever. If it had just
        been the two of us there, he would

have been vampire bait. But our
        BFFs hit it off immediately. I was more

than a little jealous of the chemistry
        between Darian and Spence, even

though helping her find Mr. Wonderful
        was supposedly my plan from the start.

I'd never experienced that kind
        of instant attraction, however. Not even

with Cole, who I found cute enough,
        but rather aloof. In retrospect, I was (am)

much the same way. It took a while
        to warm up. Not like we had much in

common, at least not on the surface.
        But with Spence and Darian crawling all

over each other, Cole and I could either
        stare off into space or attempt conversation.

Despite all the pretty vampires eyeing
        him, he chose to take a chance on me.

SOMETHING SPECIAL ABOUT THAT

For me, never the first girl
in any room who men zoomed in on.
I'm slender, and pretty enough
in a serious way. Just not what
you'd call eye candy. I didn't dress—
certainly didn't undress—to impress.

I'd had boyfriends, even semisteady
ones, but none worth giving up
dreams for. I wasn't exactly a virgin.
But neither was I looking for sex,
and I suppose that showed.
I had been called an ice queen

before, but though I didn't realize
it right away, something inside me
thawed that night. It was a slow melt,
like Arctic ice beneath high polar sun.
Maybe it was how Cole kept his eyes
locked on mine, instead of scanning

> the room for easier prey. Maybe it
> was the way he talked about home—
> the stark beauty of Wyoming.
> *I swear, you can see straight into*
> *forever. No damn buildings to get*
> *in the way. And the sky is the bluest*

blue you ever saw. You will never
look up and see gray, like here above
the ocean. Not even if a storm's blowing
in, because then the prairie sky turns
black and purple, like God balled up
his fist and bruised it. He paused. *What?*

Mesmerized, that's what I was, but
I didn't realize my face showed it.
"Uh, nothing. It's just . . ." I couldn't
not say it. "I hope this doesn't insult
you, but you're a poet." I half-expected
him to get pissed. Laugh, at least.

Instead, he smiled. *Why would that*
insult me? I write a little poetry every
now and then. Hell, the first time I got
laid was because I wrote her a love
sonnet. We broke up over the limerick
I wrote about her, though. He laughed

then, and so did I. I have no idea
if any of that was true, but in the years
since, he has written poems for me.
Hopefully, he hasn't squirreled away
an Ashley limerick to break out one
day. But the revelation that this

country-bred soldier could find poetry
in his heart and inspiration in the Wyoming
sky touched me in a way no boy had ever
come close to. Not even the ones who
had straight-out lied and told me they'd
love me forever. Poetry doesn't lie.

Turned out, Cole was feeling a little
homesick. His mom had just come
for a post–boot camp visit. *She drove
my pickup cross country, winter
weather and all,* he said. *She wanted
to surprise me. But the surprise was on*

*her. They don't let recruits have private
vehicles on base. Lucky thing, my
Uncle Jack lives close by. He said
I can keep the truck there and use
it when I'm able. Mom didn't want
to drive the interstate again. Said*

*God didn't give those Wright Brothers
brains for nothing. Goddamn, it was
good seeing her. Like she brought
a piece of home along with her
and left it here for me. California
is better with a little Wyoming in it.*

I HAD TO ENVY

Such love for home. The concept
was foreign to me. And I rather enjoyed
how this stranger opened himself up

so completely to someone he didn't
know. After that, we talked a little bit
about me. How growing up in Lodi

wasn't all that different from growing
up outside of Cheyenne, except for
the urban sprawl creeping ever closer

toward the oak-crusted California
foothills. We talked about *wanting*
to leave home. About school, and how

my dreams didn't exactly jive with
my parents' goals for me. About caving
in. We talked about best friends since

fourth grade, meaning mine. About
new buddies and boot camp, the rewards
and pitfalls of service to one's country.

He said something about Don't Ask,
Don't Tell, and though I verge on
radical liberalism, and cringe at male

posturing, when he said he had
enough things to worry about without
having to wonder why some guy

was looking at him in the shower,
I thought about it for a few. Understood.
Some things that make perfect sense

philosophically might be confusing
in a real-world scenario. "What about
gay marriage?" I asked, expecting

> a pat Bible Belt answer. Instead,
> he said, *I'm all for it, as long as they
> don't honeymoon in the barracks.*

After a drink or two, we made each
other laugh. The walls, which had
already started to crumble, collapsed.

Cole isn't much of a dancer, but when
Spencer made it a challenge, he pulled
me onto the floor. I love to dance, and

totally got into it. He liked my moves.
Still, it could have ended there. Except,
our friends had fallen insanely in lust.

IT WAS KIND OF FUN

Watching Spencer try to keep up
        with Darian. He was nineteen (no ID
        check at all for the young Marine!).

She was only a year older, but way
        more experienced when it came to
        the opposite sex. Boy, was he willing

to tap her expertise, in any and all
        of its manifestations. Her energy,
        I have to admit, was infectious,

her libidinousness almost enviable.
        Not that I'd ever try to imitate her.
        But maybe a small part of me wished

a little would rub off, cling to me,
        metal filings to magnet. One thing
        that always impressed me was how,

though the attention she sought
        was all about her, she managed
        to make men feel like every move,

every laugh, every compliment
        was instead all about them. And
        they opened themselves wide for her.

SO, SOMEHOW

Midst all the flirtation and sexual
energy, Darian coaxed Spence's
story from him. He had graduated
high school just six months before,
a year after his kindergarten classmates.

> I wasn't dumb. Just under-qualified,
> he joked before explaining, My mom
> and pop cared more about me
> helping out on the farm than going
> to school. I didn't get a lot of what
>
> you might call encouragement to
> succeed. He did discover a talent for
> "tinkering." I took my bike apart when
> I was five. Put it back together not long
> after. I was rebuilding motors by the time
>
> I was twelve. Came in handy when
> the John Deere took a dump. Auto
> mechanics was my big claim to fame
> in high school. A-plus there, let me
> tell you. Did a cheerleader or two
>
> out in the garage, too. The smell
> of motor oil is one helluva turn-on!
> Then he reached for Darian. Want
> to find out? I think Cole's truck needs
> rings. We could take a little drive.

ENDED UP

We all went for a drive to the beach.
Cole and I left Darian and Spence

inhaling motor oil fumes—and each
other—in the backseat while we took

a walk near the ocean's edge beneath
a silver spray of moonlight. I was wearing

jeans and an angora sweater, not quite
enough for a winter night, and when

I shivered, Cole lifted his jacket, inviting
me underneath and close against him.

Tequila is good for eroding inhibitions
and I didn't think twice about accepting

his offer. His body radiated heat, lifting
the scent of leather and Irish Spring soap.

Tequila also makes you say things you
wouldn't say sober. "You smell amazing."

>He laughed. *I do my best. Never know*
>*when you might have to warm up a lady.*

"Do you warm them up often?" It was
meant as a joke, but he took it seriously.

Not really. In fact, it's been a while.
Boot camp isn't conducive to romance.

I liked his answer, and his vocabulary.
"What about before? Any girls back home?"

He hesitated. *In college. There was*
a girl. But when I left, she stayed.

And when she found out I joined up,
she totally freaked. Told me war and love

are antonyms. So, no. No girls. What
about you? Boyfriend? Husband?

I snorted. "No husband. Not even
close. And no serious relationships."

He stopped walking then. *Good.*
Because if there was, I sure wouldn't

do this. He turned me toward him,
slipped his arms around my waist,

lifted me until I was just beyond tiptoes.
This time when he looked at me, his eyes

asked permission. I nodded. His mouth
covered mine. That kiss was our beginning.

WITH A KISS

Something new, some swell
of hope for what might be,
if luck can learn to rely
on patience.

                    With a

whisper of skin
against skin, a spark
of desire is fanned to flame
by an exhale of passion,
culminates within a

                    flash

of conflagration. Burns
itself out. Leaves behind
embers and the ash

                    of regret

at what is left waiting.
It is this image he carries
to warm frigid nights
in a foreign land where

                    a soldier

does not remember dreams,
except those of holding
her in the afterglow, hearts
slowing as the inferno

                    dies.

                    Cole Gleason

MY BANK ACCOUNT

Is pitiful. I did tuck most of my preschool
paychecks away, but that didn't amount
to much. My parents pay my rent, give me

an allowance, and will until I finish school.
My only other income is goodwill checks
from my Alaska grandparents. Somehow,

I make do, and only need big chunks of cash
on weeks like this one, when the best price
I can find for roundtrip airfare to Honolulu

is just shy of seven hundred dollars. So much
for "discount tickets, best prices guaranteed."
My choices: draw my savings down to zero

cushion; or ask my mom and dad to help out.
I hate to, because I know exactly how
the conversation will go. But I swallow

my pride and make the call. "Hey, Mom.
How's everything?" Simple enough
greeting, but obviously code, because

her response is, *Not bad. What's going on?*
Which is also code for, *What do you want?*
We don't exchange mundane pleasantries

often, and almost never by telephone.
Might as well get right to the point.
"I heard from Cole. He's deploying

in less than three weeks. I need to see
him before he leaves." She remains
quiet. "Uh . . . the ticket is seven hundred,

which would just about wipe me out.
I was hoping . . ." It isn't the first time
I've asked for airfare. I'm sure I'll get

> the usual lecture, and I do. *Ashley,*
> *you know how I feel about supporting*
> *the military. It makes my skin crawl.*

"You're not supporting the military,
Mom, or even supporting Cole. I guess
I shouldn't have called. I'm sorry."

> *Now, wait. I didn't say I wouldn't*
> *help out. I just want you to value*
> *my opinion. I know you love Cole*

> *very much. . . . There's a big "but"*
> *coming. But love isn't always pleasant.*
> *I worry that you're going to get hurt.*

GAME WELL-PLAYED

On both sides. She can tell me one more
time why I made a mistake falling for

a Marine. And I will receive the needed funds.
"Thanks for worrying, Mom. If I get hurt,

it was my choice, right? Do you have to
ask Dad about the airfare?" She should.

> But she won't. *You know better than that.*
> *I'll take it out of my mad money, and we'll*
>
> *keep it between you and me. You know*
> *how Dad is when it comes to unexpected*
>
> *expenses.* Dad is the master budgeter.
> Except somehow he never found out

about Mom's confidential cash stash. Over
the lifetime of their marriage, she's managed

to squirrel away thousands. I've known about
it for as long I can remember. When I was

younger, we used it for hardcover books, pricier
prom dresses, and Victoria's Secret underwear—

extravagances, Dad would have called them,
totally unnecessary. To him. But Mom

always understood my hunger for them,
the same way she gets my need to see

Cole, despite the price tag. Good thing
my brother doesn't have a taste for expensive

gadgets, or my mother's mad money hoard
likely would have vanished by now.

"Thanks, Mom. I'll probably leave
Thursday and come back on Monday.

I'll let you know for sure. Can you deposit
the money in my account ASAP? I need to

buy the tickets today to get the quote-unquote
discount." She promises she will and when

>I ask how Dad is doing, I can almost
>hear her shrug. *Your father is fine.*

>*He's always fine, isn't he? Too mean
>for "sick" to stick to, and thank God*

>*for that. Who knows what vile disease
>he might have brought home otherwise.*

Poor Mom. I'd hate to live every day
choking down a big spoonful of bitterness.

TICKETS PURCHASED

I send Cole an e-mail, let him know
next weekend is ours, and for some
complicated reason, it initiates an outbreak
of nerves. As much as I want to see him,
I don't want to say good-bye again.

As much as I want to be with him,
I don't want to think about no chance
at being with him again for seven months.
As much as I want to wrap myself up
in his arms, I don't want to consider

how lonely I'll be when I have to come
home to this love-empty apartment.
But I will suffer all those emotions,
and more. Because that's what you do
when you are crazy about a Marine.

I try to go about my day. It's funny,
but when Cole is overseas, I don't think
about him every minute. Maybe it's
a subconscious stab at self-defense.
Because if I let myself stress over where

he was and what he was doing, I'd
worry myself into a state of catatonia.
Instead, I save anxiety for the few days
before I know I'll spend time with him.
What would it be like to see him every day?

I SAVE THE QUESTION

For Saturday night, when I know
I'll have the chance to ask women
who've been there. That is, if they
want to talk about their husbands

at all. So far, an hour into our girls'
night out, the conversation has been
about what to drink, which appetizers
to order, and the relative merits

of the other women in the club.
It's still fairly early, but for a Saturday
night, this place seems pretty quiet.
As usual, Darian is the center of

      attention, even among the ladies
      at our table. There are three, plus
      Darian and me. *Jeez, where are all*
      the guys tonight? asks Darian.

            I give her a look. She ignores it.
            Like you need more men in your
            life, jokes Celine, who is maybe thirty-
            five. Her husband is career military,

and currently training grunts east
of here at Marine Corps Air Ground
Combat Center Twenty-Nine Palms—
a stretch of California desert that

pretty much simulates Middle Eastern hell.
Cole just spent a month there in intensive
training. The idea that he might have met
Celine's husband is kind of intriguing.

> *Ah, come on,* whines Darian. *All I want*
> *is a dance partner who isn't wearing a*
> *skirt. But if that's the best I can do,*
> *it's all good by me. Shall we, girls?*

She tilts her head toward the dance
floor. Meghan, who is a little older
than me, shrugs and follows her.
Carrie, who is probably younger,

laughs and does the same. I'm staying
put. Celine and I watch in silence for
a few. Finally, a question bubbles up.
"Why didn't you go to Twenty-Nine Palms?"

> Celine smiles. *Trade the ocean for desert?*
> *Not even. Anyway, it's only a temporary*
> *assignment. I'm not going to pack up the kids*
> *and move for a couple of months. He'll be back.*

Matter-of-fact. He'll be back. Sooner
or later, they all are. One way or another.
"How long have you been married?"
How many times has he come back?

EVERY SOLDIER'S STORY

Is different. Every soldier's story
        is the same, or at least has some-

thing in common with every other
        soldier's story. Ditto the narratives

of those left behind. Girlfriends.
        Wives. Husbands. Children. Parents.

What ordinary people forget is us,
        left behind. How we cheer victories.

Weep at photos of flag-draped coffins,
        even those enshrining the bodies

of warriors we have never met. Another
        day, it might be our loved ones whose

fate dictates arriving home in a box,
        shrouded by the red, white, and blue.

I keep that fact folded up and stashed
        deep inside a small closet in my brain.

The same hiding place, I suppose,
        a soldier buries the fear that feeds

aggression, the drive to lift a weapon
        and determination to pull the trigger.

CELINE'S STORY

I fell in love with Luke in high school.
He's from a long line of Navy men, and
wanted to enlist right after graduation.
His mom was dead set against it.
"Goddamn Navy took your father away
from me. I won't have it, hear?" See,
Luke's dad was a horrible husband.

Drank most of his paycheck, whored
around every time his ship anchored
in some foreign port. "You go to college,
son," his mom told him. "Take care
of your lady like a decent man should."

But Luke was determined to join up,
despite a brilliant GPA and SAT scores.
He talked to a recruiter who convinced
him he was officer material. And so he
compromised. We both attended UNLV
during the school year. But while I spent
summer vacations at home, Luke sweated

out Platoon Leaders Class at Quantico.
He graduated cum laude and accepted
his commission, then spent the next year
in Virginia, acing The Basic School and
specialized infantry officer training. When
they moved him to Camp Pendleton, we
tied the knot. That was eleven years ago.

SO HE'S A POG

Person Other than Grunt. Not
enlisted, and so, worthy of scorn,
at least in some soldiers' eyes.
Still, some fast subtraction gives
me important information about him.

"So, he deployed for the Iraq invasion?"
POG or grunt, those Marines are legend.

> *Oh, yeah. Came home a hero, too.*
> *America was all about taking out*
> *Saddam Hussein. Too bad they forgot*
> *the real-time cost of war, you know?*

I do, all too well. "It must be hard,
having kids, when he's gone."

> *Celine smiles. In a way, it's easier.*
> *We have a routine, and I'm in charge,*
> *so there's no room for discussion.*
> *When he's home, believe it or not,*
> *he's a total pushover. Even at nine*
> *and seven, the girls have learned how*
> *to work their father. What's hard . . .*

When she pauses, everything about
her softens. *What's hard is having*
to tell them he won't make a birthday
or holiday. Again. The one thing

we can count on is we can't count on
anything. Semper Gumby. After a while,
like it or not, you just get used to it.

Semper Gumby. Always flexible.
A seven-month deployment could go
eight or more. Whatever the situation
demands. I've already gotten used to it.
And I haven't even put in half the years
she has, interwoven with a Marine.

"Does it ever get . . . I don't know.
Too much? Have you ever considered
a life outside of the military?"

You mean, desertion? Her smile grows
wider. When Luke and I fight, of course
I think about leaving. But I never will.
I decided that when I agreed to marry him.

It has nothing to do with vows, though.
It's about loving him, and I do, with every
molecule of my being. If I didn't, I most
definitely wouldn't be here right now.

THE MUSIC STOPS

One last question before the others
return to the table. "What did you mean
about Darian needing more men in her life?"

> Celine's smile finally drops. *Look.*
> *It's really none of my business, and*
> *probably not yours, either. But . . .*

She glances toward the dance floor,
and my eyes follow hers. Meghan
trails Carrie down the hall toward

the bathroom. Darian, however, is at
the bar, leaning close to some generic
guy and flashing cleavage. Celine tips

> her head, explains, *Darian thrives on*
> *male attention, as you know. Marine*
> *wives talk. There are rumors. That's all.*

I can't believe I had to ask *her* that.
I should have known the answer. Or maybe
I did. Do. Whatever. Right now, all I see

is Dar, flirting. That might bother me
more, except I still enjoy flirting, too.
Not quite as overtly as Darian, though.

EASY FLIRTATION

Is everywhere. Case in point, one
extremely good-looking man is currently

checking me out. Directly enough to make
me blush. He must notice because now

he offers me a beautiful let's-do-it kind
of smile that might just lead somewhere,

if not for that little picture of Cole I carry
around in my head. Still, I color even

deeper. This time it's Celine who sees.
"Sorry." I turn my full attention back to her.

> *Don't apologize. I'd turn straight*
> *out purple if he smiled at me like that.*

"Sometimes it's just so hard, you know?
Don't you ever get lonely? I mean, for . . ."

> *Sex? A nice warm body beside me in*
> *bed? Of course. That's pretty normal.*

"But you've never . . . well, I haven't,
either. But I almost did once. Cole

had been gone, like forever. And this
guy was just so gorgeous. Sweet. Smart.

A gentleman, too. He never pushed
for anything, but God, I came close

one night. I even kissed him. And,
boy, was it hard to stop. But I did."

> *Don't beat yourself up about it.*
> *You did the right thing in the end.*

I finish my drink. "Yeah, but I was
so tempted to do the wrong thing."

> *Look. You're young. Healthy.*
> *Your body responded to pleasant*

> *external stimuli exactly the way*
> *it's supposed to. No big deal.*

I have to smile. "You make lust
sound so clinical." Logical, even.

> *It's not exactly rocket science.*
> *Especially if the guy was all that.*

> *Look, being committed doesn't*
> *make you dead, but all those months*

> *alone can make you feel that way*
> *sometimes. You never signed on*

> *for that. Embrace the moments*
> *that let you know you're alive.*

MY BEGINNING

With Cole was a long, slow kindle.
The first night we met, we sparked.
But, perhaps because we're both
cautious by nature, we guarded

the flame, kept it smoldering low.
Darian and Spencer blazed. In
a way, I was surprised. Spence
reminded me of Darian's father,

and the clichéd adage about a girl
wanting to hook up with a guy like
her dad didn't seem like it should apply.
Darian didn't much like her father,

a hard-nosed rodeo cowboy who traveled
the circuit and came home only long
enough to rest his horse, screw his wife,
and try to corral his wild child. Darian

> was having none of it. *Bastard never
> taught me to tie my shoes or ride my bike,
> and now he wants to tell me where
> I can't go and who I can't see? Hardly!*

Okay, Spence is a lot nicer than
Darian's dad, but he carries himself
in a similar way—with an overabundance
of self-confidence. Not conceited, but

so sure of himself as to never admit
being wrong. Regardless, his and Dar's
connection was immediate. Real. Primal.
I have no idea where Cole and I would be

today, if it wasn't for our friends hooking
up that night, and staying hooked up for
the next four days, until the guys' leave
was over and the next phase of training

began. Spence, who was out-of-his-head
in love with Darian from the start, wanted
to spend every minute with her, mostly
in the apartment she and I shared.

Cole had a choice—barracks, Uncle
Jack's, or said apartment. For whatever
reason, he chose the last option. Spence
slept with Darian. Cole crashed on the couch.

AT LEAST

That was the original plan. Because,
as drawn to Cole as I was that first night,
I've never been the type to jump straight

into bed with a stranger. Not even a striking,
soft-spoken stranger with eyes that hold
on to you like they can't get enough of you.

So, while Darian and Spence disappeared
inside her room, the door of which did
little to muffle all the moaning and *yessing*

behind it, Cole and I talked through the dark
hours, toward daylight. I loved the way,
when he spoke of his mom, his voice got

> all silky. *She wanted me to go to college,*
> *even though money was tight. I was almost*
> *through my second year when my kid sister*

> *got sick. Fucking cancer takes the weak,*
> *like wolves culling antelope. Annie fought*
> *hard, but not good enough. Between doctors*

> *and hospitals and the funeral, the savings*
> *dried up. Two solid years of undergrad*
> behind him, Cole was considering work

in the natural gas fields when a savvy
recruiter snagged him. Told him he could
send part of his paychecks to his mother,

and college could come, paid-for, after
he fulfilled his commitment. He was still
considering his options when word came

that an Iraqi bullet had claimed his cousin
Eugene, who signed up for the Army while
he was still in high school. He was barely

voting age when he deployed. As Cole
told the story, his body tensed visibly,
and he squinted around the anger

> that bloomed in his leonine eyes.
> *Son of a whore hajji shot Gene square*
> *in the back, right through his heart.*

> *I don't much take after my bastard*
> *father, except when it comes to revenge.*
> *Eighteen is too fucking young to die.*

I didn't say I thought twenty-one was too
young to die, and it seemed a distinct possibility
for him, or any soldier, in search of revenge.

NEITHER DID I ASK FOR SPECIFICS

About his father. I didn't know him well enough,
nor had I consumed nearly enough alcohol. Later,
I learned that Bart Gleason, who left Cole's
mom two days before Cole's ninth birthday,

was serving a life sentence for murder.
Seems the girl he left Mrs. Gleason for
wasn't such a sweet, young thing after all.
Bart heard rumors about her sleeping around.

He followed her one night. Waited long
enough for her to get naked and knotted
up with another guy, then calmly blew
out both their brains with his favorite

.357 magnum. Probably a good thing
I didn't hear the story that night. My own
parents are big subscribers to the old
"apple doesn't fall far from the tree" theory.

I'd heard it all my life, and maybe believed
it, at least a little. By the time I found out
about Cole's father, though, I loved my Marine
way too much to even think twice about it.

THAT KIND OF LOVE

For me is a once-in-a-lifetime,
        planets-aligning-at-the-exact-
                right-coordinates kind of thing.

I guess I always hoped it was
        possible, but never let myself
                believe it would happen any time.

I definitely wasn't looking and
        so I didn't see it right away.
                The kiss at the beach was sweet.

But it was only memorable in
        retrospect. The kissing on
                the couch quickly moved from

tentative cool to electric hot.
        You can tell a lot by the way
                a guy kisses. Cole kissed like

summer rain—barely wet,
        the temperature of August
                sky, thunder-punctuated. Delicious.

BREATHLESS

Heart thudding, I came very close
to giving him a lot more. I wanted to,

despite forever declarations to never,
ever invite one-night stands, and surely

that was all it would be. Cole is all-man,
and I can't say he didn't try, but when I

slowed him with a simple, "Can't. Not yet,"
he respected the request, though not without

> comment. *You positive you're a California
> girl?* He wasn't clear about whether he'd

heard all California girls were loose or only
if all the ones he'd met so far were. "Meaning . . . ?"

He started to answer just about the time
Darian came stumbling down the hall

to the kitchen, hair like an eagle's nest,
and wearing nothing but a T-shirt that

> barely covered her crotch. Barely. *Hey,*
> she slurred, sort of giving us the twice

> over. *Sorry. Thirsty.* She grabbed a couple
> of beers from the fridge. Staggered back

to her room. Cole and I looked at each
other and laughed. "Point taken," I said.

"And if I don't want to look like that"—
nodding toward Dar, who just then faded

into her room—"I probably better get
to bed. That, or scare the bejeezus out

of you in the morning." Cole accepted
that with a not-hot kiss, then asked,

> Don't suppose you've got an extra
> blanket? It's cooling off fast in here.

I went down the hall, pulled the spread
off my bed. By the time I got back, he was

lying there, still as stone, eyes closed.
I covered him, turned away, and heard him

> say, Thanks for the blanket. And for
> the great evening. See you in the morning.

I liked how that sounded. And although I
was critically tired, it took a while to fall asleep.

WHEN I WOKE UP

It was full-on morning, light crashing
through the window in brilliant waves.
It took a few minutes to figure out why
I felt so anxious to get out of bed. Then
I heard a muffled male voice, Darian's
high-pitched laugh, and the night before

tumbled back. Marines. Right. I went
straight for the bathroom to shower,
brush my teeth, and put on makeup.
Slid into silk panties, knee-length satin
shirt, a sexy-casual compromise. When
I slipped into the hall, the place was silent

except for the creak of Darian's bed
behind her closed door. God. How
many times could you do it in a twelve-
hour period? I tiptoed past, not wanting
to bother them, or Cole, who I thought
must still be asleep. But no. The couch

was empty, the bedspread folded
neatly. He wasn't there, hadn't even
bothered to say good-bye. Disappointment
clawed. I went into the kitchen, noticed
the glasses on the counter, dishes
in the sink. When did that happen?

CLUTTER ALWAYS BOTHERS ME

But the irritation I felt at the state of
my kitchen bordered on irrational.
I knew it, but couldn't say why.
I unloaded the dishwasher. Loudly.

>And, even more loudly, started
>loading the crusty dirties. *Hey!*
>*Stop! I planned on doing that.*

I jumped at the voice, strange but
not, falling over my shoulder; spun,
pointing a fork like a tined bayonet.

>Cole's eyes glittered humor. *Careful.*
>*I'm trained in hand-to-hand combat,*
>*you know. Put down the weapon.*
>*Slowly. Better yet, give it to me. Please.*

I handed him the fork, which he put
in the dishwasher. "Jesus. You scared
the crap out of me. Where did you
come from? I thought you'd left."

>He shook his head. *Everyone was*
>*still asleep when I woke up, so I sat*
>*outside and . . . wrote. Hope you don't*
>*mind I borrowed a piece of paper.*

"Of course not." It wasn't the paper
that bothered me as much as the idea
of him rooting around for it. "In fact,
you don't even have to pay me back."

      He smiled. *Maybe I want to.* Then
      he looked at me so intently I had to
      turn away, inventing some necessary

chore. "You a coffee person? I think
I could use a cup." I reached up
into the cupboard for the Folgers.

      Let me help. The weight of my long,
      still-damp hair lifted suddenly. *Mmm.*
      You smell good. His lips brushed
      my neck, and it was like stepping
      outside in a thunderstorm—a hint

of lightning initiating goose bumps
in places both seen and hidden.
I turned into him, and he lifted me,
sat me on the counter. Wrapped

my legs around his ripped torso,
pulled me into him until the pulsing
between my legs rested against
the throbbing beneath his breast bone,
zero between them but silk and skin.

It was nothing I'd ever experienced
before, this sudden blush of desire
so intense I couldn't believe it belonged
to me. And significance infused our kiss.

I think we both knew it then, though
it took time to acknowledge that some
brilliant stutter of fate had connected
us in such a profound way. I can't speak

for Cole, but for me, the world as I
understood it to be ceased to exist.
In that exact moment, I couldn't have
reasonably claimed to have fallen in love

with him. But in that exact moment,
I still wasn't sure I believed in love.
Anyway, it was enough to be snared

by passion so intense, it bordered surreal.
Swept away, unable to swim and barely
finding air, I would have let him carry

me into my bedroom, make love right
then and there. Instead he pulled back.
Not quite in unison, but staggered closely,

we both had one thing to say. "Wow."

Wow.

THAT KIND OF FOREPLAY

Without follow-through is a huge
      turn-on. While Darian and Spencer
      spent the day following through,

Cole and I wandered the hills
      of the San Diego Zoo. The air
      was winter-spiced but I barely

noticed. Everything about me
      felt warm. And, while I studied
      the animals, I noticed other things.

Like how Cole's hand was nearly
      twice as big as mine. And warm,
      when it gloved my exposed skin.

Like how I tucked completely
      under his arm, the sculpture
      of his biceps. Like the way

he adjusted his stride, my legs
      no match for his, until we walked
      in perfect step. Like how he liked

the big cats best, especially
      the jaguars, who paced in short
      strokes of sun. Every time we stopped,

we kissed, and lacing every
      kiss was desire, rising up big
      and bold, voracious as a leviathan.

LEVIATHAN

Sleeps. Dreams fitfully
of sand, unstained from
horizon to horizon, while

        overhead

silence floats in mirrored
sky. Disturbing. No pleas.
No screams. No sound
of distress. Not even

        the drone of

tear-muffled prayer.
Leviathan wakes. Yawns.
Stretches haunch and claw.
Cocks his head and finds
the ghostly moan of

        danger, distant,

but alive. Leviathan cracks
a smile, reveals fear-sharpened
fangs. Sheds the shadow

        of nightmares

born within hibernation.
Leviathan embraces blood
hunger. Rises, lifts into
the startled blue, dragon

        on the wing.

Cole Gleason

DARIAN LIVES

At Camp Pendleton. Like most military
bases, the sprawling chunk of oceanfront
California is pretty much self-contained,
with schools, fast food, golf, and religion
just beyond spitting distance from jets and
helicopters, tanks and heavy artillery.

Some spouses use their housing allowance
to live off-base nearby in one of San Diego's
neat, suburban neighborhoods. The thrifty ones
bank that money and stay with generous
relatives. But from the start, Darian wanted
to cozy up to other military wives.

> *They understand what I'm going through.*

Like I don't. Like a marriage license
somehow ups the ante on emotion. Pissed
me off when she first said it, and it still
makes me mad that she might actually
believe it. It's a chink in the once-solid
armor of our friendship. That makes me sad.

> *Anyway, on base I can get by without a car.*

Her beater Civic broke down not long
after we moved here. She'd mostly
made do bumming rides from me.
But after her wedding, she decided
to quit school, move into base housing,
and play housewife. How can she stand it?

THEY SAY MILITARY WIVES

Are, overall, a lot more fit
       than other women in their age
              groups. Uh, yeah. The gym spells
                     relief—stress relief, Mommy duty

relief, and serious tedium
       relief. Looking at Dar, I can
              see she definitely spends time
                     utilizing the workout facilities.

But is that the *only* way
       she relieves tension and
              boredom? Better to know
                     for sure than to keep guessing.

I can't ask her now. She won't
       discuss the subject here. Not
              in front of these three women.
                     Military wives talk, Celine said,

and Darian knows that's true.
       She came with them, but maybe
              she'll let me take her home.
                     I look at Celine, whose seniority

makes her the de facto team
       leader. "Would you mind if
              I drove Dar back to the base?
                     We haven't had time to catch up."

SHE GLANCES AT THE OTHERS

But they are caught up
in their own conversation
and don't notice a thing.

> Carrie: . . . *heard the draw*
> *down is going to happen*
> *sooner than they thought.*

> Meghan: *Is that good or*
> *bad? I mean, are you ready*
> *for a full-time husband?*

> Carrie laughs. *Maybe not.*
> *But don't worry. There's*
> *always another shithole . . .*

I tune back out. Trying to
second-guess the brass is
a fast track to disappointment.

> Celine smiles, as if reading
> my mind. Then she shrugs.
> *I'm good with you driving*

> *Darian back as long as she*
> *is.* We both look at Dar, who
> is slow dancing with the guy

from the bar. Slow grinding
might be a more apt description.
"I'll ask as soon as the music stops."

I'M HALF-WORRIED

Darian will be pissed at the interruption
but instead she seems almost grateful.

> *You really want to drive me home?*
> *Crazy! You can stay over, if you want.*

> It's the guy who gets pissed. *Hey,* he slurs.
> *You're supposed to come home with me.*

Darian is all Darian. *Why? Because I danced*
with you? How does one equal the other?

> *Because of* how *you danced with me.*
> He starts moving his hips, a bad imitation.

> *You know what I mean.* He grabs for her,
> but she isn't nearly as drunk and easily

sidesteps his reach. *Fuck off! You couldn't*
get that teeny pecker up if you tried.

The guy's cheeks puff out and his face
blossoms crimson. He takes a step forward

and I yank her backward. "Come on, Dar.
We'd better get going or your husband

will get back before you do." We both smile
at the joke and I take her arm, steer her

toward the table. The other ladies watch
intently, no doubt trying to decide if full-on

intervention is called for. So does
a beefy man, clearly labeled "bouncer."

One look from him moves Drunk Guy
back to the bar, muttering a fast-flowing

> stream of obscenities. Darian laughs
> it off. *Wow. He got a little testy, huh?*

>> Carrie and Meghan titter. But Celine
>> is thoughtful when she says, *Some men*

>> *would get more than testy. Maybe you*
>> *should think about that.* She stands.

>> *My babysitter turns into a pumpkin*
>> *at midnight. You girls ready to go?*

The three offer lukewarm good-byes,
head out. "What about you? Ready?"

> *Just about. Gotta pee first.* Off she goes,
> unaware of, or at least paying minimal

attention to, the way Drunk Guy watches,
scooting toward the edge of his barstool

as if he just might follow her. Bouncer
definitely notices and shoots a warning

glare. Thank God he's on it, or I'd be more
than a little afraid of the walk to my car.

WE MAKE IT SAFELY

And I rush to lock the doors.
Still, I don't hurry too quickly
to back out of the space. Last thing
I need is to bump into something.

I don't feel inebriated, but who knows
how close to .08 I might be after three
drinks, approximately one per hour?
Darian, I'm pretty sure, is beyond

legally drunk. It isn't far to the gate,
maybe fifteen minutes, driving right
at the speed limit. Not enough time
to plumb her in depth, but I have to

say something. Let's start with trite.
"So, what have you been up to?"
She sighs and leans heavily back
against the seat, making it squeak.

> Not a whole lot. I'm taking a couple
> of courses online. Might as well
> get my BA. Never know when it
> might come in handy. How's school?

"Not bad. Except for Chaucer.
It's kind of lonely living by myself,
but after you, any other roommate
would be totally boring." I smile,

> because it's so true. I know, right?
> Good thing your parents want
> to help out. Are they used to the idea
> of you and Cole yet? My dad's always

been good with Spence and me, but
five years later and Mom still thinks
I'm crazy. Of course, she's married
to Dad, so I guess that makes sense.

In addition to ranching and rodeo,
Darian's dad is in the National Guard.
He's been deployed several times.
The Guard isn't just Weekend Warriors.

Sometimes, they get called up,
regardless of age or points earned
toward a calf roping championship.
Darian's mom thinks the military

is most of the reason he's so mean.
"My parents don't agree with a lot
of my decisions. But you're right.
At least they're willing to support

me in them. Not sure how I'd pay
back a student loan as a rookie social
worker. If I can even find a job once
I get my degree." We reach the gate

and Darian starts to dig in her purse
for her ID. But the cute young MP
sticks his head in the window. *Don't*
worry. I know who you are. He grins,

waves us through. Why does that
not surprise me? "*He* knows you,
but do *you* know him?" It's a joke,
but not, and that's how she takes it.

SHE IS SERIOUS

When she answers.

> I've made it a point to get
> to know lots of people here,
> including men. Especially
> men, in fact. Life is simpler
>
> when you're in charge, even
> though you need to make others
> think they're driving the tank,
> if you know what I mean.

I do, and it's not very pretty.
But it is truthful, so that's a good
start. I have more questions.

We pull up in front of a row
of pretty, well-kept town houses.
Darian directs me to a short

> stretch of driveway. I'd let you
> park in the garage, but Spence's
> Harley takes up more space
>
> than you'd think. She laughs.
> They say buying a big bike is
> a guy's way of making up for
>
> certain personal inadequacies.
> Not true in Spencer's case, at least
> not if you're talking about cock size.

I cringe at her straightforward
language. She has changed in
the last few years. Changed a lot.

AS KIDS

Any curse word beyond "jackass"
would have resulted in a bar of
Ivory in the mouth from Dar's mom,
or giant belt welts from her dad.

Funny, but my parents never said
a thing about my language, not
that I ever used bad words within
their earshot, and rarely beyond it.

I don't have a real problem with men
cursing, unless they go overboard.
But lipstick-framed profanity somehow
seems wrong to me. If you hear it

escape my mouth, you'd better run.
It means I've totally lost it and I'll
probably throw something, too.
I have to admit I got a kick out of

Dar's "teeny pecker" comment tonight.
"Teeny cock" wouldn't have had
quite as much power, in my modest
opinion. I lock the Durango's doors,

follow Darian inside. The two-bedroom
town home is compact but pretty.
At least it would be pretty if she kept
it a little neater. As it is, dirty glasses

and crumpled wrappers decorate
tables and countertops. "Uh, Dar?
Is it the maid's day off, or did you
invite your neighbors' kids for snacks?"

LAUGHTER SNORT-CHOKES

Simultaneously from her nose
and throat. *Thus my decision*
to leave child rearing to others.
Kids are fucking messy, no doubt

about it. She gestures for me to sit
on the beige microfiber sofa. Goes
over to the wet bar, pours Campari

and soda for herself, three fingers
of some upscale (but likely bought
duty-free) Añejo tequila for me.
One velvet sip and I am convinced

that Jose Cuervo is a wannabe. No.
Take that back. A total imposter.
"W-wow . . ." It's a hoarse imitation
of the word. "That's excellent."

Right? It's not what you know,
it's who you know, et cetera. She
rewards me with a long, assessing

stare. *God, it's great to see you.*
How come we don't get together
more often? Not like you live across
the universe, or even the state!

Valid question. Why *don't* we get
together more often? Why the heck—
hell—do friends have to grow apart?

THE GREAT THING

About long-time, all-time friends
is, no matter how many hours
(days, weeks, months, and, I assume,
years) you spend in different places,
when you're finally in the same
room again, it's like you've never left

each other's side. And you realize
that your hearts have never
disconnected. You still like the same
music. Even though it's not exactly
California "in," Darian and I have
been country fans since we were kids.

> She turns on Lady Antebellum,
> who I much prefer to Lady Gaga.
> "Need You Now" plays softly and
> Darian sings along. *And I wonder
> if I ever cross your mind. For me,
> it happens all the time . . .*

Such a sad song, and somehow
it feels relevant here, where I can't
find evidence of Spencer. Cole and
I don't even live together, but there
are pieces of him everywhere
in my apartment—a favorite shirt,

still smelling of his deodorant
and cologne; stuffed animals he won
for me at carnivals; shells and sand
dollars we collected on beach walks;
the dried husks of flowers he gave
me over the years. I never tossed any.

There is no trace of Spencer here—
no flowers, no shells, no shirts.
Framed photographs grace tables
and walls. Dar and her mom. Dar
and her horse. I can see a couple
of Dar and me. But none with Spence.

Not even one of their wedding.
Wonder if there are any in their
bedroom. I'm tempted to go look.
And while I'm there, check the closet
for his clothes. Why am I suddenly
so certain everything inside there

belongs to Darian? And why should
I really care if time and distance
have jacked them apart? Because
I do, damn it. It's just sad to think
about. There was so much promise
in the two-as-one of them. I'm not

sure how to approach the subject,
other than directly. I take three
strong swallows of tequila, seeking
courage. "How are things with Spence?
Any better?" I'm hoping she'll say
yes. But it's just wishful thinking.

> About the same, I guess. It's hard
> to know, exactly. E-mail isn't
> the best way to communicate
> feelings. And it's definitely not
> the right way to discuss our future.
> If we even have one together, that is.

I'M AFRAID TO ASK

But I did start this, so here goes.
"You're not thinking about leaving
him, are you?" The divorce rate

for deployed soldiers is dependably
high. Something like seventy
percent. Can't Darian and Spencer

>be part of the thirty? She shrugs.
>*I don't know. There are reasons*
>*to stay. And reasons to go.*

I think about Celine—how she and
and her husband decided to stick
together, no matter what. "Is it because . . ."

It's so good talking to her again,
I really don't want to make her mad.
Still . . . "I heard there are rumors.

About you and other men. Don't get
pissed, okay? I just wondered, um,
if that's one of your reasons to go."

She sips her Campari. Considers
what to say. For several seconds,
she retreats so far away she might

>have visited another time zone.
>Finally, she returns to Pacific
>Standard. *What am I supposed*

to do, Ash? I'm only twenty-five.
Not like I can live without sex,
and no piece of vibrating plastic

is going to cut it for me. Yes, I've
slept with a couple of guys. I'm not
as strong as you, and maybe I lack

morals. I don't know. It's just every
now and then, I need a warm body
next to mine. I need someone real

and strong and caring to pull me
into him, hold me close, and tell
me he lo—" She skids to a sudden

stop, and certain clarity washes
over me. Why did I start this, again?
"And tell you he loves you? Is that

what you were going to say?" I wait,
but she doesn't answer. "Talk to me,
Dar. Are you in love with someone else?"

She directs her gaze until it's level with
mine. *Yes.* She gulps down the rest
of her drink. I do the same with mine.

IT TOOK ME

About two weeks to overtly insert
the word "love" into the Cole-plus-
Ashley equation. There were hints
before I accepted it. Tendrils

of that elusive emotion, infiltrating
our togetherness. Especially our
intimate togetherness. Before Cole,
I never understood the meaning

of making love. My previous sexual
adventures came in two categories.
One: tepid fumbling—no play, no
passion, no real point to the effort.

Certainly, no orgasm, at least not
for me. Or, two: overheated romps—
no concern, no caring, no real
connection. Lightweight orgasm, yes,

and short-term fun, but nothing worth
holding on to. Either way, I always
ended up disappointed. Sex and love
were two distinct entities in my mind,

as separate as east and west.
Cole fused them, and although
I refused to believe it at first,
the merge began right away.

WE SPENT OUR FIRST SUNDAY

Together at the Air and Space Museum.
We even managed to drag Darian and

Spence out of the bedroom for a few
hours. It was fun playing tourist, even

> if Darian did complain. *What's next?*
> *LEGOLAND?* But she managed to enjoy

the day. We all did. The guys were
attentive. Proprietary, even, holding

us close beside them. A couple of times
I noticed Cole watching children running

ahead of their parents. In a private
moment, I asked, "You like kids, huh?"

> He nodded. *Yeah. I want a big family*
> *one day.* He squeezed my hand. *You?*

"Considering I work at a preschool
and want to teach, I like them okay."

> That didn't quite satisfy him. *How*
> *about kids of your own?* The weird

thing was, I hadn't really thought much
about it before. Marriage was a distant

target. "Of course I want them. Ask me
how many after I've taught for a while."

THE SHORT EXCHANGE

Spoke loudly to me. Here was a man
with a heart. Not a single previous
boyfriend had ever mentioned
children or wanting a family. Whether
or not I shared Cole's dream, that he
had not been afraid to talk about it
illustrated an abstract kind of courage.

I liked him. A lot. Already. That scared me.

But not enough to close myself off.
Not enough to send him away. Cole
had roused intense curiosity. This
gentle-souled, tough-hided soldier
was an enigma. A puzzle I wanted
to solve. A stranger who felt like
someone I knew once upon a time.

I didn't consider the future at all.

Enough, to explore the museum,
hand in hand. And afterward to stop
by Cole's uncle's place, where the boys
were officially staying while on leave.
Followed that up with dinner at a little
oceanfront seafood joint, sharing platters
of crab and oysters on the half shell.

And drinking just enough decent wine.

ALL RESISTANCE WEAKENED

All barriers lowered, when we got
       back to the apartment, Darian
       and Spence were hot and heavy

through the door. They didn't waste
       a second, went straight back to her
       bedroom. Which left Cole and me

alone in the front room. I felt like
       an awkward teenager, wanting
       to kiss him but thinking I really

ought to go brush my teeth first.
       "Be right back," I said. My hand
       trembled as I loaded my toothbrush.

"Jeez. What's up with you?"
       I asked the person in the mirror.
       She didn't answer, and I thought

that was good, at least. All
       fresh-mouthed, I went back to
       the living room. Cole watched

me with those serious eyes,
       a question floating in their gold
       sea. I slid my arms up around

his neck, invitation heavy in
       the kiss I gave him. He lifted me
       as if I were weightless. Our lips

never disconnected as he
        carried me to my room, eased
        me onto my bed. It was romantic.

Sexy. And even sexier when
        he stopped, took off his shirt.
        Marines have to be fit. But Cole

was a whole different level
        of fit—every muscle chiseled
        and skin smooth as suede.

        I started to unbutton my blouse.
                No. Let me. Please? I loved how
                he asked permission, all the while

taking complete control. I also
        loved how he didn't hurry. Each
        time he loosened a button, he kissed

the skin just beneath it. When
        my entire top half was exposed,
        his tongue explored it, inch by

goose bump–covered inch. And
        by the time he unzipped my jeans,
        slid them off my quaking legs,

        my panties had soaked through.
                Jesus. Some things are worth
                waiting for, my California girl.

THE "MY"

Took me over the top. In that
moment, I wanted to be his,
and so gave him things I'd always
resisted. BC (Before Cole), oral
sex had been offered, and received,
with definite boundaries. That night,

we exchanged it with abandon.
I opened my legs wide, pushed
his face in between, urged his tongue
deep inside me, asked his fingers
to follow. I let him bring me right to
the edge. Stopped him. "My turn."

He was down to boxers by then.
BC, I'd been with a grand total
of four men. And if I were to describe
"size," I'd have to say three average,
one little. Comparing to breast size,
three B-cups, one double-A. Cole

is a C-plus, and while that didn't
surprise me, neither did I expect
it. They say size doesn't matter,
but in my estimation, it makes things
both problematic and sort of amazing.
I quickly learned to relax my jaws,

coax him inside my mouth little by
little. It was intense, and all I wanted
in those moments was to make
him feel like the most important
man in the world. I still had no clue
how quickly he would become that.

SIZE DEFINITELY MATTERED

When he finally slipped inside
me. If I hadn't been so wet,
it would have been uncomfortable.

As it was, he filled me up completely,
a sensation I had never known.
He flipped onto his back, pulled me

on top of him. His eyes never left
my face as he lifted my hips, slid
me backward, against his critically

hard erection. A gentle push and when
my own eyes jumped wide, he smiled.
There was no pain, but extreme

pressure against that deep internal
spot some people argue does not exist.
It does; at least I definitely have one,

and Cole was the first guy ever to
find it. I am not a moaner by nature
and, in fact, have always believed

all real-life sex-squeals were put on,
some sorry attempt at porn sound-
track noises or something. But, totally

unplanned, unforeseen, and unbidden,
a minuscule *ah-ah-ah* began in the back
of my throat, grew into a steady *ooooh*

as I climbed toward orgasm. It swelled
into a small scream as I reached
the plateau. A foreign place. Almost

surreal, and he wasn't finished yet.
A shift of bodies, and then he was on
top, rocking fast and faster into me.

I locked my legs around his waist,
lifting my hips to make him touch
that elusive spot again. He took a long

time. A very long time. We reached
the pinnacle together. When our bodies
were quite finished, still we stayed joined

until we had no choice but to slip apart.
Then Cole turned me on one side, urged
me into the bowl of his body, held me

> there. *Exceptional*, he whispered into
> my hair. *Extraordinary*. Within a few
> minutes, his soft, steady breathing told

me he was asleep. I closed my eyes,
but didn't tumble straight into dreams.
Rather, I thought about how quickly lives

can change. Because, while intellect
insisted this was likely a transient connection,
a sliver of emotion really hoped it wasn't.

I AM, BY NATURE

An early riser. Even watery
rays of predawn light will trigger
the built-into-my-brain wakeup
call. So the next morning, when
my eyes stuttered open at eight
oh six, my first thought was, *Wow.*

That's weird. And then, in this order:
Who is in bed with me? Cole. Right.
Wait. What day is it? Monday? No!
I'll never make my nine a.m.
I extricated myself from Cole's arm,
still resting in the U of my waist.

He moved restlessly, but the depth
of his breathing indicated sleep.
I grabbed some clothes, hurried
into the bathroom to shower off
the remnants of sweat-soaked sex.
I was already struggling a little

in my developmental learning
class and didn't want to miss it.
I wrote a quick note to Cole: *Have*
classes until four. Back by five.
Hope to see you then. If not, when?
I left it closed in the bedroom door,

where he'd see it when he got up.
Hurried to class, and managed
to make it with two minutes to spare.
Spent the rest of the day trying
to concentrate. Wondering if Cole
would be there when I got home.

NOT ONLY WAS HE THERE

He and Spence had gone grocery
shopping. The two of them were in
the kitchen, slurping beer and doing
their best to cook something resembling

> spaghetti. Darian diverted me to
> my bedroom. *Thank God for Ragu!*
> she said, laughing. *Now, if they can
> just figure out how to do al dente.*

I put my books on my desk. Noticed
that Cole had made the bed. "What's
up with all the domesticity?" I wondered
out loud. "The way to a girl's heart?"

Just saying it gave the fractured cliché
some weight. "Whose idea was it to make
us dinner, anyway?" I expected her to take
credit. But, no. Apparently it was Cole's.

> *He said he owed you.* Darian smiled.
> *He didn't say what for, but I've got
> a pretty good idea. Girl, I've never heard
> you, like, howl before!* Then she laughed.

My face ignited, but I laughed, too.
Well, a little. They *heard*? "Compared
to you, it was more like a whimper. But . . ."
I never shared the details of my sex life—

or lack thereof. But I knew she really
wanted them at that moment. I didn't
know what to tell her, except, "Cole
is amazing." In more ways than one.

THE SPAGHETTI

Wasn't half-bad. In fact, bolstered
by extra onion, garlic, and a fresh
grate of Parmesan, the Ragu proved

pretty darn good. The guys even
seemed to understand the meaning
of al dente. We ate. Drank a little.

Enjoyed dinner-table talk about past
problems and future fears. It was more
domestic than anything I'd enjoyed

since I was a little girl. The guys
cleared and washed the dishes
by hand. It was such a sweet gesture

that later, when I had to go searching
for my favorite knife, finally finding it
in the drawer with the spatulas, it

bothered me only a little. After dinner,
we watched a scary movie on HBO,
and by the evening's end, the four

of us were solidly a pair of couples.
My homework suffered (in fact,
it languished completely). But sex

that night was even better because
with the basics already accomplished,
Cole and I made it all about nuance.

I WAS UP IN TIME FOR CLASS

Darian, who had missed Monday,
        missed Tuesday, too. I have no idea

if she and Spence slept all day,
        emerging like vampires when the sun

went down, or what. Neither do
        I know for sure how Cole entertained

himself while I was at school.
        All I know is, he was waiting for me

when I got home. Some nights,
        we had dinner out. Others, we cooked

together like a regular committed
        couple. It was a pleasant holding pattern

until the fledgling soldiers had to return
        to Pendleton for SOI—School of Infantry,

where recruits learn vital warfare skills—
        Machine Gun on the Run or Grenades 101.

Cole and Spence would sort into
        different groups there—Cole to the

Infantry Training Battalion, and Spencer
        to the Marine Combat Training Battalion,

before moving on to his chosen
        Military Occupation Specialty training.

AT THE TIME

I was clueless about such details.
All I knew about the Marine Corps
was that it was about to swallow
the new guy in my life. The tall,
serious one from Wyoming, who
enjoyed staring me down with amber

eyes and making me come, first
with his tongue, and then the magic
way only he knew how to do.
I wouldn't have used the word "love"
then, but I was well on my way there.
It would take several days of silence,

brooding about what our time together
actually meant, for the first real pangs
of love to strike. But as Cole tossed
his things into his backpack, this little
voice kept whispering, "God, you're
going to miss him." And when he

went to pee before leaving, I slipped
one of his T-shirts back out of his
pack, stashed it beneath a pillow.
I wasn't exactly sure why then, but
later, when my bed seemed terribly
big and lonely, Cole's shirt, still smelling

of him, brought comfort. And when
he finally had to say good-bye, a river
of emotions—sadness, joy, regret,
hope—permeated our last kiss.
I couldn't make it last long enough.
When he turned away, he left me breathless.

A RIVER

Threads the desert
landscape, splinters
desolation,
an artery of life

                                      blood,

silver-blue. And carried
in its tepid flow,
a promise of one
more tomorrow,
each apricot dawning

                                       soaked

with hope for the young.
History is an unkind teacher.
The elders are wise
and well beyond

                                       dreams

of glory, riches,
or gentle death. Enough,
in a war-tattered land,
that thirst does not

                                       ravage

the throat. Enough
that, bellies taut
with the valley's slender
abundance,
children sleep through

                                       the night.

Cole Gleason

I'VE NEVER CONSIDERED MYSELF

A romantic. Probably because
no evidence of anything even
remotely resembling romance

existed in the house I grew up in.
Maybe, if I think way, way back
to my pre-kindergarten days,

I might catch a glimpse of Mom
and Dad kissing. But holding hands,
or whispering sweet nothings?

Nope. Not even a vague memory
of such things. I'd see them for
what they were on TV or in movies—

fiction. In high school, boyfriends
were more about status than happily
ever after. Relationships came.

Relationships went, and not only
for me. It wasn't that I didn't like
the idea of falling in love. But I settled

for fleeting passion. And then I met
Cole. And Darian met Spencer, and
their overriding love for each other

was contagious. The difference being,
mine and Cole's has grown. Matured,
even. Theirs seems destined to wither.

I CAN'T BRING MYSELF

To say it has already folded up
        into itself, passed away. But if
        Darian really believes she's in love

with someone else, she can't still
        love Spencer, too. Can she? I curl
        my legs under me, watch her refill

our drinks. Glad I'm staying over.
        I'm fuzzy-headed and an artificial
        warmth snakes through my body.

I wait for her to hand me the glass
        before asking, "Who is it, Dar? Tell
        me about him." She sits on the far

        end of the small loveseat, close
                enough so I can see her eyes. *His
                name is Kenny, and I met him at*

        a support group for military
                spouses. Not the one here on base.
                Too close to home pasture and all.

I nod, feeling like an idiot, or at
        the very least, a semistranger.
        "So, his wife's in the military?"

        Her turn to nod. *Air Force. Intel.*
                I guess Tara loves it. It "fulfills her,"
                she told Kenny. Sad, for her family.

HER FAMILY?

What is Darian thinking?
"You mean, they've got kids?"

> *Yep. Well, one. She's fifteen.*

Wait. Fifteen? That makes
her mother at least, what?
Thirty-five? "How old is Kenny?"

> *Don't freak, okay? Forty-two.*

Seriously? What the hell?
A Daddy fetish, or what? "Dar . . ."

> *I know, I know. He's old enough*
> *to be my father. He's also smart*
> *and sweet and stable . . .*

"Stable? I hate to point this out,
but he's sleeping around on his
wife." Which brings me straight
back to Dad, and Darian gets it.

> *He's nothing like your dad, Ash.*
> *I mean, it's not like your mom*
> *was traveling the world, gathering*
> *intelligence for the U.S. of A.*

> *Not like she left you behind for*
> *your father to take care of while*
> *she was off playing spy. It was*
> *Tara's choice to leave, not Kenny's.*
> *Please don't judge him. Or me.*

NOT MY PLACE

To judge. Not my place to worry,
really, except infidelity rarely turns
out well, and last time I looked,
Darian was still my best friend.
"I'd just hate to see you get hurt."

> *Hurt? A little fucking late to worry*
> *about that now!* Her jaw tightens
> and her violet-blue eyes flash anger.
> *Want to know what hurt is? It's . . .*

Her words puncture the space
between us, fangs, but I want to hear
the rest. "What is it? Tell me, Dar."

> She considers. Shakes her head.
> *Maybe someday. But not tonight.*
> *Tonight is supposed to be fun.*
> *Wait. I know . . .* She gets up, rushes

down the hall to her bedroom.
When she returns, she's wearing
red flannel pajamas. She offers a blue

> pair to me. *Get comfy. Then we can*
> *play What If?* Our old sleepover
> game. She goes to switch out CDs

while I heard toward the bathroom
to change, a little reluctant about
her plan. What If? was a blast when
we were in middle school. I'm not
sure it's such a great idea tonight.

THE RULES ARE SIMPLE

One of us asks a "What if"
          question. The other promises

to answer truthfully. When
          we were kids, the questions

          were simple enough. Dar:
               What if the hottest guy in school

          tried to kiss you? She knew
               I was petrified my first kiss

would totally suck, and guessed
          my answer: "I'd run the other way."

Or, from me: "What if your
          parents got divorced? Darian's

          answer, in eighth grade: *I'd*
               help Mom find a nice man.

In high school, the game got
          more complex. Freshman year,

          Dar: *What if Matt tried to put*
               the make on you? Matt was her

new boyfriend. I'd crushed on
          him for over a year, and she knew it.

As I considered my answer,
          it occurred to me that if things

were reversed, I wouldn't be going
　　　　out with my best friend's crush.

In that moment, what I really
　　　　wanted to say was, "I'd tell him

let's do it right here. And then,
　　　　let's do it where Darian can't help

but see us." Okay, the closest
　　　　I'd come to doing "it" was actually

enjoying my first kiss. So when
　　　　I said, "I'd deep throat him and

walk away," I meant I'd tease
　　　　my tongue down his throat, zero

follow-through, because Dar
　　　　was my BFF, and I'd never mess

with that. I swear, I had no idea
　　　　"deep throat" could mean oral sex,

but it did to Darian. Game over.
　　　　It took several days to convince

her of my naïveté, and only after
　　　　she forgave me did I pause long

enough to think that my best friend
　　　　really should have known me better.

ALL COMFY IN BLUE FLANNEL

I hope for the best, return to
the front room, where Darian
and the Dixie Chicks are singing
"Cowboy Take Me Away."

"Been a while since I've listened
to *Fly*." It was our favorite album
in seventh grade. We even thought
we might be the next Dixie Chicks—

Darian taking lead with her fine,
clear voice and me on guitar, doing
harmonies. We drove our parents
nuts, practicing over and over.

> It's the perfect lead-in for our
> game. *What if,* Darian asks, *we*
> *would have put together a band*
> *and gone on the rodeo circuit?*

We figured that was the easiest
place to break in. Plus, Dar's dad
could give us rides to events. I mull
over my answer. "If we'd actually made

it on the circuit, you and your father
would either totally hate each other
by now or we'd be so rich and famous,
he'd insist on being our manager."

> She laughs. *Pretty sure it would*
> *be the former. Or maybe both.*
> *Who knows? Okay. Your turn.*
> She waits while I think of a question.

I sip tequila, relish the crawl
of heat. "What if you hadn't broken
up with Carson Piscopo?" They were
everyone's idea of the perfect

> couple for almost two years. Dar
> smiles. *I'd be living in a trailer,
> chasing a pack of kids around
> while Carson sucked down beer.*

"He did like his Budweiser, didn't
he?" Not so unusual, of course.
The majority of the football team
overindulged, as do most Marines

I know. Then again, any soldier
worth his MREs deserves to relax
when he can, with whatever. High
school jocks? Not so much. Jeez,

> I'm showing my age. Dar clears
> her throat. *What if Cole was around
> all the time? Like, if he wasn't a Marine.
> Would you still love him as much?*

What a weird question. "Well,
of course. Why wouldn't I? I don't
love him because he's a Marine.
I love him . . ." Damn. I almost said

in spite of it, and that isn't right,
either. It's such a big part of who
he is. "If he was around all the time,
I'd have sex a lot more often."

WE BOTH LAUGH

But now it's time to get serious.
This was her idea, but I'm ready to play
tough. "What if you never met Spencer?"

> *Then you wouldn't have met Cole.*

"That's not what I mean, Dar."

> *I know. Okay. First off, I wouldn't*
> *be living at Camp Pendleton.*
> *Probably not even in San Diego.*

Grad school was never in her plans.
I'm not even sure a degree was.
She went to college to leave home.

"But would you be happier?"

> She shrugs. *Who knows? Things*
> *would be different, that's all.*
> *Anyway, happiness is overrated.*

"You don't mean that. What if . . ."

> *Hey!* she interrupts. *It's my turn.*
> *Um . . .* As she contemplates her next
> question, the Dixie Chicks launch into

"Goodbye Earl," a song about two friends
who feed poisoned black-eyed peas to
the ex-husband whose fists put one

of them in intensive care. So long,
Earl. The song is half amusing, half

scary as hell. Darian listens for a few
seconds, then finally asks, *What if
Cole got drunk and hit you?*

She looks at me so earnestly, it spins
the tiny warning lights inside my brain.
"That would never happen. But if

it did, I'd make sure it would never
happen twice. I'd . . ." What? Have him
arrested? Poison his black-eyed peas?

Or would I, just maybe, chalk it up
to the alcohol? The bigger issue is,
"Are you talking from experience?"

> Her face flushes. She starts to say
> something. Closes her mouth.
> Shakes her head. *Just wondered.*

There's more there. A lot more,
I'm guessing. "Darian, you'd tell
me if somebody hit you, right?"

> *Yeah, sure. Of course I would.*

This game is getting old. One
more round, then I'll call it quits.
"What if Kenny left his wife?"

> *Good question. What if I told
> you he's already decided to?*

THIS ISN'T FUN ANYMORE

I want to support my friend. Want
her decisions to be sound. Why do
I think those two things are opposing
forces? "Would you please stop
the coy routine? What's going on?"

> Look. I haven't totally made up
> my mind, but I'm thinking about
> divorcing Spencer. I can't tell him
> long distance, though. So I guess
> I'm stuck in limbo for now.

"And if you decide to split up,
will it be because of Kenny?"

> In a way. I didn't fall out of love
> with Spencer because of Kenny.
> But I did fall in love with Kenny
> because of Spencer. Kenny treats
> me with respect. Simple as that.

Sadness seeps into me. Through
me. And still, "I guess I understand.
I'm just sorry, you know?" I give her
a hug. "I'm fading fast. Guest room?"

> She smiles. Clean sheets on the bed
> and everything. And there's a new
> toothbrush in the medicine cabinet.
> Morning-after-tequila breath is brutal.

> As I start down the hall, she calls
> after me, So you know, I'm sorry, too.

TIRED AND BUZZED

Still, I find it hard to sleep.
The bed is bigger and softer
than mine. I sink down into
the pillow top. Eyes closed,
I could be afloat in a calm sea.

Then up blows a wind. Spiraling
impatience for the impermanent
nature of love. Can it endure?
Grow? Flourish? I love Cole more
now than I did our first year

together. Is it because I know
him better—have investigated
beyond exterior shine, discovered
the facets underneath, strong,
pure, impenetrable? I hear Darian.

What if he was around all the time?
Would seeing him every day change
the way I feel? Is my heart fonder
because of his absence? Does proximity
breed discontent? The last thing

I want is for Cole and me to become
like my parents, one finding some
slim measure of satisfaction in
the other's failures. But what about
loyalty? Faithfulness? Promises kept?

Would sharing a home make it less
welcoming—to Cole, or to me?

OUR FIRST YEAR TOGETHER

Was mostly a year apart. At first,
while Cole attended SOI, we saw
each other when he got weekend liberty.
Sometimes on base, other times off,

but only if he wasn't in the field, and only
if his platoon sergeant was so inclined.
We didn't know for sure if or when it
would happen, and anticipation built

to an insane degree. Cole could
use his cell phone only on Fridays,
after training. I'd wait breathlessly
until I got a definitive yea or nay.

Even then, there were restrictions.
Luckily, Uncle Jack lived within
the prescribed radius and also had
a daughter cute enough to lure

Cole's "battle buddies." SOI
infantrymen did not leave base
alone. The Corps believes in
chaperones. We did manage some

alone time, though. Sex, ever better,
was my reward for patience, and
"liberty" for Cole meant plummeting
toward commitment for me.

SCHOOL OF INFANTRY

Lasted not quite two months.
    By the time Cole's graduation
    loomed, I was over-the-top in love

with him. My own schoolwork
    suffered more than a little, not so
    much because of time spent with him,

as because of too much time
    fantasizing about being with him.
    Daydreams are distracting. Then

came the very real threat of
    losing him. As commencement
    day marched ever closer, anxiety

took seed. Sprouted. Grew like
    the spring weeds outside my door.
    I didn't eat much. Food had no taste.

My brain fought sleep and when
    exhaustion forced it, desolation
    framed my dreams. And snapshots

of war. I couldn't get past those
    images. They were everywhere—
    television, magazines, the Internet.

Finally, I went to a counselor
    who sent me to a therapist, who
    prescribed tiny pills that allowed

me some measure of deep night
    respite. *Non-narcotic*, he promised.
    Then he amended, *But could cause*

dependency. I still depend on
    them to silence the nightmares.
    My body has learned to work in sync

with them, sleeping straight
    through the night, waking on time
    and mostly refreshed. But those

first weeks, Ativan fogged
    every morning. The alarm couldn't
    fight the daze. I ended up missing

my morning classes, and as
    someone who had always been
    in complete control of my life

up until then, I felt like a puzzle
    that couldn't be solved because
    pieces were misplaced. But then

would come Cole's Friday call,
    and all those pieces started to fall
    right into place, except for the most

important ones around the edges,
    the ones that completed the puzzle.
    Those appeared when Cole did.

COLLEGE

Wasn't working out much better
for Darian, not that she saw Spence
much more than I saw Cole. And
not that she worried any more
about him, either. In fact, she slept

> fine, sans medication. Her problem
> was lack of motivation. *The only thing*
> *I'm good at is singing*, she said. *So why*
> *bust my butt, working for grades?*
> The only classes she kept up with

were music and screenwriting.
Spence's MCT school was only
four weeks, no liberty the first two.
By the third, he and Dar were in
regular heat for each other. They

had only a few hours together,
but made the best of it at Uncle
Jack's. The fourth week, Spence
was allowed overnight liberty, and
partway through their all-night love

fest, they began making wedding
plans. After his MCT graduation,
Spence's MOS training would continue
at Pendleton. He wanted a wife
before any chance at deployment.

And Darian wanted a husband.
Spence received special liberty
to walk down the aisle. Cole
was granted it, too, to serve as best
man, opposite my maid of honor.

The wedding night was incredible,
at least for Cole and me, who had
our own honeymoon suite right
on the beach, waves serenading
us as we made love. It was our

first time alone with no pressure
to hurry since those first days
after we met. We were starved
for each other, barely through
the door before tux and dress

fell to the floor in an inelegant
heap. There was nothing elegant
about what came next, either.
It was desperation, made flesh.
He picked me up with steel-

muscled arms, kissed me, bit
me, licked me. Tried, it seemed,
to swallow me. And I screamed
for him to climb inside me and
he did, with his lips and tongue

and fingers—one, two, three.
And then he filled me up with fire
and stone and when he poured
into me, I cried. Because I knew.

I KNEW

That would be our last night
to join in such a way before
the Marine Corps ordered him
to a place where touch would not

be possible. Unfair, when I had
just tapped into this wellspring,
need I never knew I thirsted for.
Unfair, to strip me of him, just

when I realized he was intrinsic
to the "me" I'd become. Who would
I be when he was gone? Later,
I would realize that distance was not

at the heart of my pain. It was time,
dissipated. Vanished into the ether.
Moments lost cannot be resurrected.
But, whether or not I knew the reason,

I ached for him, for us, though he held
me in his arms. When I confessed
my fear and he made love to me
the second time, it was tender, driven

by tears. And he whispered into my ear,
my hair, the plush skin of my breasts,
my belly, my thighs: *Don't be sad, Ash.*
As long as you want me, I will always

come back to you. And, no matter where
I am, you will be the first I think of every
morning, and this will be the last thing
I remember as I fall asleep each night.

ROUND THREE

Was the best one of all.
        Something to remember,
                for sure. For him. And me.

Exhausted, but not close
        to satiated, we poured
                memories into the predawn

hours, enough to last
        for the long months apart
                dangling on the near horizon.

Afterward, he held me
        so tightly I could barely
                breathe. But when he mumbled,

        I love you, Ash, I could have
                happily suffocated right there
                        in his arms. It was the first time

he'd said it. I half-suspected
        he was delirious, wasn't sure
                I believed him. Nor was I certain

he heard me when I dared
        admit out loud, "I love you,
                too." I'd never uttered those

words, to him or anyone. But
        I realized, just as I nodded
                off, how very much I meant it.

LOVE CAN COMPLETE YOU

It can also destroy you. The day Cole
graduated SOI, love annihilated me.

By then, I was helplessly, ridiculously,
out of my mind crazy about him. And

they gave us exactly fifteen minutes
to say good-bye before loading him up

to send him off to his permanent duty
station on Oahu. I don't know why they

call PDSs "permanent." "Regular" is more
accurate, at least until the brass deploys

their grunts elsewhere. Cole would have
four months in Hawaii before heading to

Iraq. San Diego felt a million miles away,
and as summer closed its fists around

spring, I felt the squeeze. Finals were
a nightmare. Despite the vastness between

Cole and me, I was every bit as distracted
as when he was "spitting distance," to borrow

a Wyoming colloquialism. Later, when
my parents wanted to know what happened

to that semester, I told them I was sick,
which wasn't a total lie. I was heartsick.

I DID GET REGULAR CALLS

They always started pretty much
like this: *Hey, sweetheart.*
What's up in the real world?

And, since I always answered,
"Not much going on here. What's
happening in *your* world?"

I got a regular rundown
about barracks cleaning
and physical training before

the poet in Cole started talking
about, *The perfume of plumeria,*
fighting the scent of sweat

in the air, or how, *The ocean's*
singing reminds me of our last
night together. Remember?

How could I possibly forget?
And that made me even
hungrier to see him or touch

him or taste him. His voice was not
nearly enough, so I'd go get his shirt
and bury my face in it until time was up

and he had to tell me, *Good-bye. Love*
you. And, *I'm in need of some serious*
Ash time. Before long, our mantra.

ALL SIGNS POINTED

To Spencer being assigned a local
PDS. He had requested Pendleton,
which is home to several helicopter
squadrons. With that likely, he put
in for on-base housing, knowing
it would take a while for approval.

Meanwhile, his housing allowance
would pay for the off-base apartment
he could come home to after completing
training. With SDSU out for summer
break, I packed up my stuff, left Darian
in San Diego, and went home.

Despite my growing feelings for Cole,
I hadn't mentioned him to my parents.
I had a pretty good idea of how they
would react, especially Mom. The only
thing that surprised me was how calm
she remained when we sat down to dinner

my first night back and the conversation
almost immediately went to if and who
I was dating. At that point, lying seemed
ridiculous, so I admitted, "Actually, I am
seeing someone. And it's kind of serious."
All silverware action came to a halt.

> *Why didn't you mention it?* asked
> Dad. *Is he, like, twice your age?*

I smiled. "Well, he is an older man.
Twenty-one, in fact. And he's kind
and smart, and really good looking . . ."

It was then or never; at least
that's how it felt, so I went ahead
and added, "And he's in the Corps."

Mom's jaw went rigid. *Surely you
don't mean the Marine Corps?* When
I looked away, she knew. Yet she kept
her voice low. *Are you actively seeking
heartbreak? Have you heard there's a war
going on? I can't believe you're that stupid.*

That smarted, but I didn't want to
argue, or even defend myself.
"Love is stupid sometimes, I guess.
Look, Mom, I didn't go looking to fall
for a soldier. Yes, I know there's a war.
Cole's heading that way very soon."

Stating it so matter-of-factly sucked
all bravado out of me. My shoulders
slumped and my eyes stung. "And
I'd really a-a . . ." A huge wad of
emotion crept up my throat. I choked
it back. "Appreciate your support."

Mom shook her head, dropped
her eyes toward her plate. It was
Dad who said, *Ashley, girl, I think
this is a huge lapse of judgment.
But I can see you're upset. We'll
talk about it after dinner, okay?*

But our appetites were crushed
beneath a relentless blitz of silence.

THE WEIGHT OF SILENCE

The plain is still,

                    emptied

of even the thinnest
sounds—the murmur
of creeping sand;
pillowed spin of tumbleweed;
susurrus of feathers trapped
in thermal lift.

The well is dry,

                    drained

to weary echo
above desiccated silt.
Thirst swells, bloats
every cell until
the body arcs
beneath its weight.

The page is blank,

                    scrubbed of

metaphor, flawless
turn of phrase. Parched
within the silence, hungered
in a desert without

                    words,

I am stranded
in your absence.

Cole Gleason

THE TIMING

For this trip couldn't be a whole
lot worse. The semester has barely
started, and I'm just settling into
my classes. I'll only miss a few days,

though. Hopefully my professors
will be understanding. I'm not so
sure about Mr. Clinger, who wears
austerity proudly. I wonder if he writes

poetry, too, or if he only analyzes it.
You can't teach poetry without truly
loving it, can you? Guess we'll see. Class
is over for the day, the room deserted

except for Mr. Clinger and me.
"Excuse me." I muster my prettiest
smile, but when he looks up, he scowls,
and I almost change my mind.

> *Yes, Ms. Patterson? What can I do*
> *for you?* His voice is flat, though
> his blue glacier eyes seem curious

enough. I study his face, subtly creased
beneath a surfer's tan. He might
be handsome, if he could find a smile.
"I won't be in class on Friday or Monday."

> *I see. And where, if I might ask,*
> *will you be?* He taps his fingers
> on the metal table top. Drumming

impatience. "I'm flying to Hawaii
on Thursday. Cole—uh, my boyfriend—
is deploying to Afghanistan. He'll be gone
seven months and . . ." Suddenly, it hits

me that Cole will spend the holidays
overseas. Again. Flimsy celebrations
this year. "It's his fourth deployment.
We'll have a few days to say good-bye."

> *I see.* His tone is not especially
> sympathetic. *You'll miss a test, but
> I suppose I can let you make it up.*

"Thank you, Mr. Clinger." I saved
some ammunition, just in case.
Apparently, I don't need it, but I'll
use it anyway, if only for punctuation.

"By the way, Cole writes poetry.
I was wondering what you thought
about this." I hold out the crinkled paper
like it's a special gift, which it is.

> He reads Cole's poem, "The Weight
> of Silence." Reads it twice, I think.
> Finally comments, *This is good.*

"Really? I thought so, too.
I'll tell him you said—"

> *I wasn't finished. I'm almost sorry
> it's this good. I hate to see talent
> wasted, and, one way or another,
> the military will squander it.*

I'M AT A LOSS

How to respond? I want to say
something, but can't find words.
"I . . . um . . . don't . . ." He stares
intently, dissecting me with

those translucent, cool eyes.
Behind the frost, there's a story.
"I'm sorry. I don't understand
what you mean. Waste it, how?"

> Now he's searching for his own
> words. That's gratifying. Finally,
> *This is a military city. Teaching here,*
> *I've seen a lot of what the service*
>
> *can do. Not much of it is good.*
> *People lose autonomy. Lose dreams.*
> *Worst of all, they lose other people.*
> *People who are important to them.*

I nod, because it's largely true. Still,
"I try not to think about losing him.
I know it could happen, sure. But if
I let myself worry, I'd be wrecked

all the time. Cole was a Marine
when I met him. That's who I fell in
love with. I have no way of divorcing
him from the Corps, so I cope."

> *I understand. To a point, anyway.*
> *I was an Army brat, so no divorce*
> *was possible. My father dragged*
> *us halfway around the world and*

back. I never had real friends. Never
knew what it meant to set down
roots until after I came here. Once
I finally sprouted some, the taproot

grew deep. I doubt I'll ever leave.
That turned out to be a problem
for my wife. Or, should I say, my
ex-wife. She was hot to travel.

Ah, the story behind the frost.
Two stories, actually, or maybe
a pair of epic poems. "So far, Cole
has only been assigned to one PDS."

Except for deployments, you
mean. Not like they'd send families
chasing their soldiers into Iraq
or Afghanistan. With the coming

draw-down, who knows where
he'll go? Are you ready to follow
him wherever? Especially if you have
kids one day? It's worth thinking about.

The military is a highly engineered
machine. It's only as good as the sum
of its parts, however, and its parts
are fragile. But easily replaced.

Cole, fragile? Not so much.
But I'm not about to argue
the point. "Thanks, Mr. Clinger.
Guess there's a lot to consider."

I START TO TURN AWAY

Ms. Patterson? Er . . . Ashley?
You forgot this. He offers me

Cole's poem. *I'm sorry if I seemed*
unsympathetic. This really is good.

Tell your boyfriend when he's done
defending freedom, he really should

do something with his writing.
The tension between us dissolves.

"Thanks. I'll be sure to let him know.
He'll probably freak that I showed

it to you, but I really wanted to get
your opinion." I reach for the paper

and our fingers brush, initiating
a totally unexpected electric jolt.

Holy crap! What was that? My hand
jerks back, zapped, and my cheeks react

with a furious blush—half shame,
half ridiculous lust for a man who is

my professor. A man who is several
years older than I. A man who most

definitely is not Cole. "S-s-sorry,"
I stutter. Stupid! What am I, twelve?

THE REAL QUESTION

Is, why am I apologizing? And,
to whom? Mr. Clinger smiles
at my obvious consternation.
Oddly, I smile back, despite
my discomfort at what just

transpired between us. Or,
maybe nothing at all did. Maybe
I imagined the whole thing.
But I don't think so. There
is some weird chemistry here.

> *Travel safely, Ashley. Let's find*
> *a good time next week for you*
> *to make up that test. By the way,*
> *we're moving to spoken word*
> *poetry next week. Here . . .*

> He scribbles some names on
> a personalized Post-it. *If you have*
> *a few minutes before I see you*
> *again, check them out on YouTube.*
> He offers the paper, and I take it

gingerly, hope he doesn't notice
the way my hand is shaking.
I glance at what he's written.
"Oh, I know Rachel McKibbens
and Taylor Mali. Alix Olson, too."

> His grin widens. *Of course*
> *you do. Have a great trip.*

I MANAGE

To make it through the rest of the day
        without getting turned on by another

professor. Or fellow student, campus
        policeman, or janitor. To be fair to myself,

it has been a few months since I've seen
        Cole, but I've successfully sequestered

the thought of sex with him, or anyone.
        Until today. But to say what happened

earlier meant nothing at all would be
        a lie. In that moment, I wanted to fuck

Mr. Clinger. Jonah. That's the name
        on the Post-it, above the slam poets.

Some tiny, niggling splinter of me
        was desperate to fuck Jonah Clinger

and all the rest of me believes that
        shard is a no-good traitor. And tonight

that's what I'm obsessing about.
        Not research. Not writing the paper due

Wednesday. Not packing bikinis
        and sexy nighties to wear for Cole. Nope.

Instead, I'm trying to drown every
        recurring image of Jonah in a huge glass

of Chardonnay. Doesn't seem to
    be working. Maybe if it was tequila

I'd have half a chance. Instead, I keep
    flashing back to ice blue (not golden) eyes.

I need someone to talk to. But who?
    Darian, my forever friend, who's likely

dumping her Marine husband for
    a guy who's definitely dumping his Air

Force–focused wife? Probably not
    my best choice. My other local friends

are UCSD students with no military
    ties. I already talked to Sophie today,

and got her to agree to watch
    my apartment. After all the hype

I just fed her about *needing* to see
    the love of my life before he leaves

for Afghanistan, how could I possibly
    discuss the seedier side of my psyche?

Brittany, who's all sass and easy sex,
    no desire for commitment, *ever* (at least

until she finds someone actually worth
    committing to?). Another wrong call.

I PACE THE APARTMENT

Putting out of place things back
into place. Tossing stuff that needs
tossed. Seeking order in disorder.

I dust. Vacuum. Clean counters,
sinks, and the toilet. At least when
I get back from Hawaii, everything

will be in its place and I can dive
straight back into my class work
without having to do this stuff first.

Finally, I refill my glass. Turn on
my computer. Cruise over to YouTube
and some of the best spoken word

poets in the world. I'm not familiar
with a couple on this list, but before
I'm through watching, I will be.

There is order in this, too. I can read
my poetry out loud, but this is pure
performance. Rhythmic. Bold. Passionate.

Sort of like great sex. The kind I'll
have in a couple of days. With Cole
Gleason. Not Jonah Clinger. Stop it,

already. I turn off my computer, reach
for my pen and the notebook I write
poetry in. Find order in formal verse.

SLOW BURN
by Ashley Patterson

What happens to kisses never kissed—
those we pretend not to have missed?

Do they fall from our lips and settle, silt,
compress into fossils, layered in guilt;

Do they crumble like wishes, their magic lost,
or wither and curl, seedlings chewed by frost;

or perhaps they take flight, buoyant as screams,
to tempt us again in the heat of our dreams.

What is the ultimate cost of kisses not kissed?
What becomes of passion we choose to resist?

Does it sink like hope on a cloudy morning,
mire us with doubt, muted forewarning;

Does it rise from the groin, seeking the brain,
creeping like quicksilver, vein into vein,

to bewilder, an answer we cannot discern,
or smolder, a candle condemned to slow burn?

What can we say about passion dismissed,
or the import of kisses consciously missed?

Scorned passion is truth we're doomed to forget,
kisses wasted, the weight of final regret.

IN THE DAYS

Right before Cole shipped out
for his first Iraq tour, his enthusiasm
was almost contagious. Almost.
When he'd call, he'd talk about
a hundred klicks (military speak

> for kilometers) a minute. *Fallujah,*
> *here we come! Get ready for a major*
> *ass-whooping. Did you hear about*
> *that sonofabitch suicide bomber*
> *at that funeral? Crazy bastard!*

If he harbored the tiniest hint
of fear, he never confessed it,
and it never, ever showed. In fact,
he felt immortal. Untouchable.
The way he'd been trained to believe.

Personally, I was thrilled for him.
Petrified for me. Fallujah.
I did my research, and it scared
the crap out of me. When this
whole Iraq mess started, Fallujah

was, according to everything I read,
the "deadliest city" in the country,
a stronghold of insurgency, and
who knew, exactly, who the bad
guys were or where they hid

their weapons? When coalition
forces first went in, casualties
were assumed—and that included
civilians. Bombs aren't selective.
And grenades truly are colorblind.

Killing women and children
is not conducive to goodwill.
It took years to rebuild, and
by the time Cole arrived in Iraq,
the corner had been turned.

That's what they were saying,
and I clung to that. Cole and his
buddies, however, were primed
for a fight. And that worried me
more than the very real threat

of IEDs or stray bullets. The peace
that had been forged was fragile.
Depending on who was doing
the talking, the silence in the streets
represented a suffocating culture.

The Iraqi police force was no kinder
to Fallujah citizens than U.S. soldiers,
looking for trouble where perhaps none
lurked. Or perhaps it did. The situation
was confused, even if it wasn't chaotic.

WHEN COLE ARRIVED

In the Anbar Province, communication
became less frequent, and actual calls

were rare. He did send fairly regular e-mails
from Camp Fallujah's Internet café.

At first, they were tinged with excitement.
YOU WOULDN'T BELIEVE THIS PLACE. IMAGINE

A GHOST TOWN. TOMBSTONE OR SOMETHING.
ONLY IT'S A GHOST CITY. MOST OF IT HASN'T

BEEN REBUILT SINCE THE 2004 OFFENSIVE.
IT LOOKS LIKE A BUNCH OF STONE SKELETONS.

BUT, SOMEWHERE IN THE GUTS OF THOSE
RUINS ARE FUCKING INSURGENTS, BUSY

BUILDING IEDS AND POKING THEIR HEADS
UP JUST LONG ENOUGH TO TAKE POTSHOTS

AT US. BY GOD, WE'RE GOING TO SMOKE
THE MOTHERFUCKERS OUT AND SQUASH

THEM LIKE HORNETS. AND IF THEY'RE PISSED
HORNETS, SO MUCH THE BETTER. ON ANOTHER

NOTE, PLEASE SEND SOUR CANDY AND CIGS.
DOESN'T MATTER WHAT KIND. I CAN TRADE.

LOVE YOU. MISS YOU. I'D SAY WISH YOU WERE
HERE BUT I DON'T. TOO MANY PERVS AROUND.

AS THE WEEKS WORE ON

E-mail often became gripe mail.
The Fallujah action had slowed
in the months before Cole's unit
arrived. Courageous Marines spent

less time actively being brave and
more time training Iraqi policemen
to handle local issues. The city
had been divided into walled-off

sections. The locals were required
to travel by foot and show military-
issued ID in order to move between
neighborhoods. As Cole wrote,

> WE MAN CHECKPOINTS AND KEEP
> CURFEWS AND HELP REBUILD
> INFRASTRUCTURE. ALL OF US ARE
> JONESING FOR ACTION. AIN'T HAPPENING.

He complained a lot that first swing,
but I was happy to hear casualty
counts for his unit remained steady
at zero. Once in a while, an e-mail

> would hint at ugliness. HAD A LITTLE
> EXCITEMENT. CAUGHT TWO DUDES
> TRYING TO PLANT AN IED. WE BLEW
> THAT MOFO SKY HIGH. ALMOST FELT
>
> SORRY FOR THOSE HAJJIS THOUGH.
> THE IRAQIS HAULED THEM OFF OUT
> OF SIGHT. CAN'T SAY FOR SURE BUT
> I DOUBT THEY MADE IT TO LOCKUP.

SOME TIME LATER

I became aware of free press
stories leaking out of Iraq. Stories
about detaining Sunni Arabs

for no other reason than that's what
they were, and locking them up for
months or more, no judge, no jury,

not even a day in court. Sometimes
their families didn't hear of their fate
for a very long time. Sometimes

they just disappeared. Other stories
made it very clear that all the American
goodwill we saw on videos—delivering

boxes of food or handing out candy
to children—was tolerated, not
celebrated, as we in the U.S. believed.

Tootsie Pops and MREs hardly
compensated for destroying
the Fallujah economy or executing

its men. Farmers and storekeepers
often met the same fate as tried-
and-true insurgents. But, who knew

who was who? Especially with
the growing Awakening movement—
former insurgents bought off by the U.S.,

in the hopes that three hundred
dollars a month would temper their
extremist ways. The Awakening forces

were paid to patrol neighborhoods,
help with the rebuilding, and maybe
do a little spying. It didn't make them

love the Americans any more, but
they didn't care much for al Qaeda,
either. In theory, the idea worked well.

In reality, it was working to a point.
Except, what if it wasn't? Iraq is a land
of tribes, and as more and more sheiks

signed on to the program, infighting
was unavoidable. Not only that, but
with millions in aid pouring in, every

> tribal leader wanted a piece of the pie.
> And, as Cole wrote, *WHO KNOWS IF ALL*
> *THESE DUDES ARE REALLY SHEIKS OR NOT?*
>
> *SEEMS LIKE HALF OF WHAT WE DO IS TRYING*
> *TO FIGURE THAT OUT, OR KEEPING SUNNI*
> *HAJJIS FROM MURDERING SHIITE HAJJIS OVER*
>
> *WHO GETS WHAT. GODDAMN. WHY DON'T*
> *WE JUST LET THOSE MOTHERFUCKERS KILL*
> *EACH OTHER AND BE DONE WITH THIS MESS?*

It was a mess, but less a mess than
before the surge that made it a mess.
At least, that's how the brass saw it.

AN UGLIER MESS WAS BREWING

In the years since the 2004 siege,
Fallujah doctors had seen a huge
swell of infant mortality and serious
birth defects, including a two-headed
baby and too many born paralyzed.

Breast and brain cancers increased
fourfold, childhood cancers
twelvefold, and leukemia cases
skyrocketed to thirty-eight times
usual levels. Not only the sheer

numbers, but also the speed of this
rise was reminiscent of another
wartime nightmare—Hiroshima.
Scientists went looking for reasons.
What they found—evidence of white

phosphorous, napalm, and uranium
in civilian neighborhoods—would
cause enough of a stir that denial
was useless. The blame rose higher
than the offices of military brass.

It went all the way to the boardroom
of the Commander in Chief and his
advisors. By that time, the grumbling
had long since begun that the war
in Iraq was a sham, a fabrication.

Six months before the initial invasion,
Congressman Dennis Kucinich took
an unpopular stand, saying there was
no credible evidence Iraq had weapons
of mass destruction, nor provided aid

to al Qaeda, either before 9/11 or since.
And, "Unilateral action against Iraq will cost
the United States the support of the world
community." Eventually, even our staunch
ally, England, would lose respect.

I was still in high school then and, though
I heard plenty of antiwar sentiment
coming out of my parents' mouths,
I had more important things on my mind.
Cheerleading. Honor choir. My latest crush.

Those are what I worried about.
Not invented excuses for a war on
the other side of the world. I would
never have predicted it would mean
one damn thing to me in the future.

But as that long, gray autumn
of 2007 wore on, I couldn't help
but wonder if what we were accomplishing—
or not—was worth sending our warriors,
especially one of them, into harm's way.

I COULD BARELY WATCH THE NEWS

The casualty count kept rising.
When they added up the number
of dead U.S. soldiers in December,
2007 would go down as the deadliest

year yet in Iraq. Sometimes I didn't
hear from Cole for days at a time.
Though I did my best not to think
about what that might mean,

I would flash on possibilities,
none of them good. I was back in
school, and at the time still thought
I'd be an educator, so I was student

teaching part-time. Nothing like
helping first graders learn to spell
and add to lift the focus off oneself,
at least for a little while. Though

I didn't mention it to Cole (a rabid
Republican), I was out stumping for
Hillary Clinton. I figured it was past
time for a woman to run the show, and

hopefully extricate us from the quagmire.
Two-thirds of the country wanted us
out of Iraq by then. And sixty percent
of military families agreed that we should

not have gone in there to begin with.
None of that helped grunt morale,
which plunged, at least for many.

IN COLE'S CASE

I didn't pick up on the exact level
        of his frustration until after he came
        back from that first tour. While he was

over there, he did what was asked
        of him without complaining within
        earshot of the POGS who ran the show.

In his mind, he was defending
        his country, his buddies, his mom,
        and me. In that order, something

I didn't figure out right away.
        Looking back, I realize how little
        we really knew about each other.

For instance, he had no clue
        that my birthday was the last day
        of November, or that it made me

a Sagittarius, which surprised
        me when I did a rudimentary
        astrology study because I felt

much more like a Capricorn.
        Later I found out Cole called
        those daily columns "horrorscopes."

I spent that birthday alone,
        even though it was a Friday
        and my girlfriends were going

dancing. It just didn't seem
        right to celebrate another year
        of living when the guy I loved

might very well be dying.
        I hadn't heard a word from him
        since Thanksgiving Day, when

he actually got to call long
        enough to let me know chow
        was a real turkey-and-trimmings

feast. Eight days with zero
        communication were a stark
        reminder that, as Cole's girlfriend,

if something bad happened,
        it might take a while for me to find
        out. I was only "somebody" to him.

I went to my classes. Taught
        first graders. Checked my e-mail
        a lot. Came away disappointed.

Nervous. Scared. The weird
        thing was, taut with anxiety,
        every day with no word only

made me love him more.
        When I finally heard from him,
        I had no room for anger. Only relief.

WHEN I FINALLY HEARD

Relief was enough. That time.
He did not tell me everything.

> SORRY FOR MY SILENCE. HOPE YOU
> DIDN'T WORRY. I WAS ON PATROL
>
> OUTSIDE THE WIRE. SAW A LITTLE
> ACTION, NONE OF IT OURS. AT LEAST
>
> NONE I CAN CONFESS. ROOTED OUT
> SOME BAD GUYS. BOUGHT OFF A LOT
>
> MORE. THIS IS GETTING OLD. WITH LUCK,
> I'LL BE BACK IN FEBRUARY. THAT MEANS
>
> CHRISTMAS AT CAMP FALLUJAH. THINK
> SANTA CAN FIND US HERE? IF YOU SEE
>
> HIM, WOULD YOU ASK HIM TO SEND
> SOMETHING TO READ? GODDAMN
>
> BOREDOM IS KILLING MY GOOD MOOD.
> AND I'M NOT THE ONLY ONE. LOVE YOU.

I sent four holidays boxes, stuffed
with books and board games, trail

mix, jerky, sardines, cigarettes, dried
fruit, and Fruit of the Looms. I figured

every soldier needs clean underwear.
I also put in a picture of me at the beach,

wearing a three-slivers-of-crochet bikini.
Thought about his buddies seeing it.

Took it back out again. Remembered
how he cherished my body those sweet,

long nights together. Tucked a different
photo of me in short shorts and a low-

cut tank top into a Christmas card with
Santa's sleigh swooping down over

the Tetons on front. *For my Wyoming
boy's eyes only,* I wrote inside. *This*

California girl is lost without you here.
Christmas lacks luster this year. That's

as close to poetry as I can get until
you come back to me. Close your eyes

at 12:01 a.m. your time Christmas
morning. I'll be kissing you. Kiss me back.

It took some research, but just past
midnight, Fallujah time, I was in Lodi,

California, kissing Cole Gleason. I'm
sure it was just a delusion, but I swear

Cole Gleason was kissing me back.
It was the saddest Christmas ever.

DELUSIONS

Maintain sanity
in those times when a man
is called to war. The mirage
of invincibility, when

           every

iota of logic embraces
the contrary, accommodates
minutiae, the day-to-day.
The wise ask no questions,
understand that a

           soldier

battles fear with violence,
masks the omnipresent scent
of death with reminders
of living—cold tavern beer,
a hot pussy chaser. He

           harbors

no illusion of love
for the whore. She is expendable,
unlike the woman who waits
at home, pretending
not to worry about such

           secrets.

Cole Gleason

SECRETS SUCK

Worse than surprises. I hate
knowing them. Despise keeping
them, when every shred of me
believes the longer I stay silent,
the harder it's all coming down.

That's always been my experience.

Lucky me. I seem to be the secret
sniffer. It's like they appear to me,
materialize, in the flesh, from
the ether. I was the first one
to discover Dad's dalliances.

Both of them. The first time,

I happened to pick up the phone
and overhear him setting a time
to meet up with a coworker.
I was twelve, but mature enough
to understand that those murmurs

of affection meant a whole lot

more than wanting to get together
for a pleasant lunch. I never said
a word. What if I was wrong?
What if I wasn't? Did I want to
be responsible for the fight

that was sure to follow? What if

my mother and father broke up?
No sixth grader wanted that!
But that's almost what happened
a year later, when Mom found
out on her own. Meanwhile,

Dad had his cake and ate it, too.

Gross, if apropos. Me? I was anxious.
Angry. Confused. This wasn't the kind
of love they showed on the sitcoms
I watched, where married couples
worried about bills and jobs and where

to stow their kids for a few hours—

long enough to enjoy a little nookie
without getting busted. As far as I knew,
my parents never did *that*, so to learn
that one of them *did*, just not with
the other one, was eye-opening.

The second time was worse.

Mom was visiting a friend in the Bay
Area. I was supposed to stay at Darian's,
but she got sick in PE so I went home
after school. That time, I caught Dad
just-post-coitus, naked in the hall.

Two drinks in hand, he was on his way

back to the bedroom, where the other
not-Mom person waited for seconds.
He had his back to me, didn't know
I was there, when I heard her call,
Hurry. I've just about got myself ready.

I was sixteen. Driving. A woman

of the world, but I didn't know what
she meant. Dad yelled, *Hey, wait
for me!* But before he could make
his way back to help her out, I slammed
the door. Pretty sure he thought I was

Mom because he spun around,

giving me a more, um, expressive
view of my father than I ever, ever
wanted to see. I put my hand over
my eyes. "Jesus, Dad. What the hell?"
I had never sworn at a parent before.

Seemed like the right time to do it.

He didn't care at all about the swearing.
*Ashley, baby, I . . . have no words.
I'm so sorry. Can you possibly keep
this to yourself? If you can, I swear . . .*
I waited for the bribe. New car? Cash?

Not even. *I'll never do it again.*

SILLY ME

I kept quiet. Never said a word.
I figured it would all work itself out
sooner or later, and it did. The woman—

a girl, really, only a few years older
than I—decided she was in love with Dad
and confronted Mom at the grocery store.

Not a pretty scene. I know, because
I was there. The one that came after,
at home, was significantly worse.

In the meantime, I was a wreck. Felt
disloyal, which I was, and all my silence
did was buy Dad a few more weeks and

a couple more rolls in the hay. He was not
in love with her. Not about to walk away
from his family, and Mom wasn't about

> to make him go. *What for? All men
> are morally bankrupt. The next one
> wouldn't be any better. At least this*
>
> *one is keeping us well. Anyway, "for
> better or worse." The priest didn't give
> me a rating system.* She might have felt

differently had she known Dad brought
his girlfriend into our home. Their bed.
But I never told. Mom never found out.

NOW, THIS NEW SECRET

This Darian subterfuge I find myself
mired in. She asked me not to say
anything to Cole, who still keeps
in touch with Spencer. Why am I

always appointed secret-keeper?
She was tricky about it, too. Called
and said she had something for me
to take to Hawaii, and would I meet

her for dinner tonight. Curiosity
nailed me. So here I am, in a really
nice Thai place, sitting across the table
from Darian and Kenny. And, damn

it all to hell, I like him a lot, as much
as I'm trying not to. He isn't quite
old enough to be her father, and for
a guy his age, he's not only great looking,

he's well preserved. The only external
signs of his four-plus decades are a few
silver streaks weaving his thick, blond
hair and a faint network of lines etching

the corners of his eyes. But only when
he smiles. Which is most of the time,
and mostly at Darian, whom he clearly
cares about. In fact, I'd say he's gaga.

He sits very close to her, some small
part of him always touching her,
laughs at every semiwitty thing
she says, but not in a gratuitous way.

Her assessment of him was spot-on,
too. He wears an air of quiet intelligence,
no hint of superciliousness or egotism.
More Cole than Spence, except nothing

military about him at all, despite
his close ties to the Air Force.
Beyond his (ex?)wife, the Intel officer,
Kenny is an aerospace engineer.

He's taking my lukewarm grilling
in stride. "Tell me about your daughter.
How does she feel about the two
of you?" Does she even know?

> Sabrina is fifteen. Everything's
> drama, he says. But it would be,
> even if everything were perfect,
> and to tell you the truth, it never
>
> has been. Not since she was born.
> Tara never really wanted a baby,
> to have her feet so firmly planted
> in regular civilian life. I thought
>
> things would be different when Sabrina
> came along. But changing diapers
> and mixing formula only made Tara
> more determined to go back out
>
> into the field. That's where her heart
> is. Sabrina only knows her mother
> in an extremely peripheral way.
> And she's a little overprotective of me.

I NUDGE HARDER

"So, are you saying she resents
having Darian in her—your life?"

> I'm not sure "resents" is the right
> word. She's not used to having
>
> my attention turned elsewhere.
> I think she likes Darian just fine.

At least she knows about her. "But
she's not happy about the relationship."

> Not especially. But she'll get used
> to the idea. He pauses long enough
>
> to give Dar a soft kiss on the cheek.
> If I have my way, they'll see each
>
> other every day before too long.
> They are the two most important
>
> people in my life. I love them both
> very much. He is so matter-of-fact,

I believe he believes every word.
"So, you and your wife are definitely

getting divorced? And Sabrina is okay
with that?" Okay, that was blunt.

> So is his answer. Tara is in the field.
> We haven't had the chance to discuss

the details, but we will as soon
as she comes back. Until then, I can't

really talk about it with Sabrina.
But she'll be fine. She . . .

You know what Sabrina told me?
interrupts Dar, who up until now

has remained completely mum.
She said her mother has never been

there for her, that her father raised
her. And that she wouldn't care one

way or another if her mother died
because who mourns for a stranger?

Fifteen, going on fifty. How sad,
if she actually feels that way. My mom

was not a shining example of motherhood,
but she was always there for me. And if

Kenny means everything he's said,
divorce is preferable to treading time

in a marriage that has bled out
of love. I think that, feeling sorry as hell

that Darian's marriage also seems to be
mortally wounded. Bleeding out.

I DON'T BLAME

Kenny for the wounding. Pretty sure
that happened before he came along.
And if Darian had to choose someone
to stitch her up, I guess I'm glad this

is the guy. Not sure she needs a teenage
"daughter" who's needy and likely to
interfere, but it's not my call. Think
I'll change the subject. "So, did you
ever work on the space shuttles?"

> He shakes his head. *But the Spaceport,*
> *yes. And some advanced extraterrestrial*
> *weaponry systems. . . .* He goes on to talk
> about this truly fascinating stuff, obviously
> proud of his contributions. A lot of it

is mind-boggling, so I don't try to
absorb the details. The overall picture
is crazy enough, and this is all unclassified.
Hate to think about what they're hiding.

The food is excellent, the company
pretty good, too. I have to admit
Kenny brings out the best in my best
friend. That, I like. When he excuses
himself to use the restroom, I know

she'll ask, so I straight out admit, "Okay.
I like him. Just, please be careful. I don't
want to see you get hurt. Promise you'll be
very sure before making any huge moves."

She smiles, but not in the "I told
you so" way I expected. *I promise.
But I want you to promise me
you won't say anything to Cole.*

How can I not tell Cole? We don't
keep things from each other. "Why
not? I mean, if you've already made
your decision to break up with Spence.
You have made that decision, right?"

She glances toward the bathroom.
Gives a weak nod. *But I'm not sure
how to tell Spence. He's supposed
to come home pretty soon, and . . .*

Her eyes tell me Kenny is headed
in this direction. "And what, Dar?"

Her voice falls to a whisper.
And I'm scared. Really scared.

Kenny drops into the seat next
to Darian. *I'm not interrupting
some covert conversation, am I?*

It's a joke of sorts, and we all laugh.
But at the moment, nothing is funny.

WHAT COALESCES

Rising from the residual smoke
      of the evening is a maelstrom

of emotions. I feel better, meeting
      Kenny, witnessing his dedication to Dar.

I feel worse, intuiting major
      problems to come, on all sides.

I feel happy, viewing a small
      glimpse of the best friend I cherish,

the one who has felt lost to me
      for much too long. I feel anxious,

knowing she is in turmoil
      and only time will tell us how

things will all shake out.
      This is a heavyweight decision,

the pressure to make it great.
      Dissolving a relationship that once

meant everything is rarely easy.
      It should make her nervous. Sad.

But why is she scared—really
      scared? That makes me scared, too.

I AM OVER THE PACIFIC

Halfway to Hawaii, eyes closed
and headphones fighting the noise
of crying babies with country music
when I remember something Dar
said the last time we played What If?

What if Cole got drunk and hit you?

I let it go. Why didn't I pursue
it? Was she talking about Spencer?
Is that what she's so afraid of?
That he'll plunge right off the deep
end? But she'd tell me that, right?

Yeah, sure. Of course I would.

Especially with Spence coming
home. She wouldn't face him
alone if that was really a concern.
Would she? God, I want to talk
to Cole about this. Ask his opinion.

*I want you to promise me
you won't say anything to Cole.*

I promised I wouldn't mention
it to Cole. But I never said I'd keep
quiet about it period. When I get back,
I'll call someone on base. A counselor.
Or chaplain. Someone who can help.

SPRING BREAK 2008

Cole had been back from Iraq
for several weeks. He had fifteen
days of leave, and his request
to take it when we could spend
uninterrupted time together

had been granted. He went
home to Wyoming his first week,
saved the second for me. The day
I picked him up at the airport
was crazy. First, I couldn't decide

what to wear. I swear, I tried on
eight different outfits, hated
everything the mirror showed
me—too slutty, too old lady,
too college student in need

of new clothes. I finally settled
on a turquoise sundress that
showed off my legs and just
enough cleavage to be tempting
without shouting, "Hey, check

out these babies!" Then I had
to shave my legs. It had been
weeks. Not like I cared most
of the time, and mostly I wore
jeans. Then I needed makeup—

not too little, not too much, and
how did that smoky-eyes thing
go again? Everything took way
too long, and when I finally felt
ready and glanced at the clock,

I was already running late. Traffic
was heavy, and when it opened
up, I drove like a maniac. It didn't
go unnoticed by a particular California
Highway Patrolman. Shit. Shit. Shit.

By the time he reached my window,
I was crying mascara and plum
eye shadow down my pretty blushed
cheeks. Apparently, he'd never
brought a driver to tears before.

> Excuse me, miss. But may I see
> your license and registration? Please?
> And could you please stop sniffling?
> Uh, is something wrong? Besides me?

Why not use it? It was the truth,
after all. "My boyfriend is just
back from Iraq and I'm supposed
to pick him up at the airport, and
I'm late and traffic, and now this . . ."

He let me off with a stern warning,
and I might have felt really good
about that, except now what the mirror
revealed was a total hag. I cried
most of the way to baggage claim.

AT LEAST

By the time I spotted Cole, I had
cried off most of the makeup. That
turned out to be a good thing, because
seeing him only made me cry more.

I ran into his arms, which were even
stronger than I remembered. He lifted
me off the ground, spun me around.
Brought my face right up into his

> and I swear, despite my streaked
> puffy eyes, the first thing he said
> was, *Goddamn, you're beautiful.* And
> then we were kissing, and we kissed

without stopping until we really
couldn't find air, and I was glad
he was wearing his uniform because
at least then everyone waiting for

suitcases didn't think we were just
plain horny or something. In fact,
they clapped and one old guy
whistled. "Careful," I whispered.

"I think he just saw my panties."
Cole tugged down my skirt in back
and we laughed and kissed until
his duffle came rolling around.

> We walked to the car, velcroed
> together. He reached for the keys.
> *Let me drive?* I slid into the passenger
> seat, studied him as he exited

the parking lot, made his way
to the freeway, merged into traffic.
His hair was freshly cut, grunt-style.
The ruddy tan of his steel-jawed face

made the gold of his eyes even more
striking. He punched the gas pedal,
and we were flying. "Careful. There's
a CHP out here somewhere who's

already a ticket short today." I told
him about my earlier encounter
without mentioning the makeup
problem. Cole just smiled.

> *Don't worry. He can't see us.*
> *Nobody can. We're invisible.*
> Maybe we were, because despite
> hitting close to a hundred miles

per hour, no one stopped us.
No one even seemed to notice
us. We made it to the apartment
in world-record time, at least for

> a beater car like mine. *Tomorrow*
> *we'll go by Uncle Jack's and get*
> *the truck. It could use a little blowing*
> *out, I bet*, Cole said, pulling into

my parking place. Less than five
minutes after turning off the ignition,
we were in the bedroom, getting
ready to make new memories.

AFTER ALL THAT HURRYING

Cole actually slowed us down.
He stopped me just inside the door.

>   *Stay right there, where I can look*
>   *at you.* He sat on the bed, unlaced

his boots, unbuttoned his shirt.
His eyes never strayed from me

>   once. *Take off your dress. Slowly.*
>   *It's been a long time. I want to savor*

>   *every second.* He watched as I slid
>   the sundress up over my head.

Very slowly. Working the tease
as if I had a real clue what to do.

I stood there, in nothing but
my prettiest pair of thong panties.

>   *Turn around. Easy. Not too fast.*
>   *Now, come here.* I floated toward him,

and when I got close to the bed,
paused. He reached out. Touched

my breasts with hands much too
gentle for their size. Then they slid

around my back, coaxed me forward,
and his lips circled my right areola,

sucked it like a baby might. Hungry.
He sat me on his lap, his incredible

erection straining against his pants,
pushing his zipper into the thin strip

of cloth covering my crotch. "Cole,"
I exhaled. "God, baby, I need you."

The statement was truth, and felt
that way. He sighed, laid back against

the quilt, loosened the closures on
his camos. I kissed his eyes, his mouth,

his neck, down his chest to granite
hard penis, urged it into my mouth.

I am no expert, but did all I could
to bring him all the way off. He came

> very close, but stopped short. *No.*
> *I jerked off this morning, twice in fact,*

> *thinking about you and what we'd do.*
> *Does that make you pissed? It shouldn't.*

> *I did it for you, because I want you to*
> *come before I do. Twice, in fact.* He smiled.

Took total control. And he made me
come before he did. More than twice.

FOR THE NEXT WEEK

We had sex three or four times
a day. Halfway through, my body
ached, but I couldn't say no.
Cole bordered on desperate.

> *When I go back, I'll just have*
> *morning wood and my fist. I want*
> *to fuck you till I'm black and blue.*
> *I need to remember you. This.*

Pretty sure it was me who wore
bruises. His muscles were concrete,
and he gripped my arms as if he
let go, I might try to escape. Not mean.

> Just determined. His eyes never
> left my face as he chanted, *That's*
> *my girl. My beautiful, beautiful Ash.*

It was cadence. Beautiful. Beautiful.
Ash. I loved listening to his voice.
After a while, orgasm was the last
thing on my mind, but the rhythm

of his voice kept me going. That, and
knowing our time together grew ever
shorter. When we weren't in bed,
we walked the beach. Watched

movies. Ate. Drank. Laughed. Held
hands as we talked, trying to learn
all we could about each other before
he was called back to work. To duty.

WE DID PICK UP

Cole's truck from his uncle Jack,
who had stored it under a metal
roof in his backyard. It was dusty,
and the tires were low, but it started
right up once Cole reconnected
the battery cables. I didn't realize

> how much Cole loved that truck—
> a 2006 Chevy Avalanche with a big
> V-8. *This puppy screams*, he said,
> proving it as we headed east toward
> Palm Springs one morning. At least,
> that's where I thought we were going.

> Instead, where the highway split,
> he drove north toward Twenty-Nine
> Palms. *We're going to train here.*
> *I want to see it, and I want you to see*
> *it, too.* The Marine Corps Air Ground
> Combat Center is a huge stretch

of yucca-and-cactus–studded sand,
where they train soldiers in the ways
of desert warfare. It is stark. Cursed.
Dry-Sahara in summer, dry-tundra in
winter. But, for a small, magical
window in spring, wildflowers paint

the landscape purple and poppy
and raspberry pink, clear to the far
horizons. It steals your breath away.
And that day, Cole and I drew
the lucky card that brought us
there at that perfect time of the year.

RATHER THAN INVESTIGATE

The base proper, Cole turned
off on a dirt track that plunged
us into all that frail beauty.

He barely slowed, fishtailing
the truck, scaring up bunnies
and flushing quail. "Hey, take
it easy. I'd like to make it out
of here all in one piece."

He backed off the gas, just a little.
What? You don't trust my driving?

I rested my hand on his thigh.
"I trust everything about you. But
it's so pretty out here, I'd like to enjoy
the view. Hard to do when you're
raising such a big cloud of dust!"

It was behind us, and that made him
laugh. *You're looking the wrong way!*
But he did slow down and, in fact,
drifted to a stop, letting the Avalanche

idle and said dust catch up to us.
Once it settled, he opened his window.
*It is pretty out here, isn't it? Empty
of people, just the way I like it.*

A muted *ka-boom* of artillery
reverberated off faraway hills,
echoed back across the valley.
"Guess we're not so alone out
here after all." An afternoon

training session must have
begun, because more reports
followed. *Definitely not alone.*

We listened to the rise and fall
of munitions fire for a few minutes.
"Is that what war sounds like?"

> *Not the war I was in.* Regret
> inflected his voice. *Damn. Look
> at the size of that critter! Wish
> I had my rifle.* It was a huge
> jackrabbit, with ears half as long

as my arms and almost as wide.
It sniffed its way out of the brush,
stopped in front of the truck
and froze right there, staring

through the window with piebald
eyes. Unafraid. Curious, even, like
it wanted to know more about us.
"You wouldn't really shoot it?"

> *Hell yeah, I would. Desert's overrun
> with the damn vermin. They ain't
> worth a shit, except in the stew pot.*
> A weird smile crept across his face.
> *Let's have a little fun. What do you say?*

HE DIDN'T WAIT

For me to answer. Before I could
      even consider what might come
            next, he put the truck in gear.

Punched it. By the time the rabbit
      realized squashation was imminent
            and reacted, it ran straight on up

the road. Big mistake. Jackrabbits
      are quick. V-8s are powerful.
            Faster than small mammals.

The rabbit feinted right. Cole
      followed. Left-right. Veer-veer.
            That would have been one dead

animal except it got lucky.
            Goddamn little bastard! Cole
                yelled at the rearview mirror.

The Avalanche had good clearance
      and went right over the top of
            the petrified bunny. Had the tires

hit it, *Taps.* By the time Cole got
      the truck turned around, Mr. Rabbit
            had taken refuge in a hole somewhere.

Cole was pissed. *Hope I scared
      it to death, anyway.* I didn't say
            a word all the way to Palm Springs.

BY THE TIME

We got there, I had mostly convinced
myself that Cole had just been messing

around. Having, as he said, a little fun.
He didn't really want to run over a poor,

defenseless rabbit. He didn't mention
it and I never brought it up to him again.

We checked in to a nice hotel with
a jetted tub in the bathroom and two

pools outside—one hot water, one cool.
I thought it must be very expensive

but Cole said not to worry about it.
What else was he saving up his money

for? We had a fabulous dinner
at a pricey French bistro. Neither of us

ordered the lapin. Just seeing rabbit
on the menu made me cringe. Cole had

the venison medallions. I chose a nice
vegetable ragout. Chocolate soufflé

for dessert. And cognac. Lots of cognac.
By the time we stumbled back into our room,

took a hot (hot!) bath together, and fell
into bed, I did not dream at all. Especially not

about wildflowers, jackrabbits, or artillery fire.

SAYING GOOD-BYE

That time wasn't too difficult.
I knew I'd see him again when
his battalion came to California
for pre-deployment training
at Twenty-Nine Palms. Plus,
he'd get leave again before
they sent him back overseas.
Best of all, we planned a summer

trip to Hawaii for me. It would be
my first time visiting the islands
and Cole would have his off-duty
hours to spend with me. With only
a couple of months until school
was out, I didn't think I'd miss
Cole nearly as much as proved
to be the case. Because that man

had insinuated himself totally
into my life, under my skin. Our
last night together before he had
to return to base was amazing.
He knew exactly what to do, how
fast—or slow—to do it for maximum
effect. He made it all about me.
Called me beautiful, and made

> me believe it. Whispered, *I love
> you. I need you. Always will. I want
> to eat you. Drink you. Breathe you
> in.* And he did. Again and again.

OH, TO BREATHE YOU

In the middle of the frozen
night, to inhale the warmth
of you, exhale the fear of you,
no longer in my life.

                       A drift

of perfume lifting
off the silk of your skin,
a waking mist

                       of heaven.

Drink it in. Drink it in.
I never understood
the desire for eternity before.
But then you appeared,

                       midst

the chaos of my youth,
taught me how to love
when I swore I never would
again, extinguished

                       the coals

of desperation singeing
me inside, branding me
untouchable. Unsalvageable.
I am exiled to the wilderness

                       of hell

no longer, because of you.
You give forever meaning.

Cole Gleason

AS WILDERNESS

Oahu must have been incredible.
So much raw beauty was bound
to draw humans, intent on messing
it up completely. First they came
from neighboring islands—who knows
how they managed to outrigger all
that way? Settle in, make the place

home, and the next thing you know,
a more advanced people come along,
conquer you, set up housekeeping
in the very huts you built! Turnabout
is fair play, however, because just
when Group Two thinks everything's
coming up pineapples, Captain Cook

and crew sail into view, carrying
fabulous stuff like cholera, measles,
and Jesus. And once white people
discovered this little corner of heaven,
next thing you know, relatively speaking,
it's high-rises on top of volcanoes,
strip clubs peddling a lot more
than leis, concrete, and asphalt

choking sand, and jet fuel blowing
in the breeze. Honolulu represents
the worst of all that. Yet every time
I fly in, anticipation begins to build
just about the time I think I'll go crazy,
stuffed into a narrow airliner seat
between honeymooners and retired
couples looking for Shangri-La.

I'd like to tell them to hold on tight
to that person beside them, because
that's where they'll find paradise.
It is not a beach or a palm tree grove
or the brim of a smoking black crater.
It's a plateau inside their hearts, one
that can only be reached in tandem.

And as the plane circles to land,
I draw closer to my Wyoming mesa,
not so very far from me now. Wonder
what he's doing right this minute.
Cleaning his weapon? Scrubbing latrines?
Running laps or lifting weights?
In my mind, he is a snapshot, frozen
in time. I don't picture him in motion.

Wonder if he's imagining me—our last
time together, where I am at this moment.
How I'll look when he sees me. What I'll be
wearing. If I've cut my hair or lost a few
pounds. Do men even think that way?

The jet bumps down on the tarmac.
Some people sigh relief. Others laugh.
Not a few are already on their cell phones.
Conversation picks up, speeds up.
We are safe on the ground in Honolulu.
People collect their things, prepare
to join tours or embark on self-guided
adventures. Few except me arrive solo.

NO LEI AWAITS ME

No soldier, either. I won't see Cole
till tonight, after his workday ends
and he can drive the fifteen or so miles
from the base to me. Meanwhile,
I'll catch some sun. Cole doesn't care

much for the beach here. Says the sand
is filthy. Dirtied by tourists and their trash.
Maybe. But it's warm this time of year,
unlike San Diego sand. I plan on a nice,
long walk, a little warm ocean swimming

and time to sit, doing nothing but watch
the surf break. I grab a cab to the Waikiki
hotel Cole suggested we try, an affordable
high-rise two blocks from the ocean.
As affordable goes, it isn't bad. At least,

> the lobby is well kept and the desk
> clerk—Sherry—seems friendly. When
> I give her my credit card and ask to leave
> a key for Cole, she smiles. *Marine wife,*
> *huh? We've had a few check in today.*

I could correct her on my marriage
status. Instead I just smile back.
"They're deploying soon. Again."
The tone was sadder than I expected.
"You'd think I'd be used to it by now."

Sherry shakes her head. *I've got one,*
too. But mine's coming home soon.
He's transitioning into the Reserves
then. It will be weird, having him
around on a regular basis.

I nod. "You kind of get used to being
alone. The waiting is hard sometimes,
though. I wish Cole and I could have
a little more time together before
he has to go, but he used up most

of his leave last summer. His mom
was really sick, and . . ." I realize
I'm running my mouth. Shut it
before too much personal stuff spills
out all over this total stranger. "Sorry."

Sherry smiles understanding. *Hey,*
no apologies. I've been there.
*Tell you what . . .*She consults her
computer. *I'll upgrade you to a room*
on the water side. Very romantic.

I thank her, carry my small bag up
to the room, and before I change, text
Cole: IN THE HOTEL. OUR ROOM IS UP
HIGH, ON THE PACIFIC SIDE. I CAN SEE
THE WATER FROM HERE. LOVE YOU.

HE WON'T GET THE MESSAGE

Until he gets off duty. But I want him
to know he's the first thing I thought
about when I arrived. I open the sliding
glass door. Step out on the balcony. Salt

wind blows warm through my hair, weaves
it with the potpourri of plumeria, jasmine,
diesel exhaust, and streets wet with recent
downpour. One day I'll explore the other

islands, inhale the tropical air outside
of this city. Cole and I never seem to
have enough time to do that when I visit.
I add it to my bucket list, go back inside.

I slip into the purple bikini Darian
sent to Hawaii with me—her excuse
to put Kenny and me in the same place
at the same time. She got what she came

for. Manipulator. I do love the swimsuit,
though. The full-length mirror says
I've dropped some weight. Can't imagine
why. But it does look good on me.

Regardless, I cover up my midsection
with a short pink shift. Tie back my hair.
Off I go. It's really lovely outside. Not too
hot. The rain has raised a gentle steam.

It wraps around me as I walk along
the quiet sidewalk. Late October lies
between the heaviest tourist seasons.
The street vendors are voracious.

THEY TURN AGGRESSIVE

As I pass by, moving
toward me and shouting,

>*Discount tickets!*
>*Sunset cruises!*
>*Learn to surf!*
>*Pearl Harbor bus tours!*
>*Best luau on Oahu, guaranteed!*

A massive Samoan guy
in a loud Hawaiian shirt
shoves a coupon into my hand.

>*That gets you in, no cover,*
>*at the Pink Cherry Club. Single*
>*women are always welcome.*

I keep walking and a greasy-
haired haole drops in beside me,
meters his steps to match mine.

>*Hey there, pretty lady.*
>*You here all by yourself?*
>*Want some company?*

I lower my head, shake
it. The negative answer
doesn't discourage him.

>*How about some pakalolo?*
>*Best green bud in Waikiki.*
>*Give you an awesome deal.*

I DECLINE

With a quiet, "No, thank you."
But when I speed up a little,
he does, too. So I brake to a halt.
He comes around in front of me,
looks into my eyes, and I can't help
but notice his pupils are completely

>dilated. When he opens his mouth,
the condition of his teeth confirms
my suspicion that he is into much
more than weed. *Don't want to go
down? I can take you up. Way up.*
He reaches into his pocket, extracts

>a small plastic bag. *Asian ice. Pure
as it comes. One little hit keep you
going for days.* His breath, when he
exhales, smells like rotten cabbage.
It makes me gag, and for the first time
a small rush of fear lifts the hair

on the back of my neck. I shove it
aside. We are on a public sidewalk,
within rock-tossing distance of one
of the most populous beaches in
the world. He's not going to hurt
me here. "Leave me the fuck alone."

>*What? You don't like me?* He grabs
my arm, jerks it, gives a strange,
little laugh and it strikes me that this
man is totally out of his head. I try to
remember the limited self-defense
moves I know, when he suddenly

releases my arm and without
a word, slinks off, a weasel into
the shadows. I turn to see what
spooked him—a hulking cop,
double-timing toward and now
past me. Looks like he's after the ice

man, who's obviously a known
quantity. All of a sudden, walking
the beach by myself—even with plenty
of other people around—has lost
its appeal. I look up at the hotel
in front of me. The flamingo pink

Royal Hawaiian. It's a Waikiki
landmark. Old. Beautiful. Safer
than the sidewalk. I duck inside,
cut through the lobby, to the alfresco
Mai Tai Bar. Find a quiet table,
overlooking the ocean. As close

to the sand as I want to be until
I have Cole by my side. A nice-looking
waiter brings me a drink menu.
I open it with tremulous hands.
Pina Colada? Not strong enough.
Blue Hawaiian? Too sweet. *Sex*

on the Beach? Really don't think
so. I order the bar's namesake drink.
Rum, liqueur, fresh juice, and more rum.
That works for me. I sip mai tais
and watch the surf for almost two hours,
accomplishing one-third of my plan.

I CONSIDER LEAVING

A couple of times. But, oddly enough,
rather than fortify my courage,
the alcohol only bolsters my fear.
Afternoon segues to early evening, and

> I might just keep on sitting here,
> except I get a call. *Hey, sweetheart.*
> *Where are you? I'm at the hotel.*
> *And what did you tell the lady*
> *at the desk? She was damn nice.*

"I told her you were a little off,
so she'd better tread carefully.
I'm at the Royal Hawaiian, and
starving. Come find me?" No

> hesitation at all, he demands,
> *What's wrong?* Is he psychic?
> Can he tell I'm buzzed? I don't know,
> but when I try to deny, he says,
> *I can hear it in your voice, Ashley.*

"Everything's fine. I promise.
What do you want to drink?
It'll be here when you get here.
And I'm buying, soldier."

It takes a half-hour for him
to shower, change into civvies,
and walk over. By the time
he gets here, a double scotch
on the rocks is waiting for him.

Much more patiently than I.

WAITING FOR A SOLDIER

Is never easy. Whether he's gone
off to war, or on duty at home.
But there is nothing quite like
that much-anticipated moment

when you first set eyes on him again
after so much time apart. When love
connects you, it's like your heart
draws you to him, though distance

eclipses the space between you.
And when he's close, no way could
you miss him, not even when he's clear
across a crowded bar. I spot him

the moment he steps through
the doorway, and before I have
the chance to wave, he has seen me,
too. That must be what they mean

by "heartstrings." Only ours are more
like heart cables, near impossible
to sever. Despite all the activity,
he reaches me in four long strides

and lifts me into his arms; we kiss
with the knowledge of Eden.
I can feel people staring, but hardly
care. For these few perfect seconds,

every minute without him is ground
into dust, left for the sea breeze
to blow into memory. "I love you,"
I breathe into his mouth. "I love you."

IT HAS BEEN ONLY

A couple of months since I last saw him.
But it feels borderline forever. We sit
very close and under the table my leg

is hooked around his. Touch is what
we need to catch up on, not gossip about
our family or friends. We discuss them

regularly, long distance. Of course, a few
questions are expected—how's his mom,
who's slowly recovering from meningitis?

(Answer: Better, though she's lost some
hearing.) Or, have I heard from my little
brother, who's backpacking Europe?

(Answer: Yes, and he's found a girlfriend
so he's staying for a while.) It's so lovely here,
we decide to hang out and order a seafood

pizza to go with our drinks, which keep
coming. I've lost count of how many,
but the fuzz which has sprouted inside

my skull is a decent clue. It actually
doesn't feel so bad until, uncomfortably,
the conversation turns to Darian.

> *How's she doing? I heard from Spence.*
> *He's a little freaked out. She doesn't*
> *return his calls. Do you know why?*

I know it's an innocent question.
But how am I supposed to answer
it honestly without betraying her

trust? An unpleasant high-tension
wire buzzing starts in the hollow
behind my lower jaw. "No clue."

> Cole takes a bite of pizza. Chews.
> Doesn't swallow before he says,
> *He thinks she's messing around.*

A few crumbs escape his mouth.
Disgusting. The buzz volume increases.
"Really? Why would he think that?"

> He shrugs. Sips his drink, chasing
> the food down his throat. *I'm not
> sure, hon. Maybe he's just paranoid.*

For some stupid reason, the "hon"
irritates me. For some stupider reason,
I actually say, "Maybe he deserves it."

> Cole's mouth drops open. Glad
> it's empty. His cool yellow eyes
> measure me. *No man deserves that.*

No *man* deserves that? I need to shut
up. Can't. "Not even a man who hits
his wife?" The buzz swells, fills my head.

FIVE MINUTES AGO

Everything was perfect. How could
it turn so bad so fast? I suspect it has

something to do with the alcohol,
this avalanche toward all-out verbal

      battle. *Is that what she told you?*
      Did she happen to mention the rest?

"The rest! What rest? Wait. You *knew*?
And you never said anything?"

      Would you have said something
      if I hadn't brought it up first?

I hate when he uses logic to turn
things on me. The couple at the next

table stands up abruptly. The lady
tosses a nervous glance in our direction,

right before they hustle toward the exit.
I lower my voice, fight to keep it steady,

attempting my own reverse logic.
"So, tell me, Cole. What is the rest?"

      I'm surprised you don't know. Darian
      was pregnant with Spence's baby.

      She got rid of it while he was gone.
      He only found out because they got

drunk and she confessed the whole
story, just to hurt him. It worked.

Oh, my God. Darian, how could
you? The far side of the tale comes

around to shade the beginning gray.
Why are things never black and

white? My stomach lurches. Still,
"But that's no excuse for violence."

      Cole snorts. *Violence doesn't need*
      an excuse. And sometimes it's called for.

I'm getting pissed all over again.
"Against women? As bad as that was,

Darian didn't deserve to get hit. I suppose
you think rape is deserved sometimes, too?"

      He is quiet much too long. Finally,
      he says, *I think maybe it can be.*

The buzz becomes an explosion.
"Seriously? What if I told you today . . ."

I relate the cabbage-man story, doing
my level best not to slur words. Or cry.

      Obviously the guy was disturbed.
      And considering how you're dressed . . .

I stand. Pick up my drink. Let it fly.

COLE AND I DON'T ARGUE

Often. In fact, we've had only a few
disagreements, and even fewer that
led to serious exchanges of anger-
driven words. I'll never forget any

of them, especially the first. It was
going into the Christmas holiday
season in 2008. Cole and I had
spent three weeks of the summer

before playing house on Oahu.
One of his buddies had gone
stateside, leaving his off-base
apartment empty. Cole tossed

a little traveling cash his way so
we could use the older one-bedroom
place as our vacation digs. Well,
my vacation. Cole had regular duty

during the weekdays. Came home
to me the rest of the time, just like
a regular married Marine might.
While he was at work, I spent days

at the beach, roller blading and taking
my elementary surfing to a whole new
level. Over that short time, we solidified
the "two-as-one" of us. I was really

starting to believe we could make it
as a couple, albeit an often separated,
half-a-world-away-from-each-other,
couple. But then a small dose of reality

intruded. I had to go back to school.
Some people would have looked at
other options—transferring to a college
in Hawaii, or maybe dropping out.

When I asked Mom what she thought,
she offered solid advice. *If you withdraw,
what will you do? Serve piña coladas
to tourists and waste the last two years?*

*Your prepaid tuition is California based.
Anyway, your young man is returning
to Iraq in a few months. What's the point?*
The point was, she had a point. Even

Cole agreed. So, back I trekked
to San Diego to start my junior year.
I settled in just fine. Once again
got used to long-distance communicating

with the man who was so central
to the woman I was growing into.
They say the military makes you older
than your years. Ask me, that applies

to more than just the soldier.

OUR FIRST ARGUMENT

Might have belied that idea, however.
Neither Cole nor I acted very mature.

I had spent another birthday alone,
though Cole did send me a dozen

yellow roses and a framed poem
he wrote especially for me. A love

poem, which meant a thousand times
more than those beautiful flowers.

I didn't really expect him to be able to
deliver them in person. A soldier only

gets so much time away from his duty.
The problem popped up when he was

granted leave to come stateside for
Christmas. I assumed he planned on

spending it with me, and decided to
surprise him with a trip to Lodi. Neither

of us had met each other's families yet.
I figured it was time to introduce him

to mine. Meanwhile, unfortunately,
he booked his flight home to Cheyenne.

When he called to let me know he'd
stop by on his way back to Kaneohe,

I freaked. "What do you mean, on
your way back? I thought we were

spending Christmas together! I told
my parents we'd be there. I promised."

>*Without even asking me? Why
>would you do a stupid thing like that?*

The "stupid" slapped. My eyes watered.
"I wanted to surprise you. Cole, you were

in Iraq last year, and you'll probably
be there next year, too. Can't we be

together on Christmas? That's what
people in love do. Or is that stupid, too?"

>*I do love you, Ashley. But I also love
>Mom. I haven't seen her in eight months.*

>*You and I had that great time over
>the summer. This will probably be*

>*my only chance to visit Wyoming
>before we deploy again, most likely*

>*in April. You have your entire family, but
>I'm all Mom's got left. You wouldn't ask*

>*me to leave her alone on Christmas.
>You're not really that selfish, right?*

IN RETROSPECT

He was totally right. His mom lived
alone, and she didn't get to see him
often. But at the time, disappointment
overwhelmed every shred of logic.

"Selfish? Really? You think I'm selfish
because we actually have the chance
to celebrate Christmas together, and
I somehow expected you to want that?

Because I was so excited to show
you off to my parents? I want them
to know you, so they can love you, too.
Or maybe you don't want that. Maybe . . ."

The thought struck suddenly, from
some hidden place, like a rattlesnake
unseen in the brush. What if . . . ?
"Maybe you don't want that. Or me."

               Don't be ridiculous, Ashley.

"Stupid." "Selfish." And now "ridiculous."
I blew. "Stop calling me names!
This is just so . . . so unfair! Fine.
Go ahead. Go to Wyoming! But don't

bother stopping here. All I do is wait
for you, Cole. I wait for you to call.
To e-mail. To deploy. To come home.
To find a little time for me in the craziness

of your life. I'm tired of waiting. Tired
of being nothing but an afterthought."

I THREW THE PHONE

Across the room. It smacked the wall
like a missile, fell to the floor. And then
I crumbled into a million pieces. A rubble
of emotion. I stormed. I cried. I cursed.
I screamed. I was lucky the neighbors
didn't call the cops on the usually-so-docile
single woman who lived next door.

Because suddenly I felt very single. Not
only that, but it felt like the last two years
of my life had been waylaid. Hijacked
by this man and his misguided devotion
to his country, his dead cousin, and his
mother, in whatever order. I wasn't even
in the top three, and I should have been
number one. That's what I was thinking.

What if he never cared for me at all? What if
his declarations of love were only so much
bullshit? Could I have been so naïve as to
construct my entire life around him, when all
he really wanted was steady, easy sex?
Why had I made it so easy? Why had I
made it so good? Why had he been so
good? Fuck. Fuck. Fuck. I hadn't been
with him (or anyone else) for weeks.

So why did I feel so dirty? I walked down
the hall to the bathroom. A dozen steps.
Turned on the shower, and while I waited
for the water to go hot, douched with vinegar
and salt. Then I scrubbed every inch of my skin
twelve times with Ivory soap. Pure as snow.

BY THE TIME I FINISHED

I wasn't angry anymore. Hurt, yes.
Confused. Numb, really. The heat
was turned up, but inside me a deep
pit of cold seethed. I dressed in sweats
and furry slippers. Wrapped a big
quilt around me. Sat on the couch.
Alone on the couch. Tried to read.

Uselessly. The noise in my head—
shrill, sharp splinters of words said,
and words left unsaid—denied
concentration. The phone rang.
Imagine that. It had survived. Sure
it was Cole, I let it go. But then
I retrieved it and called Darian.

> She took her best shot at reasoned
> response. *Of course you're hurt,*
> *Ash. Get used to it, if you want*
> *to stay with Cole. And you know*
> *you do. So you have to share him.*
> *He's totally worth it. Compromise.*

> Then she transformed back into
> the Darian I knew and loved. *Either*
> *that, or dump him and put yourself*
> *back on the market. Lots of cute*
> *guys out there, you know. In fact,*
> *let's go out and shop for a couple.*

"You're married, Dar," I reminded.

> *So? He's gone and I'm not close to dead.*

SHE WAS JOKING

At least, I was pretty sure she was.
        We made a date to go shopping—
                for Christmas gifts, not other men.

I hung up, feeling marginally better.
        Darian always could cheer me up.
                Giving advice, however, wasn't her

best thing, so I never swallowed
        it in a single dose. Instead, I let
                it percolate. After fifteen or twenty

minutes, I realized she was right.
        I did want to stay with Cole, and
                he *was* worth sharing. With his mom,

anyway. I realized I didn't need
        the quilt anymore and was folding
                it when the phone rang again. This

time, I picked up. Cole apologized
        profusely, and so did I. We worked
                out a compromise. He would go to

Wyoming for Christmas, then join
        me in Lodi. He'd meet my parents,
                and he and I would ring in 2009

together. "Compromise" is a word
        I've learned to embrace—and hate.
                It's right up there with Semper Gumby.

I'D LIKE TO SAY

That initial meeting with my parents
went well. But everything about those
few days was uncomfortable, all the way
around. Even before Cole arrived,
the energy was strange. Strained. Mom
and Dad were barely speaking, something
I'd come to associate with her finding
out about yet another of Dad's flings.

Not like I was about to ask. Instead,

I did my best to lighten the mood,
blabbing about ridiculous comments
I'd heard on campus or the funny
ideas the kids I worked with had.
"One little girl told me the way to
her teacher's heart was through
her apple." I thought it was hilarious.
Mom sort of smiled. Dad only grunted.

On Christmas day, we all slept in.

Opened presents late. If, that is, you call
cards with checks and gift certificates
tucked inside presents. Then we split
up and went to different rooms. Mom,
to the kitchen to cook. Dad and Troy,
to the family room for football. I could
have hung out with Mom, I guess.

But I was afraid of the discussion.

Instead, I went to my bedroom, propped
myself up on my bed to read and wait
for Cole to call. I waited all day, in fact.
Finally, I called him. When he answered,
there was abundant noise in the background.
Voices. Laughter. Everything our house
lacked. It made me simultaneously mad
and sad. I tried not to let my voice show it.

Failed. "I think Santa missed us this year."

Cole said not to worry, he'd be there
in a couple of days. That Santa hadn't
missed his house, had left something
there for me. Then someone announced
dinner was on the table. When I told him
I missed him, professed undying love,
his response—*Ditto*—only increased
the anxiety inflating inside me.

Pressure, seeking release in a burst.

I swallowed a pill. Went in search of
Christmas wine. Found Mom, indulging
in a little herself. I watched her work.
Wished for conversation. Settled for
her mostly silent company. Wondered
what Cole was doing. As the medication
kicked in, the stress lightened, gas leaking

out of the balloon. But not completely.

WHICH SET THE STAGE

For Cole's visit. He flew into
        Sacramento, and I picked him
        up there. Usually, when we first

see each other after many weeks
        apart, pent-up love kindles this
        amazing blaze of happiness.

That time, something felt a little
        off. But I couldn't put my finger
        on it, other than Cole seemed

a bit tense. But when I asked,
        "Hey, soldier. Is everything okay?"
        he kissed me with such tenderness

        my initial unease vanished. And
                when he promised, *I'm fine. Just
            a little tired*, I didn't look any farther

for the source of my discomfort.
        His flight arrived late afternoon,
        which meant heavy traffic from

the airport down the I-5, all the way
        to the CA-99 interchange and
        beyond. As always, Cole insisted

        on driving, but the bumper-to-
                bumper stuff whipped him into
            rage. *Who the fuck lives in a place*

like this? he screamed, flipping
          off an equally uptight driver who
          cut in front of us, seeking an exit.

"Relax, sweetheart. A few miles,
          we'll be out in the country. No
          traffic there. I promise." Eventually,

we found clear lanes, but by
          then I was gripping the seat
          and mostly kept my eyes closed,

except when I had to give him
          directions. Open highway wasn't
          much better. He drove like he was

possessed. I looked for a way
          to exorcise a little common
          sense. "Hey. Slow down, okay?

Mom's cooking a special dinner.
          I'd rather not eat hospital food
          instead. You *do* like prime rib?"

          I like it fine, he snapped. But
                    that brought him around. *Sorry.*
                    Can't stand congestion. In any crowd

          there's bound to be at least one
                    freak. If there's nowhere to run when
                    he goes off, you're pretty much toast.

WE MADE IT HOME UNTOASTED

Stepped out of the car into late-December
air, the kind that makes your breath
steam. Yet we stood in the chill, holding
hands, allowing Cole to gather a sense
of the place. My home, growing up.
So much of me. Carbon clouds crept

overhead, threatening rain there in
the valley, snow in the Sierra above.
The smoke of incense cedar puffed
from the chimney, perfuming the air.
I turned into Cole, lifted up on my toes,
kissed him with all the love I held inside.

Drew back to look into his eyes. "Well?"

> *It's not Wyoming. But it's pretty nice.*

I smiled. "With you here, it's amazing."

> *With you there, it would be perfect.*

That was the nicest conversation
we had for three days. We went inside,
out of the cold and into the deep freeze.
"Hello? We're here." It took a minute,
but finally my parents came to say hello.
My warm introduction iced over almost

immediately as Dad led Cole to the guest
room. Cole turned and glanced over
his shoulder, a question in his eyes. All
I could do was shrug. The guest room?
Really? Dad had to be kidding, right?

HE WASN'T KIDDING

My father, the king of impropriety,
expected decorum from his daughter
and her first serious boyfriend. Okay.

We figured we'd deal with that, and
we did. Sneaking into the guest room
once my parents were asleep wasn't

so difficult. Harder was sharing the dinner
table, where conversation over rare roast
beef almost immediately turned to war.

Dad asked. Cole answered. Mom squirmed.
I tried to redirect the dialogue toward
Wyoming, but it kept coming back to Iraq.

When it moved to the newly elected
Commander in Chief, Cole made it very
clear that he would have preferred John

> McCain, who had been a soldier. *And
> that awful woman? What about her?*
> asked Mom, who leans harder to the left

than I do. Cole could have chosen
not to engage. Instead, he offered
his opinion that Ms. Palin couldn't be

nearly as bad as Mr. Obama. It fell
apart from there. Though the volume
remained low, emotion ran high.

We all skipped dessert that night.

AFTER DINNER

Dad took refuge in the living room,
behind a Jon Stewart rerun. Mom

disappeared into her bedroom. Cole
and I took drinks to the solarium, sat

very close on the wicker loveseat,
listening to rain pelt the glass overhead.

We exchanged belated Christmas
gifts. I gave him a leather journal

and an expensive pen. "So you'll think
of me when you write your poetry."

He gave me my favorite perfume,
Secret Obsession. "How did you know?"

> *Darian told me. She forgot to mention
> how pricey it was. But you're worth it.*

I opened the bottle, daubed a couple
of drops. "It's worth it, too. See?"

That led to some seriously hot kissing.
All would have been forgiven right

there, except I felt the need to say,
"I'm sorry about what happened earlier."

> And he responded, *How could someone
> like you come from people like them?*

RARELY

Do I jump squarely to my parents'
defense. Neither am I likely to argue
politics, especially with someone
I know I can't sway. But that night,

Cole's intransigence bordered on
arrogant, and I pretty much blew.
Our second argument was worse
than the first, because we were both

in the same room. Neither of us wanted
my parents to hear, but angry words
don't want to be whispered. We did
manage to avoid swearing at each

other, unless you call words like
"ignorant" and "intractable" cussing.
But we were both tired, a little drunk,
and neither wanted to back off.

Finally, we straight out wore out
and decided to go to bed. The house
was dark by then. Silent. Anger
still prickled my skin, but there was

something else—a primal need
threading my body. I could have
crawled solo beneath my own
blankets. Instead, I followed Cole

through the door of the guest room.
It wasn't makeup sex. It was "fuck
me so I can sleep tonight" sex. By
morning, forgiveness came easily.

ONE THING YOU LEARN

When you love a soldier is to expect
pre-deployment arguments. They are,
as any military counselor will tell you,
a way into the separation to come.

As bad as those Christmas spats
had been, the one we had just weeks
before Cole's second Iraq tour was
a whole lot worse. Psychologically,

it pushed us apart. Cole's unit had
been training at Twenty-Nine Palms,
and we arranged to meet up for drinks
one Saturday night at a little off-base dive.

He'd had a rough day and showed up
late, already pretty much pissed at
the universe. I'd been waiting awhile,
fending off advances by an obviously

inebriated grunt who was loitering
by my table when Cole stormed
in. The guy had just made a totally
inappropriate remark, or tried to.

He was so drunk, he could barely
spit the word "ejaculate." I happened
to be laughing at his poor attempt. Cole
assessed the situation, took it all wrong.

IT WAS THE FIRST TIME

I ever saw those beautiful eyes
go all crazy. Scary crazy. He came
stomping toward the table. "Uh, I think
you'd better go," I told the stranger,

> right about the time Cole reached
> the table and spun him around.
> *Get the fuck away from her, asshole.*

>> The guy had two choices: compliance
>> or belligerence. He chose the latter.
>> *Who you calling asshole, asshole?*

The two squared off and things
were headed straight toward ugly.
But then the bartender, hyperaware
of the situation, called them out.

He told Cole to relax and the other guy
to find a designated driver. The drunk
slunk away, muttering obscenities.

I swear, I never thought Cole would
blame me, or I might have realized things
were headed south when he didn't kiss

me hello. Instead, he went straight
to the bar, called for whiskey, neat.
The double was already half gone

when he plopped into the chair next
to me. I reached out one hand, touched
his cheek with two fingers. "Hey, soldier."

I thought he relaxed a little. Silly me.
"Do you know how much I've missed
you?" Cole sipped his drink before

> answering, taking plenty of time
> to deliberate. *That was sure a funny
> way of showing it, don't you think?*

"I don't . . . oh, you mean that guy?
I didn't do anything, Cole. *He* came
on to *me*." Prickles of anger started

> up my spine. *Yeah, well, you didn't
> exactly discourage him, did you?
> Fucking women are all alike.*

Okay, that pissed me off. "First off,
women are *not* all alike! And believe
it or not, I asked him to leave me alone

three or four times. Jesus, Cole, I drove
all the way here to be with *you*, not some
drunk jerk who I don't even know."

I finished my own drink in one long
swallow. Softened my voice. "Guess
maybe you're the one I don't even know."

> I got up, started to leave. Cole caught
> my arm. *I'm sorry. Goddamn sorry.
> Sit back down, Ashley. Please?*

MY FIRST INSTINCT

Was to jerk my arm from his grasp,
collect my stuff, drive back to San
Diego and quit taking his calls.
But then, I looked into his eyes,
found every hint of crazy gone,
and in its place, overriding love.

I sat, disquiet building a wall
between us. We'd been together
for two years. Shared laughter
and tears and beds and dreams.
I'd never glimpsed that side of him.
Had he really seen something

> different in me? *Ashley, baby,*
> *I love you so much. I can't stand*
> *the thought of losing you. Please . . .*

"The only way you'll ever lose me
is by accusing me of something awful
I didn't do, Cole. I can't believe
you have so little respect for me,
after all we've been through. I-I-I wait
for you for months at a time. Worry

about you. Stress over you. I put my life
on hold for you while you're away,
doing God knows what in some foreign
hellhole . . ." I was crying by then, tears
of frustration. "You're the only man
I've ever loved. I would never cheat on you."

I WAS GENUINELY HURT

Leveled, in fact. What I failed to see
was how hurt Cole was, too, even though

he had zero reason to be. It's rare
for him to display emotion, but he did

then. He reached for me, gathered me
into his arms. Kissed me so, so sweetly.

> I don't know what I'd do if you left
> me. Something brig-worthy, no doubt.

> You are the absolute best thing
> in my life. Without you, I'd be just

> another lonely grunt, searching
> for a good reason to come home.

"I'm not going anywhere, Cole,"
I whispered into his ear. "But I am

moving over now. People are staring."
It was true. Not sure if they were

hoping we'd get back into it, or
totally make out right there. Either

way, I wanted to take it private.
We finished our drinks. Skipped

dinner and went straight to the motel
for a couple of rounds of makeup sex.

PEOPLE STARE

When you walk into a room.
You don't notice. But I do.
It's one of the things
I love most about

        you,

this lack of self-
awareness. You wear
beauty like April
wears blossoms,

        only

spring shows off
an impatient display,
hurries away;

        you

stay. Knowing
you're there, waiting
for time to

        bring

meaning to your pause,
delaying your own dreams
to soothe mine, this keeps

        me

sane midst the chaos.
Without you, I have no reason
to find my way

        home.

Cole Gleason

I LEAVE COLE DRIPPING

Mai tai. Find my way back to the hotel,
sober enough to walk a straight line,
drunk enough not to worry about
the creep who accosted me earlier.
It's a different desk clerk, and I'm glad.
The last thing I want is to have to make
small talk about my wonderful Marine.

The same grunt who basically just called
me a slut. Every time he's about to deploy
he questions my moral fiber. Fucker. Wow.
And every time we have another pretour
sendoff, my language devolves. At least
I didn't say it out loud. I must look as
pissed as I feel, though, because people

are moving out of my way as I cross
the lobby, stomp into the elevator, head
up to the room. Our nice, romantic
suite, overlooking the Pacific. Damn.
Damn. Damn. Damn. I throw my stuff
on the big comfy-looking chair. Start to
pace. Pacing lowers my blood pressure.

Helps put things in order. I count steps.
One-two-three-four. All the way to twelve.
Turn. Count backward. Eleven-ten-nine.
Good thing we've got a big room. Fewer
than a dozen steps would make me crazier
than I am. Yeah, I know I'm a little touched.
Who wouldn't be, all things considered?

I WAS ALWAYS

On the obsessive side—
needing cleanliness.
Wanting order. But
the compulsive thing

started after falling
in love with Cole and
so much of my life spun
totally out of control.

Can't control:

           Where he is.
           Where he goes.
           When I'll hear from him.
           When I'll see him next.

Let alone:

           If he'll be safe.
           If he'll stay sane.
           If he'll come back whole.
           If he'll come back at all.

Or what he'll be like
post-deployment. Post-
retirement. I've never
known him as a civilian.

Never known him as just
a regular guy, something
I'm not sure he—or any
warrior—can ever be again.

SO I CONTROL

My own life, best as I can.
My grades are back in order.
It took a while, but I finally
figured out how to concentrate
on my classes, even with Cole gone.

I like the fieldwork, like helping
people, though I miss working
with the preschool kids. Teaching
still calls to me, despite the years
I've put into my master's.

Okay, I don't like to think about
that. Pace-pace-pace-pace. Two
times two is four. That is order.
Three groups of four is perfect.
Why twelve? Not sure. Eggs,

maybe. Two straight lines of
ovals, in their safe cardboard
nests. Picturing that makes me
calmer. Which is good, because
I hear the whir of Cole's key

in the lock. I turn toward the door,
brace myself for a wave of anger.
He comes through and, without
a word, comes straight to me,
lifts me off the floor, sweeps me

into the bedroom, throws me
onto the bed. Anger may feed
what follows. He rips himself
out of his pants, lifts my shift,
yanks off the bikini bottoms.

> His hands lace into my hair,
> hold my head against the pillow.
> He is inside me before he says,
> *Don't you ever leave me like that*
> *again. Do you understand?*

He punctuates each word with
a thrust of his hips. I lift my own,
wrap my legs around him, open
myself to accept his metered
plunging. "Yes," is the most I can

manage as he drives the air from
my lungs. The smell of rum and
whiskey clings to him, and his face
is sticky. I lick away the dried
mai tai, stoking his building frenzy.

Too soon, we crest, hard, sticky wet.
Together. Too soon, but there will
be an encore. And tonight, I'll sleep
with him circled around me, one
hand claiming my breast as his.

THE SOUND OF SIRENS

Is our alarm this morning. I left
the slider cracked, and the loud shriek
jumps us awake. Cole shoves me
over the side of the bed, onto the floor.

>*Get down!* He covers me with
>his body until the wailing fades.
>It takes a few seconds for him to
>realize where he is and exactly what
>all the noise was. *Goddamn it. You*
>*must think I'm a basket case, huh?*

"Not really," I huff. "But could you
please get off me? I can't breathe."
I try to keep it light. Truth is, my
heart is booming and the reason
I'm having a hard time breathing
is because he scared the crap out of me.

He draws himself up to sit on the side
of the bed. I get to my knees, crawl
over to him, and when I look up
into his eyes, I see fear. No, terror,
only just now receding. "You okay?"

>He nods. *On an FOB, a siren means*
>*incoming. Generally those fucking*
>*Hajji mortars hit pretty damn wide.*
>*But a couple of times, man. Way*
>*too close for comfort. I got lucky*
>*once or tw—* He stops short. We
>never talk about close calls. Never
>discuss danger. Especially not now
>that he's going back. Totally bad juju.

Still, I climb into his lap, reveling
in the feel of his nakedness beneath
my own. I slide my arms around
his neck. Kiss his forehead. Dare
to ask, "Do you ever get scared?
Over there, I mean." I have not

> ever asked him this question,
> assuming he must but that he
> probably wouldn't want to confess
> it. *Fear is your friend over there,*
> *sweetheart. If you're not at least*
> *a little scared, you're stupid, and*
> *stupid guys die faster than the rest.*

I push him back on the bed.
"I want you to be scared, then."
This time I make love to him.
Long. Lazy. Unselfish. Giving.
Ask me, that kind of sex is better
than the kind you demand.

After we both shudder release,
we lie, semidozing. His gentle
snoring tells me his fear has passed,
for the moment, at least. My own
unease is growing. Can't say why.
I count by fours. Eight. Twelve.

IT IS ALMOST NOON

When we pry ourselves from bed.
Shower. Dress for the day. I reach
for my purple bikini bottom, lying
on the floor next to the bed. Pull

> back, then ask myself why. Cole
> bends over. Picks it up. Hands
> it to me. *I want to see how you*
> *look in it. Please wear it today.*

I think that's an apology. I smile.
"Even at the beach? Even at
the pool? Even at all those places
where the other guys drool?"

> Cole laughs. *Yes, even there,*
> *Theodor. I'm not sure your*
> *poetry class is making you*
> *reach deep enough, though.*

"Maybe not. But my teacher
has excellent taste. I showed
him one of your poems. He said
to tell you it's really good, and

you should do something with
your writing one day. I happen
to agree. And so, I bet, would
Dr. Seuss." Cole's face is the color

> of an overripe tomato. *What?*
> *Ashley, no one but you has ever*
> *seen my poetry. Why would*
> *you show it to your teacher?*

"To get a second opinion. Also,
to gain a little sympathy. I missed
his class yesterday, and I'll miss
it Monday, too. You're not mad

because I used you to buy some
goodwill? Anyway, don't let it
go to your head. Chaucer, I'm sure,
would not agree with the rest of us."

> Cole still looks embarrassed,
> but at least he's smiling. Then
> he asks, *Which poem?* When
> I tell him, he nods. *Good one.*

"They all are, Cole. Take it from me,
you've got talent. We've studied a lot
of poets. Some great. Some not so. In
my humble opinion, you could be great."

It's close to one when we finally
emerge from the hotel. Famished,
but only for food. "I'm starving.
Where should we go for lunch?"

> *Leave it to me. I've got it all
> planned. Come on.* I follow him
> a few blocks, to where he has parked
> a rusting Jeep borrowed from

> his buddy, Brian. *He was going
> to use it today, but when I told him
> what I needed it for . . .* He shrugs.
> *We've got each other's backs.*

THE GRUNT CODE OF HONOR

Keep each other's backs, at all costs.
Your buddy is your brother. I'm grateful
for that. In more ways than one. Today,

I'm happy to be driving up to the North
Shore with Cole. We cut up the center
of the island, where it's mostly pineapple

> fields. *It's prettier driving up the East
> Shore, but it takes longer,* Cole explains.
> *Since we got such a late start, I figured
> this way would be better.* It's forty-five

minutes from Honolulu, with Cole
driving sort of like a maniac. It might
not be so bad, but the Jeep is both window-

free and roofless. Nothing but a roll bar
between our heads and the cloudless azure
sky. "Glad we've got a windshield. Not big

on bugs in my teeth." That makes Cole
laugh. When we get to Haleiwa, he pulls
into the parking lot of a little market.

> *Stay here. I'll be right back.* He goes
> inside and I wait, stomach growling,
> enjoying the tepid breeze blowing off
> the sea. The day is perfect. This time

of year is usually the start of the rainy
season. The weatherman on the radio
complains about how dry it's been, but

considering the state of the Jeep,
I'm quite content. Cole emerges,
carrying two big shopping bags

and grinning like a leprechaun.
A very tall, very buff leprechaun.
"You look unusually happy."

Maybe the happiest I've ever seen
him, an observation I don't make
out loud. He puts the groceries

> in back, jumps over the rocker
> panel, into the seat. *I am, my lady.*
> *I am. I thought we could lunch at*
> *Waimea Bay. You'll like it there.*

It's a short drive to one of the most
famous beaches in the world. Rain
or no rain, the ocean is rough,

the breaks big. I'd love to see them
when they swell to thirty feet. "Wish
you would have borrowed a board, too."

> *Oh, hell no. You might think you're*
> *Surfer Girl, but I wouldn't let you*
> *out there on a board. The guys who*
> *ride over here are fucking insane.*

I bristle more than a little at the idea
of him thinking I need his permission
to do anything. But I refuse to argue.

THERE'S A NICE PICNIC AREA

With tables beneath a fringe of palms.
We find one empty, and Cole spreads

his feast—deli sandwiches, papaya
and pineapple salad, baked barbecue

chips. My favorite. He remembered.
And now, the piece de resistance.

"Champagne? Are we celebrating
something?" Surely not deployment.

> *Maybe.* He pops the bottle—the first
> bottle. He bought three. Pours two

> plastic glasses. Hands me one, lifts
> the second. *Here's to you and me.*

It's even good champagne. My curiosity
is screaming, but this is his party. We

sip. Eat. Surf watch. People watch.
Several climb a huge rock, jutting out

into the ocean. They jump, catching
the turquoise water swirling around

the outcropping's feet. As my head grows
fuzzy, I ask, "Think we should do that?"

> *Are you kidding? I know it's supposed
> to be safe. I also know there's a major*

*rip out there. A wise grunt only
takes measured risks. Not that*

*every Marine follows the Corps
recommendation. Some guys are,*

*like, total jerk-offs when it comes
to offering up their necks.* He thinks

awhile. *Once, I watched this kid—
he wasn't much more than eighteen—*

*mess with a fucking sand viper,
just to prove it couldn't bite through*

*his boot. You know what? It couldn't.
But when the snake struck, the kid*

*fell backward and his weapon went
off. Asshole shot himself in the foot.*

*His boot couldn't stop a goddamn
bullet.* He laughs. Mean laughter.

A little shiver runs up my spine
and the mouthful of sandwich

I'm trying to swallow sort of lodges
in my throat. Champagne takes care

of that. It takes care of a lot, including
chasing away the image of a striking viper.

AFTER LUNCH

Wearing my hot purple bikini
and a cool champagne haze
I open a big beach blanket,
spread it over the tree-shaded
sand. Cole lies next to me, and

we smoosh into the cushion
of the sand. It folds up around
us. I snuggle my head against
his shoulder. "Hey. I thought
you didn't like the beach."

> *This one is better than most,*
> he admits. *But anyplace is better*
> *when you're this close to me.*

We fall quiet for a while. Listen
to the *wish-wish* of gentle surf.
"One day we need to play tourist.
Visit the other islands. Maybe ride
bikes down a volcano or something."

> He shakes his head. *Once I leave*
> *here, I'm never coming back.*
> *Can't stand being on an island.*
> *No place to go but round and round.*

We haven't really talked about
life after the Marines. His initial
commitment is another three
years. But after that . . . What?
"So, you're thinking about leaving?"

Eventually. I mean, everyone
does, right? I can only advance
so far as an enlisted. And who
knows what vile new conflict
the Pentagon has in mind?

A nervous thrill rushes through
me. Does he really mean it?
I kind of thought he might just
stay entrenched in the Corps
forever. This is all news to me.

Would you still love me if you
had to put up with me every day?

I nuzzle tighter against him.
Kiss his chest. "Of course I would.
Especially if you promised to take
the trash out. Dumpsters scare me."

Hang on. He gets up, goes over
to the table. When he returns,
he has two glasses of champagne.
Remember I told you I had a surprise?
He hands me both glasses, reaches

into his shorts pocket. Extracts
a small gold box and opens it,
anticipation in his eyes. Inside
the box is a diamond ring. Blood
rushes so loudly in my ears, I barely

hear, *Ashley. I love you. Marry me.*

COLE LEFT FOR IRAQ

The second time in the spring
of 2009. Our relationship
was a little over two years
old. It still felt very young.

Time together. Two baby steps
forward. Longer time apart.
Half a dozen giant steps back.
Figure in a major argument

just weeks before deployment,
everything felt shaky, at least
to me, when he shipped out.
He would have disputed that.

As far as he was concerned,
we stood, inextricably linked,
atop rock-solid ground. I'm not
really sure why I let him believe

that. Maybe it was, at least in
part, because Darian often shared
Spence's accusation-filled letters
with me. I didn't want Cole to think

those things about me. I would
never fool around with someone
else unless Cole and I severed
our relationship completely.

At least, that's what I told myself.

COLE'S BATTALION TOUCHED DOWN

At Al Asad Airbase in the lovely
sandstorm-ridden Al Anbar province,
where summer temperatures hover
around one hundred ten. Not long
after they arrived, he e-mailed:

THE BASE ITSELF ISN'T SO BAD.
WE'VE GOT A POOL. AND A GYM.
AND BECAUSE BRASS AND POLITICOS
FLY IN HERE A LOT, THE FOOD IS GOOD.
I MISS YOU ALREADY. LOVE YOU ALWAYS.

Their mission was security—keeping
the local citizenry safe, whether or not
they liked the idea. Running regional
detention facilities. Those guys definitely
didn't like the idea. Manning checkpoints.

Handling dogs trained to sniff out IEDs
and insurgent weapons caches. Some
units stayed on-base while performing
their duties. Off-hours were spent taking
online courses and improving their fitness

in general and martial arts in particular.
For most, boredom was once again
their most obvious enemy. They got
regular care packages and mail, and
computer time was generous. The "lucky"

ones, however, were sent to COP Heider,
a joint operations command outpost on
the Syrian border. Here, they were also
charged with security. High-priority,
much-more-dangerous security.

LIVING CONDITIONS

At COP Heider were austere, as Cole
later explained. Later, because when
he first arrived, there were no computers.

They were on order, but it would be some
months before they were installed. Mail
was delivered, but it crawled in and out.

With communication largely impossible,
I didn't hear from him for many weeks.
Unless you've experienced the stress

of not knowing your soldier's status,
you can't possibly understand it.
Is he or she safe outside the wire?

Uninjured? Alive? You stumble through
each day the best you can, pretending
everything is fine. It simply has to be,

in your waking mind, or you'd dissolve
into a useless mass of shattered hope
and broken promises. Promises like:

> I'll always come back to you, Ashley.
> You are my collateral. My reason
> to return, no matter what. Believe it.

Belief is easier when your soldier can
contact you. When "collateral" isn't
paired in your paranoia with "damage."

I COMBED THE INTERNET

For news of casualties. Found
a nameless few. Since Cole and I
weren't married, the Corps wasn't
bound to release information to me.
It was probably my biggest frustration.
At least, it was until I met Jaden.

He was a senior at State. Everything
Cole wasn't. California native. Liberal
arts major, focused on film. Fact:
he had more money than ambition,
something his parents didn't argue
with. He was stunningly Irish, with

black hair, fair skin and indigo eyes.
Worst of all, he was unfailingly patient,
when I made it clear from the get-go
I was not on the hunt for a new man.
I wasn't. But goddamn it, I was lonely.
More than a little scared. Tired of playing

lady-in-waiting to a tiger-eyed soldier
who might very well be dead. The night
I met Jaden, I'd finally decided enough
worry was enough worry, and sleep
would come easier under the influence.
I called up Brittany, my effervescent,

fun-hungry friend, and out we went to
binge drink, which for me meant three
or four, and for her meant a couple
more. We did take a cab. Planned
a return cab, too. Okay, maybe I knew
all that planning might lead to a little flirting.

But I did not predict the amazing
guy who would start flirting with me.
Brittany and I picked a favorite dance
club. Ear-hurting noisy, but we weren't
looking for conversation. Lucky us
(or not, depending on how you look

>at what happened later), the SDSU
>crew team was there, drinking, too.
>I went to the bar, ordered well tequila.
>For some reason, the guy—Jaden—
>standing next to me noticed. *Have
>you ever tried Trago? It's brilliant.*

I started to say something flip,
but then I turned to look at him.
Despite my certainty that no guy except
Cole could ever again make my pulse
pick up speed . . . I caught my breath.
"Trago? I bet it's expensive, huh?"

>Speaking of brilliant. His smile?
>Totally. *More expensive than Cuervo,
>for sure. Would you like to try it?*
>He pointed to the full bottle on the top
>shelf of the bar. Obviously, it was too
>pricey for most of the clientele. *My treat.*

I should have smiled, thanked him,
and said no. Instead, I shrugged.
Next thing you know, I was drinking
shots of the best tequila I'd ever tasted—
with a gorgeous guy, so not my Cole.
He was a pretty good dancer, too.

216

THE THING ABOUT TEQUILA

Is it creeps up on you. Good tequila
is even sneakier. Especially when
you're totally enjoying the company
of the guy who keeps pouring shots
for you. He bought the whole bottle.

Truthfully, I was grateful to spend
the evening with him. Brittany deserted
me early for some guy she hit it off with.
The last thing I wanted to do was sit
there, drinking alone, with increasingly

drunk guys hitting on me. Jaden,
of course, was hitting on me, too. But
at least he was respectful about it,
especially when the Trago loosened
my mouth and I started talking about

> Cole. He was sympathetic. *No
> one in my family was ever drawn
> to the military. Certainly, I would
> never join up. I respect those who
> do, but it must be really hard for you.*

At some point, I started to feel
selfish—for wanting to talk to any
guy other than Cole, and for hoarding
this one, when I had no plans to do
more than talk. "I should probably go

and let you tempt some other girl
with the rest of this tequila." I started
to stand, but he put his hand on
my arm. Stopped me with a simple: *Don't go.*

EVERY NOW AND THEN

You run into a guy who actually
appreciates your IQ as much as
your bra size. Okay, often those

guys are gay. But not always.
Jaden and I connected in a very
special way. As friends. Turned out

> he had regular fuck buddies. *No*
> *one I could get serious about.*
> *No one as interesting as you.*

I'm not sure what he found so
interesting. I didn't feel special.
But I was glad that he thought

I was. Over the next month—May,
and heading into another summer
vacation for me and graduation

for Jaden—we hung out regularly.
Anyone seeing us together would
have thought we were a couple,

and other than the sex thing,
I suppose we were. Under other
circumstances, I would have fallen

totally in love with him and if I were
to be honest with myself, I'd have
had to admit complete infatuation.

What I wasn't at all sure about
was if our budding relationship
was because of Cole or in spite

of him. When I stopped to worry
about that, guilt crashed into me.
I'd given Cole my word that I'd

never cheat on him. I wasn't. Not
really. Was I? Was it okay to carve
my heart, give a tiny fraction to Jaden?

I knew Cole wouldn't think so. But
I still hadn't heard a single word.
If he really cared, couldn't he find

a way to let me know he was alive,
he was whole, he was still in love
with me? Instinct told me he was fine.

Logic insisted the silence wasn't
his fault. I had a pretty fair idea of how
things worked beyond the wire.

So what was up with me? It all came
down to hormone-rattled emotions,
confusion at my confusion. Love,

I thought, should be straightforward
commitment, unencumbered by private
doubt, internal debate. It should be static.

IT FELT ANYTHING BUT

As that summer rolled in,
hotter than usual. I decided
to stay in San Diego. In Lodi,
there would be questions.

About school.
Which was relatively good.

About my major.
Which I hadn't changed yet.

About Darian.
Who I hadn't seen in months.

About Cole.
Who . . . I couldn't say.

Mostly, I wanted to surf.
To work and save a little money.
To wait to hear from my soldier.
To spend time with Jaden.

My dad didn't seem to care one
way or another. But when I told
Mom I wasn't going home,
the first thing she said was

What aren't you telling me?

For whatever reason, I broke
down and confessed. I steeled
myself, waiting for her to berate
me. After all, she was the one
who had been cheated on for years.

Instead, she commiserated.
You're young. You should
be having fun, not spending
so much time alone. Tell me
about Jaden. What's he like?

"He's smart."
No smarter than Cole.

"He's ambitious."
Ditto Cole. Just with different goals.

"He's wealthy."
That one impressed her. Me, not
so much. I planned to make my own
way, regardless.

"He's gorgeous."
No more so than Cole. One dark,
one blond. One blue-eyed, one
amber-eyed. And I had no preference.

"He's athletic."
Tennis champ. Rowing champ.
Decent surfer, too. Cole could
no doubt run circles around him,
even if he couldn't ride a board.

The comparisons were inevitable.
Eventually, it came down to one
very major difference.

Jaden was a civilian.
Cole was a Marine.

IT WAS A BREEZE-SOFT KISS

That made me decide not to see
Jaden anymore. We'd had a lovely
day at the beach. Dinner after. Drinks.
We stood, arm to arm, leaning against
the deck railing outside Jaden's Spartan
little house. A huge harvest moon smiled

over the horizon and the sky was clear
enough to reveal a feast of stars. We
were talking about the future. His. Mine.
Not ours. But that felt like a given. So
when he leaned down, brushed my lips
sweetly with his, it felt right. For a moment.

Then the wrong of it came crashing
down. It wasn't a demanding kiss, not
even suggestive. But it wasn't Cole's,
and I knew before I could ever welcome
another man's kiss, I'd have to say good-bye
to my soldier. "I love you," I said, and I

meant it. "Please take me home." And
he understood that I had made a decision.
Jaden and I are long-distance friends now.
We talk from time to time. He's getting
married soon. They sent an invitation,
but I can't be at the wedding.

That night, I wasn't near certain
I'd made the right choice. I wasn't even
sure the day after, when I finally got
word from my close-to-promotion soldier.

HE DID NOT APOLOGIZE

In his mind, I shouldn't have worried.
Besides, all those silent days were
just a part of the job description.

He didn't see, would never know,
how relief barrel rolled over me
when his handwritten letter arrived.

*Hello, my beautiful lady. How I wish
I were there with you, instead of killing
time in this god-forsaken land. Seriously.
God probably looks down on this place,
wondering what the fuck he was thinking.
As I write this, the thermometer outside claims
it's one hundred nine degrees. That's well after
the motherfucking sun has set. It is relentless,
only rivaled by the wind, which I think is doing
its level best to clear the desert of sand.*

*I can't share too many details about what I've
been up to. Suffice it to say the great American
masses only know as much as they're allowed
to by The Machine. It's all good. No need to know.
I volunteer for the ugliest stuff, not only to fight
the oppressive boredom, but also to impress those
who can give me a leg up. Rank means more
than better pay. It means plum assignments.*

*Once I get back to Al Asad, I'll test for lance
corporal, and will make it no problem. Then I
plan to put in for sniper training. I'm the best
shot in my unit. That includes moving targets...*

HIS CARE PACKAGE WISH LIST

Did not include chocolate or soap.
Or anything else that would melt
easily, sitting in the back of a truck,
stalled in the brutal heat. He did ask
for cigarettes. He always did, though
I never saw him smoke when we were
together, never smelled tobacco on him.

Every time he requested them, I had
to wonder who he became "over there."
This letter told me not to ask the dirty
details. How filthy were they, really?
On some level, I understood he was
trained to kill. His unspoken words
shouted, *I have killed!* But just who

did he kill? Combatants? Innocents?
Scorpions, rats, snakes, and dogs?
Did they all die the same way? Did he
watch? Laugh? Desecrate death, sick
celebration? Despite his assertion
that the average Joe shouldn't know,
video footage was surfacing via

the Internet. I never found Cole's face
among the most reviled. Had I, would
I have forgiven him summarily, or might
it have tarnished my belief in us?
Because, despite Jaden, despite weeks
of worry, despite the unsettling image
of moving targets in Cole's crosshairs,

one fact remained. I loved him.

MOVING TARGETS

Are primo. If I were
a girl, they'd make me wet.
As it is, they make me

        hard.

It's about being the best.
Truth be told, any
half-ass grunt can manage

        to

aim a SAW at a milling
crowd, flatten it out.
And most civilians can

        understand

how to draw a straight
bead on a paper bull's-eye.
What's infinitely

        harder

is assessing wind and
distance to intelligent prey,
aware of you trying

        to

estimate their path and
speed. Thwart evasive
action, it's impossible to

        deny

unparalleled skill at the kill.

Cole Gleason

EVASION

Of a marriage proposal can only
look like one thing: a solid no.
"Let me think it over" means,
"I'm really not sure." But whether
that's not sure of "you" or "me"
or "us" doesn't much matter.
Uncertainty is tantamount
to "something here is wrong."

And yet, I say yes, and I say
it with little hesitation. Maybe it's
the five-year-old-on-Christmas-
morning expression on Cole's face.
Or maybe it's the two bottles
of champagne we've consumed.
Possibly, it's the craving to bring
a higher level of legitimacy

to our relationship, in the eyes
of the Corps, not to mention
the rest of the world. Whatever
it is, I push away every notion
of "something here isn't quite
right," and accept the gorgeous
two-carat diamond in platinum.
Cole slides it on my finger.
"It's a little big, but it's beautiful."

> We'll get it sized. And it should be
> beautiful. It cost a good chunk
> of ten paychecks. I love you, Ashley.
> I'll be back in May, so we can have
> a June wedding. If that suits you.

I breathe a huge, silent sigh
of relief. I half-thought he might
suggest doing the deed right now.
"I think I can pull it together by
June. There's a lot of planning
to do." Despite my reservations,
excitement trills. Every girl dreams
of her wedding. Including me.

> Cole rushes ahead. *When I get*
> *back, I'll go active reserves, and*
> *we can move to Wyoming. We can*
> *stay with Mom until I find work.*
> *Then we can start a family. Two*
> *kids. Maybe three, depending.*

"Whoa! Slow down. Wedding first.
Family later. And don't you think
we should discuss little details like
where we'll live?" It vaguely creeps
me out that he's thought so much
about this without consulting me.

> *Well, sure. It's just, I want us to*
> *start out ahead of the game. Mom*
> *could use some help, and Dale*
> *made sure the ranch was paid for.*
> Cole's stepfather passed away last
April, leaving his mom alone again.
No rent would be a good thing, right?

I can't exactly argue with that.
"Well, sure. And, hey, we've got lots
of time to work out all the details."

THAT THOUGHT

Comforts me the rest of the day. Cole
had that all worked out, too. After
our bubbly-soaked afternoon, rather
than risk driving back to Honolulu,

> he has us booked at a bed-and-breakfast–
> type room here on the North Shore. *Nothing*
> *fancy, and we have to share a bathroom,*
> *but it's just overnight.* We make the best

of it, and the celebration continues
with local mahi burgers, the last bottle
of champagne, and Cole's crazy idea
for dessert—banana cream pie, using

our bodies as plates. I shudder to think
what sort of magazine or movie might
have made him come up with that.
But I have to admit it's kind of fun,

especially since I don't have to wash
the sheets. The bed is a small double,
and after we finish, we lie sticky (in more
ways than one) in each other's arms.

It will be our last night together
for several months. So we don't waste
a lot of time sleeping. Toward morning,
totally spent, Cole dozes. I'm wasted tired

but the tornado of thoughts twisting
inside my head defeat sleep for me.
By checkout time, shadows semicircle
my eyes and I'm mostly incoherent.

TWO HOURS OF SLEEP

Have done wonders for Cole,
and he chatters all the way back
to the Waikiki hotel. We return
via the East Shore route, which
takes us past Kaneohe Bay.

The base sits on a jut of land
surrounded by ocean. "You know,
some people would kill to work
in a place like this," I observe.

> *Some people have.* The offhand
> comment bears a lot of weight.
> It's more like many men, and maybe
> even a few women stationed here
> have taken lives. Innocent people,

no doubt, dropped right along with
deserving insurgents. "Does it ever
bother you? The death?" I've avoided
prodding him for details. Once in a while,
my curiosity won't leave me alone.

> *Not when I'm over there. Death*
> *is a part of the landscape. Dead dogs,*
> *dead donkeys. Dead camels. Dead*
> *people. The only thing you don't get*
> *used to is the fucking bloat-rot smell.*

He steers around a pothole. *When*
I get home, the memories get to me
once in a while. You see things . . .
the things humans do to each other
sometimes are downright sickening.

229

"I can only imagine." Not that I
want to. Except I have this morbid
need to understand. "Even guys
you know?" I expect him to deny
it. Unfortunately, he doesn't.

> Oh, yeah. Even guys I know. One
> time, I saw an MP let his dog go
> on a prisoner. A kid, really. Maybe
> sixteen. He acted all tough, but not
> for long. After the fourth or fifth

> chomp, his thigh looked like sausage.
> When the dog aimed for his personal
> sausage, the kid talked. Cole laughs,
> with neither malice nor genuine humor.
> Not sure his information was any good,

> though. If I were that boy, and someone
> sic'd his dog on my huevos, I would
> have come up with some information,
> accurate or not. It is a problem with
> that particular method of interrogation.

Cole seems so comfortable talking,
I decide to try a more direct approach.
"So, you're saying the boy was innocent?"

> This time derision laces his laughter.
> Nope. I'm not saying that at all. No one
> over there is innocent. Every single one
> of them is guilty of wanting us dead.

HE'S SO SINCERE

He almost sways me. I haven't been
"over there," so it's hard for me to
dispute his obviously heartfelt opinion.

However, his callousness remains, and
maybe always will, a wedge between us.
Because I simply can't *not* believe that

a common string of humanity ties me—
us—to the Iraqi and Afghani people. Some
of them are hell-bent to serve evil, yes. But

so are plenty of Westerners. Hard to tell
who is who sometimes. And when one
of the ones you're unsure about is someone

you love—uh, someone you just agreed
to marry—things get really watery.
Arguing would serve no purpose, though.

Maybe asking this question won't, either.
But I'm going to, anyway. "Have you done
things over there that you're not proud of?"

> *Everyone has, Ashley. It goes with*
> *the territory. You get bored, you get*
> *scared, you go looking for an outlet.*

> *But the thing is, for the most part,*
> *I can sleep just fine at night. Not*
> *everyone I know can say that.*

HE DOESN'T ELABORATE

And I'm not really sure I want him to,
so I lean back in the seat, close my eyes.
Next thing I hear is the sound of a city
bus shifting gears. I jump awake right
about the time Cole maneuvers the Jeep
into a tight parking space. "You're good
at that." My voice is husky from sleep.

> I'm good at a lot of things, as I would
> hope you know by now. He glances
> at his watch. I have to be back on base
> by five. It's a little after three now.
> Are you hungry, or . . . ? We agree

to the "or." It will be the last time for
many months, so we take special care
to make it memorable. I even wear
my engagement ring, though I have
to put it on my middle finger so it
doesn't fall off. By the time we finish,

exhaustion has claimed me—muscles,
bones, brain. I want food, but I need
sleep more. I sit against the headboard,
watching Cole get dressed. "Did anyone
ever tell you how graceful you are?"
Like a gazelle—built to escape death.

> Uh, no. And I hope that isn't in
> any way questioning my manhood.
> Somehow, I doubt it. He comes over.
> Kisses a bittersweet good-bye. I'll be back
> before you know it. I love you.

THE DOOR CLOSES

Behind him, leaves me here,
counting tears. They brim, fall,
splat in syncopated rhythm.

The door is closed. Cole is gone.
I will never get used to this.
Hollowed. Emptied. Drained.

I put the pillow over my head.
Inhale the darkness, pungent
with the smell of Cole's sweat

and our sex. How *would* it be
to see him every day? Is it even
possible that we can be a regular

married couple, both of us off
to work in the morning. Dinner
at home together each night?

And children. Babies? Am I
the only girl my age who hasn't
thought about having a family?

I'm still figuring out what I want
to be when I grow up. Wife and
mother is not at the top of my list.

Then again, neither is childless
spinster. It's just too much to think
about right now. Sleep deprived.

That's what I am. Once I'm rested,
the answers will come easier. Right?

IT'S INSANELY BRIGHT

So many crystals of sand, reflecting
the high, hot sun. No shade to speak of,

no shelter from the inexorable heat
lifting off the rutted street. Footsteps

slap behind me. I turn, ready to fight.
No one. The sidewalk is empty. Silent.

Where am I? I'm hungry, and looking
for the marketplace. Did I take a wrong

turn? I walk faster but don't know
which way to go, and there's no one

here to ask for help. Suddenly, I hear
yelling. Dogs barking. Laughter. The noise

is to my right. I follow it down a deserted
avenue. And now I see kennels. Men.

Soldiers. Standing in front of wire
enclosures. Laughing. "Hello?" I call,

but they can't hear me past the barking.
Snapping. And now, someone is crying.

Praying. I reach the first pen. Two soldiers
stand back, let me look inside. A boy

is chained there, on his knees. Naked.
A huge Doberman is mounting him.

And the soldiers laugh. "Bastards!"
I run along the chain link, eyes in front

of me. Suddenly, a German shepherd
lunges at its gate. When I turn, I see

it has something in its mouth. Red
drool drips, and the dog bites down,

crunching bones. "Drop it!" I scream,
and the shepherd obeys. What falls

to the ground is a hand. A lady's hand.
On its third finger is a diamond ring.

"No, no, no, no!" The keen of my own
voice yanks me from the nightmare.

Pale light leaks in through the window.
Evening? Morning? I lie, panting like

the dogs in my dream. My stomach
growls and I reach for my cell to check

the time. Seven eighteen. Morning.
I slept for fifteen hours. No wonder

I'm starving. I put the phone back on
the table and when I do, the glint

of a two-carat diamond catches my eyes.
All of a sudden, I don't feel so hungry.

BUT BY THE TIME

I clean up, get dressed, and start
to pack, I'm famished again.
Checkout is eleven. My flight,
barring delays, is a little after one.

I've got time for room service.
I think about steak and eggs.
Order an omelet instead. Cheese.
Spinach. Onions. Bell peppers.

No meat. While I wait, I organize
my suitcase. Cosmetics in the middle.
Running shoes at the bottom. Tank tops,
shifts, and shorts, folded in fourths,

placed around the sides. Flat over
all, the sweater I brought, just in case.
I've never needed to use it here.
But what if I did, and didn't have it?

Breakfast arrives and I eat it
out on the lanai, watching white-
tipped Pacific waves break gently
in the distance. That same ocean

is breaking against California
cliffs and sand. Connecting here
and there. Connecting Cole and me,
at least until he leaves for Afghanistan.

And then, the sky is what we'll share,
the earth's spin, forward movement
of time. That, and the love that makes
all things seem forgivable. Most of the time.

I AM IN THE CAB

On my way to the airport before I check
my cell for messages. The first is from Cole.

> *WOULD HAVE CALLED BUT*
> *DIDN'T WANT TO WAKE YOU.*
> *I LET MOM KNOW ABOUT*
> *THE ENGAGEMENT. SHE SAID*
> *TO GET IN TOUCH IF YOU NEED*
> *HELP PLANNING. IT'S THE BEST*
> *I'VE HEARD HER SOUND SINCE*
> *BEFORE SHE GOT SICK. WEDDINGS*
> *ARE GOOD MEDICINE, I THINK.*
>
> *FLY SAFE AND LET ME KNOW*
> *WHEN YOU GET THERE. I ALWAYS*
> *WORRY UNTIL YOU'RE OVER THE*
> *OCEAN AND STANDING ON SOLID*
> *GROUND. SPEAKING OF OVER THE*
> *OCEAN, WE LEAVE ON FRIDAY.*
> *DON'T TELL THE TALIBAN WE'RE*
> *COMING. I WANT IT TO BE A SURPRISE.*
> *I LOVE YOU ASHLEY, GIRL. ALWAYS.*

He told his mom. Guess I'll have to tell my
parents, too, which will make the idea legit.
I need a few days. The second text is from Dar.

> *WHEN WILL YOU BE HOME?*
> *I NEED YOU, ASH. IT'S SPENCE.*
> *THERE WAS AN ACCIDENT.*
> *HE MIGHT NOT MAKE IT.*

LANCE CORPORAL GLEASON

Returned early from his second tour
in Iraq, and he did qualify for sniper
school. Cole was a crack shot. No
brag. Just fact. What I didn't know
then is that all those silent weeks,
he was off on voluntary patrols with
the sniper platoon and had impressed

the right people. Just how remains
a mystery. I keep tiptoeing around
asking for details. Maybe one day
I'll find the courage. Maybe it's better
not to know. They say U.S. Marine
scout-snipers are the cream, and I
don't doubt it at all. I've seen videos

documenting what Cole went through
in his eight and a half weeks of training.
It's intense. Those soldiers must be in
top physical condition. More even than
that, they have to be prepared mentally
to run miles, swim with heavy weights,
crawl through smelly, slimy muck, then

get to their feet, run some more, drop
to their bellies, sight in and hit targets
spot-on at awe-inspiring distances.
Attrition is something like sixty percent.
Cole, of course, made the cut and
became a member of an elite squad
of single-shot kill marksmen. Woot.

I DIDN'T SEE HIM

Until after his training was complete.
I was okay with that. I'd just started
my senior year and wanted to focus
on my classes without distraction.

Plus, I was still shaken over the idea
that Jaden had made me question
my relationship with Cole. Was it pure
loneliness, or did I have some moral

defect I'd never realized existed before?
I was afraid if I saw Cole too soon,
the guilt in my eyes would give me away.
After several weeks, it did start to fade.

So I was happy enough to find out
that Cole was taking leave to help
celebrate my twenty-third birthday.
Not only that, but Spence was coming

home, too. He, Darian, Cole, and I
would be together for the first time
in almost three years. It was a reunion
we'd talked about and hoped for,

but only coincidence could make it
actually happen. Darian and I worked
hard to plan something special—
an overnight trip to Disneyland.

Neither of us had visited since we
were teens. Cole and Spence were
Disney virgins. It sounded like fun.
A real celebration, reminding us

that we were still young. The problem
was, despite our relatively youthful ages,
in too many ways, we were no longer
young. Cole had just graduated

from a school that taught him to be
a better—no, the best—killer. Spence
had recently seen three of his buddies
wiped out by a suicide bomber. Oh,

and he should have been right there
with them in the same vehicle, but
for a providential case of dysentery.
Survivor's guilt adds figurative years.

As for Dar and me, well, we still
believed in our youth. But face it, forever
commitment—whether sanctioned by
a license or not—when you've barely

entered your third decade of life
makes you older than your friends
who are still out there playing the field.
It's play that keeps you young.

PLAY

Is what we had in mind.
It sort of started out that way.
I asked my Mom for mad money
to book a room on property.
"That's all I want for my birthday,"
I told her. She seemed to understand,

although I found out later
she also added funds to my
savings account. Moms. You have
to love them, or at least appreciate
how they care for you covertly, despite
your pulling away. Overtly, she sent

enough for adjoining rooms
at the Grand Californian Hotel,
a spectacular resort adjacent California
Adventure. Disneyland, Phase Two.
Sometimes my birthday abuts
the busy Thanksgiving weekend.

This was one of those years, so it
took some planning to make it happen.
Cole flew directly into Orange County.
I maneuvered the obnoxious freeways
alone, picked him up at the airport,
and we checked in late Saturday

afternoon. Dar and Spence drove
up together. The plan was to meet
for dinner, enjoy the evening,
then do the parks the following day,
when hopefully most of the crowds
would be on their way home.

I WAS SO LOOKING FORWARD

To seeing Spencer again. My first
thought, when I spotted him and Dar,
waiting at the restaurant entrance
was, "Is he sick or something?"

I saw no sign of Spence's signature
swagger. In its place was . . . I don't
know. Caution, I guess. Where once
he held Darian with downright prideful

possessiveness, that evening,
the way his arm rested around
her shoulder seemed needful, like
if he let go, his knees might buckle.

>   Cole took a good, long look at Spence.
>   *I haven't talked to him in a while,*
>   he commented. *But he does look
>   a little unenthusiastic, doesn't he?*

"Maybe he's just scared of giant
Mickey Mouses? Or would that be
Mickey Mice?" We both snickered
at my stupid joke, but straightened

up before Spence noticed our
inappropriate laughter. I didn't think
he'd appreciate our acting all concerned,
either, so I found just the right kind

of smile and offered him a long,
affectionate hug, which he returned.
"God, it's great to see you. How have
you been?" Innocent enough.

Spence pulled back. *Ah, you know,*
I've been better. But being home
for a while is bound to help. I missed
my girl. He leaned over and kissed Dar.

She kissed back enthusiastically,
but when she glanced over at me,
her eyes held apprehension.
The hostess came to seat us for our

seven p.m. reservation. And, even
though we had just come from upstairs,
the first thing I did was excuse myself
to use the ladies' room, hoping Darian

would follow. She did. I went straight
to the sink to wash my hands. Dar did
the same. I looked at her in the mirror.
"What's up with Spence? Is he okay?"

She shook her head. *I'm not really*
sure. He's had a weird cough since
he's been back. Says it's walking
pneumonia. Whatever it is, he's not

eating right and he's skinny as hell.
And I think he's depressed. I hope
this trip picks him up a little. At home,
he just sits around, playing Xbox.

"Has he been to the doctor?"
I asked, knowing her answer.
"Any way you can get him to go?"
I knew the answer to that one, too.

HE DID COUGH AT DINNER

A deep rattle that could, in fact,
be pneumonia. But Marines—real
men—don't need doctors unless
they're bleeding out. And after
dinner, he went straight outside
for a smoke, claiming it would help

dry out his chest. Cole went with
him while Dar and I headed for
the lounge for prebirthday drinks.
We ordered a round for the four
of us before I said, "I've never
seen Spence so quiet. If you can't

get him to go in on his own, isn't
there someone at the base you
can call?" Depression is common
among soldiers, and those with
too little to keep them busy often
act out in not-so-good ways.

> *I'm on it. But with all the Iraqi*
> *returnees, they're really busy.*
> *Spouses take a backseat, and*
> *he isn't asking for help. I've got*
> *an appointment in three weeks.*

"Shush. Here they come."
Amazingly, Spence's cough
seemed a little better. Maybe
tobacco was good for walking
pneumonia. What did I know? Still,
he directed most of his attention

244

inward. It was a pleasant evening,
regardless. We all kept conversation
light. No talk of war or torture except
for some commentary about Sea
Stallion helicopters wearing out from
use, and what kind of replacements

might be coming. I might have
been totally bored, except Spence
lit up, jabbering excitedly about
his area of expertise. Just watching
him pull himself out of whatever dark
place he'd been stuck in made me

smile and pretend my total attention.
Dar, I could tell, felt the same way.
It was like old times. The four of us,
drinking and laughing and cementing
our friendship. Spencer only coughed
a couple of times, and he barely leaned

on Darian at all. By the evening's
end, while I was still worried about
Spence, his problems, whatever
they were, didn't seem quite as
distressing. Until the next day.

IT STARTED OUT FINE

We did California Adventure first,
and we got there just past opening.

There were no crowds to speak of.
No major lines. I loved Soarin' Over

California, a simulated hang glider ride.
Cole was partial to the big coaster,

which blasts you one hundred-plus
vertical feet before accelerating into

a loop-the-loop. Dar wanted to do
the Tower of Terror twice, but straight

drops give me a headache. Cole rode it
with her the second time. Spence waited

>with me. *I could really use a smoke*
>*right about now,* he said sincerely.

"Think maybe you should lay off
those things until you see a doctor?"

>*Thanks for caring, Mom. But I'll be*
>*fine. I'm better today, you know?*

As if on cue, a fresh round of hacking
punctuated the sentence. "If you say so."

>He put his arm around me. Squeezed.
>*I meant when I said thanks for caring.*

HE LEFT SOMETHING UNSAID

And I knew it. But just then, Cole
and Dar appeared, arm in arm,
laughing. Spencer tensed. Softly
pushed me away. We claimed
our partners, finished park number
one, skipping the water rides. Who

gets wet in November? After lunch
we walked over to Disneyland proper
and by then people had definitely
arrived. Down Main Street, walking
was elbow to elbow. People yelling.
Kids laughing. Babies crying. The noise

level just kept rising, the deeper
we pushed into the park. "Let's get
Fast Passes for Indiana Jones, then
go do Thunder Mountain Railroad,"
I suggested. Fast Passes let you come
back within a certain window of time

and use a quicker line. You have to
know how to maneuver, but if you work
them right, they're awesome, especially
when the park is as crowded as it was
that day. The problem was, the Thunder
Mountain line was crazy long, too.

Between working our way through
that queue, doing the ride, locating
a designated smoking spot for Spencer,
waiting for him to indulge—twice—
then finding our way back to Indiana
Jones, our Fast Passes had expired.

SPENCE WENT BALLISTIC

Had he been in uniform, or at the very
least been decent to the Fast Pass Line
guy, things would probably have worked
out very differently. Instead, when the guy
tried to turn us away, Spence shoved him.

> *What the fuck do you mean, expired?*
> *You want us to wait in the other line,*
> *just because we're a couple of minutes*
> *late? You'd better think again, asshole.*

People started moving away. Spence
grabbed the guy by the collar, and I looked
at Cole, expecting him to pull Spence off.
Instead, he stood there with an amused
grin on his face. "Cole. Please." Before

he could react, Security arrived. Bad
became worse when two uniformed
men tried to pull Spencer off Fast Pass
Man. As soon as they touched him,
Spence started swinging. Let's just say

the U.S. Marine Corps trains its men
better than Disney Security does.
It took Darian screaming and Cole
interfering to make Spencer back off.
By then, blood was flowing. None

of it was Spence's. We convinced
him to follow two bleeding guys to
the Security office. Cole had a long talk
with the man in charge, and managed
to persuade him to let Spencer go.

Darian worked her own magic,
and the injured security duo decided
not to press charges. We promised
to leave the park and not return
or ask for a refund. By that time,

Spence had chilled completely,
and really looked sort of remorseful.
At least, the guys who escorted us
to the gate didn't seem too worried.
They probably should have been.

Even Corps mechanics train in
hand-to-hand combat and lethal
force. Those two Security dudes
got off lucky with black eyes and
bloody noses. Later, over drinks,

Cole and Spencer had a good laugh
about it. Darian actually joined them.
Personally, I was more than a little
worried that the three of them
thought kicking ass on a couple of

guys just trying to do their jobs
was funny. But I let it go. I let lots
of stuff go, and that worries me
some, too. The rest of the evening
went by without incident. We didn't

return to the park, but we did take
a walk to where we could see fireworks
over Cinderella's castle, all decked out
in holiday lights. It almost made up for the day.

IN THE MORNING

We caravanned back to San Diego.
The guys, of course, drove, and their
playful game of chicken was truly

terrifying. "Please don't tailgate,
Cole," I finally begged, one hand
against the dash, the other gripping

> the side of the seat. *This is how
> infantrymen drive. Don't worry.
> I've never rear-ended anyone yet.*

Worrying—or arguing—was pointless.
In front of us, Spencer cut to the right
in front of a semi. The truck driver

laid on his horn. Spence flipped him
off. "Think there's any way we can
convince Spence to see a doctor?"

> *They already put him on antibiotics.*

"Not that kind of a doctor."

> *You mean a shrink? What for?*

"Depression. Anger. Impulse
control. Posing a threat to society."

> He laughed. *You're describing every
> soldier I know. There aren't enough
> shrinks in the world to fix all of us.*

YOU CAN TAKE A SOLDIER OUT OF WAR

Confiscate his weapons.
Send him home, reunite
him with his family.

But you

don't want to turn your back
on him. Better not hand
him a knife. And if you

can't take

his nightmares, consider
the guest room. His dreams
won't ever desert him.
The true cost of

war

can't be measured
in dollars, infrastructure,
or body counts.
It is tomorrows, wrung

out of

hope by yesterdays
that refuse to retreat,
vanish into the smoke
of memory. Ask

a soldier

what he believes in.
He'll tell you God. Country.
The patient hands of death—
the ones he's wearing.

Cole Gleason

IT'S A VERY LONG PLANE RIDE

As soon as we land, I call Dar,
but her phone goes to voice mail.
"Just got in. Where are you? Call me."

Everything seems to move
in slow motion—disembarking,
making my way to Baggage. Waiting

for my suitcase. I don't know why
I'm in such a hurry. I have no idea
how to get ahold of Dar . . . wait. Yes,

I do. When we were kids, I called
her house at least once a day, often
more. I remember the number.

> Her dad answers, and I ask for her
> mom, but he says, *She's on her way*
> *down. Darian's beside herself.*

"What happened? Do you know?"

> *Copter crash. Three guys died.*
> *Spencer's hanging on, just barely.*
> *He's in intensive care at the base hospital.*

"Okay. Thanks." I start to hang up.

> He stops me. *Wait. Will you please*
> *tell Darian I love her? I'd come, too,*
> *but the livestock . . . I'm so damn sorry.*

MEN ARE AWFUL COMMUNICATORS

What they leave, dangling
between the lines, is what
they need to learn to say.
What he told me was like a book
cover, hinting at all the words
locked up inside. I'm a good
reader. Then again, I'm privy
to the inspiration for the story.

What, I think, he wanted to
say, if he only knew how, is that
if he could do it over, he'd be
a better dad. More caring.
More involved. More here,
less there. That his daughter
means more to him than his
horse. More than a silver
buckle. Maybe even that we

should have pushed him to
take us out on the circuit, let
us show the world—his world,
especially—that we were special.
That his daughter was every bit
as brilliant a singer as Carrie
Underwood or LeAnn Rimes.
She could have been somebody.

Instead, she ran. From home.
From him. Straight into the arms
of a soldier. A brash, half-crazy
Marine, currently lying in a sterile
intensive care bed, thinking about dying.

AS THE BAGS

Plop from the belt onto the carousel,
my thoughts go to my own Marine,

off soon for another chance at accidental
crash, or completely planned bullet. Why

do we continue to do this? Why have I
volunteered for this kind of worry?

It occurs to me that he ought to know
about Spencer. I give him a call. Catch

him post-mess. "I've got bad news,"
is how our conversation begins. Not,

"I made it home safely." When I tell
him the little I know, he is not totally

        surprised. *Ah, fuck. I heard about*
        the crash. News like that travels fast.

        I didn't know Spencer was one of them.
        Sucks when they go down at home after

        making it back safe from no-man's-land.
        Goddamn Sea Stallion. Freaking ironic.

His matter-of-factness bothers me. This
is his friend, not just some grunt. I promise

to call as soon as I know more, snag
my suitcase, walk to the car, lugging

much more weight than my bag.

I GO STRAIGHT TO THE BASE

When I tell the MP at the gate why
I'm here, his tough stance softens.
He takes my ID, notes it in his log,

> hands it back. *Really sorry. Give*
> *Darian my best, please.* As he directs
> me to the hospital, I study his face

better. Oh, yes. He's the same guy
who was here the last time I came
through with Dar, no ID check necessary.

It could just be my imagination, but
his somber mood seems to be reflected
everywhere—the streets are a little quieter.

The people I do see aren't smiling.
When something bad happens to Marines,
their extended military family shares

the experience. I still haven't heard
from Darian, but I assume she's here
at the hospital. I ask a receptionist,

who directs me to a small waiting room
outside the intensive care unit. Dar
is there, rocking gently forward and back,

staring at the floor. No television.
No magazine. No company at all.
Just Darian. Dwarfed by worry.

I KNOCK GENTLY

On the doorframe. "Hey," I say
quietly. "How're you doing? I tried
to call you when I landed, but . . ."

> Her head jerks toward me. *Jesus,*
> *Ash, you scared the hell out of me.*
> *You can't just sneak up on a person.*
> Then she melts. *This is . . . insane.*

She gestures for me to sit next
to her. I do, searching for the right
thing to say. We have been friends
for fifteen years and never shared

anything quite as profound as this.
"I talked to your dad. He told me
a little about what happened. He also
said to tell you he loves you and that
he's really sorry about Spence."

> She stiffens. Frosts. *Really? Isn't that nice?*
> *It bugs me—all this outpouring of love*
> *in times of trouble. People are hypocrites.*
> *And that includes my goddamn dad.*

Wow. Does she think that about me,
too? "Dar, I'm pretty sure he meant it.
Some people aren't good at expressing
emotion. When they're worried
about you it's easier." I change

the subject to something more
pressing. "Tell me about Spence.
What do the doctors have to say?"

She looks at me with bloodshot
eyes. Straightforward says,
He's got second- and third-degree
burns over sixty percent of his body.
If he makes it—and that's a big

if—his recovery will be prolonged
and excruciating. Multiple skin
grafts. Physical therapy. And even
with all that, he'll never be the same.

"Jesus." It's impossible to picture
Spencer like that. He's a fighter, not
a victim. But you can't fight flames.
I invoke my not-quite-forgotten
religion, send a silent prayer to

the universe. Darian interrupts.
I don't know how to feel. At all.
I've been thinking and thinking.
She lowers her voice. *Please don't*
hate me for this, but know the first

thing I thought when I heard?
Problem solved. Yep, that's right.
Sick, I know. But that was my gut
reaction. But then when I got here
and saw him, bandaged and burned . . .

Burned! All the love I ever felt for him
came crashing back. Oh, God.
He can't die, Ashley. Not like this!
She leans into me, cries a long time,
soaking my shirt with her tears.

AN IMPORTANT
QUESTION DANGLES

Just there. I'm afraid to reach out
for it, but when she finally pulls
away, some inappropriate need
to know makes me ask anyway.
"So . . . what about Kenny?"

Tears glaze her eyes. *I don't know.*
I mean, I was ready to tell Spence
that it was over between us. I had
my speech all planned out. The truth

is, I'm still in love with Kenny.
Nothing can change that, not
even this. God. Why does life
have to be so goddamn cruel?

Don't look at me like that, okay?
I get the whole karma thing, and
if you don't believe I haven't been
thinking about it, you're wrong.

Maybe I'm a bad person. Maybe
I deserve to get my ass kicked.
But like this? As I understand it,
karma's supposed to be about

squaring things up. Making them
fair. What's so goddamn fair
about Spencer being the one lying
in there? Karma's fucked up!

HER VOICE HAS RISEN

With each sentence. A nurse passing
by in the hallway ducks her head
through the door, asks if everything's
okay. Darian deflates her with a sharp

> scowl. *Fine. Wonderful. Awesome,*
> *in fact. Just having a little chitchat*
> *about karma. Have an opinion*
> *you'd care to share with us?*

> > When the nurse smiles, her age
> > shows in the way her face creases.
> > *My daughter has a hamster named*
> > *Karma. I put my faith in science.*

Apparently satisfied we aren't at
each other's throats, the nurse—
Cheryl, her name tag said—goes
about her business. "Look, Dar,

I don't think you deserve this.
Accidents happen, and they have
nothing to do with karma. This must
be incredibly confusing. I know you

love Kenny. And he's definitely crazy
about you. I also know that a little part
of you still loves Spence, or you wouldn't
be here, beating yourself up. Speaking

of that, how long have you been here?"
She looks like hell—rat's-nest hair and
wrinkle-scarred clothes. "And when
was the last time you ate something?"

She shrugs. *I don't even know*
what time it is. They called really
early this morning. Woke me up.
The accident happened yesterday

but it took a while to . . . She winces.
Figure out who everyone was. One
of the other guys came in alive,
but died before his wife could get

here. He and Spence were in back.
The two in front took the worst
of it. They could only ID them by
process of elimination. It was awful.

Knowing Darian like I do, sitting
around here, waiting for . . . whatever
is going to get her all wound up
again. "Hey. Have any food in your

fridge? Why don't I cook you dinner,
and you can get cleaned up? Maybe
even catch a few z's. Seems like
everything's in a holding pattern."

She starts to say no. Reconsiders.
I'll go check with the nurse. Be right
back. While she does, I send Cole
a text message with the news I know.

WHEN WE GET TO HER TOWNHOUSE

I strongly suggest, "Go take a shower.
I'll root through your fridge. See what
I can find." She goes off in search of hot

water. I go off in search of sustenance.
Not much in the refrigerator. I try
the freezer and score calzones. Preheat

the oven. Put them in to bake for twenty
minutes. About the time they start to smell
really good, Dar comes into the kitchen, trailing

the scent of Garnier Fructis shampoo. I know
because I use it, too. We discovered it together.
"Calzones, okay? You need to go to the store."

> *I hate eating alone, so I don't grocery shop
> very often. Usually I just grab a bite after
> the gym. If I see Kenny, we eat out or he cooks.*

She sits on a stool at the granite-skinned
bar. *Actually, I had planned on moving in
with Kenny after I told Spence. We picked*

*out this nice little house at Hermosa
Beach. Kenny says I don't have to work.
I thought I could finish my degree and*

after we got married, maybe have a baby. . . .
She had picked up speed with every word,
until the last. The sudden stop reminds me.

BUT I CAN'T ASK HER NOW

If ever. The buzzer rings. Calzones
        are ready. I put them on the counter
                to cool, reach up into the cupboard

        for plates. When I put them down
                on the bar in front of Dar, she puts
                        her hand on mine. *Hey. What's that?*

The ring. I'd forgotten about it.
        My cheeks sizzle. "Uh, that was
                Cole's surprise. We're getting

married. He wants a June
        wedding. That's about as far
                as our planning got, so I'm going

to need all kinds of help from
        you. You'll be my maid of honor,
                right?" I didn't realize it, but my own

vocal tempo had picked up, too.
        It was almost as if I didn't want
                her to comment too quickly. Not

that I should have worried, I guess.
        She is quiet as I slide a calzone
                onto each plate, put forks beside them.

        When I ask about napkins, she
                points to paper towels and says,
                        Are you fucking out of your mind?

WORDS HAVE POWER

The power to soothe. The power
to skewer someone through
the heart. The power to render
someone speechless. I manage
to stutter, "Wha-what do you mean?"
The expression on her face is something

approaching fury. *A Marine? Who
in their right mind would marry
a Marine? I mean, when Spence
and I got married, I had no idea
what I was getting into. But you?
How could you marry Cole, knowing*

*what you do? Jesus, Ashley! I like Cole,
I do. but he's a soldier, and that
means he'll never belong completely
to you. What about your dreams?
They'll always come second because
what the good ol' U.S. of A. desires*

*has to come first. Why do you feel
the need to mess with the good thing
you've got going? Without that stupid
piece of paper, you can walk any time
you decide you've had enough. It's not
like you have to get married, right?*

"Have to? You mean, like, am I
pregnant? How old-fashioned of
you, Dar. And glad you have such
a high opinion of me. Like I don't
understand how to use birth control?
Even if I didn't, I'd never use it as

an excuse to get married. You didn't
marry Spence because you were
pregnant, ri—?" Holy crap. This
is so not the time to bring up
her possible pregnancy. Besides, if
they got married because of that,

why would she have had an abortion?
No, that doesn't make sense. And now
I've gone and put my foot in my mouth.
All I had to do was complete the word.
Instead, I skidded to a stop one consonant
sound short and now she looks at me

with suspicion, like I've been spading
her personal ground. "Sorry. Look, I've
dissected the marriage idea for years.
Alternately dismissed and embraced it.
I've stuck with Cole through amazing
highs and impossible lows. That has to

be worth something. This has nothing
to do with being pregnant, although
I wouldn't mind having kids at some
point. Don't you want a family, Dar?"
Why do I keep shooting off my mouth?
Then again, I've opened the door.

> She sighs. *I don't know. Maybe.*
> *But it isn't high on my list. Right*
> *now I have to get through this*
> *mess before I can even think about*
> *the future. Any future. But whatever*
> *happens, I won't have kids with Spence.*

SHE LEAVES THE CALZONE

Untouched. Goes to her liquor cabinet.
Doesn't ask if I want some, doesn't try
to explain why she does. She pours two
glasses of something clear. I can't see
the label from here. Alcohol to smudge
the edges—the grunt way. "Please eat

too, okay? I mean, I slaved all day to
make that incredible calzone for you."
The humor blunts the tension. Dar nibbles
a little, drinks a lot. Gin, it turns out. Not
my favorite, especially straight, but I go
ahead and join her. When things get a bit

> fuzzy, she clears her throat. *Ah-um.*
> *I was pregnant when I married Spencer,*
> *Ash. Everything just happened so fast,*
> *you know? My mom would probably*
> *have supported me, but my dad would*
> *have killed me. A wedding seemed like*
>
> *the easiest solution. Spence was so happy.*
> *But then he went away, and he was gone*
> *for so long. I couldn't imagine raising*
> *a baby alone. I mean, I was just a kid*
> *myself. I wanted to go out. Wanted to*
> *party. Diapers and bottles and whatever?*
>
> *I just couldn't do it.* She pauses, and her
> face contorts, a precursor to the tears
> that follow. *I had an abortion, Ash. I*
> *thought it would be easy, but it was*
> *awful. I'm sorry I didn't tell you.*
> *Some things shouldn't be kept secret.*

SOME SECRETS BITE

And sometimes it's just a fluke that
they are dragged out into the light.

After the Disneyland birthday fiasco,
Cole put in for holiday leave and we

actually celebrated Christmas together.
He had met my parents the previous

year, and since we were still a thing,
he decided it was finally time to take

me home to Wyoming. It was blowing
Christmas Eve snow when we landed at

      the little airport. A white-knuckle landing,
      which had me uptight. *I've been through*

      worse, Cole soothed. *And so has this pilot,*
      I'm guessing. Anyway, God's smiling.

Felt more like God was pissed off
to me, but he arranged for a safe

touchdown on the small runway.
Cole's mom was there to meet us,

along with her new leading man, Dale.
I was so nervous, I was shaking, and

not just because of the weather.
What if she hated me? She and Cole

were so tight. I had crazy ideas about
some imposing Wild West woman wanting

to keep Cole and me apart. Instead, I met
a gentle lady, countrified, to be sure, but more

Bridges of Madison County than *True Grit.*
I'm not sure how someone so petite

could have created a son as beefy as Cole,
but next to him she resembled a fairy—tiny.

Delicate. Almost gossamer. All she needed
was wings. When she saw us, her smile

was a bonfire against the blizzard outside.
It was a small surprise, midst bigger ones

soon to come. Cole's embrace lifted her
off her feet. When he spun her around,

> she insisted, *Put me down, you. I want
> to meet your girl.* She took my cold hand

> in her warm one. *So happy to meet you,
> Ashley. I'm Rochelle, and this is Dale.*

COLE HAD MET DALE

The year before. Dale was dating
Rochelle then, but she still lived
in town. On her own. Turned out,
things had recently changed. A lot.

>Rochelle directed us to Dale's big
>Suburban. *Guess you should know*
>*that Dale moved me out to his ranch.*
>*Me, and everything I own. You'll love*
>*the place. Even under all this snow.*

The ten-minute drive took us
almost thirty, at blizzard-driving
speed. Finally, we pulled up in front
of a low ranch-style house. We fought
our way through the pelting ice to
the front door. Inside, it was warm

>and inviting, and Rochelle had done
>the place up right, with garland and
>mistletoe and a huge Christmas tree.
>Cole whistled, and she said, *I could*
>*never give you this kind of Christmas*
>*before. Glad I can give it to you now.*

>*I only wish your sister could be here*
>*to share it with us.* I wished then that
>I could have met her, to have known
>someone he cared so much for. We
>would never share that connection.
>Chalk up yet another small regret.

DALE'S HOUSE

Was enormous. It must have been
awful living out there alone. No wonder
he was anxious to move Rochelle in.

> *Your bedroom here is exactly like it*
> *was at home, she told Cole. Except,*
> *there's a whole lot of extra space*
>
> *around the furniture. It's a little bigger.*
> It was big, all right. Like the rest of
> the house, it had aging wood floors

brightened—and warmed—with
Southwestern-style throw rugs in
turquoise and orange. Two big

> windows looked south, toward
> the frosted hills. *See?* said Rochelle,
> proudly, *I even arranged it just like*
>
> *it was before. Same lamp on your*
> *desk. Same clothes in your drawers.*
> *I want it to feel like home to you.*

> *It's great, Mom,* he said, perhaps a bit
> stiffly. *Will you give us a few minutes*
> *to unpack, please?* She gave us a funny

look and when she left, I asked, "Is it
okay that we sleep in here together?
Not being married?" No guest room?

> *Don't worry about it. They're not*
> *married, either, you know.*

THAT WOULD CHANGE

Practically right away. The smell
of roasting turkey woke us late morning
on Christmas day. Rochelle was up
early to bake pies and put the bird in
the oven. By the time we dressed and

went in search of coffee, the kitchen
looked like a page out of *Martha Stewart
Living*. My mom always made the holidays
nice. This was amazing. Later, Cole
assured me it was not Christmas-as-usual.

> There was a reason beyond Rochelle's
> wanting to make the holiday special.
> *I hate to spring this on you*, she told Cole,
> as she handed him a mug of Christmas
> blend "Joe." *But we just made the decision*
>
> *a couple of days ago. See, Dale and I*
> *want to get married, and we want to do*
> *the deed while you're here. Today, in fact,*
> *if Reverend Scott can get his butt out here*
> *through all this snow. You good with that?*

Cole is not the type to wear emotion
on his face. He sat very still for several
seconds, turning it over in his mind.
Finally, he nodded. *I never liked you*
living all on your own. Dale seems like

a decent guy, though you'd know more
about that than I would. If you want to
make it legal, I guess I'm good with it.

IT WAS A MEMORABLE CHRISTMAS

Dale had wanted Rochelle to break
the news without him present. Not sure
if he thought Cole would react badly or
what. Once he knew Cole had, in fact,
given his blessing, we all exchanged
gifts. Cole gave me a pretty filigreed

gold locket. I gave him a Christopher
medal. "To keep you safe over there
and here at home." Remnants of my
Catholic upbringing. I don't embrace
it, but can't quite let it go completely.

Reverend Scott fought his way through
the driving snow and arrived just past
one p.m. Cole let him in, took his coat,
and by the time the minister had warmed
his hands in front of the fire, the happy

couple was ready to tie the knot. All
decked out in his very best sapphire
silk shirt, string tie, and Stetson hat,
Dale looked every ounce the cowboy.
Rochelle wore a plain peach-colored
dress and the prettiest smile ever.

A soft, sweet kiss served as the amen
for the simple nuptials. Reverend Scott
stayed for turkey and trimmings, with
pie and eggnog for dessert. It was merry,
indeed. None of us knew then that some
covert cancer cell had infiltrated
Dale's stomach. And it was multiplying.

BUT THAT WAS THE LAST THING

On any of our minds.
It probably would have
been the perfect trip
except for a random
discovery that almost
dissolved the bond
between Cole and me.

Over time, his mom and
I had learned to divvy up
Cole's love. I might have
been his heart, but she was
his blood. Both, we knew, were
necessary to keep a guy alive.

I think she was used to letting
go of those she loved—her
awful husband. Her lovely
little girl, who went home
too young. With them, she
had no choice, but she opened

the door for Cole. And, like
the old saying goes, he came
back to her. He always would.
I had no problem with that,
or with knowing he loved her
at least as much as me.

Probably more. I wasn't
jealous of that. It was time,
lost to her, that I sometimes
resented. As the years marched
on, even that stung less.

COLE'S MOM

Was not responsible for
the extreme attack of jealousy
I suffered a couple of days
after Christmas, although when

the whole thing first went down,
I wondered if she had encouraged
the source. At the time, I was feeling
isolated. Unsure of the trembling

ground I stood on. I had no clear
idea if Rochelle was in my corner,
or wanted to slam her front door
in my face. She had seemed so

welcoming. Had I just been naïve?
My own mom, who has had plenty
of reasons to suffer the bite of
the little green monster, once told me,

> The only person jealousy hurts
> is the one who's feeling its sting.
> You can't make someone love you.
> You can't force faithfulness.

> If those things don't exist for your
> partner, you have the choice to stay
> or go. Either way, you are in charge.
> Jealousy works against you. It takes

> control away from you, hands it over
> to the opposition. Maintain control.

PROBABLY A VALID PHILOSOPHY

Truthfully, throughout most of my life,
I had nothing to be jealous about.
Yeah, a few parts in plays that went
to less talented people—at least
I thought so at the time. Who knows?

But as far as relationships, the only
one who mattered enough for me to feel
that sort of possessiveness about
is the one I have now. So far, there
have been only a few green monster

attacks. Most were of the "little" variety.
Other women at bars—vampires, mostly.
Sometimes those girls were downright
"don't take no for an answer" pushy,
trying to steal Cole away from me right

under my nose. He laughed it off, but
I didn't find it funny. And after enough
alcohol, it led to an argument or two.
But nothing he couldn't get me to laugh
about later, not to mention his making me

> feel just the slightest bit petty. *There*
> *are lots of pretty girls in the world,*
> he would say. *But I fell in love with*
> *you. No girl can ever change that,*
> *or tempt me away.* I believed him.

Felt like a total jerk for thinking bad
of him. Until the day I came across
Lara's letters. Then, I didn't know what
to believe. Then, I almost hated him.

LARA WAS HIS COLLEGE SWEETHEART

The one he claimed to be nothing
more than a dusty memory.

It was the last day of the Christmas
visit to Wyoming—a Sunday.

Cole got up and went to church with
his mom and Dale. I lounged in bed.

When I finally roused myself, the house
was cool. Jeans and a long-sleeved T

couldn't fight the chill, but my jacket
was too much. My Southern California

"warm clothes" were laughable, so I dove
into Cole's drawers, looking for a sweater.

I found a nice green one, and underneath
it, a small bundle of handwritten letters.

Well, who wouldn't look? Up until that
minute, I hadn't given a second thought

to Cole's ex-girlfriend. Didn't even know
her name was Lara, or that she lived

in Denver. Loved to ski, and sometimes
took her Australian shepherd with her.

Had no idea that before Cole left school
they had talked about getting married,

or that his decision to join the Marines
was the only reason she had changed

her mind. One of her letters made it
very clear that she was staunchly

antiwar, anti-Bush/Cheney, anti-
anything or anyone who supported

them. If I had stopped reading there,
I would have been okay. But others

came after—love-drenched apologies
and entreaties to be safe overseas.

And this one:

> So happy you're safe and sound, back on American
> ground. I was out of my mind, worried about you.
> Without your emails, I would have freaked completely.
>
> I would love to visit you in Hawaii. Maybe next
> summer. Meanwhile, I can't wait to see you at
> Christmas. Your mom invited me to dinner.
> Hope that's okay. Don't want you to feel awkward.
>
> Love always,
> Lara

Christmas 2008, while I waited in Lodi
for him to join me, he was with her?

I FOLDED THE GREEN SWEATER

Put it back in the drawer.
               I didn't feel cold anymore.
    At least, not the kind of cold

a sweater could fix. The pulse
               at my temples picked up until
    it beat so hard I could see it

in the mirror, pushing against
               my skin like it wanted to burst.
    I restacked the letters exactly

as I found them, bound them
               with the same rubber band.
    But I didn't put them back in

the drawer. Instead, I stretched
               the sheets over the bed, left
    the evidence there, on the foot

of the homemade quilt. It did
               strike me then that Rochelle
    knew about the letters. She had to.

She had moved Cole's dresser,
               and his clothes. Folded them,
    put them inside the drawers.

No way could she have missed
               the letters there. And she'd asked
    Lara to dinner the year before.

What must she have thought
                    of me? That I was a romance
          wrecker? Or maybe just stupid?

I picked up Cole's clothes, folded
                    them, too. Put my suitcase right.
          Everything neat. Everything orderly.

Everything except my life. No way
                    could I reconcile my Cole with
          the person who had lied to me.

How could he promise the things
                    he did, all the while plotting such
          treachery? Under other circumstances,

I probably would have packed
                    up and left, but I was alone
          there, somewhere in the frozen

wilds of Wyoming, with no available
                    transportation. I was pretty sure
          I could not convince a cab to come

all the way to the ranch, if Cheyenne
                    even had such a thing as taxis.
          I thought about walking, but even

if I could have found my way on foot
                    to the airport, it would have been
          a very long, cold hike. I was trapped.

I STARTED TO PACE

Six steps one way, six steps back,
all the while having a conversation—
no, more like an argument—with myself.

Logical me: The last letter
was dated over a year ago.

Emotional me: Doesn't mean
there haven't been others since.
Oh, yeah, and what about e-mail?

Logical me: You don't know when
he e-mailed her last. Maybe it was
just his first deployment.

Emotional me: Right. And even if
it was, computer time is limited.
He could have e-mailed me instead.

Logical me: Your relationship
was fledgling. Theirs had ended.
Sometimes it's hard to let go.

Emotional me: He told me it was
over. He totally lied to me.

Logical me: Most men are liars.
I thought you understood that.

Emotional me: I can't believe
that. All men are not my dad.

Logical me: You sound like me.

I WAS IN A SHADOWED SPACE

When they got home from church.
It's a place inside my head I crawl
into, when things get too overwhelming.
Cole hasn't found me there very often.
But he did that day. He came in, all

smiles. The look on my face told
him a lot. But when I asked him to
please come back in the bedroom,
he definitely did not expect to see
those letters soiling the quilt.
All I could say was, "You lied to me."

>He offered no excuse, only apology.
>*I don't know what to say, Ash. I . . .*

"You told me there was no girl back
home. No other girl at all. Why did
you tell me that if it wasn't true?"

>*There wasn't. Not really. As far as*
>*I knew, she had vacated my life*
>*completely. I never thought she'd*
>*change her mind. Besides, by*
>*the time she did, I was in love*
>*with you. She means nothing to me.*

"Shut up, Cole. If she means nothing
to you, why did you see her last
Christmas? How dare you make me
think I was being unfair, wanting to
be with you, when you . . . God, what
else have you lied to me about?"

*Nothing. Ashley, she and my mom set
up the Christmas thing. That was before
I let my mother know for sure that Lara
and I will not be getting back together.
I swear, I wasn't plotting to see her.*

"Really? You mean, she doesn't
write you in Hawaii, or when you're
overseas? Looks like she e-mails
you, and that you reply. If you love
me so damn much, have you told her
about me?" I was out of breath and

*my heart was beating furiously. He
started toward me, but I backed away.
Please, Ash, calm down. She e-mailed
a couple of times to make sure I was
okay. Not to set up a date. All I did
was respond so she wouldn't worry.*

He had left my last question
unanswered. Suddenly, it took
on tremendous importance.
"Cole, have you told Lara about
you and me? I really need to know,
and please tell me the truth."

*He couldn't have lied if he tried.
His eyes held nothing but guilt.
No. It just never came up, and
it didn't seem that impor—*

I AM BY NATURE

Silent in anger. When I blow off
steam, it's generally internal. If
I hadn't exploded outwardly
right then, I probably would have
imploded soon after. Instead,
I picked up the letters, threw

them in his face. "Fuck you!"
I screamed, loud enough to
pierce the bedroom walls.
I hardly cared. "I tell everyone
about you. Brag about you.
The only possible reason

for you not to tell her about me
is because you want her, too.
Well, sorry, but you can't have
us both." I grabbed my jacket,
stomped out of the room, down
the hall, past Cole's bewildered

mom. If she hadn't been standing
there, I might have slammed
the door. I was probably a half
mile away from the house before
Cole caught up with me. By then,
the glittering rage had faded

to a muted halo. So when Cole
stopped me, pulled me into
his arms, I didn't resist. But when
he apologized again, promised
to make things right, I didn't believe
him. Didn't forgive him. Not right away.

TO RAGE

Against an enemy
is no more than what's
expected. And yet, such
an outpour of energy
might very well be

                      better

directed toward
a silent stalk, circuitous
and unexpected,
far, far beyond the

                      watch

of sentry or spy.
To rage against an act
of nature may be instinct,
but it is tantamount
to full-bore drilling a hole in

                      your

skull to free frustration
with what cannot be
changed. To rage
against the woman
you love when your

                      back

is against the wall,
and she holds you there
with the truth in her eyes,
well that is the time-proven
folly of a man.

Cole Gleason

IT HAS BEEN A LONG WHILE

Since I've felt Spence here, in
his own home. But his spirit, so
obviously missing in recent visits,
is present this evening. So it is more
than a little disquieting when
the doorbell rings and on the far

side of the threshold stands Kenny.
Darian opens the door and he opens
his arms, and she leans wordlessly
into his embrace. They stay that way
for what seems like a very long time.
Finally, he steers her back to the bar,

> helps her up on the stool. *I'm glad*
> *you're here for her,* he says to me.
> His smile is slight, but genuine.
> Then, back to Darian, *How's Spencer*
> *doing? Anything new to report?*

Darian shakes her head, looking
vaguely uncomfortable that Kenny's
here. Her discomfort bothers me.
"I should probably go. It's been
a really long day." One that began
in Hawaii and ended in a big pile

of ugly. I gather the plates, put
them in the dishwasher, and as I
gather my things, the doorbell rings
again. All three of us react with
jerks of surprise. Dread starts a slow
roll in the pit of my belly. It can't be.

CAN'T BE

That visit every
>   military spouse
>   pretends can never
>   ever happen. Yes,
>   to their neighbor,
>   maybe. But not to
>   them. Not to them.

Can't be two
>   uniformed goons
>   on the front step
>   wearing apology
>   like cheap cologne,
>   here to thank you
>   for your ultimate
>   sacrifice, and your
>   deceased loved one
>   for his patriotism.

Darian's face
>   goes slack and her
>   shoulders sag and
>   she would likely fall
>   from the stool, but
>   for Kenny, catching
>   her. Propping her up.

She looks at me
>   with fear-lit eyes. I
>   nod, go to the door.
>   A flood of relief slams
>   into me when I look
>   through the peephole,
>   see no Casualty Officer.

I HAVEN'T SEEN

Mrs. Watson for almost three years.
Time has not been gentle to her.
She seems to have aged a decade.
"It's your mother," I tell Dar
before I open the door, giving

her time to pull out of Kenny's
arms. I have no idea how much
she knows about this complicated
situation. But the way Darian
puts space between Kenny and

her makes me think she must
be pretty much in the dark. I stand
back to let Mrs. Watson by. "Long
time, no see," I say, too pleasantly.

> She stops long enough to give
> me a hug, then rushes over
> to Dar. *Is he okay? How are you?*
> *And*—she gives Kenny a long,
> almost rude once-over—*who is this?*

Darian and Kenny both look
at me, as if I should have an
acceptable answer at the ready.
"I'm sorry. This is my, uh . . . friend,
Kenny." Mrs. Watson's eyes

dart between Kenny and me.
She's probably thinking the same
thing I did when I first met him—
he's old enough to be my father.

NO MATTER

Let her think what she will.
This is no more than a small eddy

of concern. Surely it will be consumed
by this vortex of bigger worry.

"I really do need to go now. Kenny?"
I give him the out, and he takes it.

Darian's meager smile is grateful.
She promises to keep us informed

       and we make a graceful exit. Kenny
       walks me to my car. *Thanks for that.*

I shrug. "I've got her back. Always
have." At least when she lets me in

on her secrets. "I'm really sorry.
I hope everything turns out okay."

       Yeah. Me, too. But we don't always
       get what we want. He turns away,

shuffles over to his Prius, eyes fixed
on the townhouse as if he could see

through the walls. Wonder if Mrs.
Watson will notice two cars gone.

BONE WEARY

Soul heavy, I get home, carry
      my suitcase inside. Don't bother

with unpacking, except for
      my toothbrush. Wash my face, fall

into bed, certain sleep will
      swallow me. But no. It nibbles.

I *have* always had Darian's
      back. A regular battle buddette.

Once, that meant singing
      backup for her. Self-confidence

was not her best thing. Despite
      having a brilliant voice, she never

      believed in herself. *I need you*
            behind me, she told me once. *If*

      I fall, you promise to catch me?
            She meant it figuratively, and I sang

my truest alto so if her soprano
      faltered the tiniest bit, I was there

to cover up for her. It strikes me
      that everyone tightens the slack

for her. I think it's about time
      Darian faces her audience solo.

BEING AN ADULT

Kinda pretty much sucks sometimes.
When you're in high school, you want
to be eighteen so you can go where you
want, do what you want. That's the theory,

anyway, though it's not exactly accurate.
After that, the goal is twenty-one, so you
can go out and legally continue the bad
behaviors you've already been practicing.

That birthday comes, nothing changes
except now you're looking toward graduating
college. With that goal in your sight,
you realize you're expected to embark

on the career you envisioned. Except,
at least in my case, someone changes
your mind for you. So, it's grad school,
which is really a way to avoid adulthood

a little longer. Pretty soon, everything
is going to come crashing into me. Social
work? I know there's a need and all, but
the truth is, I can't see myself there.

Problem is, when I try to find my future,
I can't quite make it materialize. I'm going
to be twenty-five. I should have a clue, yeah?
Marriage and kids? Housewifery on a Wyoming

ranch? Teaching? Counseling? Interventions?
Too much to think about. Too many
questions. Sleep lies somewhere in the rubble
of answers over there, far beyond my reach.

DEEP IN THE DARK HEART

Of morning, I find myself
hovering in that strangest
of places—not asleep,
because I'm aware, and yet
I must be dreaming because
everything looks filmy. Misty.

I come to this place, I believe,
when my brain refuses to turn
off. When whatever problem
it's working on keeps dancing.
This is where I often discover
solutions, and tonight is no

exception. The reason I can't
find answers to my questions
is clutter. I had left my suitcase
open in the living room and
rummaged through for my
toothbrush. Such a simple fix!

Now that I know what it is,
I have to get up and put things
right. I haul myself out of
Dozeville, reach for the light.
Twenty minutes later, I'm
unpacked, everything in its

place. I glance at the clock.
Almost four. Might as well
stay up. I can nap after class.
I take a shower. Get dressed.
Make my bed. Drink a Red Bull.
Read. Try not to think about answers.

I STUMBLE THROUGH THE DAY

Focusing on the lectures is tough.
The fieldwork would be killer,
but I call in. Beg off one more day.

I'm heading for my car, pretty much
thinking it's all in the bag, when I hear
my name swim out of the murk.

> *Excuse me! Ms. Patterson. One*
> *minute, if you will.* Damn. Jonah.

Or maybe I'd better think of him
as Mr. Clinger. I turn, wait for him
to catch up. Hope he doesn't want

me to make up the test I missed
right now. As he approaches, I can't
help but watch the strength of his stride.

Funny. The most athletic thing I've
ever seen him do is stand for an hour,
holding a heavy book. He's no Marine,

but he definitely works out. And outside,
beyond the fearsome pallor of fluorescent
lights, his polished good looks are obvious.

> *I wanted to ask a favor of you.*
> His syntax is irritating, but at least

I'm pretty sure he isn't going to ask
me to make up that test. A smile slithers
across my face. "Uh . . . really? What?"

He draws even and when he looks at
me, his eyes catch the slanted sunlight.
Aquamarine, like the gemstone.

> *Listen. A local high school has asked*
> *me to judge their spoken word poetry*
>
> *competition. They could use another*
> *judge and, naturally, I thought of you.*

Naturally? "Uh, well, I guess so.
Sounds like fun. Um, if I'm open,
of course." Like why wouldn't I be?

> *Of course. I'll e-mail the details.*
> *How was your trip?* Suddenly,

I'm hyperaware of the scent lifting
off his skin—rich, spicy. Yum. He's
waiting for an answer, Ashley.

"Uh, it was great. I got to see north-
shore Oahu. It's beautiful. Have you
ever been there?" His smile tells me

> I've struck a chord. *Actually, I lived there*
> *for a while, back in my crazy surfer*
>
> *days. I rode Waimea and the Banzai.*
> *Couldn't wait for winter and the big*
>
> *waves. When I start to feel too old and*
> *staid, I go back, looking for that rush.*

OF COURSE HE DOES

And I probably never will. I hear

> Cole's voice, *I wouldn't let you out*
> *there on a board.* And, *Once I leave*
> *here, I'm never coming back.*

Yet, I say, "I didn't get the chance
to ride. I hope to go back myself
and remedy that one day." It's true,
I realize, for whatever that's worth.

> His dimples deepen. *You're talking*
> *about some sizeable water. Hope*
> *you get the chance. It's life changing.*

For a second I thought he was going
to try and talk me out of it. Instead,
he encouraged the idea. I like it.

> *Okay, then. Guess I'll see you in class*
> *tomorrow. Will you carve out an hour*
> *to make up the test you missed?*

I promise I will and start again
toward my car. I can feel Jonah's
eyes on my back, watching me

> walk away. *Hey,* he calls, making me
> look over my shoulder. *Why haven't*
> *I seen a surfing poem from you?*

WHY IS HE

So damn attractive?
So damn interesting?
So damn supportive?

At first, when I never
noticed him smile or act
anything but scholarly,
I pretty much saw him
as just another professor,
and a rather uptight one
at that, despite his leather
jackets. But now I have

glimpsed the boy inside
the man. The one who
beach bummed in Hawaii,
anticipating giant surf.
Wonder how an army
brat ended up a surfer.
Wonder how an army
brat wound up teaching
creative writing courses
on the university level.

There's so much about
him I'd really like to know.
That must be wrong, but
I'm not sure why. It's all
just so confusing. A wide
stripe of gray sandwiched
between the unforgiving black
and white of my comfort zone.

I CHALK IT UP

To the sleep-deprived twilight
zone I'm currently wandering.
I manage the short drive home
without too much difficulty.
But when it comes to finding
my keys in my bag, I might as
well be legally blind. I'm still

fumbling when my apartment
door opens. "Darian! Good God!
Are you trying to give me a heart
attack?" She has the key, of course
she does. I never took it back.

> S-s-sorry. I just . . . didn't know
> where else to go. Come inside.

Uh, yeah. What else would I do?
Leave? "What's up? Is everything
okay?" She doesn't look too distraught.

> Yeah. Uh, no. I mean, it's not that.
> Spence's condition hasn't changed.

I follow her to the living room,
put my book bag down as she says,

> Spence's parents arrived today.
> Mom and I were at the hospital
> when they got there. It was . . . ugly.

THE ONE TIME

I met Spence's parents was a few months
after he and Darian got married. They had
not attended the wedding. The last thing
a couple of Kansans want for their patriot
son's wife is some leftie California girl. Really.

Spence was barreling toward his first
deployment. Unlike Cole, whose mom
has always come just a nudge ahead
of me, Spencer was never focused
on going home to his native cornfields.

What energy he didn't invest in training
was sucked up by his spitfire wife.
Dar does demand attention, and their
marriage was young. Mostly what he
wanted when he got home in the evenings

was a few beers. Dinner. A little TV.
And Darian, who he would be leaving
behind when he went off to the Middle
East in only weeks. They were wading
through paperwork—wills and banking

> and such. Both felt overwhelmed.
> Drowning in details and "just in case"
> preparations. *I hate thinking about*
> *him dying,* Dar complained. *I never*
> *signed up for that.* Like, who does?

A TRIP TO KANSAS

Wasn't happening. Spence's parents
had to come to him, which influenced
the visit's tone. Cole was already in Hawaii,

so it was just me, helping Darian make
salad for the occasion. She's not much
of a cook, and that includes chopping

lettuce. Spence was outside, firing up
the barbecue, when his parents arrived.
I answered the door, and had to smile.

Picture a forever farm couple—the mister
tall and burly, the missus petite and plump.
Now, reverse that. Mr. Blaisdel wasn't

much taller than me, with a gently-rolling-
hills physique. Mrs. Blaisdel was a regular
she-bear. She looked at me. Cocked her head.

> *You're not her,* she said. Apparently,
> Spence had sent photos. Mrs. Blaisdel
> stormed past me, toward the kitchen.

Mr. Blaisdel shrugged an apology,
stepped inside. I extended my hand.
"I'm Ashley, Darian's friend." His grip

> surprised me. I expected Play-Doh,
> instead got iron. Despite his stature,
> he could probably carry a cow. *I'm Jim.*

> *Pleased to meet you. And don't let
> Clara fool you. She's mostly bluff.*

Clara was at that moment mostly
bluffing Darian in the kitchen.
Jim and I arrived, not quite in time

> to interfere. *Our Spencer tells us*
> *you're born and bred California.*
> *This is my first time here. So far,*

> *I'm not impressed.* Never mind
> that all they'd seen was the airport,
> freeways and a military base.

Darian, terrified, kept chopping
vegetables. "California is a very
big state, Mrs. Blaisdel," I said.

"Darian and I grew up in Lodi, in
the Sierra foothills in the northern
part of the state. It's mostly ranchland.

I bet you'd love it. And while you're
here, I hope you get the chance to go
to the beach. The Pacific's beautiful."

Spence came in through the side
door. He kissed Dar as he walked by,
then went to shake his dad's hand

> before hugging his mother. *Hey,*
> *Mom.* His goofy grin alone should
> have melted her ice shell. But, no.

SHE WAS PISSED

And she wanted us all to know it,
and I was pretty sure she wasn't
faking her anger one little bit when

> she said, *I really don't understand
> why you made us travel all this way.
> Like you couldn't spare a little of
> your paycheck on airfare to come
> home before you leave? Where's
> your respect for your family, son?*

Bam! Darian and I exchanged
anxious glances. Spence stayed
totally calm, calling her bluff, if
that's what it was. He kissed her

> cheek. Went to the fridge and
> grabbed a beer. *Anyone want one?*
> He was still shy of twenty, and his
> mother reacted like it was a sin.

> *Beer? You're drinking now? Is
> this what California teaches
> young men?* The way she glared
> at her daughter-in-law made it very
> clear that in her mind, California
> and Darian were synonymous.

> Spence forged straight ahead.
> *The thing is, Mom, I'm about to lay
> my life on the line for my country.
> I'd think my enjoying a brew should
> be at the bottom of your worry list.*

I HAD TO HAND IT TO SPENCE

He knew exactly how to manipulate
his mother. She retreated. A little.

Still, the afternoon was not pleasant.
I probably would have begged off

early, except I didn't want to leave
Darian to face the she-bear alone.

Neither of us drank beer. But when
the Blaisdels went outside to watch

Spencer flip the burgers, Dar and I
chugged from a bottle of Jäger.

It helped us paste obviously phony
smiles on our faces throughout dinner.

In retrospect, I can see how Spence's
mom looked at him as a stranger. Or

maybe more like an alien, who had
invaded her son's body. He had yet

to leave American ground, though
to her California was a foreign land.

But Spence had changed, evolved
from Kansas farmer into U.S. Marine.

Darian was not to blame for that,
of course. But she was responsible

for another, subtler transformation,
one many a mother has regretted

for her son. And that was the shift
from boy into man. For some women,

this translates to loss, and so the source
of that loss becomes someone to envy.

Jealousy is never pretty. But when
a mother becomes jealous of her son's

love interest, it can become hideous.
I felt so sorry for Dar. Despite everyone

else's best efforts to divert the negative
attention away from her, Mrs. Blaisdel

kept refocusing it squarely Darian's way.
There was dust on the living room shelves.

The ketchup bottle was gooey and there
wasn't enough mayonnaise. The burgers

were burnt—that one squarely Spence's
doing, but somehow she blamed Dar.

By the time they took off for their hotel,
the Jägermeister bottle was drained.

I HAVE TO ADMIT

I've helped drain a lot of bottles
since I met Cole. Not that I was

even close to a teetotaler before
we hooked up. In high school,

there were plenty of postgame
Friday-night parties. Keggers up

in the hills. Jello shots at friends'
houses whenever their parents

took off for a couple of days. And,
once Dar and I started school

in San Diego, oh those frat parties.
Weekend benders. The odd midweek

celebration. But I was pretty much
a lightweight. Hated hangovers.

The one time I woke up in my bed
and couldn't remember how I got

home, I almost swore off drinking
completely. Never did I imbibe

to deal with stress. Never to help
me fall asleep, dunk me deeper

than nightmares could follow.
Never, ever to make me forget.

THE REPORTED STATISTICS

Are harrowing. Triple the amount
      of problem military drinking since

the war in Iraq began. Not to mention
      how said drinking figures into suicide

attempts and victories, and vehicular
      deaths. Marines—especially frontline

warriors—top the lists. Why wouldn't
      they? Oh, the things they've seen!

The things they try to scrub from
      their brains, through self-medication.

I've seen it too often at the VA hospital.
      But dope only masks their memories.

I'm sure many of their significant
      others are much like me—we drink, too.

We drink, playing hide-and-seek
      with the omnipresent fear. We drink

to find a pathway into sleep.
      We drink to believe The Reaper

cannot harvest us. To attempt
      common ground with our soldiers.

We are too young, most of us,
      to go looking for hope in a bottle.

I ASKED COLE ONCE

If soldiers can drink while deployed
to Iraq or Afghanistan, where alcohol
is frowned upon—or rejected completely—
by the Muslim population. He laughed.

> Believe it or not, with the influx
> of Westerners, not to mention
> the exodus of the Taliban, you can
> find bars in big cities like Bagdad
> and Kabul. Good Muslims won't

> drink in them, and bad Muslims
> get kicked out of them, but foreign
> business is much appreciated.
> Soldiers aren't supposed to drink
> except every now and again, for

> a special occasion, with a two-beer
> limit. But it isn't hard to find liquor.
> Some guys get it in care packages.
> They're not supposed to, but it
> comes, looking like mouthwash.

> And local moonshine is plentiful.
> That there is some crazy shit,
> let me tell you. I've seen guys go
> totally off the deep end drinking
> that loco-juice. Gotta be careful.

We were drinking together at
the time. When he's home, it's one
way he tries to fight the depression
that sometimes gulps him down.

That night, I also saw him pop
a pill. Prescription. Maybe his,
maybe not. I couldn't see the label,
but I recognized the Prozac. My mom
took them for years. Cole's voice

> got all thick, heavy. *The brass*
> *don't condone alcohol. Shit happens*
> *when soldiers go a little out of*
> *their heads, you know? This one*
> *dude got all fucked up and started*
>
> *shooting stuff, just for kicks.*
> *Took out four or five Humvee*
> *tires and the side of a crapper.*
> *Good thing no one was inside.*
> *I mean, that was kind of funny*
>
> *and all. But another time, these*
> *guys drank a whole lot of moonshine*
> *and went all apeshit. Grabbed*
> *a little girl, like thirteen or fourteen.*
> *Gang raped her. Jesus, man.*
>
> *She didn't even have titties.*
> *And then, when her father tried*
> *to stop them, they up and killed*
> *him. The girl, too. Blew 'em away,*
> *left them bleeding in the street.*

ALL OF THOSE MEN

Were court-martialed, even the one
who shot up the outhouse—for conduct
unbecoming. But others got away with
much worse. Like assaulting their fellow
grunts. Female and not. Rape among
the deployed reached epidemic proportions

in Iraq and Afghanistan. And, while those
in command got a little better about coming
down on the offenders, often they looked
the other way, or blamed the victims. Many
never reported being assaulted. Those who
did were insulted, even called traitors, for

turning on their battle buddies. Some buddies.
As emotional as Cole got when he told me
about the Iraqi girl, when I mentioned
the story I read about rape in the ranks,
he actually jumped on the defensive.

> We're under a lot of pressure. Some guys
> can't handle it, and it's how they blow off
> steam. Anyway, some of those women
> ask for it, the way they wear shorts and all.

I blew off a little steam myself. "Are you
kidding me? Do you wear shorts when
it's a hundred degrees, Cole? And do you
really believe anyone deserves to get raped?
Rape isn't about sex. It's about violence."

> Why do women want to be soldiers?
> If they can't stand the heat, they should
> go back to the kitchen. War is violence.

WAR IS ALL KINDS OF UGLY

It is putrefaction, steaming
upon sun-brittled clay,
flesh-chewed corpses
staring with vacant eyes
at the steel-edged sky.

War

is a shivering child, alone
in the street, mourning
the father dragged off
to hell, the home that

is

burned to ashes,
a smoldering memory.
War is men, fueled
by hatred for a philosophy
they don't understand and

a

soul-deep fear of what
they can't see, but suspect
is on the far side
of any wall. And when a

man's

instinct screams,
he hears a voice much
louder than his own.
All bets are off. In the

game

of war, there are no rules,
no codes of honor.
Civility loses all meaning.

Cole Gleason

THEY SAY TRUTH

Is a double-edged sword. I see
it more like a multibladed gyroscope,
spinning one direction, then the next,
with minimum external input.

I love Darian, with that deep kind
of best-friend love that forgives
almost anything. But this . . . goes
against more than my grain. This

is contrary to the core of who I am.
It's hard to side with Spence's parents.
But the purest elements of my belief
system insist they're right in wanting

to take Spencer home to Kansas,
if and when he can be moved.
Darian isn't equipped to nurse him.
Changing bandages, soaked through

with body fluids? Not even close
to her thing. So why does she feel
the need to push back? Even her mom
agreed, which is why Darian fumed

out of the hospital and, instead of
going home where she could be easily
located, wound up taking a taxi here.

> *His mom insisted I divorce him,*
> *so she can collect his disability*
> *money,* Dar explains. *Can you believe*
> *she thinks she can dictate something*

like that? I told her any decision
to divorce was totally up to Spence
and me, and that it seemed premature
to plan on collecting any disability.

"But, Dar, weren't you going to
ask Spencer for a divorce anyway?
I mean, I know this isn't exactly
the perfect time, but still . . ."

    I don't know what I'm going to do,
    Ash! Why does everyone keep
    pressuring me? Anyway, until
    I decide, I need income. I'm entitled

    to Spencer's paychecks until those stop,
    and his disability or death benefits,
    depending. I'm not giving those away.
    His mother's just a greedy bitch.

Who is this person? What did
my best friend become when I
wasn't looking? "Take it easy, Dar.
I'm just playing devil's advocate, okay?"

    No! That's exactly what my mom said.
    She's supposed to be in my corner,
    and so are you! God, the only one
    I can trust anymore is Kenny.

"That's not true. We've been
friends for a long time, Darian.
I only want what's best for you."

WRONG THING TO SAY

Her body language is a scream.
What comes out of her mouth

      is closer to a petulant whine. *Shut up!*
      You sound just like my mother.

      How do you know what's best
      for me, if I don't know it myself?

      Can't you all just give it some time?
      Can't you just let me breathe?

You can't fight this kind of emotion
with logic. "I'm sorry, Dar. Of course,

you need time. Just, please, try to
understand where we're coming

from. I know your mom wants
to support you, and I do, too.

Whatever you decide, I'm there
for you, okay?" I go over to her,

try to give her a hug. She balls up,
as if protecting her heart. "Listen.

I didn't sleep much last night. I need
a nap, and I might just sleep through

until morning. You're welcome
to stay as long as you want. And

just so you know, I love you, Dar."

I GO INTO MY ROOM

Shut the door. Close the blinds.
Create a dark, safe lair. My bed
is soft. Warm. Inviting. All I want
to do is turn off. Slip away. Fade
into gentle dreams. Why won't

my brain cooperate? Scattered
thoughts litter my pillow. Darian.
Spencer. The two of them, together.
Happy, once. Together. His mother,
demanding they not be together, before

even knowing for sure he will survive.
Kenny. Dar. Does that make two
or three? Stop. Stop. Stop. Stop.
You are on the beach, your back
settling into autumn-warmed sand.

Surf breaks. Soft. Not so. Loud.
You should grab your board, accept
the challenge of big water. The boys
are out there. And Jonah, calling.
But it's nice here, on the cushion

of sand. Close your eyes. Somewhere
a door closes. Door? Far, far away.
You'll find it later. Pull your pillow
over your head. Swim. No, float
upon the midnight sea. Toward winter.

I DO SLEEP THROUGH

The night, wake right at dawn,
starving. I go to the kitchen,
where Darian has left a note.

> *Kenny picked me up. Thanks*
> *for letting me vent. I know*
> *you care. And I love you, too.*

I microwave a breakfast sandwich,
check my phone for messages. Find
a couple. One from Mom, asking

if I'll be home for Thanksgiving.
Another from Cole, saying his mom
is thrilled about the engagement.

A small attack of guilt threatens
my decent mood. I probably should
have called to tell my parents

about the upcoming wedding. In
a big way, however, I'd rather tell
them in person. I text Mom to confirm

my presence at her Thanksgiving
table. Text Cole, with a tiny white
lie: MY PARENTS ARE HAPPY, TOO.

Because, of course, they'll have
to be. Not like they have any choice
in this decision. Or Darian, either.

THE REST OF THE WEEK

Is an emotional roller coaster.
Long, slow ups and belly-twisting
downs, with plenty of loops to
keep me guessing. I manage
to make up missed class work
and tests. The fieldwork—intake
at a woman's shelter—is daunting.

Some of them run, urged
by the knowledge that death
cannot be far behind the regular
onslaught of callous fists.
This ain't their first rodeo.

Others must be talked into flight.
They arrive in silent shame,
the terror, loud in their eyes,
the only testament to what
they have escaped. Maybe escaped.

The ones that rip my heart
from my chest are the little ones.
The children, with tangled hair
and dirty clothes, covering
their own ugly secrets.
And all they ask of me
is shelter, food to warm
their hollowness,
a bed free of nightmares.

They look at me, and through
me. And it's hard to tell
who's more haunted—
them or me.

I DON'T HEAR

From Dar, which must mean
       good news, though it would

be nice to know that for sure.
       I'm afraid to call her. Don't want

her to think I'm her mother,
       checking on her welfare. I wait

for her to get in touch with me.
       After three communication-free

days, I call the hospital directly.
       All they can tell me is that Spencer

remains in ICU. He's there, alive.
       That must mean he's improving.

At least, that's what I must believe
       until his wife, my friend, who knows

more than some receptionist,
       says otherwise. I have faith. And that

in itself is strange, because I could
       have sworn any personal relationship

with the Master of Faith had long
       since passed away. Does every strayed

believer return to faith in times of
       crisis? Does God use that to his advantage?

SATURDAY AFTERNOON

Is the spoken word poetry competition.
I decided to ride over with Jonah, who
claims the parking lot is going to be full.
Somehow, I doubt that. How many high
school kids are likely to compete? How
many parents and friends will give up

a Saturday afternoon to support them?
The event kicks into gear at one p.m.
We're supposed to get there at eleven
thirty, to go over the judging rules
and read through the poems ahead
of time. Jonah knocks on my door

at ten forty-five. I'm just about ready.
"Come in. Give me five minutes." I go
back to finish brushing my damp hair,
slip into my well-loved Doc Martens.
When I exit my bedroom, I find Jonah
looking at the picture of Cole I keep

> on the end table. It's a favorite, with
> him in cammie pants and a khaki T-shirt
> which shows off his superbly defined
> biceps and pecs. Jonah smiles. *I could*
> *never be a Marine.* He imitates a body
> builder's pose. *They'd laugh me out of there.*

"No one starts out looking like that,
you know. It's called conditioning."
I go over to him, touch the small
bulge he has pumped up on one arm.
"Besides, I kind of like this. It's cute."
When we laugh, it cuts the sudden tension.

THE SUDDEN SEXUAL TENSION

Caused by my touching him in
such a semi-intimate way. Wow.
Did I really just do that? Again,
I'm struck by a charge of energy
that can only be described as desire.

Our eyes meet, and his inform me
he feels it, too. In the movies,
a kiss would come next. But this
is real life, my life, and I turn away
instead. "Okay, muscle man, let's go."

I follow him to his car, a newer BMW
two-seater, midnight blue out,
silver leather in. "Wow. They must
pay poetry professors really well.
I've been considering changing

my course of study, and this reinforces
that idea. I don't think too many
social workers drive BMWs. But, hey.
Wait a minute. Where do you put
your surfboard?" I wait as he opens

> the door for me, chuckling. *I've
> also got a restored '39 Ford Woodie
> wagon. Plenty of room for a board.
> The Beamer gets better mileage, though.*

A Woodie. Wow. I can definitely
picture him behind the wheel,
longish sun-streaked hair tossed
and crazy from the sea breeze blowing
in through the open windows.

Then again, he looks perfectly
fine behind the wheel of his BMW
Z4. I watch him shift, admire
his profile. When he punches the gas
to merge onto the freeway, my renegade

eyes are drawn to his slender
thighs. *So, are you really thinking*
about changing your field of study?
I mean, why social work, when you
seem so drawn to writing and lit?

"My BA is in English, and I always
meant to teach. But so many people
need help. Volunteering at the VA
Hospital has shown me that. Working
at the women's shelter, too."

But you've had second, or third
thoughts? Switching now wouldn't
be impossible, but it would be
expensive, I'm afraid. Personally,
I think you'd make an amazing teacher.

"I think I would, too. I'm not
sure why I keep vacillating. My dad,
who is underwriting my education,
is becoming irritated. Of course, he'd rather
I just get an MBA and forget all this

'service to others crap,' as he calls
it. 'Too little money and even less
respect,' he says. Maybe he's right.
But there's more to life than money."

HE'S NODDING

Like he agrees. God, he's cute
in profile, and I really wish I'd quit
thinking about how cute he is.
Even if I were free, he's my professor,

for Pete's sake. It's probably not illegal
to flirt with him. But there's a high
probability that it would be frowned
upon in pretty much every circle.

> What about your mother? Is she
> against your teaching as well?

"My mom is a high school librarian.
She has nothing but respect for
teachers. And, anyway, she supports
most of my decisions." It's like

> he knows exactly what my answer
> will be when he asks, *Most?*

I have nothing to hide, nothing
to apologize for. "Neither of
my parents is very happy about
my relationship with Cole. I mean,

they like him. But they are not
pro-military at all. My dad actually
thinks following orders emasculates
him. My mom has personal reasons."

> *I see,* he says, and leaves it there.
> Maybe—or maybe not—because
> apparently we have arrived.

THE PARKING LOT

Isn't overflowing, but we are here
ninety minutes early, and it is half
full already. "Wow. Who knew so

many people liked poetry? I'm
impressed." We follow the human
stream into the gym, where we're

directed to the judges' green room.
Jonah greets a pretty brunette
with a kiss to one cheek. My face

     heats, and when he turns to
     introduce me, I hope neither
     of them notice. *This is Heather*

     Marshall, who teaches English
     here. She's wholly responsible
     for this event. And this is Ashley

     Patterson, one of my favorite
     students, and a very good poet
     herself. The jealous wave passes

and Heather hands us a sheaf
of papers, pointing out the judging
rubric. Jonah adds a few words

about what he looks for and I absorb
all that, despite thinking about poetry
and changing lives and how teachers,

not just social workers, do that, and
about a major shift of direction.

IF I REALLY WERE TO DISSECT

My reasoning for choosing
my grad-school path, I'd probably
have to start with the way I felt
after finding Lara's letters. I came
home from Wyoming, already
reassessing my life. Changing
career paths seemed like a brave,

new start. Until then, social work
hadn't even been a consideration,
but when I went over the SDSU grad
school web page, that's where I
ended up. Psychology had always
fascinated me and the idea that you
could manipulate that for the better

was appealing. There were kids
at the preschool whose families needed
interventions. And it was becoming
clear that so many returning soldiers
would need services. The damage wasn't
always obvious. Sometimes it hid
for years before surfacing. I wanted

to help those already home. Those
coming home soon. One day, Cole
might even be among them. I wanted
to be able to recognize the signs, know
what to do if I saw them. Because,
as furious as I was with Cole, I really
needed to believe he loved only me.

IT WAS A BAD TIME

For shaky faith. Cole would be
deploying to Afghanistan in just

a few months. Meanwhile, he would
spend some weeks at Pendleton's

sniper academy, if that's what you
could call the obnoxious tract of

swampy coastal land he crawled
through, across, and over. I did get

to see him on his off-hours, and that
was crucial to our survival as a couple.

I needed every fiber of me to believe
he would come home. Not to Lara, ever.

Always, to his Ashley. What bothered
me most was my eroded certainty in

his code of honor—that intrinsic
element that had first pulled me to

him. My inner cynic had long insisted
that no man truly respected such

a thing. Cole had changed that for me.
Or had he? I just wasn't sure anymore.

And in that fertile ground of doubt,
a garden of nightmares took root.

WAR WIDOWS

Sometimes pick up the phone, certain
their man will be on the other end,
speaking to them from wherever it is
his spirit now wanders. Sometimes,
I'm told, they even hear his voice.

My nightmares were kind of like
that. Cole would come to me in
the middle of the night, and even
though I knew he wasn't really there,
he was. We would talk about life—

his, mine. Ours, together. We would
plan. Remember. Commiserate.
When he touched me, my skin grew
warm. When he kissed me, he wetted
my lips. When he made love to me,

orgasm came easily. And it was real.
The nightmare was waking up, sure
he was there, and not finding him
beside me. When he finally went
off to Afghanistan, the dreams grew

scarier. Sometimes when he came
to me, he would describe a kill
in all its gore and glory. Sometimes,
he would show me the shrapnel-
strewn landscape. Once in a while,

when he talked, his voice sounded
foreign. And on more than one occasion,
he tried to kiss me without a mouth,
because he was missing half of his face.

THAT IMAGE

Must have come from one of the many
video clips I watched about the war.
Okay, it wasn't a brilliant thing to do,

but I wanted to know what he would
be facing in Helmand Province.
It became something of an obsession.

Truthfully, as Cole's third deployment
approached, I was more afraid than
ever before. Afghanistan wasn't Iraq.

Fed by al Qaeda, the Taliban claimed
much of the country, teaming with
the drug trade in the poppy-rich land.

There was more money there, more
resources, and a deep-seated hatred
of the American infidels. Used to war-

fare and shifts of power, the Afghan
farmers simply went with the flow,
tending their crops and pretending

friendship to whomever wandered
their fields with weapons. Charged
with identifying insurgents, detaining

or removing them, American soldiers
might have been better equipped
than their enemies. But they were dying.

WE DIDN'T KNOW IT THEN

Of course, but 2010 would prove
to be the most deadly of the war
up until that point. All I knew in
the few months leading up to

Cole's deployment was the casualty
counts were high. Rising. President
Obama had ordered thousands more
troops into the region. Cole was one

of those troops. And he was raring
to go. I flew to Hawaii to say good-bye.
He could only give me a few hours.
And, though I understood, it made

me incredibly sad. Made me angry,
because his excitement eclipsed
my disappointment. He was leaving,
and I didn't want to let him go. I stood

glued to him, kissing him as if I had
some sort of insider knowledge
that he would not return all in one
piece. He dismissed my fear.

> *How many times must I promise*
> *that I will always come home*
> *to you? I love you. And that's*
> *a magical force field, all around me.*

But then he had to go. When he tore
himself out of my arms, I thought
I heard the *chink* of a new crack
in our plaster. Splintering hope.

THE CHASM WIDENED

With the dearth of communication.
The battalion was split by company,
and moved to different operating bases
within the Helmand Province.
Conditions, according to the battalion

newsletter, were "spartan," computers
only available at a few locations. The men
would rotate between them, and a satellite
phone would get passed around, but
we were told to expect long periods

without hearing from our soldiers.
On top of that, "River City" often denied
communication. This happened when
a secret operation was in the works,
or if there was a casualty, to allow

time for the family to be notified
before the press could get wind of it.
And there were casualties, and the press
let us know, sometimes with photos
of flag-draped coffins. As I finished

my senior year, my BA mattered
a whole lot less to me than knowing
I wouldn't spend an afternoon
in Arlington National Cemetery,
mourning for my beloved Marine.

I SPENT A LOT OF JUNE

Combing the desert, as if navigating
    California's heat-shimmering sand
        could somehow bring me closer

to Cole. I even borrowed his truck
    from Uncle Jack, who seemed to
        understand my growing obsession.

I did not chase rabbits, though
    they were plentiful enough. I did
        pick late wildflowers, pre-annual

wilt. Determined to avoid any echo
    of the summer before—no Jaden-
        type temptation—I didn't go out

much. In fact, I became quite
    the hermit. My only real human
        contact was at my job, where

most of that was with young kids,
    who I did not have to worry about
        crushing on. I did take a special

interest in one little girl. Soleil
    was extremely quiet, and had a hard
        time making eye contact. It took a lot

of work, but when I won enough
    trust to be able to push her on
        the swings, it felt like a real victory.

COLE FINALLY CAUGHT UP

With me at home, via sat phone.
It had been some seven weeks
since I'd heard a word, and when
the call finally came, the words
I heard were disturbing. Not:

> *The Afghani people are so happy*
> *we're here. They say they'll feel*
> *safer with us patrolling their fields.*
> More like: *Bastards can't even*
> *thank us for keeping their women*
>
> *and kids safe. Probably wish*
> *they'd die so they don't have to*
> *feed them. I'm not allowed to tell*
> *you what all kind of patrols we're*
> *doing. Suffice it to say we've wiped*
>
> *our fair share of Taliban assholes*
> *off the face of the earth. Praise Allah.*
> *Lost a good buddy last week, though.*
> *Motherfucking IED. I swear I'll get*
> *the guy who did it and if not him,*
>
> *his brother or father or fucking*
> *grandfather. Sight. Lock in. BLAM!*
> *Oops, there goes another hajji head.*
> *Hey. I have to go. Keep the home*
> *fires burning. I love you, Ash.*

And he was gone. The voice
of a ghost. I didn't even get to tell
him I loved him, too. So I sent that
off in a letter. Hoped it reached him.

CLOSE TO MORNING

A noise brought me up out of sleep.
Was it a door? My bedroom door?
I couldn't quite tell. Wasn't exactly
awake. So I stayed very still. In
the silence came the whisper
of feet. "Who's there?" I asked,

but when I tried to see, the room
was empty except for the sound
of footsteps, soft and sinking into
the carpet. I wanted to move but
crushing fear kept me pressed
against the mattress. "Go away!"

It came out barely a whisper.
The foot of the bed compressed,
as if someone had dropped there
on their hands and knees. I saw
no one, and yet the presence—
ghost?—came crawling toward me.

I tried to scream, but the weight
of something invisible and needy
fell against my body, cutting off
all sound. "No!" I tried. "No."
I choked on the "n." Then a hand
covered my mouth and the thing

> whispered, *I love you, Ash. I'll
> always come back to you.* This
> time noise escaped my mouth—
> the high, anguished keen of a new
> widow. I woke, certain Cole had
> just returned for a final good-bye.

SOMETHING INVISIBLE

Lurks there, just this side
of the battlefield, at the fringe
of the poppy field. If I were
a romantic, I might call it

                evil

but that would signal intent.
It's more like invitation,
a test of will. It is what

                remains

when hyenas and buzzards
have finished their work,
picked the bones
clean, and it

                calls

with the voice of the siren,
the song of wind-tossed
sand. It is a ripple
of enlightenment, teasing

                the weak

into its embrace
and squeezing the air
from their lungs, pressing
them to their knees

                to worship.

Cole Gleason

SPOKEN WORD POETRY

Is an amazing experience. First
of all, the gym fills up completely.
As Jonah and I take our seats
at the judges' table, I whisper,

"This is like the *American Idol*
of poetry. Why are they all here?
Only twenty-six kids are performing."

> He smiles. *Some teachers give
> extra credit. And some kids
> strong-arm their friends. No
> one wants to be the only one
> who doesn't get cheered for.*

That is not a problem. Everyone
cheers as each poet finishes
reciting a memorized piece.

Some are more theatrical, but
that doesn't necessarily make
for the best performance. In fact,
we're supposed to deduct points

if theatrics outweigh the correct
interpretation of the piece. I'm glad
I know most of these poems, and
understand the poets' intent.

Still, seeing them in this way
brings a deeper meaning. I love
it. A few kids definitely rise to
the top. We narrow it to five, ask

them to perform again so we can
rank them. The winner will go
on to represent San Diego at
the state level. There are five
of us judging, and our scores

are averaged. The girl who finishes
first totally rocked it. "Thanks for
inviting me to do this," I tell

Jonah, once we've wrapped it up.
"If you ever need another judge
for one of these, I'd do it in a heartbeat.
These kids have such great energy."

> How's your *energy*? I'd love to take
> you to dinner. To thank you. And
> then, if you're not too tired, there's
> a slam downtown tonight. Have you
> ever been to one? If you enjoyed
> this, you'll go crazy over that.

I should say no. But he's so sweet,
and I am hungry. And I've never
been to an actual slam, though

I've always meant to go to one. Oh,
why not? It's Saturday, and all I'll
do is go home and wonder what
Cole's up to. So I say, "I'd like that."

HE CHOOSES AN UPSCALE
STEAKHOUSE

I've never eaten here. Too pricey
for my budget. But I've heard
about it. The décor is simple
dark wood, polished so it glows
in the low light. Brass and crystal
embellishments add glitter.

It's early yet, but the place hums.
"Are you sure we can get in?"

> He grins. *I was an Eagle Scout,*
> *you know, and I live by the motto,*
> *"Always be prepared." I made*
> *a reservation. Hoping you'd say yes.*

We wait only a few minutes before
the maître d' escorts us to a table
in back. Jonah pulls out the chair
for me, more gentleman than explorer.
"Were you really an Eagle Scout?"

> *You betcha.* He sits across from me,
> stretching his long legs toward mine,
> the warmth of them obvious, even
> without contact. *My dad signed me up*
> *for Cub Scouts the day I turned seven.*

I glance at his hair, which hangs
straight down to his collar.
My expression must change

> because he says, *What? You*
> *don't think I look like a scout?*
> *I think my feelings are hurt.*

But he laughs, so he must be
joking. Why is it so hard to tell?
Maybe because Cole is always
so serious. And why must I over-
think everything, anyway?

> The waiter arrives to take our
> drink order. *Red wine okay?* I nod,
> so he orders an expensive Napa
> Valley cabernet. The waiter seems
> pleased. *So, what looks good?*

I scan the menu. Oh, my God.
How much do college professors
make? "I, uh . . . don't know. Maybe
a dinner salad?" Maybe just water.

> *Hey, now. I didn't ask you to*
> *go dutch, you know. You're not*
> *a vegetarian, are you? All the beef*
> *here is locally raised and hormone*
> *free. I suggest the blackened filet.*

I refuse to look at the price.
I haven't had a really brilliant
steak for a long time. "I'll take
your word for it. Sounds good."

> Back comes the waiter, plus wine.
> He opens it, invites Jonah to taste.
> *Very good, thanks.* Once our glasses
> are poured, Jonah orders our meals.
> Filets, medium for me, rare for himself.
> Baked potatoes. Salads with balsamic.

I'M ALWAYS JUST

The slightest bit suspicious when a guy
seems to intuit things like the way
I like my steak cooked, or that balsamic
is my favorite dressing. He looks at me
for approval, of course. What can I do,

but give it? "Did you do a background
check on me? Or maybe you've been
peeking in my windows?" The thought
makes me blush. I'm glad it's dark
in here. "Or, are you just psychic?"

> *No background checks and not*
> *psychic. I'll keep you guessing*
> *about the windows. Um, but if*
> *I were a betting man, I'd say*
> *blinds, not curtains. At my raised*

> eyebrows, he laughs. *I'm just good*
> *at assessing people. You watch*
> *your weight. Balsamic. You have taste*
> *but are conservative. Medium beef.*

Okay, I like that he thinks I watch
my weight. Not much, but whatever.
I have taste. Good. But the conservative
thing bugs me. "Wait a minute.
I'm one hundred percent progressive."

> *Really? Not sure how I missed that.*
> *A dedicated liberal would be hard*
> *pressed to give up her dreams to make*
> *other people happy. Don't get mad.*
> *That's only what you've told me.*

HE'S INFURIATING

But only because this little voice
keeps whispering, "He's right."

Okay, I've told him more than
I should have. Given him insights

few enough even care to know.
What is it about him that makes

me want to expose my innermost
eccentricities? Did I just think

of myself as eccentric? Damn it.
He's eccentric. I mean, he teaches

poetry, at a university. Does he have
a PhD in poetry? What does that take?

And why does he have to be so freaking
intriguing? Okay, I really must chill.

The best defense is a solid offense.
I'm ready to spar. "So, how did an Army

brat end up teaching poetry? What did
your parents have to say about that?"

> *You know, I blame my mom. All that*
> *Dr. Seuss got me completely hooked.*

He's funny. And totally charming.
"No, really. I'm being serious."

*So am I. Growing up, we didn't have
a lot of things because we moved*

*pretty often and Mom hated all that
packing and unpacking. But she was*

*a rabid book lover, and insisted on
reading out loud to my brothers and me.*

*Wherever we went, one of our first
stops was always the library. Books*

*were our entertainment. Books, and
BB guns. That was pretty much it.*

The salads come and the waiter
refills our glasses. I wait until

he's finished before I ask Jonah,
"How many brothers do you have?"

*I had three. But I lost one four years
ago. In Fallujah. The other two*

*are still in the Army. Lifers, like Dad.
They used to tease that I must have*

*been adopted because I just never
had an interest in artillery. I was,*

*in fact, born a pacifist. A hippie gene
must have snuck in there somewhere.*

CONVERSATION SLOWS

As we eat our salads—the dressing
is exceptional—and move on to
the perfectly seasoned steaks.
I keep stealing glances at Jonah,
who cuts his meat delicately.

Gracefully. Some might find it
borderline feminine, but he is all
man. Enigmatic, because despite
a definite hippie gene influence,
he maintains the self-assurance

of a soldier. Nurture, nature, or
both. He is utterly fascinating.
Teacher. Wine connoisseur.
Rider of the Banzai Pipeline.
"So, where did you learn to surf?"

> He takes the time to swallow.
> *In Hawaii. My dad was stationed*
> *at Fort Shafter when I was in high*
> *school. It was the first place I really*
> *felt at home. Like I belonged there.*
>
> *I went to a public high school, and*
> *pretty much everyone surfed. Not*
> *only did I pick it up right away, but*
> *when I discovered riding, I found*
> *myself. Right there in the ocean.*
>
> *Riding big water? That liberated*
> *me. It's something my brothers*
> *would never do. And it takes almost*
> *as much courage as facing bullets.*

LIBERATED

I like the sound of that. I think
I need to ride bigger water.
We finish dinner. Turn down
dessert in favor of getting to
the theater a little earlier.

The poetry slam is similar to
the spoken word competition,
except the poets perform their
own original work. Some of it
is funny. Some of it is sexy.

Some of it reflects the time—
unemployment, foreclosure.
War. Depression. Loss. A couple
of times as people take the stage
Jonah lets me know they were
in his classes at some point.

> *See that guy there?* he whispers.
> *He actually gets paid to teach*
> *performance poetry at schools.*
> *Pretty cool gig, don't you think?*

I do, actually. Making a living
doing something creative, not
to mention something you love,
has immense appeal. It's a great
evening, topping off a fabulous day.

On the way home, I find myself
happy. Why does that strike
me as strange? How long has it
been since I've felt content?

What's even more interesting
is this feeling has nothing to do
with alcohol—two glasses of wine
at dinner, and that was hours ago—
or pills. It's all about the activity,

and the company, and the idea
that life brims with possibility.
When we get to the apartment,
Jonah walks me to the door.
"Thanks so much for today."

Suddenly, I'm afraid to go inside,
back to the isolation I've created
for myself. I put my key in the lock,
wishing I could invite him in for
a nightcap. But that could go all

> kinds of wrong. Jonah smiles.
> Reading my mind again? *Thanks*
> *for helping out today, and for your*
> *company tonight. I really enjoyed*
> *the day. See you in class Monday.*

Before he can turn away, I give
him a quick hug, more thank you
than invitation. He looks surprised,
but pleasantly so. "Night." I go inside,
surprised by myself. In many ways.

INSIDE, ALONE

I find myself wishing I had
       taken Jonah's hand, coaxed

him in for that nightcap.
       Sometimes it's just so tiresome

playing the martyr role.
       Before I really understood

what sex could be, it was
       easy enough to convince myself

I didn't need it. I mean, if you
       don't enjoy it, shun it! Cole taught

me how to love it. And I do,
       with him. But every now and then

I wonder if it's only because
       I'm with Cole, or if the lessons

he's taught me could make me
       love it as much, or more, with someone

else. Is an orgasm the same with
       every partner? Sitting here, buzzed,

I imagine being with Jonah.
       My hand slips down between my legs

where fantasy has made me wet.
       When I finish, I write it as a pantoum.

GHOSTS
by Ashley Patterson

Even a small bed is too big, alone.
She lies half-awake, draws stuttered breath,
listens to memory's bittersweet drone,
wonders if silence comes cloaked in death.

Not quite awake, she draws stuttered breath,
promises shattering on her pillow.
She wonders if silence comes cloaked in death,
as her storm clouds begin to billow.

Promises shattering on her pillow,
she conjures the image she cannot dismiss,
seeding her storm clouds. They billow
with the black remembrance of his kiss.

She conjures the image she cannot dismiss,
summons the heat of his skin on her skin,
the black remembrance of his kiss,
desire, abandoned somewhere within.

She summons the heat of his skin on her skin,
opens herself to herself, in disguise,
recovers desire, abandoned within.
Heart beating ghosts, she closes her eyes

And opens herself to herself, in disguise,
listens to memory's bittersweet drone.
Heart beating ghosts, she closes her eyes,
knowing her small bed is too big, alone.

SLEEP STUDIES

Suggest the belief that someone
is in your room, in your bed, where
you can hear them breathing and
feel their hands at your throat,
even though, in reality, no one
is actually there, can be explained
by coming up out of REM sleep
too quickly. This produces a state
of sleep paralysis. Part of your brain
is aware, the other part is still dreaming.

You can't move, can't speak, can't
chase away the imaginary monster.
There was a time when sleep paralysis
could only be explained through
the paranormal. Some people still
believe it is the presence of evil
and if you only pray hard enough,
God will chase it away, allow you
to wake completely and go about
your day. I'd rather accept science.

The morning I woke up, positive
Cole's ghost was in my bed, needing
to say good-bye, was the scariest
experience of my life. I deal with fear
by research, and what I learned was
sleep paralysis can be linked to periods
of high anxiety. Anxious? Me? Well, yeah.

COLE WAS IN AFGHANISTAN

Where they were ramping up security
ahead of the coming elections.

A Taliban spokesperson warned,
*Everything and everyone affiliated
with the election is our target—*

*candidates, security forces,
campaigners, election workers,
and voters. All are our targets.*

Cole's unit was one of several
charged with keeping those targets
safe, and it would not be easy.

Pre-election, three candidates
and at least eleven campaign
workers were killed, and his unit

lost a soldier. During the voting,
across the country, dozens of bomb
and rocket attacks led to even more

deaths at the polls. But the district
Cole was protecting suffered no
casualties. The official word on

that credited good communication
between the locals and the Marines
who oversaw their safety. According

to Cole, it had more to do with
the accuracy of the sniper squad's
scopes. I pretty much believed him.

HE TOOK PRIDE IN THAT

But he was not exactly
enthusiastic about it being
his mission. He e-mailed:

> *WHAT THE FUCK ARE WE DOING?*
> *THESE ELECTIONS ARE A FARCE.*
> *THAT FUCKING KARZAI STOLE*
> *THE PRESIDENCY LAST YEAR.*
> *THIS ELECTION IS STINKO, TOO.*
>
> *ALL WE'RE HERE FOR IS SECURING*
> *THE PLACE FOR MORE FUCKING*
> *FRAUD. PEOPLE ARE AFRAID TO*
> *VOTE. YOU CAN BET THE ONES*
> *WHO DO WILL STUFF THE BOXES.*

He was right, of course.
Widespread fraud tainted
the election. A fifth of the ballots
were tossed. Winners eventually
lost, and losers took their seats

in the Afghanistan parliament.
None of that mattered to me.
All I cared about was knowing
Cole was not among the reported
casualties. They continued to swell.

At that point, he was over half-
way through his deployment.
I was counting down the weeks.
Checking them off the calendar.
Obsessing about dates.

CHRISTMAS 2010

Was still up in the air.
Some from his battalion
would be home. Others
would have to wait for
January to take leave.

I started thinking about
holidays and birthdays
and other celebrations,
how the Marine Corps
defined those for us,

and for every military
family. Would their
soldier make it home in
time? And if not this year,
then next? No promises.

As bad as that was for
me, what would that mean
to a child, waiting for Daddy,
only to be told, sorry, he
won't help you blow out

your birthday candles this
year? You turn four only
once. And what if you turned
five without him there, too?
And what if an insurgent's

bullet meant you'd never
share another birthday
with your father? And why
did I decide to worry about it?

I HAD ENOUGH

To worry about. Besides Cole, flushing
insurgents, and largely incommunicado,

I was starting grad school, unsure
about the program and the direction

it was pulling me in. My summer hermit
phase had made me uncomfortable

in new situations or around large crowds
of people—like on a university campus.

I was definitely anxious about pretty
much every facet of my life. And sleep

paralysis was only one manifestation.
I also started having mild panic attacks.

Sleep paralysis, only totally awake
and even on my feet. I'd be walking

along, all good, and suddenly it was like
the world began to shrink, everything

closing in around me. Too many people.
Too many voices. Closer. Smaller. Tighter.

Suffocating. I'd freeze in place, unable
to move. My heart would race, crowding

my lungs. All I could manage was shallow,
breaths, ragged and pitiful. A hollow

ringing in my ears disallowed balance.
I had to sit or fall. I learned to drop

my head between my knees and close
my eyes until the world began to grow

wider again. After the fourth "event,"
I went to my doctor and asked for

chemical help. He prescribed Xanax,
told me to avoid alcohol while taking it.

I thought that was probably a good
idea anyway. I'd been drinking more

than I knew was wise. I needed
an excuse to stop. And I did. Mostly.

I wasn't an alcoholic. I didn't drink every
day, didn't often drink to excess or binge.

And could leave it alone completely
for large swaths of time. But I did drink

to be social. To have fun with friends.
Sometimes, to sleep. Sometimes, to forget.

WITH THE XANAX

School was okay, though I was glad
I had only two classes that semester.
There was a lot of reading. A lot of writing.

A lot of research. I learned more
than I ever wanted to about human
behavior. Unfortunately, it made me

very aware of some very bad things.
Especially at my job. I still loved
taking care of the little ones, teaching

them things that would jump-start
their regular school experience.
Colors. Letters. Numbers. Telling time.

But every now and again, I couldn't
help but notice signs. Things that
made me uncomfortable. With Soleil,

especially. Over the summer, I'd broken
through the barrier she'd erected
between herself and the rest of the world.

I could even make her laugh once
in a while, chase the thunderheads
from her eyes. And when she finally

conquered a difficult concept,
her face lit and she transformed
into the prettiest child, ever.

But some days she retreated
to a place inside where I couldn't
reach her. A place she created

where no one could touch her.
I started watching the interaction
with her mother, a stiff young woman

who rarely smiled and seemed to
communicate by snapping and
barking. If Soleil didn't move

quickly enough, sometimes her
mother would grab her and jerk.
One day, I finally had enough.

I stepped in front of her. "Excuse me,
but do you think that's an appropriate
way to deal with a child?" When I

looked into the woman's eyes,
there was something scary there,
and it went beyond how dilated

> her pupils were. *How I handle*
> *my daughter is really none*
> *of your business, now, is it?*

She stepped around me, yanking
Soleil out the door. The little
girl had to run to not get dragged.

A WEEK LATER

Soleil arrived at school dressed
in jeans and a long-sleeved shirt.
Not so unusual, except it happened
to be unseasonably warm. All
the other kids were in shorts.

I already had my suspicions, so
I decided to set up the easels for
some painting. The kids all slipped
into smocks. When I helped Soleil
into hers, I told her we had to roll

      up her sleeves. I've never seen
      anyone look quite so scared.
      I can't. Mommy will get mad at me.

"But if you get paint on your shirt,
she'll really get mad," I coaxed.
"We'll just turn them up a little."
She let me, and the finger-shaped
bruises on her arms were apparent

immediately. I prodded one gently.
"Does that hurt?" In answer,
an obvious wince. "Are there more?"
She trusted me enough to give
a small nod. "Can I see, please?"

Fear clung to her like sweat. I soothed
it as best I could. "Soleil, honey,
I don't want anyone to hurt you.
Ever. I can stop it if you let me see."
Her eyes, which had been focused

on the floor, turned slowly up
to meet mine. She must have
found what she needed there
because she took my hand, led me
to the bathroom, closed the door.

She turned away from me, lifted
her shirt. The bruising began
in the small of her back, disappeared
beneath the waistband of her jeans.
It was dark. Fresh. "Who did this?"

> Her voice was mouse-quiet.
> *Mommy. She's very sorry.*

Of course she was. "Okay, honey.
You want to go paint now?"
Anger seethed. Red. Frothy. How
could anyone do something like
this to a child? We returned to

the playroom and I gave Soleil
a paintbrush. Then I went to call
Child Protective Services. It was no
more than my duty, but it felt
really good to report what I saw.

Later, however, it hit me that
Soleil's mother would probably
blame her for the trouble coming
their way. I went home. Popped
a Xanax. Washed it down with tequila.

I NEVER SAW HER AGAIN

Once Child Protective Services
stepped in, it was completely
out of my hands. I knew I'd done

the right thing, but I was concerned
about her safety. Especially as I learned
more about what happened after

someone—like me—reported abuse.
Often the child remained in her home,
if the parents seemed cooperative

and mostly sane. I had a hunch
Soleil's mom was using some
sort of controlled substance. Crystal

meth, maybe. I hoped they looked
for that. Hoped their investigation
was more involved than asking

a couple of questions and accepting
easy answers. The bruising I saw
looked massive. But what if Ms. Bruiser

managed to make them believe
it was only an accident, or admitted
she went overboard, but only that once.

There were just too many variables.
And I never learned the outcome.
One more checkmark on my worry list.

PRISONER

Mine is the dream of the caged
wolf. He has forgotten his howl
but still remembers long lopes
through stiletto woods,   drawn by desire.

He is adrift on a current of night.
Summer trails humid perfume
and the forest yields a feast
of decay, but there is more—   blood scent.

A notion of movement quickens
his gait, the chase becomes game.
She cannot match his speed,
but he must overtake her to win
her. Respect is born of   power.

At his demand, she flags reverence.
Some might call their joining
savage—the mesh of fang
and fur, the singe of lupine thrust.
But at the tie,   he lays her down

on a pillow of forest. Begs patience.
Mine is the heart of the caged
wolf. Roused from nocturnal reverie,
he paces the perimeter of sleep
rattled bars. The waxing moon
casts a pale shadow. He   looks to the amber sky

listens to a distant plea,
water on the wind.   Finds his song.

Cole Gleason

COLE IS A MONTH

Into his fourth deployment—deep
in the Helmand Province—when I go
home for Thanksgiving. It has been
a casualty-heavy period for coalition
forces. Roadside explosions and suicide

bombers have taken their toll.
Cole sounds grim when I'm able
to talk to him. Hopefully the troops'
own turkey-and-trimmings feast
will boost morale. Maybe they'll even

get to have a couple of beers.
It's a long drive from San Diego
to Lodi, and I'm making it alone.
I asked Dar if she wanted to come
along, get away from the hospital

for a couple of days. Spence will
survive, something to be thankful
for. But it will still be a while before
he's strong enough for skin grafts.
Darian can't do much but wait.

She turned me down, however.
I'm pretty sure she plans to spend
the holiday with Kenny. And that's
all right by me. I leave very early
Thursday morning. Driving seventy,

it will take around six hours. I nudge
the speedometer to seventy-five. Hope
the highway patrol feels generous today.

WITH A STOP

For coffee and another to pee
it out, I arrive home a little after
one. Nostalgia sweeps over me
as I turn up the long, curved driveway.

It's been a dry autumn. The hills
are parchment brown, beneath
sprawling, green oak canopies.
Representative California. I park

in front of our low stucco ranch-
style house with a red-tile roof.
Buster, our golden retriever, lifts
his head from the front porch, too

lazy to come investigate. Besides,
he knows it's me. I can see his tail
thumping. I get out of the car, stretch
a minute, inhaling familiar air.

Why is it appreciating home comes
easier after you've been away for
a while? I stop long enough to pat
Buster's head, go on inside.

I hear football in the family room.
That will be Dad, and I know Mom's
in the kitchen. What I don't expect
is to see my brother, no longer in Europe.

> Three heads swivel toward me—
> Dad's, Troy's, and one very blond one,
> with a cute, freckled face I don't recognize.
> *Hey, Sis. Come meet Gretchen.*

She's a very sweet German, who
speaks delicate English and hangs
on to Troy like he's her anchor
here in this crazy country. I say

hi, hug Troy, and give Dad a quick kiss
right before the Niners score.
He and Troy both jump to their feet,
cheering. Gretchen looks anxious.

"I'm going to go help Mom with
dinner. Want to come?" I invite.
Now Gretchen looks grateful.
She follows me to the kitchen,

where Mom is peeling potatoes.
"Hey. Can we help you with that?"

>   *Hi sweetheart. How was your*
>   *drive?* She keeps on peeling.

"Uneventful." I look for something
for Gretchen and I to do. "How about
if we open some wine? I know it's early,
but hey, it's Thanksgiving, right?"

>   *Go for it. The wineglasses are in*
>   *the hutch. Gretchen, white or red?*

Gretchen barely looks old enough
to drink. But she chooses white.
I hand her a bottle of each and
a corkscrew, go off to find the glasses.

356

WITH ONLY COFFEE

And a muffin for breakfast,
the wine produces a nice, little
buzz before very long. I try to

keep it in check, sipping slowly.
I also try to let everyone else
do most of the talking. We learn

Gretchen is from Dresden, but
she met Troy at a café in Munich.
Her dream is to work in publishing.

As an editor, perhaps, or public
relations. Whatever will get her foot
in the door. Meanwhile, she's living

> off a small inheritance. *This is the time*
> *to travel,* she says. *Before I must get*
> *serious. I think then I will grow old.*

> Mom laughs. *Getting serious*
> *about a man will make you grow*
> *old. Don't you think so, Ashley?*

"Depends on the man, I guess."
I've been hoping to steer clear
of talking about Cole. No such luck.

> *Ashley's boyfriend is a soldier.*
> Mom tells Gretchen. *This war*
> *has made her much older.*

I WOULD PROTEST

Except she's right. I turn twenty-five
in a week. I feel ten years older.
It's the war, yes, and Cole's fighting
there. It's a consequence of worry.

The oven buzzer sounds. I go to take
out the turkey. Open the door. Find
ham. No wonder the smell wasn't
familiar. I guess I'd noticed that on

some level. "Ham this year? Was
there a turkey shortage I didn't hear
about?" We've never had ham for
Thanksgiving dinner. Mom drains

> the potatoes. *Nope. Plenty of turkeys.*
> *Just thought it was time to shake*
> *things up a little. It's a lovely spiral*
> *cut. There's some pineapple-cherry*
>
> *sauce on the stove. Would you mind*
> *basting it? It should sit a few minutes*
> *before we carve it. By then, I'll have*
> *these potatoes mashed.* Gretchen

beats me to the pan and baster,
so I refill our glasses. When I reach
into the fridge for the Pinot Grigio,
I notice a beautiful chocolate cheesecake.

"No apple pie, either?" This shaking
stuff up thing is slightly disturbing.
Wonder what else she's agitating.
This feels a little bit like a revolt.

THAT FEELING ONLY GROWS

As we sit down to dinner. Mom's chair used
to always be right next to Dad's. Today,
they're at opposite ends of the table.

Putting Gretchen and Troy straight
across from me. We say grace, then
Mom and I go into the kitchen to get

> the serving platters. Dad gives
> the sauced-up ham slices a hard
> double take. *What the hell is that?*

Okay, he has been drinking rum
most of the afternoon. But that
was pretty harsh. "It's ham, Dad."

> *Yes,* chirps Mom. *And you paid*
> *a pretty penny for it, and I've spent*
> *most of the day making it special*
>
> *for you. Us. Is there a problem?*
> *It's not like you don't eat pork.*
> *We have ham all the time.*

> He looks at her like she's crazy.
> *Not for Thanksgiving. But I guess*
> *there's a first time for everything.*

Troy and I exchange "phews."
Gretchen looks alternately terrified
and relieved. We start passing trays,

bowls, and baskets of meat, veggies,
and Mom's homemade buttermilk
biscuits. And I think it might all

>be perfectly fine until suddenly Troy
>whistles. *Hey, Ashley. What's that?*
>*Did you forget to tell us something,*

>uh . . . *kind of important?* He's staring
>at my left hand, and now everyone
>else is, too. I swear, I forgot all about

the ring, which I just got back, sized,
from the jeweler's two days ago.
"Uh, well, yeah. I guess I did.

Cole and I are getting married.
Probably in June. We haven't set
a date yet or anything, but that's

what we were thinking. I know,
relatively speaking, that's not a whole
lot of time, but I think we can pull

it together. . . ." Troy is grinning.
Gretchen is nodding. Dad is shaking
his head. But Mom . . . I don't know.

All color has drained from her face,
and any hint of a smile went with it.
Did she have too much wine?

She kind of looks sick. "Are you okay,
Mom? I'm sorry I didn't mention it."

MOM FINDS SOMETHING

Approximating a smile.
Says she's fine. Turns
her attention back to
her dinner, though she's
really only picking at it
now. It is Dad who says,

> *Have you thought this*
> *through, Ashley? I mean,*
> *all the way through? Why*
> *get married now? Aren't*
> *things good just as they are?*

Déjà vu, and annoying
déjà vu, at that. "You sound
like Darian. God, Dad, I'm
almost twenty-five. Don't
you think that's old enough?"

> *It's not exactly over the hill.*
> *Why rush into marriage?*
> *You're not . . .* Okay, now
> it's anger-inspiring déjà vu.

"Pregnant? No, Dad. No
shotguns involved. And
as far as 'rushing,' Cole
and I have been together
for five years. Not exactly
jumping the gun. Why do
I have to keep defending
this decision? Everyone
should be happy for me."

EYES STINGING

I push back from the table, carry
my plate into the kitchen. Rinse
it, put it in the dishwasher, along
with the pots and pans Mom left
in the sink. Then I step outside

to cry in private. The back patio
is in the sun, and warm. But I'm
shivering. Nerves. Anger. Hurt.
I'm cold, from the inside out.
It's quiet behind the dining room

window. At least they're not talking
about me—about what a fool I am
or how I'm too young to know
what I want. Ha. What would
they say if I told them I'm not sure

about social work, either? Dad
would freak, that's for sure. I can
hear him now. *After all that time
and money invested you want
to change your mind now?*

      I sit on the old porch glider.
      It has seen better days, for sure.
      The door opens, and Mom comes
      outside. *May I join you?* She sits
      beside me, knowing I'd never say

      no. We rock gently back and forth
      for a minute. Finally, she says,
      *I need to tell you something I've
      never shared with you before.*

You know my mother and father
died in a car accident, right? What
you don't know is that it wasn't
really an accident. It was a murder
suicide. Daddy was never right

after he got back from Viet Nam.
It was a long time ago, and I was
little, but I remember how the sound
of a helicopter sent him to the floor.
How he heard noises that I never

did. How if someone looked at him
in a certain way, he'd go ballistic.
He was arrested a couple of times
for starting a fight in a bar. Drinking
made everything worse because

then he saw ghosts. Really. I know
he did horrible things in the jungle.
Things no amount of alcohol or pills
could erase. War stains soldiers,
all the way through their psyches,

into their souls. I understand that,
and could almost forgive him for taking
his own life, to quiet the ghosts. But
I can never forgive him for taking
my mother with him. He thought

of her as a possession. One he wouldn't
leave behind for someone else to own.
And I worry about that for you.
Cole reminds me of my father.

IT'S A STUNNING REVELATION

One I never even suspected.
I am trembling. Mom slides
her arm around my shoulder,

pulls me into her embrace.
I can't remember the last time
we sat like this. Now I am young.

Like, four or five. We freeze
in this place, wordlessly watching
a covey of fat quail foraging

for several minutes. Finally,
I clear my throat. "I understand
why you're worried for me, Mom.

But I've never seen Cole do
any of the things you described."
Wait. Not true. There was the time

he heard the helicopter and
pushed me to the floor. Except,
he was protecting me, so that

was not the same thing at all.
"Cole would never, ever hurt me.
It would go against his code of honor."

> Her arm falls away. *That's what*
> *Momma thought. I want to support*
> *your decision. I'm just not sure I can.*

THE DOOR OPENS AGAIN

It's Troy, checking up on us, though
he pretends it's all about cheesecake.

>   *Dad said I had to ask you before*
>   *I cut it. He also said to ask if you*
>   *bought brandy for the eggnog.*

>   Mom vacates the slider. *I'll cut*
>   *the cheesecake. Think I'd leave that*
>   *to a man? You up for eggnog, Ashley?*

"A little, I guess. Actually, maybe
straight brandy. Save the calories
for the cheesecake. I'll be right in."

>   Mom brushes past Troy, who
>   doesn't follow. Instead, he comes
>   over to me. *So you know, I think*
>   *it's cool you're getting married.*

I have to smile. "Thanks, Troy.
You going to be here this summer?
I don't think we can have a wedding
if you're not going to be part of it."

>   *No worries. I'll be here. I like*
>   *Europe. But it's not California.*

"What about Gretchen? You
two look pretty darn tight."

>   *Yeah, well. Don't tell Mom and*
>   *Dad just yet. But Gretchen and*
>   *I might be getting married, too.*

LAST FALL

As the nighttime temperatures
in San Diego slid lower and lower,
toward forty degrees, in Helmand
Province, Afghanistan, Cole and crew

celebrated ninetyish daytime temps,
with nights in the upper sixties.
They were ecstatic. Up until the first
week in November, I talked to Cole

fairly regularly. He was in decent
spirits. Coming home in just six weeks.
We knew by then he'd spend Christmas
in Kaneohe Bay. I'd see him in January.

Ramadan had ended. Rumor had it
that during the holy month, the locals
were grouchier than normal, having
to fast from sunrise to sunset. Skirmishes

were common. The Marines worked
closely with the Afghan National Army
and Afghan National Police, in an effort
to allow children to safely attend school

and allow farmers to harvest their crops
without Taliban interference. Problem
was, every now and then a sneaky
insurgent would find a job within the ANA

or ANP. And then, all bets were off.

WHETHER FROM WITHIN

Or from direct enemy fire, there
were Marines among the coalition
casualties. But as the time for Cole
to return to Hawaii grew nearer,
my anxiety lessened, despite the fact
that his final weeks carried him out

beyond the wire, closer to the heart
of Taliban country. Some people,
probably wiser than I, grow more
nervous as their soldier's homecoming
nears. They know that every day
that passes problem-free increases

the odds that something bad might
happen. But I wasn't seeing things
that way. Maybe it was because
I kept myself busy, or because I kept
myself medicated, but I didn't worry
too much about Cole, not even when

communication dried up. I knew his
patrols were sending him beyond
the reach of phones or computers,
expected I would hear from him once
he was back behind the wire at Camp
Leatherneck. There was a rhythm

to his life, a rhythm to mine, and
before long our rhythms would mesh
into a gentle syncopation of time
together. That's how it had been for
almost four years, despite a few hiccups
that threw us completely off-beat.

SO I WAS SURPRISED

No, shocked, really, when I got
a late-November call from Cole's

> mom. *Ashley, honey, now don't*
> *worry. Everything's fine. Cole's okay . . .*
> Not a good start to any phone call.

> *But there was . . . uh, something*
> *happened.* At that point, her voice
> kind of caught in her throat.

> *Um, a roadside bomb went off*
> *and the Humvee he was riding in*
> *flipped over into a drainage ditch.*

> *The guys in the truck behind them*
> *pulled everyone out. Cole was wearing*
> *body armor, so he wasn't hurt. Well,*

> *he had a slight concussion, but that*
> *barely slowed him down. Stubborn*
> *kid wanted to go straight back to work.*

> *Can you believe it? They kept him*
> *overnight for observation, but he walked*
> *out on his own after that. Said a little*

> *bell ringing in his helmet wasn't any*
> *big deal. That is just so much like Cole,*
> *isn't it? Ashley? Are you there?*

I was, and I was speechless. "I'm
here. Thanks for letting me know."

I COULDN'T MANAGE MORE

Small talk about the ranch
or Dale or to ask if any letters
had arrived from Lara. A shock
wave of nausea shook my body.
Just like that, he could have been

gone, erased from my life as if
he'd never been part of it. And
I would have heard that news
secondhand, too. I resented
that, but not as much as I hated

the overall implication. What
must it be like to get that call,
or the ring of the doorbell? To
have your other half severed
completely, or returned to you

with pieces missing? Cole got
lucky. In my belief system, luck
and God are interchangeable.
God was watching over him,
allowed him to walk away with

a few scratches and a shaken
brain. Hopefully, not shaken too
hard. But on another day, God
might have been busy elsewhere.
It was a wakeup call I didn't need.

SPEAKING OF CALLS

I did not get one from Cole, giving
me any sort of details. I kept waiting,

but it never came. Finally, I e-mailed
him. Said his mom had mentioned

something about a little accident. Still,
I had to wait several days to hear

> back from him, via return e-mail.
> *OH BABY, IT WAS NO BIG DEAL. I KNEW*
>
> *YOU'D BE WORRIED OVER NOTHING,*
> *SO I DIDN'T WANT YOU TO KNOW.*
>
> *I WOULDN'T HAVE TOLD MOM, EITHER,*
> *BUT IT'S PROTOCOL TO INFORM NEXT*
>
> *OF KIN. ANYWAY, I WENT STRAIGHT*
> *BACK OUT ON PATROL. GOOD AS NEW,*
>
> *EXCEPT FOR A HEADACHE THAT WENT*
> *AWAY AFTER A COUPLE OF DAYS.*
>
> *MY BUDDY, TIM, SAID WHEN THAT BOMB*
> *BLEW IT WAS PRETTY EXCITING.*
>
> *I DON'T KNOW. I DON'T REMEMBER*
> *IT AT ALL. NOT THE EXPLOSION,*
>
> *OR GETTING EXTRICATED FROM*
> *THE VEHICLE. THEY TELL ME I WAS*
>
> *UNCONSCIOUS FOR TEN OR FIFTEEN*
> *MINUTES. FIRST THING I REMEMBER*
>
> *WAS SEEING TIM'S SHIT-EATING GRIN*
> *AND HIS LIPS SAYING, "WELCOME BACK,*

BUDDY." I COULN'T HEAR HIM AT ALL.
NOT FOR THE ROARING IN MY EARS.

I COULDN'T HEAR MUCH FOR A FEW
HOURS. TELL YOU THE TRUTH, I WAS

A TEENSY BIT WORRIED I MIGHT BE
DEAF. BUT, LITTLE BY LITTLE, THE NOISE

IN MY HEAD WENT AWAY AND MY HEARING
CAME BACK, GOOD AS NEW. PHEW.

Curiosity got the best of me and
I had to ask if everyone else

      involved made it out okay, too.
      ALL BUT ONE. HIS BACK TOOK

      THE PRESSURE FROM THE BLAST.
      BUSTED A VERTEBRAE. THEY'RE NOT

      SURE, BUT HE MIGHT BE PARALYZED.
      TOTAL SUCKAGE. FUCKING BASTARDS.

One more thing to be thankful
for. In fact, I was so grateful,

I almost forgot to be mad. But
not quite. Whatever his reasons,

Cole had no right to try to keep
me in the dark about something

as important as that. I didn't want
to be protected. I wanted the truth.

TRUTH

I turned the word over in my head.
Distrust surfaced from beneath
the shimmer of anger that remained.
Lara. Why did she cross my mind
when Cole's mom got hold of me?
I had this sudden desire to know
more about her. All I knew was

her name and that she lived near
Denver. How could I find her?
Facebook, of course. It took about
two minutes. I expected her to be
a knockout. Maybe even a model
or something. Not quite. According
to her profile, she worked ski patrol

in the winter, lifeguarded in the summer.
She was cute, not beautiful, but
probably looked great in a swimsuit.
Her photos showed her on skis,
drinking with friends, and playing
Frisbee with her dogs. She liked
reading, reality TV, and Adele.

Her status showed "in a relationship."
At first that made me feel better.
But then I got to thinking. I started
scanning her wall, hoping Cole
didn't show up there somewhere.
I scrolled down a very long way.
But I saw no sign of him there.

THAT WAS WHAT I HOPED FOR

But somehow it wasn't quite enough.
Cole had a Facebook page, too.
Not that he ever used it much, at least
not when he was deployed and his

computer time was limited. I rarely
went looking there, but was tempted
to that day. His posts were dated
very far apart. The most recent

> was a couple months old. *FUCKING*
> *118 DEGREES IN THE SHADE. TOO*
> *GODDAMN HOT TO CAUSE TROUBLE.*

> And, by God, the one comment
> there was from her. GOOD. YOU
> NEED TO STAY OUT OF TROUBLE.

That was it. Nothing more. No
words of love, or even affection.
They were Facebook friends. So what?
They didn't seem to communicate

very often. Although, I had no idea
if they were messaging each other.
Or e-mailing each other. Or writing
each other. And if I really had to worry

about any of that, it's not like I could
change it. I had to believe in Cole.
In us. And I did. Except when I didn't.
Why did I have to find out about Lara?

SUSPICION BREEDS BAD DREAMS

Now that I had her face
embedded in my brain,
I had a doozer about Lara.

I was in the desert, picking
wildflowers, when it started
to rain. The sky opened up
and it poured. I was soaked
in seconds. The sand sponged
the water but couldn't hold it.
Soon, a wet sheet covered
the land, to the far horizon.

Flash flood. It picked me up,
carried me along, and it was all
I could do to keep my head
above the flow. Faster. Faster.
I swam hard, a long way, but
my shoulders grew tired, my legs
went weak, so I flipped onto
my back, and the river enfolded
me with pewter arms. Pulled

me under. I held my breath,
struggled for more, looked
up, seeking help. There, in
her lifeguard tower, Lara smiled
down at me as my lungs filled.
He doesn't want you, anyway.
Woke, soaked and shivering,
between sweat-drenched sheets.

SOMETHING ABOUT NOVEMBER

Touches me.
How, splendid in nutshell
skin, she exposes the green lies
of June, swollen ego unsustainable
beyond a single shot of

summer.

Something about November
touches me like a lover.
How she bares herself
beneath autumn's iced blue
sky, defiance in her tarried
striptease, the low slink

of shadow.

Something about November
touches me like a lover's kiss.
How she shivers, wet
with rain too long coming,
soaks her earth
with the heady sweat of

downpour.

Something about November
touches me like you do.
How she waits for gray
December tendrils to infiltrate
secret places, infuse
her with the ephemeral light

of solstice.

Cole Gleason

PLANNING A WEDDING

Begins with a couple of basics—
when and where. I'm thinking
the end of June, to give Cole
time to return from Afghanistan,
debrief, and decompress. Plus,
the Lodi weather can still be cool

early in the month. While I would
love to get married in the same
church my parents did, Cole isn't
Catholic. We'd have to jump through
too many hoops. A nice outdoor
venue should do. Maybe up-country,

in the woods. Or at a winery.
Pricey, and it might be late to find
one that can accommodate us. But
there are many in the area. If I get
right on it . . . Or maybe I'll put Mom
on it. That way, at least I'll know how

much my parents will help out with
this financially, and if I get Mom
involved, hopefully she'll become more
enthusiastic about the day. I need
her in my corner. Like, really a lot.
I should probably shoot the idea

past Cole first. But he told me to go
ahead and make the plans, and anyway,
that's the bride's prerogative, right?
Besides, who could argue with a wedding
at a California winery? It's perfect.

I CHECK MY CALENDAR

Saturdays, late June. The twenty-third
or the thirtieth. Could go the Friday
evenings before or the Sundays after.

That's, like, nine dates. Surely we can
find a winery that can accommodate
one of them. I call Mom, ask her what

> she thinks of my plan, and if she'd be
> willing to help out. Avoidance. *Well,*
> *you know, I'm pretty busy with school.*

Redirect. "But, Mom, winter break
is pretty soon. Can't you spare a few
hours to make some calls for me?"

> Change of subject. *You're coming*
> *home for Christmas, right? You could*
> *make the calls yourself then.* Wow.

Tactic shift. "I guess I could. So,
what do you think of the idea?
It might be kind of expensive."

> Long sigh. *I guess we'll know that*
> *after you make those calls. How*
> *much were you thinking of investing*
> *in this wedding, Ashley? Look, I put*

> *a little money away for your day.*
> *You might want to consider the best*
> *way to spend it, though. Big wedding*
> *or maybe the down payment on a house?*

I HATE LOGIC

But only when it's applied
to something as emotional
as this. "I'll think about it.
Can you give me a ballpark
figure, though? It will help."

> *I've got around twenty*
> *five thousand earmarked.*
> *If you're careful, you could*
> *do a very nice wedding for*
> *half of that. Or less. Or . . .*

Or I could just wait. That's
what she wants to say.
I won't give her the chance.
"Thanks, Mom. I'll make
some calls and then we can

decide. How many people
do you think we should plan
for?" Way to keep her involved.
"I should probably make
a guest list. Can you help?"

> Another, bigger sigh. *Of*
> *course. When you're home*
> *at Christmas we can do it*
> *together. You should get*
> *hold of Cole's mom, too.*

Good point. "I will. Hey, Mom?
I really appreciate your support.
Love you lots. Bye." All things
considered, that went okay.

I SPEND A COUPLE OF HOURS

Looking at websites. The average
cost of a wedding is just about
the amount of money Mom has
put aside. The average cost
of a winery wedding . . . well,
there are just so many variables.

The brides are beautiful, in white
dresses, among the grapevines.
The handsome grooms stand
happily by them, all decked out
in tuxes. We'll save a little there.
Cole will wear his dress blues.

Catering, per person. DJ or band?
Flowers. Rings. Invitations. Do
we really need "save the date"
cards? So much to consider. No
wonder it takes so long to plan
a wedding. And I'm just getting

started. We definitely need those
guest lists to do very much. I can
start mine now, let Mom add to
it later. I put in a call to Cole's mom.
Feel relieved when it goes to voice
mail. "Hi Rochelle. This is Ashley.

How are you feeling? Cole says
you're doing much better. Listen,
I'm starting to make wedding plans
and before I can do much, I need
a guest list. Can you please help out on
your end? Thanks and I'll be in touch."

I START MY OWN LIST

Relatives. Friends. Many of whom
I haven't spoken to in years. My bad.

I mean, school has been my focus. Well,
school and Cole. I used to be popular,

but I really have turned into something
of a recluse. Who will I even ask to be

in the wedding party? Darian, of course.
Hopefully, she'll come around and agree

to be my maid of honor. Bridesmaids?
Sophie and Brittany, I suppose, though

it's been weeks since we've gone out
together. I haven't even told them

I'm engaged yet. Note to self: Call
Sophie and Brittany. Invite them out

so you can break the news in person.
And maybe have a little fun in the process.

I am considering just how little fun
I've allowed myself when my phone rings.

Rochelle, calling me back already?
Nope. Local number. Wow. It's Jonah.

> *Morning, Ashley. Do you have a wetsuit?*
> *I hear they're breaking large at Swami's.*

LET'S SEE

Spend the day alone, perusing
wedding websites and stressing
over not getting out enough and
having fun or . . . surfing with Jonah.
Kind of a no-brainer, except,
"Actually, I don't have a wetsuit.
I don't surf much in the winter."

> *Oh, but December is prime*
> *riding. Massive storms up north*
> *mean big breaks down here.*
> *And no worries. I've got an extra*
> *wetsuit that should fit you.*

"Does this mean I get to ride
in your Woodie?" That sounds
vaguely vulgar, but we both
let it go and he says he'll pick me
up in a half hour. Guess that
means I should get dressed. I've
been sitting here in my jammies.

I slip into the purple bikini I
haven't even looked at since
Hawaii. It reminds me of Cole,
chiding me for dressing too
provocatively. Wonder what he'd
think about my going surfing
with Jonah. Scratch that.

I don't wonder at all. I know
exactly what he'd think.

AND YET

I'm going. I leave my ring stashed
        beneath my underwear. Probably
                the first place a burglar would look,

but still. I don't want to wear it
        riding big water. If it came off,
                I'd lose it forever. I hide the bikini

beneath jeans and a sweatshirt,
        French braid my hair. Grab my
                board, hoping it's long enough.

I've never attempted swells
        much bigger than six feet.
                These could easily be twice that.

Excitement and fear collide
        in a heady torrent of blood
                through my veins. For about

a half second, I consider
        a Xanax. Toss the notion
                aside. This particular variety

of anxiousness is righteous.
        I want to stay sharp, not feel
                all blurred around the edges.

I walk by my laptop, where
        a beaming bride poses midst
                a vineyard. Hit *Hibernate*.

THE WOODIE IS TOTALLY COOL

Cooler than the BMW. It's cherry
red, with big polished wood panels
in back. Super clean. Super Jonah.
"I didn't know cars like this really
existed. It's so . . . Beach Boys."

> Jonah slides my board up on
> the roof rack, secures it carefully.
> *You know the Beach Boys?*

"Well, sure. Doesn't everyone?
They're quintessential California."

> *Yeah, like forty years ago.*
> *Don't tell me you've heard*
> *of Jan and Dean, too.*

I wink at him. "She's the little
old lady from Pasadena." It's a fair
imitation of the original.

> *You are just full of surprises.*
> He gives me a lightning-quick sideways
> hug, then opens the car door for me.

I can still feel the grip of his hand
on my shoulder as I squish into
the cushy leather seat. "They built 'em
for comfort back then, didn't they?"

> *That, they did. Make yourself*
> *at home.* He looks just like I pictured
> him as he motors us to Encinitas,
> except it's too cool to put down

the windows so his hair can blow
back. Still, he's so Jan and Dean.
I glance over the seat, where two
neoprene suits, one Jonah-size, one
smaller, look a lot like beheaded seals.

"So, do you keep an extra wetsuit
around, just in case some girl
wants to go winter riding with you?"
It's a flip throwaway question, so
I don't expect the serious answer.

> *You're the first girl I've gone*
> *surfing with since my wife left.*
> *It was hers. Hope you don't mind.*

"Uh, no. Not at all." I forgot he had
a wife once. He mentioned her
wanderlust in passing that time.
"How long were you married?"

> *Five years. Well, officially five.*
> *Velia split after three and a half.*
> *Met a guy she liked better. An Aussie.*
> *Last I heard, they'd moved Down Under.*

When I tell him I'm sorry, he shrugs.
Don't be. She and I were worse
than oil and water. We were more
like kerosene and flame. Volatile.
Definitely not meant to be together.

RELATIONSHIPS

Are just weird. You think
you belong together. Find
out you don't. Some people
stay. Smart people go. Except
sometimes you can't. You have
kids together or your bank
account is empty or there are
special circumstances like your
husband being a burn victim.

Or, like my parents, you're just
too damn stubborn to admit you
made a major mistake. How many
people meet, hook up, commit,
and find themselves glad they did
after a decade or two together?

I muse out loud, "Do you think
it's possible for two people to
stay in love forever? Or at least
to stay content together forever?"

> *Yes.* No hesitation at all. *I do.*
> *Too many people get together*
> *for the wrong reasons—sexual*
> *attraction. Or escape. If they can't*
> *find common interests, build*
> *a friendship, those relationships*
>
> *are probably doomed.* He turns
> onto a long boulevard. *Too bad*
> *it doesn't work the other way*
> *more often. When love evolves*
> *from friendship, it must be stronger.*

SWAMI'S

Is an elongated stretch of beautiful
beach. I can see why it's so popular.

Especially today, with big, rolling breaks.
Probably ten- or eleven-foot swells.

As Jonah gathers the gear, I watch
a couple of rides. Again, that blend

of fear and anticipation quickens
my heartbeat. The slight trepidation

      I feel must be obvious somehow
      because Jonah asks, *Nervous?*

"A little," I admit. "They're a bit bigger
than what I'm used to. Any tips?"

      First of all, a bit of fear is good.
      It keeps you thinking. Be patient.

      Don't take the first wave in the set.
      If you're not sure, watch me or one

      of the others to know when to go.
      Then paddle in hard. Harder than

      you might normally. Use the power
      of the wave to your advantage.

      Once you've done one or two, you'll
      be fine. And remember, this is fun.

ALL SQUEEZED

Into Velia's wetsuit, I follow Jonah
to the water's edge. Stand for a minute,
watching the surf, and the two dozen
or so guys and exactly three girls
working it already. They're good,
but I don't think they're better than
I am, so when Jonah asks if I'm ready,

I flip my head in answer. The initial
splash into the winter Pacific takes
my breath. But almost immediately,
the neoprene goes to work. I'm warm.
I paddle out after Jonah, admiring
his contours. We push hard over the breaks,
finally reach the semistill water beyond.

> Be smart, be safe, and if those two
> things fail, I've got your back, says
> Jonah. We watch a couple of sets.

Finally, I give him a nod meaning
I understand the water's rhythm.
The perfect wave starts to roll in front
of me. I don't look right nor left, but
rely on my instinct and paddle hard.
Harder than I've ever paddled before.

Instinct yells, "Stand up." Next thing
I know, I'm on my feet and a powerful
force is pushing me forward and it curls
behind me in excellent fashion. I don't
panic or fall. I just ride. And it is the best
thing I've ever done. At least, for myself.

AS THE TIME APPROACHED

For Cole's last homecoming, I was equal
parts relieved and worried-as-hell. His
e-mails were coherent. Outlined, maybe.
Plotted to sound as reasonable as I hoped

they would be. Had I only heard from him
via the web, I would probably have felt fine.
But his infrequent calls were vaguely disturbing.
Not so much because of what he said.

Because of how he didn't say much
of anything. "Are you feeling okay?"
I always asked. "Headaches gone?"

> *Mostly,* he always answered. *Except
> when they're not. Sometimes they're
> regular motherfuckers.* He was manning

up, I thought. But I wanted the truth,
not that I knew how to pry it from him.
I checked out his Facebook page
more regularly than at any other time

in our relationship. His posts remained
few and spare. From time to time, I saw
replies from his mother. From Spence.
Other grunts he knew, or didn't. A school

> buddy or two. But from Lara, just that
> one post for weeks and weeks. And then
> came a second. YOUR MOM TOLD ME YOU
> WERE INJURED. PROMISE ME YOU'RE OKAY.

Cole's response was nothing more
than congenial. *AH, YOU KNOW MOM.*
SHE WORRIES WHEN I GET A BLISTER.
I'M ONE HUNDRED PERCENT EXCEPTIONAL
BUT YOU KNOW THAT ALREADY, RIGHT?

Nothing in the exchange sounded
like anything but a concerned ex-girlfriend,
stress on the "ex," asking about Cole's
welfare. His reply was rather ambiguous.

A little flirty but with no overt hints
of romantic entanglement. My jealous
reaction to their ongoing communication
was totally unreasonable. Probably.

And my anger at Rochelle was completely
off the charts. Why were she and Lara
in such obvious touch? Rochelle knew
about me. Had welcomed me into her home,
let me stand next to her son as witness

to her vows with Dale. Did she prefer
Lara? Maybe even want Cole to break
up with me so he could get back with his
ex? I thought about the letter stash, especially
the most recent one, which had to have

been mailed in care of Rochelle, and
suddenly I felt like a fool, caught up in
some soap opera conspiracy. Since
Rochelle and Lara were on speaking
terms, had they spoken about me at all?

IT WAS A WOUND

Left to fester. Truthfully, I might have
said something except just about
the time Cole touched down in Kaneohe
Bay, we got the news about Dale.
Those bouts of indigestion and heartburn?
Well, everybody got those, right? And

what was a little nausea but a bad case
of the flu? Okay, several bad cases.
Bloating. Middle-aged spread, and maybe
he should eat a little more fiber. But then
the blood in his stools became regular.
It was probably just an ulcer. His dad

got ulcers. Cured them with cream.
But even drinking all that cream
didn't help the burn or keep the weight
from dropping off. Finally, Rochelle insisted
he go see the doctor. And by then it
was much too late. When Cole took

his leave, we went back to Wyoming
together. The cheerful ranch house
was shrouded with sadness. Cancer.
It struck viciously. Without regard
for the life it had already made ragged
once. Rochelle had lost her daughter

to it, and now she would lose her husband.
Oh, they would try radical treatment,
but Dale should have gone in sooner.
He already looked wraithlike—ghostly
white and skeleton thin. I barely recognized
him. And I didn't know what to say.

WHAT DO YOU SAY

To a man you've met only once—
one you like, but don't really know—
when it's obvious his time is short?

What do you say to his wife, your
boyfriend's mother, who might be
subtly interfering with the relationship

you're trying to build, when worrying
about that seems trite and petty, in
the shadow of her tomorrow? What

do you say to your boyfriend, who
is struggling to shore up his mother,
when it's clear she's crumbling, but

determined not to show it because
that would mean she's acquiesced
to the will of fate—not God's will, no,

because the God of love could not
be so capricious or cruel? There was
nothing to say. So I kept mostly quiet

for the best part of three days. I held
Cole when it seemed he wanted me
to. Gave him space when he required

that instead. It was boring, and the silence,
oppressing. Maybe that's why when
things finally blew, they blew wide.

THE ROTTING LESION

Turned gangrenous with a chiming
of the telephone. Rochelle and Dale

had gone to church. Cole was outside,
tossing hay to the livestock, when the call

came. It wasn't my phone. Not sure why
I answered it. Maybe I was starving for

two sentences of conversation, but I did
pick up, and a woman on the other end

      inquired, *Is Rochelle there?* When I told
      her no, she said, *Will you please tell her*

      that Lara called? It's not important. Just
      wanted to ask how Dale is doing. She must

      have thought about who had answered.
      Uh . . . may I ask who this is? A big part

of me wanted to tell her to mind her own
damn business, but then I realized it was

a golden moment. "This is Ashley. Cole's
girlfriend." I waited for that to sink in,

      wondering if she'd be gracious or bitchy.
      Neither, actually. *Oh. Well, is Cole there?*

It was a non-reaction, and I couldn't
gauge its meaning, but the wound

threatened to bleed. I started
to say no, but just then I heard

the front door close as Cole returned
from the barn. "Just a minute. Cole!"

I called, and when he came looking,
I mouthed, "Lara," and handed him the phone.

His face flushed, and as he talked
into the mouthpiece, closing the distance

between Lara and him with words,
his eyes closed and his hand lifted against

his temple, as if his head had begun
to throb. He told her about Dale's condition,

> and said his mom wasn't taking it well.
> *Please do*, he said at one point. *I know*
>
> *she'd like that.* As Lara talked into his
> ear, I felt like gum stuck on his shoe.
>
> Finally, he finished the conversation
> with a not unexpected, *You, too.* Which,

no, didn't have to mean, "I love you,
too." But that's sure what it seemed

like to me. By the time he hung up,
my own head was pounding blood.

THE PRESSURE

Inside me was intense, and even though
I knew it was the wrong time, wrong
place, I opened the release valve wide.
"How would you feel if I kept an old
boyfriend holding on? How can you tell me

you love me, then keep in touch with her?
Up until this minute, she still didn't know
about me, did she? What the fuck, Cole?
How can you do this to me? How can . . . ?"

> *Stop it!* His hands cinched my shoulders.
> Squeezed. *I'm sick of you bitching*
> *about Lara. Goddamn it, just shut the fuck*
> *up about her, hear? I don't keep in touch . . .*

"Liar!" I shouted. "You do. I've seen
her posts on your Facebook page.
What do you think I am, stupid?"

> He squeezed even harder, started
> to shake me. My head snapped back
> and forth. *Don't you ever call me a liar.*
> Fury shaded his golden eyes red.

"Cole, stop. You're hurting me."
Tears spilled down my face. "Please."
Some piece of Cole snapped back
into the proper place. He let go.

> *Oh, Jesus, Ash, I'm so sorry. I . . .*
> He stepped back and I did, too.
> The space between us was a billion
> times wider than those inches.

I STUMBLED TO COLE'S ROOM

On legs as unsteady as a newborn
        foal's. I thought they might buckle,

so I sat in the rocking chair by
        the window, staring at the Wyoming

terrain. Sparse. Ice choked. Alien.
        That place didn't belong to me, nor

I to it. It could have easily been
        another planet. As the froth of fear

and anger inside began to dissipate,
        for some reason I thought about Cole,

forced into alien environments,
        and charged with taming them, all

the while knowing that, despite
        every effort, they would likely return

to wilderness once left to go fallow.
        His call to duty was greater than mine

could ever be. I understood that
        before, trusted his motives implicitly.

How could I let this phantom girl—
        a whisper of his past—quake my faith?

THEN HE CAME TO ME

Knelt in front of me, laid his head
in my lap, wrapped his arms
around my hips. I stroked his hair
and at practically the exact same

instant, we both said, "I'm sorry."   *I'm sorry.*

He looked up at me, and there
was nothing in his topaz eyes
but apology, and a question.
My favorite question. I didn't

have to speak my answer.

> He stood, pulled me to my feet,
> led me to his bed. *Wait. Let me*
> *lock the door. They'll be home*
> *soon.* When he turned back to

me, I had taken off my sweater,

> thrown it to the rocking chair. He
> whistled. *Jesus. What did I do?*
> He traced the bruises, patterned
> exactly in the shape of his fingers,

and turning the gunmetal gray

of night, lifting over the ocean.
"It's okay," I promised. And only
a tiny disbelieving sliver of me
kept whispering that it wasn't.

THERE WAS SOMETHING FRANTIC

About the way he made love
to me then. It had nothing to do
with hurrying to finish before

his mom got home. It was more
like he thought I might change
my mind midstroke, decide to leave

forever. He pinned my wrists over
my head. His mouth roamed my body
freely, and every time his tongue

made me squirm, he gripped harder.
His kisses were laced with lust. Only
later did I question the stimulus of

his passion. I don't know if I'll ever
trust him completely, but I did in that
moment. I had to. He was taking me

places I'd rarely been before, even
with him. He plunged his face between
my legs, driving into me with tongue

    and teeth and fingers until I begged
    him to stop. *No.* It was a growl.
    Give me your cream. I had no choice,

he made me come, but then I pleaded
for, "More. Fuck me." I'd never said
those words before. Not to Cole.

Not to anyone. He hesitated, and I
worried I'd made him angry or turned
him off. Not even close. He smiled.

> *Say it again. Louder.* I did, and when
> I did, in a single strong move, he slid
> one arm under me, flipped me over

onto my stomach, tugged me to
the foot of the bed. He stood there,
just looking at me, for what seemed

like a very long time. Suddenly,
he was inside of me, driving into me
with animal ferocity. Wilderness,

personified. There was lust there,
yes. And more—the fear of a soldier,
flushing an enemy he cannot see.

The anger of a man who has watched
his buddy blown to bits. The tension
of a sniper, waiting endlessly for

an uncertain outcome. The brittleness
of a boy, trapped in a man's uniform.
In one gigantic shudder, it was all

released, right there in me. We crept
up onto the pillows, covered our nakedness
with quilts. And, snug in each other,

we escaped into the haven of dreams.

HAVEN

So much I want to say,
wish I could confess,
but silence swells,

            black

as midsummer
clouds, stacked upon hills
between us. Black as the

            demons

shrieking inside my head.
My heart rumbles, heavy
with snippets of memory
that must not be

            conjured.

Alone in this untamed
empty place, I free
a relentless volley
of words. They

            rage

against the pages, a torrent
of what was, what is,
what yet may come.
And when at last the spirits

            recede,

I find echoed
in their retreat, stories
I dare not give voice to—

            nightmares set adrift

in my paper harbor.

Cole Gleason

SOME THINGS YOU DO

Whether or not you want to. Especially
when a friend is involved. Case in point.
Darian promised to go to Lodi with me
over the holiday break. We're supposed
to check out wineries, even though she still

insists I'm crazy to even consider getting
married to Cole. Not only that, but she
agreed to be my matron of honor, even
though she said the word "matron"
makes her sound like a prison warden.

> We discussed colors. I was thinking
> sort of pale green, maybe with lavender
> accents. *Oh, no. Check out the purple*
> *dresses on this website. Dark is in*
> *this year. And purple is memorable.*

I have to admit, she was right. So, I'm
thinking purple, with turquoise accents,
to go with Cole's dress blues. We've still
got time to decide, though. Darian's got
lots of great ideas. I told her she should

> consider becoming a wedding planner.
> *I'm definitely better at making plans*
> *for other people,* she said. *Every time*
> *I try to plan for myself, something*
> *always fucks up forward motion.*

SEEMS TO BE THE CASE

For my forever friend. That makes
me sad. Sometimes it's all her doing.

Sometimes it's just the fickleness
of the gods or whatever. And I suppose

at times everyone feels the same way.
But without a friend to prop you up,

see you through the tough periods,
it could start to feel overwhelming.

So, because we're best friends, and
since turnabout is fair play, I'll support

Dar's decision to stay with Spencer,
at least until he's able to care for himself,

or agrees to move home. When his mom
brought it up, he was as resistant as Darian

> to the idea. *Oh, hell, no. Go back home*
> *so Mommy can feed me and change*
>
> *my diapers? Not on a dead damn bet.*
> *I'll do this all on my own if I have to.*

It was about then we all figured Spence
will recover. It's been a slow, painful process.

But he is progressing. He's scheduled
for an artificial skin graft right after

the first of the year. Artificial, because
he doesn't have enough undamaged

skin to serve as his own donor. And as
organs go, I've learned, skin is among

the pickiest, almost always rejecting
donations from other people or animals.

Spence's face, neck, shoulders, and arms
were burned the worst. Somehow,

his hands mostly escaped. The doctors
believe he tucked them under himself,

protecting them instinctively. Beyond
the burns, there is some impact nerve

damage to his spine. They're not sure if
he'll walk again. But, supine or straight

up and down, the part of Spencer that
makes him uniquely Spence is alive

and kicking inside him. That gives
everyone hope that he'll find his way

back onto his feet. Yes, no, or maybe,
he's going to need all the help he can

get, both medically and emotionally.
I really hope Darian is up to the task.

EITHER WAY

She and I are going out tonight
for a belated birthday celebration.
I'm officially twenty-five. (Is that all?)
Dinner. Drinks. And slam poetry.
She was a little resistant to the last,
but hey, it's my party and I'll do what

I want to. Argh! More sixties-era
lyrics. I pull into Dar's driveway
a little before six. When I ring the bell,
she yells for me to come inside, make
myself at home while she finishes
her makeup. The TV is on, so I sit

and wait for a commercial to finish
and the local news to fire up,
They flash a picture for the lead story,
and my stomach drops. I know this
woman. I haven't seen her in well
over a year. She's thinner. Rougher

      around the edges. But it's definitely
      Soleil's mother. *New developments*
      in the drive-by shooting that claimed
      two victims in Santee on Tuesday,
      says the announcer. *10News has learned*
      that twenty-two-year-old Chandra Baird,

      who resides in the bullet-strafed house,
      allegedly has ties to a Mexican drug cartel.
      A large quantity of methamphetamine
      was recovered. Baird's boyfriend, Max Lemoore,
      was killed in the incident. Her four-year-old
      daughter remains in guarded condition. . . .

NO!

The blood drains from my face. I feel it
turn white and cold. "No-o-o-o." It escapes
my mouth in a single protracted whimper.
The next is a shout. "Why, goddamn it?

How could they let her go back?" Didn't
anyone notice? Did they even bother
to look? Isn't that what Child Protective
Services is supposed to do? What the hell?

> Darian materializes suddenly. *Ash?*
> *What's wrong? Hey, are you all right?*
> *You look like you just saw a spook.*

"Can I have a drink?" I don't wait
for an answer. Tequila. And a lot of it.
I pour a fat glass for me. "Want one?'

> *Not until you tell me what in God's*
> *name the matter is.* She watches
> me down a long, slow swallow.

"Did you hear about a drive-by in
Santee? The little girl who was shot
went to the preschool for a while. I
noticed some problems and called CPS.

What good did it do, Dar? What good
did I do? What's the point of a so-called
safety net if it can't catch kids who are
are obviously falling?" I think about

how long it took to convince Soleil
to let me push her on the swings.

The trust she finally gifted me with.
The trust her own mother shattered.
"I knew, goddamn it. I knew she was using.
Now they're saying it was drug related."

> Darian puts her hand on my arm,
> which is shaking enough to make
> the drink look dangerous. *It's not
> your fault. You did all you could.*
>
> *I'm sorry it wasn't enough. So much
> of the system is broken. They want
> to keep families together. Sometimes
> it works. But when it doesn't, you can't*
>
> *always fix the outcome. It sucks,
> but you'd better get used to it. You're
> going to see it a lot as a social worker.*

I set my drink on the counter.
"Maybe, maybe not. I'm not sure
I could handle stuff like this all the time."

> *So, do something else. It's not too
> late to change your mind. Look.
> I'm going to finish getting ready.
> Then we're having some fun, okay?
> Don't forget you're driving, though.*

She eyes my drink and goes to put on
her shoes. I reach for something
close to belief, toss a prayer toward
heaven. I couldn't save her. Will He?

I TRY TO PUT AWAY

All thoughts of Soleil,
but I keep picturing

> her spindly legs
> pumping air beneath
> the swing. Kicking.

I sip my tequila, relish
the slow warm trickle
down my throat. See

> her thin lips, coaxed
> into a small gap-toothed
> smile. Fleeting.

One more small taste,
wishing the slender
buzz could make me
forget about

> her purpling back,
> the way she reached
> deep for courage, showed
> me the corded welts. Lifting.

I close my eyes, but
the darkness behind
the lids can't obscure
the nightmarish pictures
forming in my mind of

> her, beaten, bruised,
> and crying out for help
> she could never find.
> Of her, lying still and
> quiet in a rivulet of blood.

THE DISEMBODIED VOICE

Of another newscaster pulls me
from my self-absorbed reverie.
He's . . . on the TV. Darian's TV.
And he's saying something about

> *A strong unexpected Taliban*
> *offensive in the Helmand*
> *Province of Afghanistan.*

Not that. Not more. Turn it off.
Hurry. I try not to listen, but I
can't help but hear

> *. . . numerous casualties among*
> *the civilian population, as well*
> *as coalition forces . . .*

A flick of the remote. Blessed
silence. I can't watch the news.
Too much information bloats
the omnipresent fear, floating

like high, thin clouds on the far
horizon. Better not to wonder
or suspect. Better simply to know,
even if that knowledge brings pain.

> Finally, Darian sweeps back
> into the room. *Okay. Let's go.*
> *You're still good to drive, right?*

"If I'm not, you still remember
how, right? Anyway, when did you
become an adult?" Necessary banter.

BANTER AS DISTRACTION

Works well, as does an evening
out, away from the confinement
of home, where I know I'd do nothing
but stress over bad things beyond
my control. It's good, being with

Darian, who has somehow found
her way back into her comfort zone.
Since it's my birthday dinner,
I get to choose the restaurant, and
settle on a favorite Mexican place

> on the beach. *Glad you went cheap,*
> *since I'm buying,* says Dar. *Happy*
> *birthday. Oh, keep it around five*
> *bucks, okay?* I think she's kidding
> but I'm not sure until she laughs.

It's the high, pure Darian laugh
I know and really appreciate tonight,
because it's been a while since
I've heard it. She orders drinks—
margaritas on the rocks, with pricey

tequila that flashes me back to
Jaden, but only momentarily.
At least it's a pleasant snapshot.
We decide to share a huge platter
of sizzling fajitas, *con guacamole*

y salsa verde, and as we wait for
the food, I consider asking for details
about her and Kenny. Decide not to
risk it. I don't want to spoil the mood.

I AM, IN FACT

A little surprised when Dar brings
up the subject herself. Sort of, anyway.
We've been talking about the wedding,
and maybe going shopping for a dress.

> *If you want something kind of unique,*
> *I know a great, little boutique with*
> *decent prices,* she says. *Sabrina and I*
> *picked out her prom formal there.*

"Sabrina is Kenny's daughter,
right?" She nods, opening the door.
"So, what's going on with you two?
You're not still moving in together."

> The last sentence was a statement.
> That decision had been made.
> *No. But he did still buy the house*
> *at Hermosa Beach. I'm glad.*

> *I loved that little place.* Her voice
> is sad, and now I'm sorry the subject
> came up. *I keep telling myself things*
> *happen for a reason. I'll always love*

> *Kenny. No man has ever been that*
> *good to me. But I still love Spence,*
> *too, despite the water stagnating*
> *under our bridge. And right now,*

> *he needs me. Funny, but when you*
> *mentioned I became an adult, you were*
> *right. Don't know if that's good or bad.*
> *But it had to happen sooner or later.*

GROWN-UP OR NOT

I'm having a great time with Dar tonight,
despite brief flashes of Soleil's face
intruding now and then. We finish dinner,
take it relatively easy on the tequila,

and I feel totally capable of driving
the short distance to the coffee house
that's hosting the slam tonight.
It's not quite as crowded as the last

one, and much more informal.
A gig more for fun than a chance
at prizes. We arrive a little before eight,
when it's supposed to get underway,

 and are looking for a place to sit
 when I hear my name over my shoulder.
 Ashley. It's Jonah. *I'm glad you came*
 tonight. Darian and I both turn,

and Jonah kisses me on the cheek.
Darian shoots me a look meaning,
how about an introduction? "Oh.
Sorry. Darian, this is Jonah. Uh . . .

Mr. Clinger. My poetry teacher."
Awkward. But Darian smiles
and Jonah grins and I guess that

 means it's all good. *Great to meet*
 you, Darian. May I join you ladies?
 Poetry is better with excellent company.

Darian shrugs. *Okay by me. Ash?*
It's your party. She looks at Jonah,
and amends, *Her birthday party.*

"Belated birthday, actually. And
sure, please join us." I consider
playing coy, but I think at this point

confession is the better path.
"Jonah took me to my first slam."
That elicits a single eyebrow raise

>from Dar, and that might be as far
>as it goes, except Jonah adds, *I also*
>*watched her ride her first big waves.*

>*I don't know if she told you or not,*
>*but she was amazing. Twelve-foot*
>*breaks, and she totally rocked 'em.*

I can see Darian trying to process
all this, and am infinitely relieved
when the lights flash, signaling

the start of the slam. I'll have some
explaining to do later. But right now,
Darian is laughing at something

Jonah said—I seem to have missed
it—and all I want to do is immerse
myself for a little while in the energy

of my best friend and my . . . If I had
to label him, my best male friend.

I NEVER HASSLED COLE

About Lara again. It wasn't fear,
    although the way I covered the bruises

reminded me of how abused women
    have hidden secrets beneath fabric

ever since the invention of the loom.
    Before that, no one cared. Few enough

cared after. I was warier of Cole's
    moods. But I wasn't afraid. Not really.

No, the reason I quit worrying about
    Lara was because I had no choice.

As my mom had once counseled, I
    could either believe him or leave him.

I had invested too much time in us
    to throw it all away. I even stopped

combing posts on his Facebook
    page, decided it was best to accept

his word that she was only a whisper
    from his past, echoed. Echoed loudly.

I never expected to actually meet
    her. But as bad luck would have it, I did.

IT WAS A ROTTEN DAY

All the way around. Funerals
generally are, and Dale's was
a particularly sorrow-steeped affair.

He passed on Good Friday. Something
significant there, to someone of faith
anyway. Mine continued to waver.

God. Dude. Why did you bring
Dale and Rochelle together, only
to force them apart so quickly?

That's what I was thinking as I flew
to Denver. Cole, who was granted
emergency leave, joined me

there and, rather than puddle jump
into Cheyenne, we rented an SUV.
Spring had officially started more than

a month before, but Old Man Winter
was stubborn, if fickle. One day it was
sixty; the next topped out at forty.

> *That's life on the prairie*, said Cole.
> *Capricious, any time of the year.*

The funeral itself was at Rochelle's
church, officiated by Reverend Scott.
He was nowhere near as jolly as when

I met him the first time, at the Christmas
nuptials. In fact, he looked almost as sad
as Rochelle, though his sermon argued,

We must celebrate Dale's death
as a beginning. Like opening a new
journal with crisp, clean pages inside.

I sat next to Cole, who sat beside
his mom at the front of the church.
On her far side was Dale's brother,

Donald, and beyond him his wife,
Carlene, their four grown children
and a passel of grandkids. I'd been

introduced, but their names were
lost somewhere in the swirling sadness.
The pews filled in behind us—old

friends and rows of family members
I had yet to meet. And though Cole
knew most of them very well, he became

noticeably nervous, especially as
the noise of voices built. He cocked
himself sideways, and I could see

him throw several anxious glances
over his right shoulder. Always,
his face rotated past mine, which

seemed to ground him in the there
and then. So did familiar music.
Especially "Amazing Grace," which

allowed him to close his eyes,
comfort in what could be trusted.

THERE WERE NO TALIBAN

At the funeral. No insurgents,
sneaking through the sacristy
or hiding in the pews. Every single
person was a "honor the red, white,
and blue American," and as Anglo
as they came. Still, Cole teetered

on the edge of nerve-driven
claustrophobia. I'd never seen him
like that before and it was more than
a little disquieting. There was only
one bad guy—or girl, I guess—there,
though I didn't realize it until after

the benediction, when we finally
stood and walked to the rear
of the sanctuary to form a reception
line. Lara sat midrow, toward
the back. Cole spotted her right
away, and when his attention turned

toward her, she drew mine as well.
Her face was a little rounder than
in her Facebook photo. She'd put
on a few pounds. That satisfied
me immensely. I knew it was not
a good way to feel, so I did my best

to retract my claws. I looked her
straight in the eyes. Smiled. Her wistful
expression didn't change at all. Oh,
she was good. But I belonged to Cole.
And she was here all alone. Had
she believed Cole would be, too?

DECORUM

Is my middle name, at least in public
situations, sans alcohol and scaffolded
with Xanax. I could hear my mother

reminding me, "Always act like a lady
in front of closed doors. Never show
emotion if it means risking your power."

She had plenty of practice. I conjured
her face, steeled my own in the same way.
I was a lady. I only hoped that meant

something to the man I plastered myself
to. I couldn't hold his hand because we
were expected to shake hands with those

who came by, offering condolences.
Truthfully, I felt like an imposter. I liked
Dale just fine, but I didn't really know

him that well. Lara could have accused
me of stealing her commiseration, like
some petty pickpocket, pretending

> to be a lady. She didn't, though. In fact,
> she was gracious. She shook my hand
> gently. *So happy to finally meet you.*

> *Cole has told me so much about you.*
> Okay, she got me there. I couldn't really
> offer an honest reciprocal greeting.

So I relied on a detour. "You, too, Lara.
I feel like I know everything about you."

NO NEED TO ADMIT

I was a snoop. She moved down
the line, gave Cole a small kiss, mouth
on mouth. Which, oh yeah, bothered
me mightily. Not that I'd let it show.
And not that I'd bring it up to him later.

I was sleeping with him that night.
She'd be on her own in a lonely hotel
bed. Or back in Denver, if she decided
to drive that far after the burial and wake.
She attended both. Of course she did.

The cemetery was like something out
of a nightmare. Iced-over headstones.
Once-lush grass crunching beneath
our feet. It must have taken a bulldozer
to dig Dale's final resting place. Grave.

That's what it was. A three-by-eight-
by-four-foot-deep trench in the frozen
earth. It may sound strange, but it was
the first time I'd ever seen a casket
lowered. It was fascinating and awe-

inspiring, at the same time. I hoped
I'd never have to witness such a thing
again, knowing, of course, I would
some day. Cole's mom. Or my own.
That was the natural order of things.

> Reverend Scott seemed almost
> as uncomfortable as I was. He muttered
> some basic words, the usual . . . *ashes*
> *to ashes*, capped off with a simple, *Amen*.

I CARRIED THE VISION

Of that coffin all the way back out
to the ranch. It faded once I went
inside to help spread out all the
food on the tables. It seemed like
everyone brought something, most

of it sugary or otherwise carb laden.
As more and more people arrived,
cloying the rooms with body heat
and swelling noise, Cole began to
get anxious again. I fixed him a plate,

found him a beer. "Why don't you
eat outside? It's not so bad in the sun."
Besides, by then, Lara was perched
on a chair in the living room. I kept
looking at her few extra pounds

and this little voice inside my head
insisted I should skip eating, go
straight for the alcohol. Not brilliant.
Two drinks on an empty stomach
beelined to my brain. There's a paragraph

in the *Book of Drunk* that begins
when your head fuzzes over and
your tongue swells to twice its normal
size. The first sentence starts, "You really
don't want to say this, but . . ."

AND, YOU KNOW

Had she respected me, my space,
my relationship with her ex—who, by

the way, she dumped, not vice versa—
I might not have said a thing. Might

have listened to my mom and maintained
the loftier plane. Instead, after watching

Lara buddy up to Cole's mom, knowing
they maintained a relationship—one I had

yet to establish with Rochelle—I soft-core
freaked. I waited until Cole took his plate

outside and joined a few other men on
the porch. Until Rochelle's attention diverted

to a kid spill. Then I sidled over to Lara,
who was working on a plate of pasta—

Hamburger Helper, was my best guess.
"Can I ask you something?" I worked

really hard not to slur in the slightest.
Her mouth was full, so she nodded.

What I wanted to ask was why the hell
didn't she leave my boyfriend alone?

But caution kicked in. "How long did
you and Cole go out?" I waited for her

to swallow. She looked at me with
curious eyes. *Not quite two years.*

"He and I have been together more than
four—the hardest years of my life.

As I understand it, you broke up with
him because he joined the Marines."

          I wanted her acknowledgment.
          She gave it to me. *Pretty much, yes.*

"Well, I fell in love with him despite that.
I've stuck it out through three deployments.

I've stressed. Cried. Celebrated every
homecoming. Been destroyed when he

couldn't make it for some special occasion.
I've done all those things for Cole, and you

refused to . . ." Bolstered by what I'd already
said, emboldened by alcohol, still I calculated

my words carefully. "So why won't you
just go away? Leave him alone. Please."

She might have gotten angry. Maybe
it was the "please." Her shoulders dropped.

          It's hard to let go of love. I tried. But once
          the anger faded, the love was still there.

IT WAS THE ADMISSION

I'd been looking for. So why didn't I
feel righteously vindicated? I felt sorry
for her. Regardless, I wanted her out
of Cole's life. Not to mention my life.

"Cole's still a Marine. I support him
in that. You can't take it away from
him. And I don't believe you can
take him away from me, if that's what

you have in mind. I don't know if it is.
But you have no right to interfere
in our relationship." It was a strong
statement, and I thought it a good

place to truncate the conversation.
Rochelle had finished her cleanup
and focused her attention our way.
The smile I flashed her was more

triumphant than friendly. Not that
I knew for sure if I had triumphed.
But, at the very least, I had said
my peace. And all the suspicion

and resentment I'd been harboring
came pouring out. I turned my back
on Lara. Went to the food table.
Skipped the pasta. Gorged on salad.

LATER, AFTER

Most everyone had gone, Rochelle
sank into an overstuffed leather chair.
Dale's favorite, where she could

still smell him, she said. I could relate.
The weight of the occasion seemed
to settle down onto her shoulders.

She shrunk. And so did my ego.
I sat on the ottoman in front of her.
"Will you be okay out here alone?"

> Cole was worried about it, I knew.
> But Rochelle was adamant. *This*
> *is my home, even with Dale gone.*
>
> *Everything he loved is all right here.*
> *Horses. Cattle. Dogs. The land.*
> *I won't be alone. He won't go far.*
>
> *And he left me plenty to do, too.*
> *So, yes, I'll be okay. He made sure*
> *of that. But what about you?*

"Me?" I had no clue what she was
asking. "What do you mean?"

> She shrugged. *Lara told me what*
> *you said to her. Cole loves you.*
> *But love is like water. You have to*
>
> *let it run its natural course. Dam*
> *it up, you're asking for trouble. It's*
> *gonna go looking for a way to escape.*

WATER NEVER DISAPPEARS

It only reinvents itself,
liquid, solid

                        liquid

gas, liquid,
forever
in random echo.

Every drop
encapsulates
the beginning, its

                        undulating

glass a window,
opening
into Genesis.

Wake to platinum
beads of dew,
the very first
morning breaking

                        within

the clutch
of dawn
dampened grass,

consider
that we are essentially
water and wonder
how many eons
we squander, every

                        time

we allow
ourselves to cry.

Cole Gleason

FOR THE SECOND TIME

In a month, I find myself hitting
the highway to Lodi. Only this
time, I have Darian for company.
"You're sure Spencer's okay with this?"

> *Yeah. They're having a big to-do*
> *at the hospital. Pretty sure his*
> *physical therapist is dressing up*
> *as Santa. She won't need a pillow.*

The plan is for Dar to stay a couple
of days with me, while we scope
out the wine country. Then she'll
spend Christmas with her parents.

> *Mom says Dad cut a giant tree.*
> *Not sure why. Guess he's trying*
> *to make up for the last four years.*

"What does he have to make up for?
You're the one who stayed away."

> *I know. She actually sounds contrite.*
> *Since the accident, Dad has been so*
> *supportive. He even offered to let us*
> *move home when Spence is released.*

"Really? Are you thinking about it?"
I'd kind of hate for them to leave
San Diego. Then again, who knows
where I'll be living after the wedding?

I'm not sure. Coming home seems
like backward motion, you know?
Still, if we can find a good VA
hospital not too far away, we'd
probably have to consider it.

She goes on to outline courses
of treatment, physical therapy
requirements, etc. Poor Spence.
"How's he doing, attitude-wise?"

> *Depends on the day. It's like he built*
> *a big wall around himself. Sometimes*
> *you can't break through it at all.*
> *Other times you can peek through*
> *a crack and see the old Spencer inside.*

That brings up a lot of reminiscing.
Swallowed up by yesterday, the drive
passes quickly. Finally she asks if I've
heard from Cole. "Not lately. But I don't
expect to when he's outside the wire."

> *Don't you get sick of that? God,*
> *I couldn't stand not knowing.*
> *Even this is better, I think.*

"He promised he'd ask for stateside
deployment, or go into the reserves."

> She's quiet for a minute. Chewing
> on it. *You don't really believe that?*
> *This is Cole we're talking about.*

I'M ABOUT TO ASK

For an explanation, when the radio,
which has been playing country
since San Diego, launches news.

> *Twenty-two-year-old Chandra Baird*
> *was arraigned today, on a half-dozen*
> *charges, ranging from child endangerment*
> *to trafficking methamphetamine.*
>
> *Baird, who plead not guilty . . .* I don't
> want to listen to it all. But as I reach
> to turn down the volume, I do hear
> him say Soleil's condition has been

upgraded to critical. Hang in there,
Soleil. She's marginally improved.
Better than going the other direction.
"Thanks." I send it to the universe,

> mumbling the last word out loud.
> *You talking to me?* asks Dar, knowing,

I'm sure, that I'm going to say, "Nope."
But now I reconsider. "Well, yes.
Thanks for riding along. Thanks for
supporting me. Thanks for being you."

> *I think I'm blushing. You're welcome.*
> *But when did you get God again?*

Fair question. "I haven't exactly
acquired Him again. Just hedging
my bets, you know? I figure if
He's out there, I might as well be polite."

Darian laughs. *I don't suppose*
it could hurt. I've said a prayer
or two myself in the last few months.
If it worked for Spence . . .

"Like you said. Can't hurt. Poor
baby. Some people just shouldn't
have kids, you know what I mean?"
I turn the radio back up, encourage

Dar to sing along. Her voice is still
beautiful. "If you won't take up wedding
planning, I think you should try out
for *Idol,* or *The Voice,* or one of those

shows. Even if you didn't win, it would
give you great exposure. You could
make it in the business." I mean every
word, but she acts like I'm joking.

> *Oh, definitely. And you know where*
> *I'd get the leg up? Having a disabled*
> *husband. "Please let me win. I need*
> *to take care of my disfigured war vet."*

"Hey, whatever works. But just so
you know, you're talented enough
to do it all on your own." We fall into
idle conversation, and the day dissolves.

It's late afternoon when we pull into
my parent's driveway. It's choked
with cars, so I pull around, park on
the street. "Wow. Wonder what's up."

WHAT'S UP

Is a reception for Troy and Gretchen,
who chose a quickie wedding in front
of a justice of the peace. The cars
belong to Troy's friends, who are
here, I think, for the champagne
and nice, little canapés, care of

Mom's favorite delicatessen. I know
they came from there because
the longtime owners, the Ellisons,
are here, celebrating with
the small crowd. I recognize a few
who were just behind me in high

school. Most are complete strangers.
Whatever. A party's a party. Darian
and I mingle. I survey the house.
Nudge Dar. "Looks like my mom
is compensating for your dad going
overboard this year. We don't even

have a tree. Or mistletoe. Or stockings
hung by the chimney, with or without
care." The house is too obviously bare
of accoutrement, a rare occurrence
over the span of my lifetime. In fact,
it has never happened before. My mom

is the Martha Stewart of Christmas.
"I'd better go find her," I whisper
to Dar. "Something's up." I leave
Darian to her own devices. Which
only worries me a little. These young
inebriated men don't stand a chance.

I WEAVE, ROOM TO ROOM

Finally locate Mom, alone and sipping
tea, in the solarium. "There you are."

The low winter sun lights the window
behind her, painting her platinum hair

with a gentle glow, almost like a halo.
It softens her features and I can almost

see the girl she was in our family photo
albums. Oh my God. I can almost see me.

> *You made it. How was the drive?*
> Generic. She makes no move to get

up, so I go sit beside her. "The drive
was fine. Definitely more interesting

with Darian along. She's the life of any
party. And speaking of parties, what's up?

This party's out there. So, why are you
back here?" She sips her tea before

> answering. *It's still a party without
> me there. I just needed a little quiet.*

This is so unlike Mom, who is ever
the hostess. "You okay? Where's Dad?"

> She shrugs. *He's here somewhere,
> I guess. Didn't you see him?*

"No, but I didn't look very hard.
And I wanted to talk to you first.

So, talk to me. Something's wrong.
Tell me what it is. You're not . . . sick?"

> She smiles, but it's a smile defined
> by sadness. *No. Nothing like that.*
>
> *It's just . . . everything's changing.*
> *Oh, news flash. The school district's*
>
> *cutting jobs. Librarians are at the top*
> *of the list. I'm lucky, I suppose. They're*
>
> *only slicing mine back to part-time.*
> *I don't know what I'll do with myself.*
>
> *Find some insipid hobby? Volunteer?*
> She pauses. Thinks for a few seconds.
>
> *Once, I thought if we had the energy*
> *and resources, your father and I would*
>
> *travel together. But, unfortunately,*
> *your father prefers to travel "alone."*

The last word is weighted, leaving no
doubt what she means. "Why do you stay?"

> *Where would I go? This is my home.*
> *Anyway, you know me. Ms. Propriety.*

THAT'S MOM, ALL RIGHT

Always doing the right thing.
Except maybe not for her.
I hate that. Mostly because

she reminds me of me—
always trying to please others
first. It's an annoying habit.

One I'm struggling to break.
This probably isn't the right
time to bring this up, but I doubt

there is a perfect time. So, here
goes. The new me. Ashley, who
is not worried about pleasing

everyone else first. "So, Mom.
I've been thinking things over
and I'm seriously considering

changing my course of study."
I can't say Ms. Propriety looks
totally surprised. Still, she says,

> Now? But, Ashley, you're halfway
> there. Do you really think that's wise?

Unbidden, my fingers start tapping.
Tap-tap-tap-tap. Tap-tap-tap-tap.
"Maybe not. But I think it's necessary."

I OUTLINE MY REASONS

"I just don't believe I can spend my
life failing the people who most need
help. There's too much at stake. I think
it takes a stronger person than me.

There are things I love about it.
Working at the VA Hospital, for one.
But I could still help out there, even
if it wasn't in an official capacity."

> Mom has listened without comment.
> Finally, she says, *But creative writing?*
> *What can you do with a master's*
> *except teach?* Immediately, she answers
>
> herself, *Which is what you always*
> *wanted to do, anyway. That was*
> *your plan, ever since you were little,*
> *wasn't it? To be totally honest*
>
> *here, your father is probably right*
> *about teaching. Too little pay, less*
> *respect, and that's only getting worse.*
> *I'm not sure how people expect*
>
> *their children to succeed without*
> *a good education. But that seems*
> *to be the tenor of our country right*
> *now. You need to understand that.*

"I know, Mom. I'm not worried
about the money, although I guess
I should be. It's more about making
a difference. If I can, that is."

I'm sure you could. You'd make
a great teacher, Ashley. As long
as you remember you'll probably
fail a few of your students, too.

I wish it were possible to save
them all. It's not. Some will fall
through the cracks, same as social
work. You'll see ugly things you might

not be able to change. But someone
needs to try. Your father, of course,
will be livid. But if this is really what
you want, I'll support your decision.

My fingers quiet. "Thanks, Mom."
I change the subject, before she can
reconsider. "Hey. What happened
to Christmas? Did the Grinch come by?"

Her smile is sad. I figured I should
get used to it. Both you and Troy
are starting new lives and will build
your own traditions. It doesn't make

sense to go crazy with decorating
if I'm going to spend the holidays
alone. The last word is worrisome.
Why would she spend them alone?

I WANT TO PROMISE

That would never happen,
        that Troy or I or both of us
                will always come home
                        for the holidays, with spouses

and maybe children, who
        knows? That Dad would
                never leave her solo on
                        Christmas, if for no other

reason than to show up
        at mass and let Father
                Frank see him there.
                        But I don't know for sure

if any of that is true. Cole
        might insist we spend
                Christmas in Wyoming.
                        And Troy could very well

be in Germany. Those two
        things could happen at
                the same time on any
                        given year. And as for Dad,

he's always been a wild
        card. Not to mention,
                a selfish bastard. Mom
                        deserves better. A lot better.

THE PARTY GOES

Until the champagne is gone.
Dad has been drinking right
along with the younger crowd,
getting sloppy and slurring and
outright flirting with a few of

the girls. They seem to find it
funny, maybe even flattering.
I think it's disgusting. No wonder
Mom wasn't anxious to join
the party. She finally emerges

from her sunroom asylum,
takes one look, and hustles
off to the kitchen, ostensibly
to refill the goody trays. She
doesn't reappear until Troy

and Gretchen see their guests
to the door. Ever the hostess,
after all. With the other girls
gone, Dad comes over, sits on
the recliner adjacent the sofa

> where Dar and I are talking.
> *Great party, huh?* he asks.

A jolt of anger zaps me. "Looked
like you were having fun. Poor
Mom got stuck with kitchen duty."

> *Right where she belongs. Right*
> *where all decent women belong.*

THE JOKE

If it was a joke, it was so not funny.
It was ignorant. I chalk it up to
booze. Dad sways slightly, and
his eyes have a hard time focusing.
This is not the time to discuss
anything of importance.

"It's been a really long day, Dad.
I'm going to bed. You coming,
Dar?" On the way to my room,
we pass Troy and Gretchen.
I hug my brother. "I'm so happy
for you guys. Sorry about Dad."

> He gives me a "so what's new?"
> shrug. Dar doesn't have to follow
> me. She knows the way to my room.
> *Wow. It hasn't changed at all.*
> *First thing my mom did was paint*
> *mine blue and make it the guest room.*

Mine is still lavender, with white
furniture, curtains, and throw
rugs over the hardwood floor.
The same framed prints of irises
and white roses hang on the walls.
"It's kind of like a shrine, isn't it?"

> Darian laughs. *I like it. Sort of*
> *comforting to know everything*
> *doesn't have to change. Hope*
> *the mattress is still comfortable.* We
> change into warm pajamas, fall
> into bed, and barely talk at all.

DAR MAKES UP

For the lack of conversation last
night as we tour the foothill wineries,
seeking the perfect combination
of amenities, availability, and price.

Darian knows all the right questions
to ask. Basic venue fees. Vendor
recommendations. Hours weddings
are allowed. Some places make you

wait until their tasting rooms are
closed, which can push a wedding
pretty late into the evening. It takes
all day. Some wineries are close

together. Others require a good deal
of driving time. And while we're on
the road, we talk. I mention I told
Mom about changing my major.

> *Good. I'm glad she's in your corner.*

About my dad, his inappropriate
behavior. What a jerk he can be.

> *Your poor mom. She's so complacent.*

Which leads to a discussion about
fidelity. If it's necessary. If it's possible.
If a marriage can survive without it.

> *It's possible. Look at your parents.*

"Thirty years. But was it worth it?"

WHICH SOMEHOW BRINGS US

Around to Jonah. Not sure why
it took her so long. I expected
her questions before today.

> *So, what's up between you*
> *and your cute poetry teacher?*

"Jonah?" Like there's another
one. "Nothing. What do you mean?"

> *First of all, you call him Jonah.*
> *Pretty friendly, if you ask me.*
> *Plus poetry slams. Surfing?*
> *Since when do you own a board?*

"Since you moved out and I quit
going to the gym. I decided I prefer
exercise that doesn't involve inhaling
other people's sweat stench."

> *Fair enough. But when did you*
> *start hanging out with Jonah?*

"We don't hang out. He asked me
to help judge a poetry competition.
Took me to dinner and a slam after.
We've only been surfing once. That's it."

> *Sounds like hanging out to me.*
> *Come on. What else? Any, you know?*

"Absolutely not! He's never even
tried to kiss me. Let alone, you know."

Okay, fine. But, just in case you don't
know, and I'm not sure how you
couldn't, he'd "you know" with you
in a hot damn second. I'd consider it.

"Hello, Darian? I'm getting married.
To Cole, remember? That's why
we're uh . . . here." We pull into
the final winery of the day—a huge

Spanish-style stucco affair on a hill
with a magnificent view. "Ooh. I like
this one, don't you?" She agrees,
and we go inside to do some talking.

Driving back to Lodi, we go over
copious notes. Discuss pros and cons
of the five possible venues. "Now
that we've narrowed it down, I'll see

if Mom wants to check them out
with me. She still isn't too excited
about the whole idea. But at least
she isn't trying to talk me out of it."

Darian reflects. Says softly, I wish
someone would have talked me out
of it. I love Spence. Then, and now. But
I don't love much about being married.

LATE CHRISTMAS EVE MORNING

I drop Dar at her parents' house.
Stay long enough to say hello
and walk with her out to the paddock
where her aging bay mare, Snaps,
is sniffing the ground, looking for

grass. Not much out there this time
of year. When she hears Dar's voice,
her head springs up and she whinnies
a greeting, comes over for a scratch
behind the ear. "At least she's the same."

> *Yeah, but getting up there. One day*
> *I'll come home and she'll be gone.*

"Way to mess up my high, Dar.
I was hoping to hold onto it a little
longer. Guess that means I might
as well head home. So looking
forward to mass this afternoon."

> *You used to be such a good, little*
> *Catholic. What happened?*

"My parental role models. All
that confessing going on
and not enough genuine apology.
I still like the incense, though."
We arrange for me to pick her up

> in a couple of days. *Say a Hail Mary*
> *for me. I could use some forgiveness.*

WHEN I WAS A KID

Christmas Eve mass was critical.
My obligation was fulfilled. I had
been forgiven. Baby Jesus was almost
born, and he was happy with me
(okay, slight logic lapse, but whatever),
and that meant Santa was definitely

on his way. That last part I deciphered
all by myself. We always had a nice
dinner out, so Mom wouldn't have
to cook or wash dishes. Enough of
that to come the next day. Then it
was overdosing on sappy holiday

flicks. My parents let Troy and me
stay up really late, hoping we'd sleep
in a little. As if. He and I were up
before dawn broke. We'd sneak into
the living room to count all the gifts
Santa had delivered overnight.

It was magical. Over the years, little
by little, the magic has faded away.
The only person up early today is me,
and only because my phone rings
a little after five a.m. It's five thirty
p.m. in Afghanistan. "Hey, baby."

> *Merry Christmas, lady. Sorry*
> *to get you up at the crack of dawn.*
> *Everyone wants the phone. I can't*
> *talk more than a second. But I want*
> *you to know I love you. Miss you.*
> *I'm in need of some serious Ash time.*

JUST LIKE SANTA

Up the chimney, he's gone.
I lie in bed, visions of Afghanistan
dancing in my head. I expect to find

an e-mail from Cole later, with a little
more information. Probably what
they're having for dinner. Some

prank some grunt pulled on another.
Possibly a hint of what he's been
doing during those long stretches

when I hear not a word from him.
The usual minutiae on this less-
than-ordinary day. That's what

it should be, anyway. I'll settle for
mellow. A little conversation would
be nice. Something to melt the silent

ice between Mom and Dad. Troy
and Gretchen and I have done our
best, but so far, no dice. I get out

of bed, snuggle into a robe. Maybe
Santa showed up last night after
all, with a tree and trimmings and

lots of presents. I extract the ones
I brought from my suitcase, tiptoe
down the hall to the living room.

See no sign that Santa was there.
I turn up the heat, root through
the entertainment center shelves,

locate a CD of Christmas music.
Old rock 'n' rollers, singing carols.
If no one else wants Christmas, I do.

It's only a little after six, but I put
on the music, turn it up loud enough
so I can hear it in the kitchen. Go

start coffee. Glance in the fridge.
Looks like prime rib for dinner.
Perfect. There are lots of apples

in the drawer. I'm thinking pie.
I start peeling and slicing and by
the time the rich, bitter scent of

> Sumatran perfumes the air, Mom
> comes padding into the room.
> *Merry Christmas, Ashley.* She hands

> me a small box, wrapped in gold
> foil. Inside it are two filigreed rings.
> *Mom and Dad's wedding rings.*

> *I thought you'd appreciate them*
> *the most. Hope Cole likes them.*
> Her long, deep hug makes me cry.

AFTER DALE'S FUNERAL

Cole flew back to San Diego with me.
The whole way, I wondered if his mom

had mentioned the thing with Lara,
but if she had, he didn't bring it up.

I decided confession was every bit
as useless as my confronting Lara

had been. Rochelle was right. Love
without trust is nothing more than

infatuation. Pointless, considering
the loosely woven fabric of my relationship

with Cole. It's impossible to weave
the threads tighter when you spend

so much time apart. We felt like gauze.
I had to have faith that the filaments

were strong. Easier, when you're
sitting close, holding hands, making

plans for a future together. Easier,
when you're laughing over a couple

of beers, fish and chips, and a shared
piece of chocolate decadence cake.

Much easier when, buzzed and needy,
you tumble into a familiar bed together.

WE SLEPT TOGETHER

At Rochelle's, but not comfortably.
It felt strange, sharing a bed there,
like maybe the walls possessed ears.
The sex was muted. Low-volume
fumbling. Satisfaction-free. At least,
for me. By the time we got back to

my apartment, I was starving for more.
And, doubtless because of my recent
run-in with Lara, I felt like I had something
to prove. To Cole. And to myself. I was sick
of playing passive. I wanted to try on
the power role, and so I didn't crawl

to one side of the bed and wait for Cole
to make love to me. I pushed him
backward into the bedroom. Dropped
to my knees in front of him, unbuckled
his belt, unzipped his jeans, slid them
off. Watched him stir, helped him grow

completely hard with my hands. Mouth.
I brought him right to the brink. Stopped.
Stood. Took off my own clothes. "Lie
down. And don't move." Oh yes, I liked
taking control. I kissed my way up on
top of him. Licked his face. His neck.

His chest. I straddled him, pushed
him in, rocking hard. Harder. Not enough,
with him still inside me, I turned around,
faced the other way, and that angle
created exquisite pressure. I made it
last as long as I could. We both howled.

SATIATED

I slept backed up into the curve
        of his body, luxuriating in his warmth,

the tautness of his muscles.
        He could, I thought, snap me in half.

Instead, his marble arms held
        me carefully. Gently. Like you hold

a baby. He fell asleep first.
        The rhythm of his breathing told

me his dreams were effortless,
        devoid of memory. He wandered

fantasy. I hoped to find him
        when I, too, slipped off the edge,

into the netherworld of sleep.
        Eventually, I dozed. But somewhere

in the watery depths of night,
        I was pulled from my own dreams

into Cole's arms. And when
        he made love to me, I couldn't fight

passivity. His turn to take control.
        But even in the power role, he confessed

his love for me, his soft repetition
        a lullaby carrying me back into sleep.

THE NEXT DAY

We woke to this incredible news,
announced the night before, while
we tangled ourselves together.

> *OSAMA BIN LADEN, THE MOST HUNTED*
> *MAN IN THE WORLD, HAS BEEN KILLED*
> *IN A FIREFIGHT WITH UNITED STATES*
> *FORCES IN PAKISTAN. BIN LADEN*
> *RESISTED AND WAS SHOT IN THE HEAD.*

I thought Cole would celebrate,
stand up and salute the Commander
in Chief, or at least his special forces
brethren. Instead, he was almost gloomy.

> *Fuck, and I had to miss all the fun?*
> *Goddamn Obama gives the mission*
> *to the fucking SEALS, after we laid*
> *all the groundwork? That's just not right.*

I knew better than to argue.
And then came details, some
of them pretty damn dirty.

> *IN THIRTY-EIGHT MINUTES, FIVE PEOPLE*
> *WERE KILLED—BIN LADEN AND SON,*
> *HIS COURIER, COURIER'S BROTHER*
> *AND COURIER'S BROTHER'S WIFE.*
> *ONLY ONE WAS ARMED, BUT THE OTHERS*
> *HAD GUNS NEARBY. ALSO IN THE HOUSE*

> *WERE SEVERAL OF BIN LADEN'S WIVES*
> *AND CHILDREN. HIS TWELVE-YEAR-OLD*
> *DAUGHTER WAS HIT IN THE FOOT WITH*
> *A PIECE OF FLYING DEBRIS. ALL CHILDREN*
> *AND WOMEN WERE HANDCUFFED AND*
> *REMOVED FORCIBLY FROM THE COMPOUND.*

COLE'S REACTION

To that was also unexpected.

> *They should have lined them all*
> *right up against a wall and strafed*
> *'em. Period. See y'all in hell.*

"You can't mean that, Cole."

> *Women, children, fucking Qaeda*
> *dogs, even. All they're going to do*
> *is breed more fucking terrorists.*

"You're telling me you could kill
kids just because they were al Qaeda?"

> *In a heartbeat. Those kids are all*
> *brainwashed. They'd kill you, too,*
> *and you can take that to the bank.*

I couldn't believe he felt that way.
A sudden chill ran through me.
I thought back to a day right after
we met. We were at the museum.

I remembered how Cole had watched
the children running in the hallways
with nothing but affection in his eyes.
His heart had been tender then.

I thought that would last forever.
But there was something new under
Cole's skin. Some dark vapor. War,
they say, leaves no soldier unchanged.
Could it shred every hint of compassion?

THE COLOR OF PASSION

Some say passion colors

up like autumn, maple
weaving dreams into crimson
veils, and shedding them one
by one in seductive dance,

to stand naked and frail
in the court of the woodland king.
Others see passion as brittle
winter silver, whispers

buried within a thick hush
of white, promises
held captive by bonds of prismatic light,

awaiting the lash's redemption.
You find passion
in springtime pastel,

a riotous fusion
of blossom and blade,
joining wet in placid rain, scenting
garden and glade with the pale

perfume of goddesses.
I think of passion as brown
summer skin, mine wrapped
in yours, on a beige strand of beach,
temperate souls, grown feverish
beneath cool amber pearls of moonlight.

Cole Gleason

JUMPING SHIP

Out of social work and into creative
writing is fairly straightforward. It's
too late to apply for the spring semester,

so I focus on next fall. I need to complete
the application, pull together transcripts,
writing samples, and three letters of

recommendation, all by February first.
Since I need good grades, I have
to either withdraw from my current classes

or work diligently enough to maintain
my GPA. I choose the latter course
of action. No use wasting the money

that's already been spent on my behalf.
And who knows? Maybe studying social
work will make my writing deeper.

> Dad about blew a gasket when I told
> him my plan. *Who needs an MFA*
> *in creative writing, for God's sake?*

> *Anyway, if you're getting married,*
> *graduate school is a waste of time.*
> *You don't even know where you'll*

> *be living next year. Why don't you*
> *just withdraw and think about*
> *playing house for a while?*

That pissed me off, but I managed
to stay calm. "Married or not, I want
to make my own way, Dad. Cole

will probably ask for assignment
at Pendleton, so SDSU will suit me
fine." I don't know if that's true, but

I hope we can work it out. I do not
want to live in Wyoming. Not enough
ocean. I am sticking to my grand plan,

    working on the application, when
    the phone rings. It's Darian. *Hey,
    Ash. I got some bad news today*

    and I thought you should know.
    Remember Celine? Her husband,
    Luke, was killed a couple of days

    ago. He was training ANA soldiers on
    the Pakistan border. Took a bullet.
    They're shipping him home next week.

"No." It's not enough. Denial
can't change it. But what else
is there to say? Jesus, it's so not fair.

I conjure a familiar image of a flag-
shrouded coffin, embracing some
anonymous soldier. Heartbreaking,

yes, but much, much more so when
the remains inside are recognized.

I NEVER MET LUKE

But I feel like I know him. Celine
was clear in her description of him.
I could have picked him out of a crowd.
And her love for him imbued her spirit.
It was like he was there with her.
Will that stay the same? Or has it died

with him? It's so close to home.
And yet, it could be closer. It could be
lounging on my doorstep, even now.
I wouldn't know until I tripped over
it. Would I break my neck? Could
I get over it? Will Celine? I realize

Darian is still on the line. "Sorry.
I'm just so damn sorry." Wait.
"Hey. How's Spence doing?" It's been
over a week since his skin-graft surgery.

> *Better than expected. I mean,*
> *he's still confined to bed and wrapped*
> *up pretty tightly. But his doctors*
> *are pleased with his progress. They gave*
> *him good pills, so he's not in much pain.*

"That's great to hear. Give him my love,
okay? Oh, and let me know when
you can get away for a few hours so
you can take me to that boutique.
I do want something unique. Maybe red.
That would go well with purple, right?"

THE JOKE

Falls flat on a field of sadness,
sinks into the well-cultivated soil.

Dar and I return to the minutiae
that swallows up so many days.

I check them off the calendar, one
after another. Amazing how fast

weeks can disappear into months,
into years. School. Fieldwork.

Spare hours at the VA Hospital.
Each day can only hold so much.

My MFA application goes in on time,
bolstered by recommendations from

one third-year and one senior-year
teacher plus, of course, Jonah.

His class is the brightest slot on
my schedule. I love learning poetry.

Love writing poetry. Love watching
Jonah teach poetry. I asked him to

help me choose the necessary writing
samples. He picked some favorites,

and some I had forgotten about, including
a couple I wrote about the VA hospital.

ROUGH DAY AT THE VA
by Ashley Patterson

Fog unfolds
across a sea cliff silhouette, thin
linen over a sandstone cadaver,
and I think of Harry.

I didn't know him, just a grizzled
face beneath a prim ball cap,
red, white and blue;
eyes like movie reels, rewinding
long term memory,
replaying jungle films,
one scene bleeding
into the next.

He was hardly noticeable,
in a far corner of the waiting
room, every chair filled.
On first glance, the men
were all the same.
Pepper-haired.
Ochre-fingered.
Ember-eyed.

But there were differences.
Cowboy boots. Nikes.
Bedroom slippers, one pair
complete with lions' heads.
Flashy team jackets.
Tattered flannel shirts.
Imperfect postures.
Limbs, lost to sacrifice.

It was an island of wait,
fogged by skin in want
of soap, breath forgetful
of mint, patchwork bodies
incapable of propriety.
Hours, plunged into magazines
with faded dates, TV sets
that talked in whispers.

Tests followed tests,
gastro-this, thyroid-that,
administered by personnel weary
of routine, impolite in response
to complaint, impatient
with pain not their own.

Brain scans.
Drug screens.
Pressure checks.
And in between nutrition
consultations and post-surgical
follow-ups, the intercom warned:
Code 99, waiting room.
The island emptied.

Fifteen minutes later,
the resuscitation team lifted
Harry onto a gurney, gentled
thin, white linen up over
the crumbled sandstone of his face.

THAT ONE

Jonah claimed, was what a poem
should be. Emotion, wrapped in
imagery. A complete story, in eight
perfect stanzas. To me, it was one

small truth I observed while trying
to help wounded warriors. Some people
who worked at the hospital were healers
of physical wounds. Others mitigated

broken psyches. We did our level
damndest. But there were so many!
Daily, it seemed, their numbers
multiplied. Depression. Post-traumatic

stress disorder. Garden-variety anxiety.
Thoughts of suicide. Alcoholism
and drug abuse. Domestic violence.
Brains, in need of long vacations.

Most were salvageable. Some would
need services the rest of their days.
A few would shun them, and wind up
on the streets. But they were alive.

It's been a couple of weeks since Luke
came home, in a box beneath a flag.
Celine must be drowning in a riptide
of shock and pain. Possibility

is a placid sea, easy to navigate until
roiled up by a random wind of fate.
If it were me, how long would it take
to surface and suck in air again?

I HAVE YET TO RECEIVE

The wedding guest list from Cole's mom.
I can't move forward without it, so I

give her another call. She picks up this
time. "Hi, Rochelle. I was wondering

about your guest list. I need it to book
the caterer. Oh, I chose the venue.

It's this beautiful winery . . ." I go on
to describe the place and she doesn't

utter a word until I say, "By the way,
my mom wondered if you'd like to stay

in our guest room, so you could save
a little money on a hotel room."

> *I'm confused. I thought you were*
> *getting married out here. That's*
>
> *what Cole told me. He said it would*
> *only be a few people so not to worry*
>
> *about a guest list, just go ahead and*
> *invite who I want. June thirtieth, right?*

"Wait. What? When did you talk to
Cole about it? Because, he and I never

decided to have the wedding in Wyoming.
We didn't even pick the date. Not together."

HOW COULD HE

Possibly think it was okay to choose
both date and location for our wedding?
Oh, and then not even bother to let
me know. That is seriously messed up.

> *I'm sorry, Ashley. I had no idea*
> *Cole had made this decision on*
> *his own. You discuss it with him,*
> *then let me know what you want to do.*

"Oh, I'll discuss it with him, okay."
I try not to sound as angry as I feel.
Not sure it's working, though.
This is unbelievable. I hang up

with Rochelle, shoot Cole an e-mail.
It definitely reflects how pissed I am
right now. YOUR MOM TELLS ME YOU'VE
MADE ALL THE PLANS FOR OUR WEDDING.

LAST TIME I LOOKED, THAT WAS UP TO
THE BRIDE. THAT WOULD BE ME, IN CASE
YOU DIDN'T REALIZE THAT. OR HAVE YOU
DECIDED ON A DIFFERENT BRIDE, TOO?

I have no idea where he is or what
he's up to. Can't guess when he might
get back to me. One thing I know
is I can't sit here and wait. Neither

do I want to spend this Sunday alone.
It's late morning. I call Darian, but
there's no answer. Probably still asleep.
Who sleeps in until eleven? Not Jonah,

I bet. Of course, what makes me
think he's alone, or that he'd
want to do something with me,
even if he is? Conceited, much?

Whatever. Nothing ventured, nothing
gained. I really like being with him.
I feel weird calling, so I text him
instead. That way, if he wants, he can

just ignore it and pretend he didn't
see it. SORRY TO BUG YOU ON SUNDAY.
DO YOU ROLLERBLADE? I'M THINKING
ABOUT GOING TO MISSION BEACH.

There's a great, touristy boardwalk
and plenty of paved skating. It's kind
of cool in early February, but it's clear
today, and sunny. That, in itself, should

cheer me up. I go get dressed and by
the time I'm ready, there is a return
text. *MEET YOU THERE OR PICK YOU UP?*
YOU CAN ALWAYS CALL IF IT'S EASIER.

I call and he comes to get me,
in the Beamer, which is plenty
big enough for a couple of pairs
of Rollerblades. Cole would never

blade with me, or surf, either. And
I bet Jonah would never go around
his fiancé, to his mother, to plan
his wedding, either. Wait. Rocky ground.

I REFUSE

To think about the wedding.
Refuse to talk about Cole.
But I should talk about something
or it will be a very quiet ride to
Mission Beach. Maybe a joke.

"So, were you just sitting by your
phone, waiting for me to text you?"

> *In fact . . . Okay, no, not exactly.*
> *Actually, I was going through*
> *some of the early submissions*
> *to our Poetry International Prize.*

"Sounds like a semi-serious way
to spend your Sunday. Sunshine
and exercise sounds better to me."

> *To me, too, obviously. Thanks*
> *for the invitation. Sometimes I*
> *totally forget about having fun.*
> *In fact, seems like all the fun I've*
> *had in a very long time is with you.*

I have to admit that's mostly true
for me, too. Don't dare say it, though.
"Can I ask you something personal?
Why don't you have a girlfriend?"

> *Gun shy, I guess. I've dated*
> *a few women since my wife left.*
> *They wanted to get serious right*
> *away and I wasn't ready for that.*

"So, I'm a safe date?" It's meant
to be funny, and he does laugh.

> But then he says, *I suppose you*
> *could look at it that way. But*
> *I also really enjoy your company.*
> *There's so much to like about you.*

I'm glad his eyes are on the road.
My face must be a fabulous shade
of raspberry. "Thank you, Jonah."
Time for a change of subject, I think.
"Tell me about the poetry prize."

> *You've never entered? You should.*
> *There's a thousand-dollar prize.*
> *Have you ever submitted to our lit*
> *mag?* He goes on to list submission

requirements, deadlines, and details.
By the time he's done, we're there.
We lace up our blades, head down
the bike path and, unlike surfing,

I can most definitely hold my own
with Jonah on Rollerblades. It's a great
workout and I'm so glad I came, and
doubly glad I asked Jonah to come along.

IT'S THREE DAYS

Before I hear from Cole. His e-mail is a gentle rebuke:

SORRY I COULDN'T GET BACK TO YOU
SOONER. IT'S BEEN CRAZY HERE,
WITH ALL THE PROTESTERS. ARE
YOU SEEING IT IN THE NEWS THERE?
KORAN BURNING ISN'T A BRILLIANT
IDEA. EVERYTHING WE'VE BUSTED
OUR BALLS TO BUILD IS CRUMBLING.
IT'S SCARY AS HELL AND I'M BETTING
A WEEK AFTER WE PULL OUT OF HERE
THE TALIBAN WILL OWN THE PLACE.

AS FOR THE WEDDING, GUESS I SHOULD
HAVE CLEARED IT WITH YOU FIRST.
BUT I FIGURED YOU'D BE OKAY WITH IT.
MOM STICKS CLOSE TO HOME. WE CAN
TAKE THE WEDDING TO HER, RIGHT?
MAKES THE MOST SENSE TO ME. OKAY,
NOW THAT'S SETTLED, IF YOU'RE GOING
TO SEND A CARE PACKAGE, DO IT SOON.
OH, AND WHAT'S UP WITH SPENCE?

He thinks things are settled? My reply is terse:

SPENCE IS BETTER. I HOPE IT'S OKAY
THAT I ASKED HIM TO BE AN USHER.
HE CAN'T TRAVEL TO WYOMING WHICH
SHOULDN'T BE A PROBLEM, SINCE I'M
PLANNING A CALIFORNIA WEDDING.
AT A WINERY. WITH FLOWERS AND
CAKE AND A WHOLE LOT OF GUESTS.
HOPE YOU CAN MAKE IT. I PUT YOUR
NAME ON THE INVITATIONS.

THAT'S BULL

I haven't actually ordered
the invitations. And now
I'm not sure if I should, or
even if I want to. How can
he flat dismiss me and what
I want in such a condescending
way? He's as bad as my dad.
Maybe even worse. We'll see,

when he gets my e-mail. Am
I ridiculous, expecting a big
wedding—my first and, with
luck, only wedding, the one
I've thought about practically
forever? Am I out of line, refusing
to do it his way, and "take it
to her"? Am I psycho, wondering

who is more important to Cole,
me or his mother? Am I selfish,
wanting it to be me? I know he's
got a lot on his mind. Bigger stuff
than guest lists, DJs, and floral
arrangements. Stuff like bullets
and bombs and body armor.
Unique boutique gowns are not

high on his priority ladder.
Maybe they shouldn't be on
mine, either. I really don't know
anymore. Am I just premenstrual?
Am I just being totally petty?

JANUARY 2012

Five years after Cole and I met,
we had come an incredible distance,
together and apart. We had transformed.

Morphed into different people, because
of each other and in spite of each other.
In almost every way, we had grown up.

My growth came from self-discovery.
Choosing one path, journeying awhile,
changing direction. I had learned much

along the way. The elation of first love.
The anguish of separation. The meaning
of sacrifice. Courage. Overwhelming fear.

Patience. Impatience. Wresting control.
Relinquishing control. I still wasn't always
certain when to wrest and when to relinquish,

but time is perhaps the best teacher.
I had withdrawn into self-inflicted solitary.
Clawed my way out. Retreated again.

I had pushed envelopes. Pushed buttons,
allowed mine to be pushed. Decided
I'd rather be the pusher than the pushee.

I had come to realize that life is fluid,
and while that can be a very scary thing,
riding the flow is better than trying to stop it.

COLE'S GROWTH

Had largely been imposed on him.
Yes, he had volunteered for the ride.
But how many young people truly

comprehend the face of war until
it's staring them down? You can't patrol
unfriendly villages without embracing

paranoia. You can't watch your battle
buddies blown to bits without jonesing
for revenge. You can't take a blow to

the helmet without learning to duck.
And you can't put people in your crosshairs,
celebrate dropping them to the ground,

without catching a little bloodlust. Paranoia.
Revenge. Bloodlust. These things turn
boys into men. But what kind of men?

I had experienced much in that five
years. But it was nothing, compared
to what Cole had witnessed. Suffered. Done.

Each returning soldier is an in-the-flesh
memoir of war. Their chapters might vary,
but similar imagery fills the pages, and

the theme of every book is the same—
profound change. The big question
became, could I live with that kind of change?

AS I WAS FILLING OUT

The application to segue out of social
work and into creative writing, Cole

was earning the respect of his fellow
grunts, and working toward the rank

of sergeant. Getting there involved
some incidents deemed necessary

by the NATO forces, and atrocities
by many Afghani people. Nighttime

raids netted insurgents, but also flushed
harmless villagers from their homes.

Many never returned. In an effort to thwart
IED planting, some soldiers fired into

vehicles at checkpoints. As often
as not, they found no IEDs. Intelligence,

perhaps faulty, perhaps not, resulted
in indiscriminate U.S. bombs killing

innocent civilians, including women
and children. To be fair, the Taliban

felt no compunction about using kids
to carry weapons, serve as screens

and even as suicide bombers. Children
as young as six were gathered and taken

to training camps where they learned
the fine points of sacrificing themselves

to Allah. When someone comes at you
with explosives obviously strapped around

their middles, you take them out, no matter
how young they are. Even if they remind

you of a kid you know back home. Maybe
even your own kid. Soldiering was ugly.

After all that, the Taliban wanted to come
to the table and talk. ANA and ANP troops

were defecting, or just plain scared of
what might happen once the coalition

forces deserted the country. Despite years
of training and working hand in hand

to guarantee they would be in control,
that outcome was anything but assured.

U.S. troops, including Cole, began to feel
frustrated. Unappreciated. Downright angry.

Paranoia, revenge, and bloodlust
were natural consequences of survival.

I WAS IN THE DARK

About most of that. Cole bottled
his feelings, kept them inside
where every event shook them
up like carbonated water. I only
knew when they finally blew.
He wasn't supposed to rant, but

now and then it happened. Better
to fire off a barrage of words than
a spray of bullets, like soldiers who
wandered all the way off the deep
end. Some waited until they got home
and memory or boredom riled

them up. Then they'd go looking
for action. Sometimes they took
it out on strangers—crowds at
political rallies or random homeless
guys on the street. Other times,
it came down on people they knew.

Maybe even loved. One woman at
the shelter was married to an Army
vet. It took more than two years for
his PTSD to kick all the way into gear.
He never scared me, she said. *But
one day, it was like the light went out*

*in his eyes. I swear I was looking
evil in the face. I thought he'd kill me.*
He claimed it was the heat that set
him off, taking him back to Fallujah.
I made a mental note to make sure
Cole and I always had air-conditioning.

TRIPLE DIGITS

Days, defined by axial lean,
stretched long and longer
toward

          the soft release of

summer night.
Awaken to the predawn
caress,

          cool silver light

wrapped around eastern
hills, a lover. Slow
rotation into mid-morning
cerulean, warm and

          flawless

as high Rockies hot
springs. Perpetual
revolution, the mercury
pushes past twin digit

          luxury

into the realm of risk.
Terrestrial self-defense,
June's mad celebration

          lifts,

wet, on sprays
of July heat, darkens
the sky, thunders,

          stuns the earth,

and for one black,
electric moment . . .

          Everything is still.

                  Cole Gleason

EARLY MAY

When I'm not studying for finals,
I'm working out the tiniest details
of my wedding. Eight weeks away.
And there's still so much to do.

Cole came around, not that I gave
him a choice. I refused to budge
on the location. I'd already given
them a deposit. "We can't afford

to lose a thousand dollars," was
my excuse. "And, anyway, your
mom said she's happy to fly out."
So that was mostly that. Darian

and I picked out an amazing dress.
It's knee length, strapless, ice blue.
I'm not such a formal girl after all.
And it was only four hundred dollars.

I decided to save as much as I could,
through simplicity. It's turned into
kind of a game, one I'm mostly winning.
Except when Cole goes all silent

on me. I try to ignore it when
it becomes obvious he's pissed
at something I've said or done.
I'm sort of getting used to it, though.

WHEN I TOLD HIM

About my plans for grad school
next year, he went completely mute

for quite a while. Like, a week.
Finally, he e-mailed back:

> *I THOUGHT WE DISCUSSED MOVING*
> *TO CHEYENNE. BUT I'VE BEEN THINKING,*
> *AND ANOTHER YEAR IN SAN DIEGO IS FINE.*
> *FOR ME TO QUALIFY FOR THE GI BILL, I NEED*
> *TO PUT IN SIX YEARS BEFORE MOVING INTO*
> *ACTIVE RESERVES. AS FOR CHANGING PATHS,*
> *WE ALL HAVE TO FOLLOW OUR HEARTS.*

It's good to know he's in my corner,
not that I expected anything else.

I asked about him requesting a transfer
to Camp Pendleton. I got this back:

> *ALREADY TAKEN CARE OF, AND I EXPECT*
> *APPROVAL. I'LL KNOW FOR SURE WHEN*
> *I GET BACK TO KANEOHE. NOT LONG NOW.*
> *I WANT WHAT'S BEST FOR YOU. FOR US.*

He'll be back in two weeks. By then,
I'll have finished up this semester.

Each year seems to rush by faster. I hope
next year tarries. I'm scared, in a way.

Half of me loves the idea of seeing Cole
every day. Sleeping with him every night.

The other half loves my freedom and
is afraid of losing me to his dreams.

FRIDAY EVENING

Postfinals, I go over to Darian
and Spence's to celebrate. It will
be the first time I've seen him
since before the accident. He's had
two skin grafts and is healing
"like a stubborn grunt," according

> to his nurses. It's been seven
> months. Still, Darian warned,
> *He's not beautiful. But he has*
> *come so far, mostly through sheer*
> *will. He's even using a walker*
> *to get around now. It's amazing.*

Amazing, and he's more than good
enough to stand up with Cole
as his best man. He even answers
the door. "Hey, soldier." I give
him a quick kiss on one cheek,
trying not to stare at what's left

of his ear. There isn't much.
His face has a strange texture,
too. But it's definitely Spencer
beneath it, reconstructed or not.
"God, it's so great to see you."
So great he's standing here in

> front of me. *Not as good as it*
> *is seeing you. Hey, Dar. We need*
> *more pretty girls around here.*
> *Can you work on that, please?*
> Yep, most definitely Spence.
> Some things are hard to change.

OVER LASAGNA

And beer, we talk about school. Poetry.
About surfing and nurses (hot and not)
and wedding plans. Just like old times.

Except someone's missing. "Too bad
Cole's not here. But he might be soon.
He asked for a transfer to San Diego."

> *I know,* says Spence. *No worries.*
> *He'll get in, no problem. Cole is*
> *everything MARSOC could ask for.*

"He put in for MARSOC? He didn't
tell me that." There is a Marine Special
Operations Command battalion

at Camp Pendleton. "But that's extra
training and more years of active duty,
right?" I already know the answer.

> *Well, yeah. But if anyone was ever*
> *cut out for special ops, it's Cole.*
> *What else is he going to do? Be a cop?*

The question is what else is he going
to do without consulting with me first?
Lasagna starts churning in my gut.

"I . . . just . . . he never said a word
about it." Not to me, only to Spence.
Why the hell does he think that's okay?

ANXIETY BUILDS STEADILY

The rest of the evening. I decide
to leave early. Don't need to freak
out in front of my friends. Darian
walks me to the door. "Sorry, but
I'm not sure I can deal with this
pharm-free." Xanax is calling to me.

> *What did you expect, Ashley?*
> *I told you there's no happily-*
> *ever-after married to a Marine.*

"But I love him, Dar." That, above
all, is true. "And after everything
we've been through, it has to work."

> *I'd take some time to seriously*
> *think it over. Think about what you*
> *want. Not about what he wants.*
> *Call me if you need to talk. I'm not*
> *going anywhere. Not for a long time.*

I drive home a little too quickly.
Rush inside, hurrying to e-mail him
and ask what the fuck he's doing.
But as I turn on my laptop, I reconsider.
Instead, go take a pill. With tequila.
Dar is right. I really need to get my head

on straight. It's feeling a little crooked
right now. I need order. I drink tequila.
Reorganize my kitchen drawers. Salad
forks. Dinner forks. Teaspoons. Soup
spoons. Perfectly stacked. Steak knives.
Boning knives. Butcher knives. Ordered.

SATURDAY MORNING

I wake up, slightly hung over.
My head aches, but at least it
doesn't feel crooked anymore.
I take an ibuprofen, drink a quart
of water. Glance at my computer,
still dark, on the table. I leave

it that way. Get dressed and head
to the beach. The last thing I'm
going to do is sit inside moping.
Or make wedding plans. It's gorgeous
outside, the kind of day late spring
gifts Southern California with.

I'm not alone here. Not nearly.
I skirt the ocean's edge, avoiding
children as best I can. They run in front
of me, into the water. Duck behind
me, toward their towels. No bombs
strapped to their middles. Lucky kids.

I keep walking, listening to laughter.
Yelling. The build-crash-lap of gentle
surf. Noises, lacking danger. I am
blessed. California is my home. And
this ocean is my heart. I can't give
this up for Wyoming. Was I naïve

to believe he'd give up Wyoming
for me? I picture his face. His grin.
His gold agate eyes, holding on to me
like treasure. I see him in camouflage.
In dress blues, surrounded by grapevines.
I hear him say, *I want what's best for us.*

I STAY OUT ALL DAY

Walk miles of beach, moving in and out
along with the tide. By the time evening
falls, my legs are sore. But my head

doesn't hurt, except from thinking
so much. I will sleep well tonight,
regardless. When I get home, I realize

I haven't eaten all day. I go straight
to the kitchen, don't find much except
eggs, cheese, and enough veggies to create

a semi-interesting omelet. I get busy on
that, pull out the skillet, and have just turned
on the heat when I get a call, not an e-mail,

> from Cole. *Hey, beautiful lady.*
> He's working it, and I can't say I hate
> that. *Just arrived back in Kaneohe.*

> *They brought me home a little early,*
> *to facilitate training. I'll be in San Diego*
> *soon. My transfer was approved.*

I turn off the burner. All of a sudden,
I've lost my appetite. "Oh. Good. Um . . ."
Just go ahead and say it. "I heard you put

in for MARSOC. Is that right?" My stomach
growls, but when I look at the beaten eggs,
it kind of turns. Tequila might be better.

*Yeah. About that, I didn't want to tell
you until I knew for sure I got the transfer.
I didn't want to get your hopes up.*

Hopes up? What? "Cole, a transfer here
is one thing. Special ops is something
else. You never even mentioned it to me.

You can't make a decision like that
without talking to me first. What's your
commitment, if you pass the screening?

Two years? Four?" I don't care about
the answer. That isn't the point. "I can't
do this much longer. That wasn't our deal."

*There's someone else, isn't there?
Where have you been? I've tried
calling all day. Is he there right now?*

What? How did we get from figurative war
widow status to screwing around?
"There isn't anyone else! Do you really

not understand what the last five years
have been like for me?" I'm glad he can't
see me break down. Especially when he

*says, What they've been like for you?
What about me, Ashley? I'm doing this
for you. For us, and our future family.*

DENSE

Is not a strong enough description.
Doesn't come within a klick of the distance
between us. Distance that has nothing
to do with miles. He sincerely believes
what he's saying. I know that. And I also

understand that what I've been through
because of loving him can't compare
to what he's experienced. But where
does sacrifice end? "Cole . . ." I let him
hear tears, inflecting my voice. "I love you

more than I ever thought was possible.
There is no one but you. I've spent
the last six months planning a wedding.
Our wedding, you know like in 'I take
thee forever.' But you and I have a problem.

We don't communicate like married
people need to. Grad school was a big
decision, one I definitely should have
asked your opinion about. But MARSOC?
That's huge." More like life changing.

Maybe game changing, too. "Look.
I don't think we can rationally discuss
this on the phone. I'm glad you made
it back safely, and that you got the transfer.
See you when you get here. Love you, Cole."

I HANG UP

Before he can argue or offer reasons
why special ops was his best path
going forward. I'm sure he has plenty
of them stashed inside his head.

I could deal with another year
of him on active duty. Maybe even two.
We're pulling troops out of Afghanistan.
But, according to news stories,

we'll be replacing regular combat
grunts with special operations forces.
The leaner, meaner units will target
insurgent leaders and encourage

their ANP brethren to do the same.
It's the warfare of the future. Along
with drones that do their dirty business,
piloted remotely by guys sitting in comfy

trailers in the Nevada desert, where
cameras can show them the damage,
but not the collateral carnage. I talked
to a couple of them at the VA hospital,

fighting PTSD. Sometimes they see
the results of their surgical strikes on
TV and it clicks. The video games they've
been playing? Those are real people

on the far end. Not aliens. Not zombies.
The Bible counsels an eye for an eye.
Wonder how many eyes Cole has plucked.
I'm sure his debt to his cousin has been paid.

ONE BIG QUESTION

Comes marching out of the cerebral
      prison I've confined it to. I've invested

five years in our relationship, and Cole
      has rewarded me with his amazing love.

If something were to happen to him
      now, would that half-decade have been

worth it? And if we get married, ride
      yet another wave of time together, only

for me to lose him to a bullet, would
      I celebrate those years, or curse them?

I need to talk to Celine. Almost four
      months since she buried Luke, the shine

must have worn off the pain by now.
      I give her a call, ask if I can interrupt

her Sunday for a short visit. She gives
      me directions to her house. On the way,

I stop off for flowers—a huge spring
      bouquet, yellow roses and orange daffodils.

I sent an arrangement to the funeral,
      but it likely got lost midst the dozens, most

of them red, white, and purple/blue.
      Thus the yellow and orange. No reminders.

EXCEPT THERE ARE REMINDERS

Of him everywhere. Small flags
decorate the white picket fence
protecting Celine's immaculate
front yard. They flap, red, white,
and blue, in the breeze. Inside,

framed photos of Luke hang
on the walls, and take up space
on end tables. Luke, in uniform.
Luke, holding his girls. Luke,
kissing Celine. Luke, Luke, Luke.

A shadow box holds the folded
flag that had draped his coffin.
That sits on the mantel of the little
stone fireplace that takes up most
of one wall of the living room.

I'm not sure I could look at Cole
like this. Not if he was never
coming back to me. I'm not sure
how to open the conversation.
Celine saves me the trouble.

> *Sit, please. Can I get you some*
> *coffee?* When I decline, she says,
> *Okay, so tell me. What's up?*
> *Still planning a June wedding?*

"That's just about all I've been
doing . . ." I give her a quick rundown
so we can push small talk to one side.
I finish with, "Cole's being transferred
to Pendleton. He wants MARSOC."

Ah. And that's counterintuitive
to planning for a future together.
I understand completely. Luke and I
had a similar discussion once.

"But you encouraged him to stay
in, right?" Of course she did. That's
what all military wives do—support
their soldiers, no matter what.

Celine shakes her head. I told him if
he reenlisted, it would be the end
of us. Obviously, he convinced me
otherwise. Love can be stubborn.

"So . . . I don't know how else to ask
this, other than straight out. And I'm
sorry, but you're the only person I know
who can answer it. Was it worth it?
I mean, if you had it to do over, would you?"

I've thought about this a lot, Ashley.
Every day with Luke was a better
day than one without him. But there
were way too many of those days.
I'll always love Luke, and what

we were together. But I'm watching
my children suffer. And when I'm
alone at night, I get so mad at him!
How could he do this to us? Her eyes
brim. Spill. Was it worth it? Probably.

Would I do it again? No fucking way.

I SPEND THE WEEK

Tying up loose ends. Finishing
my time at the women's shelter.
Finding a replacement volunteer
for the VA hospital. After all, I'm
getting married. Probably.

I should be ecstatic. Barely able
to control my excitement. Counting
down the days. Somehow, I'm not.
But how could I call it off now?
All the plans are finalized. Except

for the honeymoon, which will
have to wait until after Cole's training,
assuming he'll be accepted, and no
one believes he won't be. People
are coming from all over to witness

our "I do's." Even Dad's parents,
all the way from their retirement
heaven in Alaska. Weird to retire
in Ketchikan, yes. But they are
the tree my father fell from.

Mainstream is so not the family
thing. At least, not on my side.
Cole's side? Well, they'll just have
to get used to us, I guess. I hope.
I've spent a lot of time hoping lately.

FRIDAY MORNING

Jonah calls. *A couple of things. One,*
I would really like for you to help out
with the lit mag next year. We need
an assistant editor. Interested?

I'm flattered he thought of me.
"Absolutely, if you're sure
I'm capable." I wait for the second

thing. *More than capable. You'll*
be a great addition to our staff.
I also need some help screening
the poetry contest entries.

Most of them will go to the judge,
but we usually don't send the ones
with obvious problems. Like, not
actually qualifying as poetry.

I laugh. "People pay an entry fee
to send nonpoems to a big contest?"

You'd be surprised, my dear.
Can you invest a few hours this
afternoon? I'll buy you dinner.

"I'm a starving student, with time
to kill. When do you want me?"

He doesn't let that one go. Only
every time I think about you. But
if you could be here by three,
that would be great. See you then.

EVERY TIME

He thinks about me? Joke or no,
that makes me warm. Makes me
blush, most of the way to his office.

Luckily, the walk from the parking
lot cools me off just enough. We spend
close to three hours screening contest

entries and tossing obvious rejections
into a pile after pulling their entry-
fee checks. Some have obvious

misspellings or grammar problems
(and since it's poetry, that means
lack of grammar of any kind). Others

are simply very weak. "I kind of like
this one. 'You make me go weak in
the knees. Like the birds make the bees.' "

> Jonah looks at me with disbelieving
> eyes. *You've got to be kidding, right?*

"Yeah, actually, I am. I'm about
finished here, though. And hungry."
I leave my car, ride with Jonah.

We settle on a brewpub. Order giant
burgers and dark beer. Not my usual
thing, but Jonah convinces me to try it.

> *You've got to live large once in*
> *a while. Veer from the norm, away*
> *from what is or isn't expected of you.*

Yeah, like being here with him.
But it's been such a hard week,
tossing stuff back and forth in

my head. I really need to let it all
go. And I'm starting with dark beer.
We eat. Drink. Talk. Joke. Laugh.

Drink some more. And before I know
it, evening has slipped well into night.
"The wai'ress is givning us funny looks."

> Wow. I'm buzzed. Jonah smiles.
> *Probably time to get you home. Darn*
> *dark beer. I think I should drive you.*

I think he's right. I don't dare drive
like this. But, "Wha' 'bout my car?"

> *I can pick you up tomorrow and*
> *bring you to get it. Not a problem.*

He settles up, steers me to his car.
Drives me home without a single
swerve, missed stop sign, or other

indication he's feeling anywhere
near as messed up as I am. "Glad you
can hol' your beer better than I can."

> *Just takes practice. And body mass.*
> *I've got a few years on you. A few*
> *pounds, too. Okay, a lot of pounds.*

THE APARTMENT ISN'T FAR

We're there in less than ten minutes.
Jonah walks me to the door, waits
while I fumble for my keys. I find
them and am just sliding the correct
one into the lock when a familiar

truck comes screeching to a halt
in the parking lot, right behind
Jonah's car. The driver's door jerks
open, and out jumps Cole. It isn't
the first time I've seen him crazy-eyed,

but never has he directed those eyes
toward me in such a menacing way.
He moves like a soldier. Confident.
Fast. And pissed off at the world, or
at least this particular island of it.

> Jonah reacts quickly, moving in
> front of me just as Cole reaches
> the sidewalk, hands clenching.
> *Where the fuck have you been?*
> *And who the fuck is this?* He reeks

of whiskey, tobacco, and anger
sweat. "Cole! What are you doing
here?" His eyes focus on me, and
just for a second, seem to soften.
But when he looks at Jonah, fury

> glazes them over. *What are you*
> *doing here?* He mimics, slurring.
> *Didn't expect me, did you? Didn't*
> *think I'd be watching you, huh, bitch?*

Watching me? A cold wave of fear
washes over me. Jonah feels it, too.
His body tenses. But somehow
he keeps his voice steady. *Wait
a minute. Don't talk to her like that.*

       Cole takes a step toward him.
       He's wearing a tight khaki T-shirt,
       and I can see his biceps twitching.
       *Or what? You gonna kick my ass,
       queer?* He gives Jonah a hard push

with two hands, knocking him
backward, into me. "Cole, please.
Stop it. You need to quit now."
Unlike Jonah's voice, mine is
quivery. Cole moves back as if

       he might listen, but now Jonah
       says, *I think you should go. Come
       back tomorrow, when you're sober.*

       It's enough to set Cole off again.
       *I'm not taking orders from you,
       motherfucker!* He's screaming
       now. *You either, you goddamn whore.
       I knew you were fucking around!*

NEXT DOOR

The neighbor flips on her porch
light and now everything is in motion.
Cole comes at Jonah, who does
his best to defend himself. But he
is no match for a Marine trained

in hand-to-hand combat. Jonah goes
down on one knee. Cole circles to do
more damage. I move between them.
"Please, Cole. You don't understand.
Nothing's . . ." My jaw explodes.

Pain shoots through me and now
I am falling. Someone catches me,
keeps my head from snapping back.
Jonah lays me down, covers me
with his body, expecting more blows.

But Cole freezes. I look up at him,
through a haze of red. Blood. From
me or Jonah, or both of us. I'm not
sure. I try to say something, but
my mouth won't work. And, oh God,

> it hurts. *Don't move,* says Jonah,
> *and don't try to talk.* He reaches
> for his cell phone, dials for help.
> Still, Cole doesn't move. Just stares
> at me, shaking his head, as if he can't

believe what he just did. That
makes two of us. "Go," I manage
to tell him. "Get out of here." I don't
know if he understands. But he runs.

BY THE TIME

The paramedics arrive, I am
sitting up, propped against
the wall. Jonah keeps asking
if I'm okay. I must not look it,

or he'd probably quit asking.
I reach up, touch my cheek,
which feels like someone shoved
a volleyball inside it. My jaw,

I'm sure, is broken. Along with
my heart. Once Jonah and I both
swear it was not Jonah who did
this, the EMTs want to know what

happened. "My ex," I say, then
point to my jaw. "Hurts." I don't
want to talk to them or anyone.
Don't want to say who's responsible.

> Classic battered wife syndrome.
> The EMT whose name badge reads
> *Alvarez* is unsympathetic. *I see this*
> *shit all the time. You'd better file*
>
> *a police report. Get a restraining*
> *order. Especially*—he gives Jonah
> a straight-out once-over—*if your, uh,*
> *friend here is going to be around.*
>
> *Meanwhile, your jaw is busted up*
> *pretty good. We can take you into*
> *the ER, or he can drive you. Cheaper*
> *that way.* He gets to his feet and starts

packing up his stuff. Jonah says
he'll take me. He and Alvarez help me
to the BMW, and by the time we get
there, Jonah's wheezing. A quick

exam, and Alvarez tells us Cole also
cracked one of Jonah's ribs. Jonah
actually smiles. *Always wanted to
take one for the team. It hurt.*

We drive to Emergency in stunned
silence. Jonah reaches over, grabs
my hand, and holds it the whole way.
I can't believe what just happened.

I've been with Cole for over five years,
and though I've seen him angry—frozen
over, even—I never thought of him
as violent before. Okay, as a soldier, yes.

And he did shake me that one time.
But this? No. He'd never. Except,
he did. How could anyone do this
to someone they loved? Does he love

me? Can I possibly still love him?
And even if I can, do I want to? One
thing's for certain. There won't be
a wedding. All that money, down

the drain. And I'll need to start making
calls. Except, I can't talk. Can't think
very well, either, though I'm mostly
sober. Guess it can wait till tomorrow.

SCHOOL STARTS

In a couple of days. I'm looking
forward to it, with the kind of
rapt anticipation I haven't had
since I first went off to college.
Time to focus on what Ashley wants.

My jaw has healed, at least it's hard
to tell now it was broken in three
places, required surgery and wiring
my mouth shut for eight weeks.
That was a lot of soup. And Jonah

> brought regular milkshakes.
> I didn't want to press charges,
> but Darian convinced me I should.
> *Cole needs help, and he won't get it*
> *unless you do. Anyway, Jonah will.*

If I'd asked him not to, he wouldn't
have. But I decided Dar was right.
The wheels of justice turn slowly,
though, especially when the military
is involved in a civilian action. It took

months to set up a court date. Enough
time for Cole to complete his special
ops training. Next thing we knew, he'd
been sent overseas. Probably to
Afghanistan. That part is a secret.

He called me once during that time.
Told me how sorry he was. *I didn't
mean to hurt you. Never wanted
that. I just went a little off. Can you
find it in your heart to forgive me?*

By then, I'd thought it through.
Dissected it. Tried to stitch it back
together. But no matter how hard
I tried, I could not reconcile Cole
and me and the future. He'd broken

my jaw, but he had shattered
my heart. Smashed all the love
I'd felt for him into a small heap
of dust. Residue. That's all I had left
for him. The man I'd first met, the Cole

I fell in such overwhelming love with,
had been so profoundly changed
that he no longer existed. The soldier
who remained was largely a stranger.
Because I watched the transformation,

understood why it had happened,
I could tell him, "I forgive you, Cole.
But we need to end it here. Please ask
for help." After five and a half years,
there would be no more Ash time.

I DIDN'T LOSE

Much money on the wedding. Dar
helped there. Every vendor heard
a very sad story. All deposits were
returned, even the winery's. They
were able to rebook that night.

I spent it walking the beach, beneath
a thin stream of moonlight. Jonah
asked if I wanted company, but I
needed to be alone. I'm still nursing
a wound that has nothing to do

with my jaw. It's scabbed over, but
every now and then something rubs
against it, makes it bleed. When
the news broke about the soldier
who flipped out one night, took

his rifle and killed more than a dozen
women and kids, I thought it must
be Cole. But then they said he was
Army. My first reaction was relief.
It wasn't him. I couldn't have been

that wrong. Then came the certainty
that one day it could be Cole I hear
about on the news. I've witnessed
him a little crazy. He could go rogue.
He is not the type to ask for help.

I asked for help. I'm in therapy.
Working my way out of my own dark
places. Depression. Stress anxiety.
Chronic OCD. I've quit pharmaceuticals.
Still drink wine, the occasional dark beer.

But not to sleep. Not to avoid dreams.
The nightmares don't come so often
anymore. A couple of times, I have jerked
awake in bed, sure that Cole was lying
there beside me. Once, I thought

he was walking through the door.
But as the fear fades, mostly I dream
of the ocean. Surfing. Jonah. I'm treading
lightly there. I want to give him more.
But whenever I get close, I see golden eyes.

Jonah says he understands, that
he's waited a long time for the right
woman. What's a little more? For now,
he's content to help me heal. Anyway,
he's still my professor, emphasis on

the "my." I watch him pull our boards
from the back of the Woodie. Small
breaks only for a while, until I rediscover
my courage. But one day I'll ride Banzai.
And Jonah will be there to have my back.

WAKE ME LIKE SUNRISE

by Ashley Patterson

An orbit of need, aroused
by flight of morning,
feathered in tentative light.
Tempt me from this drowsy
abyss, persuade me from these tepid
dreams with the scorch
of your kiss.

But lips do not belong
to lips alone.

Bid yours to forge
fresh trails upon my earth, rich
with taste of summer skin
and muted scent of longing.
Leave no ground undisturbed,
no pebble disregarded.
No hiding place.

Drench me with your mouth,
fix your eyes on mine.

Allow me audience as you open
me wide, an empty book,
awaiting words penned by your tongue
without censor, without pause.
Fill these famished pages,
complete this passage,
write me to zenith.

Drown me with poetry
as dawning slips away.

Collateral

Ellen Hopkins

Introduction

Ashley Patterson, a graduate student and poet, never expected to become a military wife. But she and her best friend, Darian, fall for soldiers, both on separate paths to war. Darian and Spencer marry right away, for better or for worse, but Ashley and Cole choose to take it slower. Five years and four deployments later, Ashley is still passionately connected to Cole—her poetic, sensitive Marine. But as she looks back on the history of their relationship, she realizes that he has changed—the fear and tedium of war are starting to take a toll.

Ashley's doubts grow as Cole rises in the ranks, and she finds herself drawn to her poetry professor, Jonah, a laid-back surfer who encourages her to follow her dreams and never settle for anyone else's ambitions. As Cole's suppressed fury comes to the surface, Ashley must find the courage to fight her own battles.

Topics & Questions for Discussion

1. Discuss what it was like to read *Collateral*, a novel in verse. How long did it take you adapt to this narrative form? When did *Collateral* feel especially poetic, and when did it take on the fast-paced style of prose?

2. In "Poets Write Eloquently," Ashley observes that poets try to capture the horrors of war "using nothing / more than a few well-crafted words" (page 2). What aspects of war does the poetry of *Collateral* manage to depict? What kinds of trauma can no poet capture in words?

3. Consider how *Collateral* alternates between "Present" and "Rewind" sections. How did this switch between past and present enrich Ashley's story?

4. Choose your favorite poem by Cole Gleason and compare it to Ashley's "Rough Day at the VA," which Jonah thinks is her best. What are some of the similarities between Cole's style and Ashley's? How do their poems differ in style, subject, and imagery?

5. Recall your first impressions of Darian, Ashley's best friend. What did you think of Darian's preconceptions about marriage? How did your understanding of Darian's troubles change later in the novel? Did you gain or lose respect for her by the end of *Collateral*? Explain your answer.

6. "But there was something new under / Cole's skin. Some dark shadow" (page 448). Name some of the warning signs of Cole's "dark shadow" that Ashley fails to recognize.

7. Discuss the role that family history plays in Ashley and Cole's relationship. What dark secret has Ashley's mother been hiding, and how does her revelation affect Ashley's feelings about marriage and the military? How do nature and nurture—a family history of violence and the dangers of the Middle East—affect Cole's temper?

8. Cole reassures Ashley, "I'll always come back to you, Ashley. / You are my collateral. My reason / to return no matter what. Believe it" (page 214). Discuss the multiple meanings of the word "collateral." What kinds of danger and hope does the title of the novel imply?

9. Consider how gender issues affect the relationships in *Collateral*. How do Ashley and Cole's views of male and

female roles clash? When does sexual intimidation or jealousy threaten their relationship? Which couples in the novel have a more balanced relationship?

10. Jonah tells Ashley, "When love evolves / from friendship, it must be stronger" (page 385). Do you agree with Jonah's thoughts on friendship and love? Why or why not? Discuss how his theory applies to the men in Ashley's life: Cole, Jaden, and Jonah.

11. The sexual chemistry between Ashley and Cole is undeniable. Which of their love scenes is the most memorable? Why do you think they are so intensely attracted to each other?

12. Reflecting on the past five years, Ashley realizes that while Cole's maturity was imposed on him by the military, "My growth came from self discovery. / Choosing one path, journeying a while, / changing direction" (page 464). Compare how Ashley and Cole have grown over the years of their relationship. What has Ashley discovered about her strengths and weaknesses? How has Cole's military career affected his maturation?

13. Consider Ashley's career ambitions. Why did she initially choose to pursue a social work degree instead of teaching? What leads her to change her mind and study poetry?

14. The novel concludes with a "Fast Forward" section rather than a "Rewind," and is set a few days before school begins. What is the effect of this "Fast Forward?" What painful moments has Ashley skipped over in her narration?

15. Discuss how the wars in Iraq and Afghanistan are portrayed in *Collateral*. Which characters support the war and which oppose it? How does the novel manage to portray different sides of a difficult conflict?

Enhance Your Book Club

1. Check out IndieFeed, a podcast that collects spoken-word performances. Search for some of Ashley's favorite poets—Rachel McKibbens, Alix Olson, and Taylor Mali—and listen to their dynamic performances here: www.indiefeedpp.libsyn.com.

2. Ashley and Darian used to play a game called "What If:" "One of us asks a 'what if' / question. The other promises / to answer truthfully" (page 91). Play a book club version of "what if" asking other members which of their favorite books they would take to a desert island, pack on a long vacation, or hide under the mattress.

3. Set the mood at your book club meeting with the Dixie Chicks' album *Fly*—Ashley and Darian's old favorite. Find it in your local music store or buy it online, and don't forget to sing along to "Cowboy Take Me Away."

4. Consider donating time or funds to a veterans' organization in your area. Visit www.volunteer.va.gov/apps/VolunteerNow/ to find a veterans' facility near you.

5. Visit Ellen Hopkins's website, www.ellenhopkins.com, to learn more about the author's life and work, and to read her helpful tips for aspiring writers.